John Wyndham Parkes Lucas Benyon Harris was born in 1903, the son of a barrister. He tried a number of careers including farming, law, commercial art and advertising, and started writing short stories, intended for sale, in 1925. From 1930 to 1939 he wrote stories of various kinds under different names, almost exclusively for American publications, while also writing detective novels. During the war he was in the Civil Service and then the Army. In 1946 he went back to writing stories for publication in the USA and decided to try a modified form of science fiction, a form he called 'logical fantasy'. As John Wyndham he wrote *The Day of the Triffids* and *The Kraken Wakes* (both widely translated), *The Chrysalids*, *The Midwich Cuckoos* (filmed as *Village of the Damned*), *The Seeds of Time*, *Trouble With Lichen*, *The Outward Urge* (with 'Lucas Parkes'), *Consider Her Ways and Others*, *Web* and *Chocky*, all of which have been published by Penguin. John Wyndham died in March 1969. *Plan for Chaos*, which he wrote at the same time as *The Day of the Triffids*, remained unpublished for some forty years after his death.

Christopher Priest was born in Cheshire in 1943. He began selling short stories soon after leaving school and published his first novel, *Indoctrinaire*, in 1970. Since then he has published many more, including *The Affirmation* (1981), *The Prestige* (1995) and *The Separation* (2002). His books have been translated into every major European language and published around the world. A winner of many awards, including the James Tait Black Memorial Prize for Fiction, the World Fantasy Award and the Arthur C. Clarke Award, Priest has seen his books honoured in Australia, the USA, France, Germany, Italy and the UK. In 2006 a film of *The Prestige* was released, directed by Christopher Nolan and starring Christian Bale. Priest is married to the writer Leigh Kennedy. They live with their twin children Elizabeth and Simon in Hastings.

JOHN WYNDHAM

Plan for Chaos

Edited by
David Ketterer and Andy Sawyer

with an Introduction
by Christopher Priest

PENGUIN BOOKS

PENGUIN BOOKS

Published by the Penguin Group
Penguin Books Ltd, 80 Strand, London WC2R 0RL, England
Penguin Group (USA) Inc., 375 Hudson Street, New York, New York 10014, USA
Penguin Group (Canada), 90 Eglinton Avenue East, Suite 700, Toronto, Ontario, Canada M4P 2Y3
(a division of Pearson Penguin Canada Inc.)
Penguin Ireland, 25 St Stephen's Green, Dublin 2, Ireland (a division of Penguin Books Ltd)
Penguin Group (Australia), 250 Camberwell Road, Camberwell, Victoria 3124, Australia
(a division of Pearson Australia Group Pty Ltd)
Penguin Books India Pvt Ltd, 11 Community Centre, Panchsheel Park, New Delhi – 110 017, India
Penguin Group (NZ), 67 Apollo Drive, Rosedale, North Shore 0632, New Zealand
(a division of Pearson New Zealand Ltd)
Penguin Books (South Africa) (Pty) Ltd, 24 Sturdee Avenue, Rosebank,
Johannesburg 2196, South Africa

Penguin Books Ltd, Registered Offices: 80 Strand, London WC2R 0RL, England

www.penguin.com

First published by Liverpool University Press 2009
Published in Penguin Books 2010
3

Printed in England by Clays Ltd, St Ives plc

ISBN: 978–0–141–04877–2

www.greenpenguin.co.uk

Penguin Books is committed to a sustainable future
for our business, our readers and our planet.
The book in your hands is made from paper
certified by the Forest Stewardship Council.

Contents

Introduction   vii

PLAN FOR CHAOS
Part One

1 Picture   5
2 Where I Love   10
3 More Like   17
4 Pestilent Vapours   24
5 Confusion   30
6 Disguise   49
7 I Fly   60
8 Hard Rock   72
9 Constant Image   85

Part Two

10 Faded Pageant   109
11 Not Nature   129
12 Hideous Dream   145
13 I Go About   156
14 Expectation   163
15 Treachery   175
16 Grief   188
17 Not To Die   200
18 Mischiefs   206
19 Away   221
20 Finality?   226

Note on the Text   233

Introduction

When John Wyndham appeared in print in 1951, most people assumed it was his debut as a novelist. The book that launched his career was *The Day of the Triffids*, a success almost from the start, but under other circumstances it might well have been this one, *Plan for Chaos*, written at roughly the same time.

Triffids tells a story that is on the face of it a straightforward narrative. Monstrous plants with a deadly sting are developed for their high-quality edible oil, and at first are cultivated on that basis. However, they have a unique capability, which is that they are able to pull up their roots and, after a fashion, go walking around. Soon they are a novelty and with certain safeguards become features in most parks, ornamental gardens and indeed private back yards. Their day dawns unexpectedly when a global catastrophe occurs, and almost everyone on Earth becomes blind. It's not long before the sightless triffids pull up their stumps and set out for food.

That brief synopsis is probably familiar to many readers. The book has been around for a long time and has been made into a film, and twice adapted for BBC television. But a bare outline gives little idea of the effect the book has as a reading experience.

The novel is told as a first-person narrative from the point of view of one of the few people who, by chance, do not lose their sight. It is written quietly and convincingly, and with a constant sense of menace. There are moments of subtle satire. It plays against type: in the 1950s much science fiction was identified with B-movies and imported sensationalist magazines. Wyndham was different. Through the story of Bill Masen, as he discovers the sheer totality of the catastrophe, we read a gripping and believable account of London transformed into a place of constant danger. Gradually the scope of the book extends so that we realize what has happened in the rest of the country, and beyond that, the rest of the world.

At the time of the book's publication, the reviewers often compared John Wyndham with H. G. Wells. There are in fact several interesting similarities: for example, with Wells' 'The Country of the Blind'. In a remote Ecuadorian valley a sighted man puts to the test the saying that in the country of the blind the one-eyed man is king – the same notion runs pungently throughout *Triffids*. Further, the three-legged triffids were a reminder of Wells's tripodal fighting machines in *The War of the Worlds*. However, it seems likely that these niceties were not on the reviewers' minds, nor were several others. The point really was that in 1951 science fiction was perceived to be an almost exclusively American kind of writing. Wyndham, like Wells half a century earlier, was something of a novelty.

John Wyndham probably enjoyed the irony, because *Triffids* was a deliberate exercise in what these days we would call a reinvention of himself. During the 1930s he had been a regular contributor to American mass-market science-fiction magazines and had published at least three earlier novels, of which two were science fiction. All of these were published under his real name, John Beynon Harris. Sometimes he used a shorter version, John Beynon.

In fact, his full name was John Wyndham Parkes Lucas Beynon Harris. (He used several combinations of these names as pseudonyms.) He was born in Knowle, Warwickshire, in 1903. His father was a barrister and his mother was the daughter of a Birmingham ironmaster. Little is known of his early childhood, spent in Edgbaston, but when he was eight years old Wyndham's parents separated and he spent the rest of his childhood at a number of prep and boarding schools, finishing at Bedales school in Hampshire. He left Bedales when he was eighteen. It's all too possible to imagine the effect this must have had on him: the child of estranged parents, certainly hurt and depressed by what happened, probably suffering feelings of guilt, sent away to boarding schools. Although not a recipe for creating someone who will grow up to become a writer, it is a familiar kind of background for many writers of that period. After Wyndham left school he made several false starts in badly chosen careers – farming, law, commercial art and advertising – before he began writing in 1925. By 1931 he was selling short stories regularly in America.

The Second World War intervened, and afterwards public tastes changed, as did the publishing market. Wanting to relaunch his career after he was demobilized, Wyndham wrote a thriller (which got nowhere) and two new science-fiction novels. One was *The Day of the Triffids* and the other was *Plan for Chaos*. These two novels reveal his transition from the brash American kind of writing (at which he was only adequate) to the more measured British cadences for which he was to become justly famous.

Plan has never before been published in a popular edition, although an academic edition appeared from Liverpool University Press in 2009. Since the early 1950s the manuscript has been sitting in a file in John Wyndham's collected papers, now stored archivally at Liverpool University. The manuscript was in two versions, one apparently aimed at the American audience. The two versions have been edited and combined by two academics, Andy Sawyer and David Ketterer, and they have done a sensitive job of restoring the text and editing it as closely as possible to what we might presume were the author's intentions. Their note on the text appears at the end of this edition.

Plan for Chaos and *The Day of the Triffids* were written at more or less the same time. According to an interview Wyndham gave later, to write *Triffids* he took two of his pre-war stories and combined them. The book went through various drafts then was sent to be typed. However, Wyndham was dissatisfied with the ending and he requested the typist to halt work while he reconsidered. He reconsidered for about eighteen months, and it was during this period that he must have written the early drafts of *Plan for Chaos*. We know that he delivered *Triffids* by the beginning of 1950. It was published in the USA in early 1951 and the first version of *Plan* was sent to the USA in March of that year. Following discussion with his American literary agent Frederik Pohl and various editors, Wyndham revised the manuscript six months later. By that time *Triffids* had appeared in hardback in Britain too.

There are signs that the author tried hard to get *Plan for Chaos* published. Correspondence survives between him and Pohl, as well as some of the publishers' rejection letters. Much of the problem perceived at the time was the author's attempts, failed or otherwise, to depict the narrator, Johnny Farthing, as an American. Wyndham felt this was what was needed for American readers. While not actively disagreeing with him, the American professionals said that Farthing should seem either more American, or less so.

This dilemma is still visible in the novel as it stands today. Wyndham eventually came up with a complicated compromise: Farthing is said to have descended from a Danish family with a Danish/American father, been brought up in the UK with periods of education in France and Germany, emigrated to the USA and finally become a US citizen. This complication has a plot function, but it also created a difficulty in the narrative voice which was never satisfactorily resolved.

Farthing acts and speaks like an American of sorts, while retaining a kind of middle-class British reticence. (Johnny Farthing is an inactive narrator, who sees more events than he takes part in. He's practically or physically inept, as he proves when he tries to hack his way through the Amazonian jungle using a sheath knife.) Most of the real Americans in the novel call him 'Limey', which might be Wyndham's way of confessing that he hasn't got the voice quite right. Indeed he has not, at least in the early parts of the novel. Farthing tells his story in a sort of cod-hardboiled noir, redolent of 1930s' slang, where women are 'gals', notions are 'screwy', and things are 'cracko', 'swell', 'mighty'. As the action moves on later this uncertain narrative voice does seem less noticeable.

Although *Plan for Chaos* is not another *Triffids*, is it worth reading?

For curiosity value alone the answer is emphatically yes. Here is the young Wyndham on the cusp of success. We glimpse not only the early pulp-magazine writer perhaps being laid to rest, but the mature novelist emerging. It is a rare event for a book to come to light, written at such a turning point in the career of an author of worldwide reputation, and never before seen. Beyond curiosity, the novel has other rewards.

All Wyndham's mature novels contain cunning insights into the way the future might unfold. *The Day of the Triffids*, for instance, anticipated by about forty years military satellite technology (the blinding rays) and genetically modified crops (the gene-spliced triffids). *Plan for Chaos* casually anticipates radar invisibility, the foundation of stealth technology, by roughly the same period. Not bad for a writer sometimes dismissed as soft on science and technology.

And then there is the intriguing notion, central to the novel, of a Nazi resurgence led by the cultivation of carefully cloned Aryan children. When Wyndham started work on this novel, Hitler and the Third Reich had been gone for less than five years. Who would have thought at the time that some of the survivors would flee, set up compounds away from critical eyes and plan a return of the master race? An inspired guess, perhaps, because that's not far from what really happened when many camp guards, Holocaust administrators and Hitler henchmen escaped to South America.

In purely literary terms, *Plan for Chaos* was written nearly thirty years before Ira Levin's bestselling book (later filmed), *The Boys from Brazil*. Not exactly the same story, but all the same dreads, portents and reawakened fears. Wyndham was there first.

He's on less certain ground with his fleet of Nazi-controlled flying saucers, although writing at the end of the 1940s it probably seemed a defensible speculation. There is in fact evidence that in the real world the Nazi regime was experimenting with circular aircraft in the last stages of the Second World War. UFOs were first tagged as 'flying saucers' in 1947, and in the same year one was said to have crashed in New Mexico. Unbeknownst to John Wyndham, since that time a small but persistent fringe has continued to insist that UFOs are Nazi in origin, flying from a secret base in Antarctica. Depending on how you look at things, you might think that Wyndham was on to something here too.

Stylistically, *Plan for Chaos* is not such a smooth read as Wyndham's later novels, but once the story has moved on from its struggles to depict Johnny Farthing as an American, we are clearly in Wyndham's own territory. All his books are witty, and throughout *Plan for Chaos* there is an undercurrent of pointed connections, remarks, observations. The other great quality of Wyndham's writing – a quiet, ironic, understated satire – is also detectable throughout.

It's interesting with hindsight to speculate how John Wyndham's career might have taken off, if *Plan for Chaos* had been published first instead of *The Day of the Triffids*. It's clearly not as accomplished as his best books, and it seems likely Wyndham realized this and set it aside in favour of finishing and delivering *Triffids*. He probably made the right decision, but here at last is the book we never saw.

Christopher Priest, November 2009

JOHN WYNDHAM

Plan for Chaos

Part One

1

Picture

Look here, upon this picture – W.S.

Lois looked up from the switchboard as I went by.

'Oh, hey there! – Limey!' she said.

I turned back, reluctantly.

'Look,' I told her. 'Didn't somebody once call this a melting-pot? So on account of that, couldn't you just let a guy do his melting quietly?'

She thought about it. Head a little on one side. Gold hair like sliding water across a cheek like young roses. Very effective.

'Takes time, doesn't it?' she said. 'I guess Limeys have a kinda high melting point. – Got more corners than most, too.'

'Like to see my passport?' I inquired.

She shook her head.

'I know: got an eagle on it. All the same, you talk Limey, you sorta think Limey. I guess you most likely kiss Limey, too.' She looked speculative.

'I go on trying,' I told her.

'You sure do,' she agreed.

'And I go on learning. Maybe one day when I've got acclimatized – .'

'Acclimated,' she said.

'Okay, acclimated – then we'll hold a graduation test. Meanwhile, what about cutting out this "Hey, Limey" stuff, and giving me a break? My name's Johnny.'

'You look more like it ought to be Jan,' she remarked.

'Maybe, so I'd have to melt twice, making it that much harder, wouldn't I? So just try Johnny, will you?'

'Uh-huh – Johnny,' she agreed.

I started once more upon my interrupted way. I'd taken some four steps of it when she called me back again:

'Hey – Limey! I forgot to tell you. J.P.'s been burning wires all over the building for you. He said to send you right up, sooner than now.'

* * *

When I went into Jake Parton's room, he didn't address me as Johnny, either. He just grunted, and leaned back in his chair with an expression on his face like a man who has again been shown that humanity is the way he always thought it was, anyway. Then, kind of laboriously, he leaned forward, and pushed some stuff across his desk towards me. What he opened up with was:

'Will you just take a look at that, you big Swede!'

As I'd said to Lois, I do try. And I'd got around to distinguishing several local inflections of the words: 'big Swede', s.o.b., and suchlike. This one was ungenial enough to give me the feeling of trouble coming; though I didn't have any idea of the kind of trouble until I had looked at the stuff he pushed over.

There were two journals. One was a copy of next week's issue of our *Choice* magazine; the other was the current number of *Crime Hebdomadaire*, from Paris, France. Ours was open at a spread of my pictures: view of the dead woman's apartment, showing unfinished meal on table with coffee cup still half full (always a good touch, that); view down into fatal yard from fatal fire-escape; view from opposite side of yard, with dotted line showing the way the body must have hit the low roof and slithered down before it reached the ground; also, portrait of the woman concerned – the studio picture I had slipped under my jacket, frame and all, when no one was looking.

Then I took a scan at the French magazine. There was a dotted line there, too. Not, to my eye, a good job. The angle at which it ran down from a bridge, to end on a motor-barge with the number carefully effaced, was improbable. The editors then treated their readers to a pretty unpleasing view of the body as it had lain on the barge's hatch-cover. There was also a picture of the anonymous lady as she had appeared before all this took place.

I gave that last one a close look – just as I'd given a close look to the one I'd filched, before I'd handed it over to the blockmakers.

'That's funny,' I said.

'Not very,' said Jake.

I kept on looking at the two portraits. They gave me a nasty feeling. It wasn't just on account of their being so like one another that they'd be hard to tell apart – the ad men keep on rubbing it in that the world is full of doubles, though the significance of that is known only to ad men. No, the disturbance was simply an increase on the one that I'd felt when I first saw the picture of the girl from the fire-escape – and the fact that I could add a treble to those doubles... Either of them might have been a portrait of my cousin Freda...

When I'd compared them for a bit, I pulled out my wallet, and laid it down open, beside them. With the three close together the similarity was staggering. If you were to change around the differently dressed blonde hair, each might be either of the others.

'What's that, huh?' asked Jake.

I turned the wallet round for him to see, and told him.

He looked at it, and then back to me. His lips were a bit tighter.

'That's a fool game,' he said, bluntly.

It didn't latch for a moment. I was still taking the thing in.

'While you're being paid by this paper, you work for this paper *only*. And don't tell me you didn't know – it's in your contract,' he added, forthrightly. 'What's more, this paper wants the authentic dope – not that kind of hooey.'

'Now, look here – ,' I began, but he cut me short.

'You're an expert photographer, Johnny. That's the reason you're here – the reason you *were* here,' he corrected himself. 'Now, the only difference between the women in those three photographs is the hair style. And you say one of them is your cousin... So what? Some kind of syndication...?' he asked, unpleasantly.

'The only one of these three that I took is this,' I told him, tapping the wallet.

He didn't believe me, and took no trouble to hide it.

'Listen,' I said. 'I know it's queer that I happened to be the one to turn in that picture of the dame from the fire-escape. But I'm engaged to Freda. I'm going to marry her. Is it likely I'd be selling her picture around, the way you suggest – and on jobs like this, too? And even if I were, would I produce this version to show to you?' I shut up the wallet, and put it back in my pocket.

'I'd not know. There's a lot unlikely in this world. You take good pictures, Johnny. Worth peddling with an agency. But you over-reached it when you said that this – ' He pointed to the open page of *Choice* ' – came out of the woman's own apartment.'

'It did. Maybe we could trace who made it,' I said.

He shrugged.

'So?' His eyes were narrowed, in a hard look. 'Well, maybe you can.

Meanwhile, this paper has a reputation to maintain. You'd best look in on the accounts department on your way out.'

It didn't make sense. It wasn't logical. But I knew Jake when an idea had its teeth into him. Besides, he has an ulcer. You have to wait...

* * *

It was kind of nice in the Park. Restful. Quite a while had gone by since I had been able to sit on a bench in the afternoon sun and watch the time go without a tag on it. Astonishing how many other people were doing the same thing, too. Hard to understand how they managed it: they couldn't all have been fired that morning. I was glad I'd resisted the impulse to set about Jake. So much pleasanter to be out there with the flowers and the trees and the kids around than sitting in a station cell, hoping for bail.

In a very general way, of course, Jake had been right about the contract being broken – in the same general way he'd have been right if he had said it to any picture-man on *Choice*'s staff – though with this particular instance he was plumb out.

If I hadn't been fool enough to produce my own picture of Freda, it would have been just a coincidence. Doubles, as I said, aren't too rare. But I'd have been feeling uneasy myself. Triples begin to get fishy...

Besides, there was the other side to it. It hadn't seemed to me that the police were absolutely satisfied that the girl had *fallen* from the fire-escape. I had a feeling that maybe if there had been somebody raising hell they might have looked further into it. For one thing, there were marks on the escape, and, for another, people so seldom do just fall off fire-escapes...

And then, in the French affair, there was something not quite on the line, too. I mean, if you or I had opted to go jump in a river, we'd sort of see things were clear there first, wouldn't we? Whereas if we happened to be pushing a body over we might be a touch more hurried, less able to choose our own moment. I'd not press that... It was just an idea; a feeling about it...

Then the third photograph: authentically Freda's, but just the image of the other two. You don't have to be superstitious for a thing like that to set you wondering a bit...

I decided I'd wind up my afternoon by going over to haunt the hall of her office-building about the time she was due out.

* * *

Seeing that there is more empiric bunk talked about sex than pretty near anything else, you might think that I'd not fall for my cousin Freda. On the moronic theory of opposites invariably attracting, I ought to have been panting after some cute, doll-sized brunette – like all Patagonians ought to be crazy over Pygmies, or all Texans over Japanese girls. But I wasn't, any more than, as far as I know, they are. In fact, Freda and I made a well-matched pair. We're both tall, both fair, and we both shape-up, according to our different natures, in a way that's pretty complementary. Most of the time our outlooks don't interlock so badly, either. I know that could sound dull to those who prefer to live in passionate misunderstanding amid a welter of sulter, but we happen to prefer it that way. So, when Freda saw me waiting in the lobby, she didn't suspect me of prying on her life, she didn't flit into the rest-room to fix the armaments, she didn't even trouble to put on an enigmatical mood to be surprised out of: she just smiled as if she were glad to see me, and said:

'Hullo, Johnny. This is nice.'

Which it was.

And I said:

'I suppose it wouldn't do for me to kiss you here?'

And she said:

'Certainly it wouldn't, because there's Mr. Bottleton.'

And I said, like a good American and no Limey:

'The heck with Mr. Bottleton!'

And did.

2

Where I Love

Where I love I must not marry – T.M.

With a good plateful from the smörgasbord in front of me, I lifted the akvavit.

'Sköld!' I said.

Freda responded. Then she said:

'Are we celebrating something?'

'Well – not exactly,' I told her.

She looked at me rather hard.

'Then the only probable explanation of this unarranged meeting is that you've been fired. Have you?'

'Well – yes,' I admitted.

'Pity,' she said. 'Still, the best thing we can do in the circumstances is drink a toast to freedom.'

We drank.

She toyed among the smörgasbord.

'Tell me all about it.'

I did. 'A silly sort of business. Most likely Jake'll turn reasonable when he's thought it over a bit. It's queer all the same,' I finished.

She was looking pensively into her glass of lager.

'Very odd indeed,' she said, with a something in her voice, but she insisted on dropping the subject then to do justice to the food.

After that we took in a movie about a good girl whose mother had never told her anything, on account of which she fell for a bad guy. And there was a bad girl who'd been told everything, on account of which she fell for the bad guy, too. So the bad guy seemed all set, but he had to die, on account of the Purity Office. It looked like the good girl had bumped him, but naturally she couldn't have, on account of the Purity Office. A good guy proved that for her so that he could marry her. Then the bad girl, who *had* done the bumping, had to die someway, also on account of the Purity Office.

When we reached her apartment-house Freda said:

'Drink, Johnny?' So I went up

We'd have got ourselves married a year or more before if we had had our way. But... well, in the stories you frequently read about men and girls who crash triumphantly through everything in order to fetch up at the altar, and they are highly admired because Love is All. But the only crashers-through that I've known personally had it in the system. Once they'd crashed in, they crashed the restrictions they found there, too; and so, out again. It's all pretty simple if you don't give a damn who gets hurt in the rush.

Our obstacle was Freda's old man, my Uncle Nils. I'm not saying that he wasn't an old fool, but all the same, I liked him. So did Freda. In fact, he'd have been quite okay if he hadn't had a thing in his nut about cousinly marriages.

Lots of people do have that. You can Mendelize at them with nice patterns of X's and Y's; you can explain to them fully and patiently about dominants and recessives until the whole thing is as pellucid and tidy as Euclid, and you have a sore throat, but in the end it still turns out that several friends of theirs knew cousins who married and had offspring that weren't quite apple-pie. You can point out that they are statistically wrong and that only the failures get scored-up, but there is still that know-better shake of the head.

'Listen,' I'd say to the old man. 'Take the Egyptians. Their dynasties, some of 'em, lasted a heck of a long time, and there was a lot closer consanguinity than cousins about the way they kept up their chief families.'

'Maybe,' he admitted, 'but look at 'em now. And, anyway, we don't have any Egyptian blood in our family.'

And so on: getting no place, on a regular schedule.

'Your mother, Adela, was a very sweet girl – nothing wrong there,' he told me more than once; and he would say it gently, on account of he'd been very fond of my mother. 'And I'm okay – I think,' he'd add.

He'd raise a questioning eyebrow with that, and we'd assure him that he was okay. Then:

'*But*,' he'd say, '*but* we gotta remember your Aunt Marta.'

Then we would all sit awhile, considering Marta...

* * *

Maybe it's somewhere here that I should get around to explaining this business of Limeys, and Big Swedes, and so on. It came this way:

For a long time the Dahl family (my Uncle, as an immigrant, changed it to Darl) used to live near Norrköping, which isn't so far from Stockholm, Sweden. It had been around those parts in a quiet way for a century or more until in the generation before me it suddenly got kind of deciduous. First my Uncle Nils, as a young man of twenty, upped and went to America. Then my mother married a man called Georg Farthing.

Georg, my father, had been born in America, but his parents had brought him back with them as a boy when they had inherited property in the old country. The first thing that happened to him when he got married was an appointment to manage the London office of a Swedish cargo line. So when they went to live in England, my Aunt Marta, who was still a child, was the only one of the younger generation left at home.

Uncle Nils, over in America, married a girl called Evangeline, who died very soon afterwards, and it was twenty years before he got to marrying again. When he did, he chose a young woman from Varmland, called Christina, who later became Freda's mother for a few years before she too, died. (You don't need to remember all this, but it kind of explains how the family got spread around.)

My own father and mother went on living near London, England – only they weren't yet my father and mother: they weren't anybody's father and mother, which was quite a disappointment to them. Most summers they would go over to the old country to visit, but it gradually got so that England was more home to them than Sweden. Then there was a war that cut them off for six years, and did a lot more to settle them in there. A bit after that, when they'd more or less got over thinking about it, I surprised them by turning up, some nineteen years off schedule.

My father, who had never forgotten that he was technically an American, thought it a wise move to register my birth at the American Embassy, which turned out conveniently later on.

I was brought up mostly in England, but with a year and a half's school in Germany, and a year in France because my father considered that though the English do get around, they stay insular on account of not doing it young enough. There were vacations to Sweden, too, sometimes, but my background was English, and my home was in England.

My father died when I was seventeen. There wasn't a lot of money, so I managed to get a job as a press-photographer, to help out. Eighteen months later, my mother died. My grandparents, back in Sweden, had died years before, and I didn't have any ties, so when a letter came from my Uncle Nils saying that opportunity lay that side of the Atlantic, I went and talked a passport out of the Embassy.

I came across. I got a job. Then I set about this business of becoming an American – which isn't easy, and isn't made easier when people like Lois persist in calling you Limey. Still, I keep on trying mighty hard, yes, sir.

So there we were. Uncle Nils, now a sick old man, my cousin Freda, and myself. Only the three of us left of all the family – though plus the unembodied influence of Aunt Marta.

For, unfortunately, it had to be admitted that Uncle Nils did have a certain something there.

Aunt Marta, at the time my mother had left home, was not quite eight years old. She was a golden child. There is a tinted photograph of her in a locket of my mother's. The hair, as with all our family, is fair, and in her picture it seems to gleam somewhere between sunshine and moonlight. The forehead is broad, the nose, straight. Her mouth should, one feels, reveal more than it does; the draughtsmanship there, and the sculpture, is perhaps too impersonally perfect. Her wide-set blue eyes look out at you candidly: and yet there is something a little disturbing – a trace of the shimmer in the blue Baltic ice…

My mother used to see her almost every year when she made her visit home. The last time was when Marta was sixteen, and about to go to school in Germany. It was as she was then that my mother always used to think of her. She told me once:

'She was magnificent: like a young goddess out of one of the old sagas. She was so lovely. It used to make my eyes prickle when I looked at her – it seemed so sad that anyone who had been born to bloom like that, should be born, too, to grow old. I could almost cry at the waste of it.

'And yet, somehow, she frightened me a little. She had so much confidence in herself, so little need of the rest of us. Not that she rebelled, or disobeyed. It was something latent: she bloomed so – arrogantly. Less, perhaps, as a woman, than as youth itself. I could see behind her a Norse maiden in helmet and breastplate who would lash the horses of her quadriga through smoke and flame: fearless herself – but, also, with mercy for none…

'I did not like that. A myth ought to remain a myth. A woman should not be like that – no one should be like that. So it always hurt me a little to see it…'

Then Aunt Marta had gone off to her school in Germany.

Those were the fevered days there. The mad, tragi-comedy opera times when housepainters, or champagne sales-men could become potentates, when the exulting mystics burnt wisdom, emotion threw out reason, and the red streams began to trickle from under closed doors.

Marta was an immense success – the Nordic ideal in person. After only a few weeks her family began to hear less frequently from her. The later letters started and ended by heiling Hitler. Presently they ceased altogether.

The school wrote to say that she had left them, and gave no address for her. Her father went to Germany to make inquiries, but the school could not, or would not, tell him anything, and the police showed little interest.

For some time after that her parents heard nothing at all. Then they saw a picture of her in a German illustrated weekly. She was awarding a trophy to a blond young man in running-clothes, and her name was given as Fraulein Gerda Daele. After that, they were able in roundabout ways to learn something more of her.

She had renounced her Swedish nationality, and held papers to prove that her family was originally from Marienwerder, in East Prussia – which it certainly was not: more likely it was from Norway. She was high in the administration of several organizations, and seen at gatherings of the socially élite of the Party. It was said that the Führer himself was wont to refer to her at times as a pattern for German maidenhood. She was, according to these reports, utterly assured, completely intolerant, and fanatically Nazi. Whether or not she received her parents' letters, they went unanswered. She would be then in her nineteenth year.

In the course of the next two years her position strengthened so that one could scarcely open a German magazine without finding her photographed among those present at some function or gathering. Rumour coupled her first with one, and then another, influential Party name, but none of the news was hard. The references to her in print, however, underwent a subtle change; speculation was less gossipy, the tone more respectful. About the same time, too, stories by word of mouth, of a different kind began to reach even as far as Norrköping. They were dark, harsh stories. Her parents did their best not to listen to such tales, and to disbelieve those they heard; and they were still defending their feelings in that way when the war started, and rumour became less explicit for a time.

After Germany made the mistake of thinking she had permanently won the war in the west they began to hear more again; Marta was up in the high councils now. A person of deadly authority, descending like a Fury to purge one place or another, leaving behind her misery for the weak, inspiration for the fanatic, and an increased awe for the masters of Greater Germany. She flared, and lesser ranks cringed. She had, they said, a tongue to liquefy, eyes to shrivel, and a voice that spat bullets. In the brief mythology of her day, her name was Hecate.

But what, in the end, had happened to her? She was there at that last, grotesque debacle when the empire that had swollen like a boil was finally lanced. She had been, according to witnesses, some part at least of those last days in the historic bunker in Berlin; among that fantastic hierarchy waiting in the ante-room to Valhalla. But after that? Well – any one of three or four unidentifiable bodies might have been hers. The men of the Intelligence were never able to produce the proofs...

That, then, had been our Aunt Marta – Gerda Daele.

* * *

It all happened a long time ago, of course – before Freda, or I, was born – but for all that it was she who stood between us. When Uncle Nils said: 'But there's your Aunt Marta,' he was remembering those stories about her in her heyday. He was saying, in effect: 'There's a taint somewhere that came out in your Aunt Marta. She was a fanatic – unbalanced. You two might perpetuate that taint.'

To which I would reply: 'Seems to me a mighty lot of people were fanatics in those times. They didn't all need taints to help them, by any means. It was sort of in the air.'

But that kind of thing never got us any place. He was obstinate. But, also, he was a sick old man. His wife was dead, his sister, too. He had only Freda left. We didn't care to break right across his duty as he saw it, just at the last. So we let him go on hoping that each of us would find somebody else. It wouldn't have to be for so long...

* * *

'What'll you take, Johnny?' said Freda.

I chose rye and ginger-ale, and raised it to her.

'And now?' she asked.

I swirled the drink round so that the ice tinkled.

'If Jake doesn't see sense I could work the agencies while I look around. I've one or two ideas for a series.'

'But you'd sooner stay with *Choice*?'

There was something in her tone.

'What are you getting at?' I asked.

She'd gone over to her bureau and taken out a sheet of paper. She folded it, and cut a small piece out with some scissors. Then she came back to me, holding a copy of *Pictureweek*, and flipping through it. She found the page she wanted, put the thing in my lap, and sat down beside me. I looked at it. The page was headed *S. America*. There was a picture over a caption:

'ACCIDENT' CLAIMS U.S. BEER BARON
HELD ON B.A. SLAY CHARGE

The picture showed a striking young woman with her hair dressed smoothly from a centre-parting to a large knot on the back of her neck, in that latin fashion. Long swags dangled out of it from ears that were almost hidden. Even apart from the fact that she looked so much the conventionalized vamp of half-a-century ago, there was something familiar about her.

While I was still looking, Freda slid the piece of paper she had cut over the page so that just the face looked out of the hole. I stared at it.

'Well, sink me deep!' I said.

I looked from the printed face to Freda's. Darken the brows and lashes, and there was the same face again.

'Would you just tell me what seems to be going on?' I inquired, at length.

She shook her head.

'I happened to notice it. I was puzzled to know why it seemed familiar. So I covered up the hair, and saw. It was surprising, but I'd forgotten about it until you spoke of the other two, then I remembered. It certainly is queer.'

'Queer!' I said. 'It's more than queer. Either it's thundering uncanny, or there's a very funny stink some place.'

I studied the face again, laying Freda's picture beside it. Four women with the same face – and three of them sudden deaths. I thought hard, but nothing even started to inkle.

'Let me have this?' I suggested.

'Of course.'

I tore out the page, and put it away carefully in my pocket.

We left that for the time being, and passed to more congenial matters.

3

More Like

These hands are not more like – W.S.

'Come!' said Jake's voice, so I came.

It was not that I had at the moment any great love for Jake, or his paper. But it lays no eggs to have your reputation all snarled up by getting kicked off a magazine like *Choice*.

He looked up.

'Oh, you,' he said. 'You're fired. I distinctly remember.'

'Sure,' I agreed. 'I speak as a free man.'

One brow came down a trifle.

'Watch it,' he advised. 'There's lots of places a guy can do that – but it can get him lots of places where he can't.'

'I'm just coasting,' I assured him. 'Bringing in one you missed.'

I showed him the page from *Pictureweek*. Particularly I pointed out that part of the copy beneath, where it said:

Probing by the B.A. Police Department revealed that exotic, dark-haired, Southern beauty, Lola Martirez (picture above) was in reality a blonde, though maybe still exotic, at that. Said fresh-complexioned, forty-year-old, 250 pound, beer-baron, Andrew Fleischammer, of Milwaukee, Wis, held on a charge of showing Lola into an elevator when the cage happened to be ten floors below: 'What if she was a blonde? Who'd know why women do these things? I guess any dame has the right to fix her bale of straw the way she wants it.'

I said, after he had read it. 'Maybe you'll tell me how I fixed that one with an agency picture?'

He kept his eyes thoughtfully on it for a while.

'Queer – darned queer,' he said.

'Yesterday,' I reminded him, 'I got fired for saying just that.'

We laid out *Choice, Crime Hebdomadaire, Pictureweek,* and Freda's portrait all in a row, and looked them over again.

'I don't get this – I don't get it at all,' he complained. He pondered a bit longer, then he brought his hand down on the desk with a thump. 'Well, we'll find out. We'll run this thing – and maybe learn something on the side, too.'

I folded up my wallet, and put it back in my pocket.

'Hey!' he said.

'Not this one,' I told him.

'But, look here.'

'No!' I said.

'But if it looks the same, and it does, what the hell's it matter?' His view seemed to have altered from the previous day.

'No!' I said again.

He sat looking unfriendly for a space, then:

'Deadline six-thirty a week from tomorrow.'

'You – er – wouldn't be going to apologize?' I inquired.

'We all make mistakes,' he said, with a magnanimous air.

I looked in on Mary Blakey in Accounts. She wasn't all that pleased to see me.

'No consideration! No consideration at all,' said she. 'How in hell's a girl supposed to keep her books tidy in this madhouse?'

* * *

The cop they put me on to at Police Records studied Freda's photograph carefully.

'Quicker to trace if you have the finger-prints,' he told me.

I explained that I didn't have the finger-prints, and that it wasn't that girl that I wanted to know about, but someone just like her. He wasn't impressed.

'If you were in this job you'd have had enough practice to know that nobody looks *just* like anybody but himself – 'cept a very few twins, maybe. What's her lay?'

'I'd not know – unless you'd call being a corpse a lay,' I told him.

He grunted and went away. A few minutes later he was back, with a regulation-size picture in his hand.

'There you are. Fell, or was pushed, off a fire-escape in this city, 'bout a week ago.'

'I know about her. She's not the one. Another just like her,' I told him, hoping there might be.

'Can't be *just like* both,' he objected.

'These two look just alike to me,' I said.

'They would, to an amateur,' he told me, and went away again without explaining the subtleties visible to his professional eye. When he came back next time he was holding two pictures. He laid one of them down on the desk.

'Found near the westbound track, ten miles east of Flagstaff, Arizona,' he observed.

I examined it. Take away the high-arch eyebrows, put in the real ones, lighten the hair a little, flatten the perm a trifle – and there we were again.

'Smart of you,' I said, to please him.

'Filed under blondes on account of it was dyed,' he said, as if in some sort of explanation. 'Mostly, of course, it's the other way.'

'No.'

'Could we reproduce it?'

''T'ain't for me to say, but I guess so. Then there's this one,' he added, holding up the other picture.

It was a shocker.

'Fished out of the Hudson. Must've mixed it with something,' he told me.

It certainly had.

'We couldn't print that,' I said

He agreed. 'But see that side of the face,' he pointed. 'It might be – '

He was right, too. It very well might be.

I asked him how I got copies. He told me, then, looking again at the first two, he frowned. With a professional reluctance he admitted:

'Sure is pretty near a dupe. Must've been twins – though the one you've got's not quite so near a dupe. What do you know?'

'So far, less and less every minute,' I told him.

* * *

The only place I could think of starting to get a line on – on – well, whatever it was I was trying to get a line on, was the apartment-house where Dame Number One had launched off from the fire-escape. All I knew about her so far was that her name had been entered as Sadie Tufnell. There might be a chance of digging a lead out of some of the neighbours. As far as I knew, the police hadn't: but that's different. It's surprising how many people would take a flyer at white-slaving their grandmothers if they could be sure of getting their pictures printed for it.

But the house, when I reached it again, didn't promise a lot. It had the air of one where any neighbour is a dark, nervous shadow on the stairs about whom nobody knows much, and the less, the happier. Having to pitch in somewhere, I scouted out the janitor's room.

I found it with him inside, looking gloomy at a percolator. He was a big man, a slow-moving type, but with quick, sharp eyes set in an ill-used face. He might have been an ex-cop: or he might have been ex-jail, either side of the bars. He looked hard at me as I came in. Then he got up heavily from his chair. I'd a feeling that wasn't in character. Nothing about him suggested it as his usual line in courtesy.

'Maybe you'd not remember me?'

'For your money?' he asked.

He didn't hurry, but somehow he was between me and the door.

'Sure,' he said. 'I remember you okay. You're the guy that came to see the Tufnell dame a coupla times. The guy the cops are wanting a word with.' He laid his hand on the wall phone.

'I'm the guy who came to see her *once* – after the event, and with a camera,' I corrected him. I took out my card, and held it for him to see.

He looked at me, puzzled for a moment. Then he nodded:

'Sure,' he said again. 'The Limey with the blink-box – that was you. And there was me, too mussed up with the cops and the rumpus to know where I'd seen you before. Still, that's soon mended.'

He picked up the receiver. He didn't take his eyes off me to dial; he let the operator put him through.

He made himself known; then he said:

'Remember that big, straw-haired guy I told you 'bout? – The one that visited with the Tufnell dame? Well, I got him here right now, if you're still wanting him.' He listened, then: 'Okay,' he said, and hung up.

He reached across a chair, put it back to the door, and sat down on it very squarely.

'Something seems to want explaining.'

'Sure does,' he agreed.

'I've come here to get a bit of dope on this Tufnell piece,' I told him.

'So? Well, the idea now is that you'll give some,' he said.

I shrugged. I'd recognized the single-line type. The percolator was gurgling to itself on the gas-ring.

'How long do you let that thing bubble?' I asked, lifting my hand towards it.

He hunched forward on his chair, like he might be going to jump.

'Keep right away from that,' he growled.

I saw his point. I'd not want boiling coffee thrown over me, either.

Presently tyres squealed outside, and the cops came in.

It took me near an hour to get through with all the where-were-you-on-the-night-of-the-twentieth? business. I keep a pocket diary. By luck, I had been on picture assignments at both the times that were interesting them. A provisional check wasn't difficult. They turned us both out of the station into the street together.

'Smart guy, huh!' said the janitor. 'Trust a goddam Limey to have it all fixed. But what I seen, I seen, an' I'm stickin'.'

'You can go jump in a glue-pot for all I care,' I told him.

* * *

'Sweetie,' I bawled, trying to get the right inflection into it above the noise of traffic outside the call-box. 'Sweetie, usual place and time?'

'*Another* celebration?' asked Freda, pleasedly.

'It's not every day a fellow lands a job on *Choice*,' I told her.

'I'll be there,' she agreed, 'only I may be a bit late tonight because Mr. Bottleton's flapping like a – oh dear, I didn't see you there behind the cooler, Mr. Bottleton...'

* * *

Usual park, usual time, usual bench – and then another fellow had to come and sit at the other end of it. He was about my height, but dark, and with a lot more paunch under his natty business-suiting than I keep under my less formal get-up. If he'd done more about the sports so vividly pictured on his tie, there'd likely have been a lot less to spread the broad end of the tie on. His other leading feature was impressive glasses, with heavy, dark frames.

I tried frowning him off, but it didn't faze him a bit. He caught my eye once, and then quickly turned his attention to a nice bed of gladioli. Still looking at them steadily, he said:

'Why in hell did you want to go back there, you damn fool?'

Well, there's a kind of remorse or retrospective embarrassment that gets some guys like that. I've seen a fellow stop short on the sidewalk and designedly punch himself on the head before now. However, the rhetorical question to self, combined with objurgation, as here and now, is the more usual manifestation. I was just weighing the odds whether he was regretting weakening on a decision to walk out on his wife, or whether there was a babe some place that he couldn't cut loose from when he added:

'Well, *why*? You must have had some reason.'

He darted a quick look at me, and away again. I became blankly aware that he wasn't simply talking to himself.

'What, me?' I said, bemusedly.

'Who else, you fool? Did you leave something there?'

'Now, listen – ' I began. But he cut across sharply:

'Don't look at me when you talk. Haven't you *any* sense?'

'Listen,' I said again, still looking at him, 'I've an idea I know which of us is nuts. Who are you, and what do you think you want?'

'What I want to know first is what you think you left there?'

'Now, see here, if this is a mutant on the flee-at-once-all-is-known line, you can take it elsewhere,' I told him. 'It so happens that my private-life is just one load of big, glossy prints.'

I'd not like to say he actually barked, but it was a mighty odd sound he made, though subdued.

'For God's sake – ' he began. But just then I saw Freda approaching. I got up, and went to meet her.

'Sorry, darling, but there's a lunatic infesting our bench,' I explained.

We looked him over as I escorted her past. He goggled at us in a very convincingly loony manner.

'What would be wrong with him?' Freda asked, interestedly.

'How would I know why a loony's loony?' I said.

Just as we had got beyond him, he said quite loudly, and apparently to the gladioli:

'You two gone crazy? You know it's against orders.'

I was for passing on, with a large air of not hearing. But not Freda. She turned back, and stood looking at him.

'If we were crazy, how would we know what was against what orders?' she asked.

He gave that bark again.

'There's going to be trouble about this – big trouble. I'm telling you,' he said, savagely.

On that he got up abruptly, with more agility than one would expect in a man of his bulk, and walked swiftly away without looking at us again.

'See what I mean? Nutty – cracko,' I told her as we watched him go.

We sat down.

'A nice day – just nuts and cops alternately,' I remarked.

'Tell me,' said Freda.

She listened carefully while I gave her a résumé.

'It's very queer about these women,' she said, when I had finished, 'but I don't think it's so queer about the rest.'

'Darling, if you don't think nuts are queer – .'

'Well, it doesn't make the janitor nuts just because he mistook you for someone else.'

'Maybe. But this other guy – the loony…?'

'On the face of it, it looks as though he thought so, too.'

'All that stuff about leaving things behind. Leaving what where?'

'Don't you see, if he thought you were the same someone else as the janitor did, then what he was wanting to know was why you went back to that apartment-house.'

'Oh,' I said, in partial revelation. It had not occurred to me to connect the man on the bench with the rest of it at all. Until she pointed it out, I'd thought him just a bit unscrewed on his own: a detached nut, so to speak.

'Ah,' I said. 'You mean that some fellow who looks like me did push her off the fire-escape.'

That was apparently jumping a bit far in one, even for Freda. She looked questions.

'The janitor says that I was her only visitor that he ever knew of: therefore he suspects me,' I explained. 'The loony here either suspects or knows that I did it, and wants to know why I was fool enough to go back to the scene of the crime – keeping it well in mind, in the circumstances, that the word "I" means somebody else.'

'I see. And so it seems to him that you must have left some incriminating evidence there; or you'd not have gone back. Yes, that does make it clearer.'

'Glad you think so,' I told her. 'Though I would point out that your devoted lover is now under suspicion from two directions of a Number One crime. Anyway, who was this loony? I never set eyes on him until five minutes before you came. And what was that final crack to both of us about? I know you do look like the girl who went off the fire-escape, but for obvious reasons you can't be her – and he must know that, too. Then who *are* you supposed to be? Who am *I* supposed to be? Nothing welds.'

'There was something sort of vaguely familiar about that man,' Freda murmured thoughtfully.

'Well, I'm sure I've never seen him before,' I said.

All the same, I knew what she meant: there was a certain something about the look of him…

4

Pestilent Vapours

A foul and pestilent congregation of vapours – W.S.

Three days later Freda came through on the telephone at a time when I happened to be in the office.

'Do you ever read *Artemis*?' she inquired.

'I'm afraid you must have mistaken my sex,' I said.

'Well, now's the time to widen your outlook. Just take a look at page 41, this month's. It ought to interest you.' She paused. 'Doing anything tonight, Johnny?'

'I could be clear by a half after seven.'

'If you were to come round then I could have a little dinner fixed.'

'Or we could eat out, and save you the trouble,' I suggested.

'I'd rather eat here quietly.'

'What's on your mind, honey?'

'It's – oh, nothing much, Johnny. Tell you this evening.'

'Okay. I'll be there,' I told her.

I went down to Reference and inquired for the current issue of *Artemis*. Sally there found it for me.

'This is a new line for you. Afraid of getting married, Limey?' she inquired.

'I've told you before – oh, well, skip it, but the name's Johnny,' I informed her.

I looked cautiously at the lavish production she handed me.

'Would this be some kind of warning?' I asked.

'This business of being a woman does have its grimmer aspects,' she admitted.

I flipped through a mass of sophisticated sales-appeal. It might have been any issue, this year's, last year's, or the year before's, as far as I was concerned, though I supposed hips would have gone in and out a bit in that long. After a bit:

'I don't like the title,' I said.

'Now me, I thought it was pretty good – considering,' said Sally. 'What's yours?'

'How about *The Female Jungle, or What Every Girl Ought to Know About Decoys, Mantraps, and Spring-Guns*?'

'Oh, one of those crude, eighteenth-century titles,' she sighed. 'And after we've spent so much trouble learning about chocolate-covering and cellophane-wrapping, too.'

Page 41 was part of an article devoted to the strain of being socially winsome in Washington. At the top was a photograph of a semi-circled group on a dance-floor, with all the men trying to get that nicely-combined jovial-but-responsible look, and every woman in sight grinning like a Buick. For a moment I wondered what I was looking for. Then I saw it. I had never known Freda to smile in quite that way, but if, under some heavy pressure, say a large sum of money from a manufacturer of dentures, she had been forced to expand, I now saw what the result would be. Minimizing the expression as much as possible, the likeness was quite remarkable. I drew a circle round the head.

'Would there be any way of finding out who that is?' I asked Sally

'There more than might,' she said. 'Tall, blonde, statuesque type. H'm! You ought to like them small and dark you know.'

This opposites-attract business is well set – besides, Sally is, herself, not too tall, and darkish.

'Northern ice and southern fire going fizz every time they get together?' I suggested.

.... say northern ice, not really. I mean, I think – '
.... we finally got it fixed that she'd try to put a name to the picture.

* * *

I was kept later than I had reckoned, which made it close on eight when I rang the bell of Freda's apartment.

Nothing happened. But it wouldn't be Freda's way to sulk or act neglected. So I rang again, longer. Still nothing happened. I definitely lacked a fancy for that, so I put my shoulder to the door. Those rim-locks aren't a lot of good. Inside, I called: 'Freda! Hey, Freda!' but no sound came back.

The place stank of gas. In the kitchen I found the oven open, the gas turned on, but unlighted. There was a cushion half-in, half-out of it. On the cushion rested Freda's head…

*   *   *

'She'll be okay now,' said the doctor, 'but there ought to be somebody with her.'

You couldn't blame him. I'd have thought the same as he was thinking – if she hadn't been Freda. Anyway, hadn't it all been arranged to make it look just like that? And there certainly ought to be someone around to see her over it. I didn't know who would do that, so the Doc said he'd send a nurse.

'You don't need to worry,' he told me. 'She may be sick a few more times – that'll be to the good. Just look after her and keep her quiet till the nurse gets here.'

I did that, but she wasn't in a state where she needed to be kept quiet. Pretty much down, poor girl – but every now and then there would be a little pressure from the fingers of the hand I held as I sat beside the bed. That was enough for the present.

The nurse showed up. A woman of thirty-eight or forty. Kind-looking. I showed her where things were, gave her my phone number, and generally handed over, with a feeling that Freda would be in competent hands.

'Has she ever tried to do such a thing before?' she asked me as I was on the point of leaving.

'Neither before – nor this time,' I said. She just didn't believe me: I didn't have any evidence. I just knew.

I told her I'd be around in the morning, then I went home, where I didn't sleep much, or well. I kept on seeing a row of █████████████ like Freda's, but all of them with their eyes closed, de█████████ them *might* have been a suicide. Even the girl from the fire-escape was a *might*…

When I looked in at Freda's in the morning the nurse told me she was a lot improved, but sleeping now, and better undisturbed.

When I rang at noon the nurse said she was much recovered, and going to have some broth.

When I called around in the evening she was not there.

Nor was the nurse…

*   *   *

I went to the doctor. He put a call through to the nurse right away. He asked her pretty shortly what had happened to her patient, and listened to the answer for quite a while. Then he covered the transmitter, and said to me:

'She's mighty sore with you. I gather that never in all her extensive professional career has she been so insulted, et cetera, et cetera.'

I gaped at him.

'What am I supposed to have done?'

'She tells me that your attitude this afternoon left her with no alternative but to walk out on the case. So, as the patient wasn't in any real need of her any more, she did just that.'

'This afternoon, but – what time was that?' I asked.

'You ought to know,' he said, looking at me curiously.

'But does *she*? Will you ask her?'

He did.

'She says four o'clock you came. Twenty after four, she left.'

'Look,' I told him. 'From three o'clock until nearly six I was at the Airfield taking pictures of Conference Delegates marching out of airplanes – and half the Press of this city was there with me, to prove it.'

He scratched his head.

'Dear me!' he said. 'How strange!' It seemed to me an understatement.

We decided to go round to Freda's apartment and ask some questions right away.

As we climbed the stairs, we met one of the cleaners going home. She looked at me, and nodded. There was a compassionate expression on her face.

'Oh, I wouldn't now, the poor little thing?' she asked.

Well, anyway, taken off balance. It had never occurred to me that Freda could strike anyone as a 'poor little thing', whatever her discomfiture.

Her eyebrows went up. She looked at me hard, and sniffed.

'Huh! None of my business, I suppose,' she said, and made to go on.

I checked her. 'Hold it a minute,' I said. 'Who're you thinking I am?'

'Friend of Miss Number Thirty-nine, ain't you?' she said, with hostility slightly abated.

'That's right, but I don't think I've ever seen you before,' I told her.

'Too took up with her, I 'spect,' she said, with an understanding manner. 'I was standing right here in the lobby when you came through with the stretcher, though.'

'Stretcher?' I repeated, blankly.

After a bit, we began to get the thing to gel.

Somewhere before five o'clock an ambulance had arrived. Two attendants from it took a stretcher upstairs. A few minutes later they had come down carrying Miss Thirty-nine on it, poor thing. 'I' had been walking beside the stretcher, and when it had been loaded aboard the ambulance 'I' had got in after it. It had then driven off, presumably to hospital.

*   *   *

I found the police well enough disposed, but not inspiring. Most of the things they wanted me to tell them were just the things I wanted them to find out; so we didn't get ourselves a long way. Still, they put it in hand.

I rang up Uncle Nils and told him that Freda wouldn't be making the weekend trip she'd arranged on account of a girl at her office being taken sick – which was the only stall I could think of at the moment.

Next morning I told my office I'd be in late, and went round to the place where Freda worked to see if I could pick up anything there. The guy Bottleton that she secretaried seemed a nice fellow, fiftyish. I put the whole thing to him. He looked worried.

'I know, and I guess you'll know well enough, that Freda wasn't that kind of girl,' I said, apropos of the gas-oven.

'You certainly don't need to tell me,' he agreed. 'I know quite enough of her to be sure of that. Matter of fact, I've come to know quite a bit about you, too, one way and another.'

His expression lifted a moment as his eyes met mine; then he went right on looking worried.

'I wonder – ' he began. Then he broke off, thinking. 'She didn't tell you anything about the day before yesterday?' he asked.

I shook my head. 'She wasn't in any state – oh, but she did mention on the phone that she had something to tell me,' I remembered.

'She got here in the morning looking pretty shaken,' he told me. 'Not like her, at all.'

'Owing to what?' I asked.

'Seems she was waiting on the platform, and just as the train was coming in somebody shoved. She said that if the man beside her hadn't grabbed she'd have been under that train. People do jostle, of course, when they're getting ready to move. But she said this felt like a deliberate, strong push. With some of the others I might doubt that – but Miss Darl's different, kind of steady. And there *are* people with tendencies to homicide just for the hell of it…' He looked straight at me. 'I'm not telling you this just to worry you more. It's that the one thing coming so close on the other –' He let it go at that.

'She didn't manage to see who pushed?' I asked him.

'Too much crowd around. Might have been anyone of half-a-dozen, she said. Nobody seemed to have noticed anything – except the man who pulled her back.'

'And that, too, would have looked like just another suicide.'

He looked questioning. I told him about some of the others. He shook his head slowly.

'I don't get this. I don't get it at all,' he said.

'That makes you just another of us – but if you should begin to get anything on it, for God's sake let me know,' I told him.

He undertook to do that, and presently I broke it up, leaving him still looking worried.

If I could have thought of anything useful to do, I'd have done it. As it was, it looked like I might as well go to the office as any place, so I did.

I'd only been in there a couple of minutes when the phone rang. I grabbed it fast, hoping for news.

5

Confusion

Confusion now hath made his masterpiece – W.S.

A female voice said:
'That you, Limey? The name's Antonia Hander.'

It didn't sound like anything I'd be wanting to hear, however.

'That's nice,' I told her. 'I'm delighted to know you. Is there something – ?'

'Listen, mug,' said the telephone, distinctly, 'this is Sally, in Reference. I said the name's Antonia Hander.'

'That's what I thought you said. Why?'

'How in heck would I know why? It just is.'

'Let's get this straight. The name's Antonia Hander, although you're known here as – '

'God rescue me! Tune up, boy. I'm telling you that the woman you marked is called Antonia Hander.'

'Marked! Never! I always make it a strict rule not to – .' At about which point it came to me what all this was about. Other matters had banished the picture in *Artemis* from my mind. 'Oh, I see. Well – er – thanks for that,' I added.

Sally said, coldly: 'When I take on a job, I do a job. The name is Antonia Hander. But if you're looking for loopholes in the high-brackets, she's not one. That party wasn't quite the socialite crush that *Artemis* made out – not exclusively, anyway. She works days in I.S.D.R.A.C. Nights she gets seen about plenty – maybe she'd be working then too, but my information doesn't run.'

'Oh,' I said. 'What's I.S.D.R.A.C., anyway?'

'That's Inter-State Department for Radio-Activity Control. There was a kind of suggestion that she may be a bit radio-active herself – but I still say she isn't your type.'

* * *

A couple of days later I was in Washington myself.

The police at home were stalled. They'd found the ambulance. It had been hired. The stretcher, with Freda on it, had been off-loaded at Grand Central, and the men paid. After that, nothing – except one redcap seemed to remember a stretcher being loaded into a black van. It might or might not have been the same stretcher. At the time he had supposed it to have arrived by train.

Moiling over it didn't show me any place to pick up the trail. It was as clean a vanish as you'd find. In the end I went to see Jake about the one angle that struck me as a possible lead.

'Look,' I said, 'several women, all uncannily alike, all apparently suicides. Then my girl, looking just like 'em, pretty nearly made to seem a suicide – twice. But one woman in Washington, also uncannily like the rest is apparently healthy – as yet. Could be a line.'

'Could it?' said Jake. 'How?'

I had to admit that I didn't quite see how, but I did feel that there could be – and certainly no other line was showing. He frowned a little at his blotter, then he looked up at me, and said: 'Okay. Try it then. Good luck.'

Which was white of him. I knew he didn't think there was a thing in it, but I suppose I was looking – well, sometimes it turns out there are more human beings around than you'd generally notice.

So I'd taken it at that, and was trying it.

Miss Hander wasn't too difficult to get a lead on. A guy I know who gets money for syndicated exaggeration of the night-life in those parts was aware of her.

'Quite an enterprising young woman,' he said. 'Should land comfortably some place if she'd listen more and talk less, they tell me. Not your type, though.'

There seemed to be a conspiracy about that.

'Business,' I told him. 'The trouble about you is you've got a female mind. Is that what this job does to a fellow?'

'That wouldn't startle me. This whole town clacks like a tatting session. And I have to listen to it. It gets you warped the way you can only think in couples and triangles. You know those French farces, all in and out the bedrooms, and money up the garter? Only it isn't the farce side you notice so much – it's the men doing both-hands-off in order to play political cats' cradles while the women do the back-seat driving. We got two kinds of women, mostly. The ones that are and the ones that want to be. The want-to-be's work days with their claws out; nights they work with – well, anyway, they work. The already-there's go around pushing off the scaling ladders and breathing out poison gas by Chanel to repel boarders. You'd not get any place with this job thinking along purely male lines.'

I gave him time to expand a bit on that before I pulled him back by asking:

'Where'll I find her?'

'Find who?' he said, looking surprised.

'The one that touched off this indictment of Gomorrah, Miss Hander,' I said.

'Oh, her. Well, now, let's see. No receptions tonight. Then I'd try the *Hibiscus*, the *Snow Man*, and *El Paradiso*, in that order. If you're out of luck, call me at the *Hesperides*, and I'll think some more.'

It's kind of nice how many places a *Choice* reporter's card will get you into, with drinks on the house, too. I flashed my camera around a bit in the *Hibiscus*, but I didn't find her there. However, these night-club lynxes know their stuff. She was at the *Snow Man*, all right.

It made my heart kind of flop when I spotted her. She looked so like Freda that if I'd not been expecting it I'd very likely have gone right up to her – true, there was the reddened hair, but that's a thing which might happen to any girl. The height, build, face, colour of eyes, they were all of them Freda's. On the other hand, I didn't think Freda would have chosen the dress of pale-green satin she was wearing. There was a watch-bracelet, too, that would not have been Freda's taste; the kind of thing that seemed to me to coruscate more than a minor job in a Government office would rightly account for.

I leaned against one of the pillars, watching her dance, and, when the number was finished, go over to a table on the other side of the floor. It was then that I began to notice more of the things about her that were not Freda. She was with an older man who looked like a Senator would like to look, and knew it: leonine-orator type. The technique she was using on him – well, of course, to judge these things with a properly evaluating eye you have to be in the racket of being a woman yourself, but, speaking without the credentials, I'd have called it, roughly, ham, streaky with corn. The hanging on his words was a bit too; the searching of his face while he spoke was a bit too, too. The impulsive little gestures rightly belonged to someone several sizes smaller. As for the demure use of the eyelids in conjunction with a little smile – . Still, the test's in the taste. The guy had old-fashioned views, I reckoned – like those veterans of eighty-odd who will still guess it's under the left-hand thimble – for she seemed to be making out okay.

It's kind of funny seeing what your girl might have been, and thanking God for changing His mind.

A woman slunk out into a spotlight and oscillated there awhile, moaning a desperate unfulfilment number. It started more mildly than it went on:

> Wanna be somebody's darling,
> Wanna be somebody's wife,
> Wanna find someone to love me,
> To live with all of my life.

I'd not say that gal looked to me altogether set on social stability. Still she put the same kind of theme, from a different angle, in the encore:

> Take a hold on yourself! Con-trol yourself!
>   There's Judgement Day to come!
> When Gabriel makes his trumpet talk
>   You don't wanna take that cinder walk:
> When you're asked by Peter: 'How did you treat her?'
>   You wanna say sharp: 'Qualified for a harp!'
> It's strict mon-o-gamy here on Earth
>   That books a reservation for an upper berth.
> Keep a hold on yourself! Con-trol yourself!
>   There's Judgement Day to come!

When we'd finished with that, Miss Hander and her escort got up to dance again. On their second time round, I brought the camera up. He spotted me; said something in her ear, and turned her so that she faced my way. She came round, ready and smiling: then something happened...

Have you ever seen an expression drop, like it was a bit of the plaster falling off the wall?

Did she freeze! And she'd been ready for the camera, so it had to be me she was freezing at. It's likely I gaped back at her.

She picked up her act fast enough, though. They went on dancing, and then back to the table. Every now and then she'd shoot a quick glance across at me to see if I was still there. My presence seemed to distract her attention from the main job, too: the ham wasn't quite so peach-fed.

Choosing my moment, I shifted strategically behind a clump of flowers and foliage, and found a convenient peek hole in it. Sooner or later they'd part, and there'd be a chance for a word with her. If he moved, I'd go over to the table: if she did, I'd head her off. It took about a half-hour to happen, then it was she. I watched him rise politely as she got up, and then settle back in his chair. I slid across, making interception a few yards short of the powder-room. There was no one else close at hand, and the band was cutting loose.

'Excuse me, Miss Hander – ,' I began.

She turned. Her expression cracked again, the way it had before. She spoke. She spoke not only incisively, but in German, which I wasn't ready for. All the same, I took the gist of it. It was:

'You must be crazy! What do you think you're doing, going around like that, anyway? Leave me alone! Beat it! Get the hell out of here, right now!' Only, in the original, it was somewhat ruder.

By the time I'd gathered up my dropped jaw she was beyond the powder-room door.

I goggled at the door a bit, and then got around to reckoning that, with a lady who knew her own forceful mind so well, maybe it wouldn't do a lot of good waiting...

I decided I'd pull out, and think over a new approach.

* * *

Back in my hotel room, I poured myself a drink, and moiled it over a bit. In lining things up, I got around to wondering just what it was I thought I was doing – what I had come down here for. Quite suddenly it looked to me as if Freda's disappearance had knocked me a shade off the rails – and a shade's enough where rails are concerned. I'd gone off chasing a coincidence, a chance likeness that couldn't even be properly called a hunch. The thing was that there were too many chance likenesses by far in this affair. One or two coincidences may be okay, but there's a point beyond which they get cracky – or suspicious. I felt that that point was already way behind me but as yet I could see nothing solidifying...

And what to do about it? I had left the exact line to the circumstances – now I felt I had better plan one. I mean, you can't go up to a lady and say: 'Pardon me, Miss Hander, but a lot of gals who look like you have been getting mortuary tickets in mighty funny ways lately. Can you think of any reason why you're likely to join them?' Or can you?

No, I'd say you can't. It'd be difficult even to start – and that piece about 'a lot of gals who look like you' would slay any co-operation before it began, on account of they never think they do.

The more I looked at it, the more clearly I saw that the attempt at a direct approach had been a mistake. If she had been aware of any danger of that kind threatening her, she would have told either the cops or someone else about it – or, if not, she would have some very good reason for keeping quiet. If she was unaware of any danger, she'd have nothing to tell me, anyway.

However, from the reaction I had received, it seemed pretty clear that she did have something to keep quiet about – though maybe not from being scared. That crude repulse of hers had sounded like resentment of interference, plus something else… And delivered in German, too! Now, why in heck should she unhesitatingly address a perfect stranger in highly colloquial, not to say offensive, German?

I didn't get it. The answer would *seem* to be that she had thought I was *not* a perfect stranger – so what? Who, then, was I supposed to be? Again the fellow with the ambulance who had called for Freda? Well, in that case, there was a connection of some obscure kind established…

I could have wished I knew more about those other women: who they were, what they did for corn. So far, I had the names of two only: Sadie Tufnell, whose occupation no one seemed to have dug up; and Lola Martirez of B.A. whose means of livelihood, as far as stated, appeared to be (a) being an exotic, dark-haired southern beauty, and, (b) being a friend of Beer-Baron Fleischammer of Milwaukee. Well, (a) had turned out to be phoney; the name Lola Martirez sounded to me pretty much like the kind of thing the semantic genius of Hollywood throws off, and B-B Fleischammer would not be available for further details until he had succeeded in talking or greasing his way out of the jam he had got into down there. And that was as far as it went. The rest of the women were, as far as I knew, anonymous. Nobody seemed to be interested, or had shown up to identify them – which was a funny thing, too…

It struck me there might be a lead through Miss Hander's Senatorial-looking friend, someway, so I decided to develop the photographs, and get him identified.

The hotel had one of those central radio systems: they choose the programmes, you just get some switches and a volume-control. I turned it on and let it run gently while I got down to the job.

There wasn't any knock, just the click of the latch above the sound of the radio. I looked round from washing-off the film in the basin to see her taking her hand from the doorknob. I was surprised, all right, but I didn't have to wonder whether this was another walking likeness; under an open fur wrap there was the green satin dress that had knocked my eye in the *Snow Man*; there was also the neon-type bracelet-watch.

'Well, hullo, there!' I said, largely on account of I couldn't think of anything else to say just then.

She moved further into the room. Her expression at the moment was cast-concrete, and her eyes mighty like ball-bearings. It was no wonder that the archness and the eyework back there in the *Snow Man* had looked a bit appliqué; if what I saw now was the usual sub-structure, she had been working marvels. And she didn't co-ordinate another way – pale-green satin like that wants a kind of undulating slide that drifts lowly to anchor. This girl came closer in three unsuitable strides, and halted, smack.

'Now, just what in hell do you think you're doing?' she demanded, and this time she demanded it in English.

I picked up the towel, dried my hands, and replaced it on the rack. I also turned off the radio.

'Well, just at the moment – ' I began.

'I don't mean just at the moment,' she snapped. 'I mean back there in the *Snow Man*, and yesterday in Pennsylvania Avenue, and Tuesday over in Arlington. That's what I mean, and I'm telling you right now I don't like it.'

That last wasn't doubtable. She backed the statement up with every visible manifestation of distaste, short of flames from the nostrils. Now, if you try to dry up that kind of mood where facts have become, as it were, subjective, with simple denials, you don't get any place. On the other hand, keep it stoked up, and you may learn something by the way.

'So you don't like it?' I remarked.

'I certainly do not – and I'm not standing for it. I'm doing the job. If they don't like the way I'm doing it, that's one thing they can tell me – I can take it: I've got my results to show. What I will not take is all this keyhole-prying, corner-peeking, neighbour-tattling, under-bed, goddam snooping.' She paused for, I think, breath.

'Under-bed!' I said. 'Why, Miss Hander – !'

'You can cut the burlesque line, too,' she told me. 'And as if it weren't enough already, what in the flames of hell do you think you were doing going into that place looking the way you did, anyway? God, of all the wit-withered, doll-cutting clowns…'

I blinked. Almost, I dodged.

'That, at any rate,' she went on grimly,' is one thing you're not going to get away with. Maybe it was orders that set you crawling about behind the wallpaper, or brought you up out of the drains, but you don't get me up on a chair screaming – you only get me mad: until you break the rules. When you do that, my report goes right in – and I add my own piece about ham-sleuthing and incompetent interference. Now then, what's your number?'

The eyes were flashing, the lips pressed hard together. Imagine a Fury hampered by a few modern conventions, and you'll have a fair idea. I felt it ought to be getting around to my turn.

'Now, look here,' I began. 'You come crashing into this room – '

'Number?' she snapped. 'That's all I want from you.'

'Okay. Two-three-seven,' I said. 'Now what do I do? Double it?'

She looked at me more closely. 'That's not going to help you. It's one group you can't be.' Then she realized it was the number on the door she had just come in by. 'Oh, funny guy, huh!' she said. 'Now quit the fooling, and give me your own goddam number.'

I was getting tired of it.

'There's just one thing I feel inclined to give you, sister – but mother always said a gentleman doesn't,' I told her.

I expected her to flare back, but she didn't. Instead, she stood staring at me. A bit of her assurance melted off. The change was enough to set me wondering what I'd said. It could scarcely be that, though – it had sounded like some cheap crack from a second-feature movie; probably was. And yet:

'What was that about the mother?' she asked, looking puzzled now.

I decided to follow up my first bit of advantage so far.

'Forget it. Now let *me* tell *you* something. There are girls like you getting themselves bumped off. Did you know that?'

She looked straight back at me. 'You don't have anything on me. There's nothing to have,' she said, steadily.

'I'm not threatening you; I'm asking you. Do you know why?'

She shrugged. Her mouth was a hard line.

'The usual reason, I guess. But you can't pin a thing on me. I'm not denying there've been times when I've wished you could. But you don't have a hope – not with my job. Strictly business. And talk about heavy freight! Every time I see those roller-bearing ads, I say gimme. Well, you saw him.'

At the tail end of this gibberish I dimly perceived it to have something to do with her escort in the *Snow Man*, but before I could follow that up, she was back on course.

'If you won't give me your number, then I'll have them check on you. You'll not get away with it. What I can't see is what damfool idea took you there, anyway.'

Being so well into the department of utter confusion, by now, I felt that even a touch of truth might help to give the thing a new slant.

'I was taking pictures there,' I told her.

She just looked at me – like Medusa rehearsing.

'I'm on the staff of *Choice*,' I went on. 'You know *Choice* – "All the Pictures Safe to Print" – "Your Lens on Life."'

The devil of it was I couldn't make up my mind whether I would do better by telling her who I was, or by trying to find out who she thought I was: you still feel you've got something in hand as long as you're not quite tagged. I paused, but she didn't forthcome.

'Okay. You're on *Choice*: I'm in I.S.D.R.A.C. So what?' she said.

'So I wanted a picture of you and your eminent partner,' I said, hoping that he was.

She regarded me thoughtfully for some moments; then she announced: 'I give up. Which is it? Am I supposed to think *you're* crazy? – Or are you trying to persuade me *I'm* crazy?'

'It wouldn't astonish me either way,' I admitted.

So we considered one another for a bit. At last:

'Why were you sent here?' she asked. 'You're out of your area. You don't act like an American – and you've got an English accent. There's something screwy about this.'

I disregarded the last part of that.

'There was a dame like you who kind of fell off a fire-escape; another who fell out of a train; and another who – '

'I told you you can't pin anything on me. 'I – .' She stopped abruptly, as if an idea had struck her. 'Do you mean someone else did it – they're on to us? Are you trying to warn me?'

'Maybe,' I said cautiously, wondering where in thunder we might be heading now.

'Don't be a goddam fool,' she advised. 'Either you are, or you aren't.'

'Then – yes,' I said. After all, a woman warned might be a woman perturbed. And it seemed likely, for her expression become serious.

'Who's on to it?' she asked.

'I'd not know that. I thought perhaps you – '

'If I had, I'd have reported, of course,' she snapped.

'Who to?' I asked. And the moment I said that I knew I'd slipped up.

'You – ' she began. Then the door opened, and she stopped.

A man came in quickly, closing the door behind him.

It isn't only that I don't care in general for men who slip swiftly and silently into my room, without knocking. What I particularly dislike, is men who do it with the right hand in the jacket opening, as though they might be holding something there. It gets me suddenly feeling kind of naked.

My surprise was all the greater as I recognized him in one. The loony from the park-bench hundreds of miles away. Same suit, same paunch, same hand-painted, outdoor-boy tie. He put his back against the closed door, and stood looking at us.

'I warned you two to break it up. What in Sam Hill do you think you're playing at?' he demanded.

I looked over him. He was just my height. The paunch would give him more weight, but less condition. The factor of imbalance was that under *my* left armpit I had nothing but shirt.

'God!' said Miss Hander, with suffering. 'Not another of you!'

At the sound of her voice he looked at her more closely. Their inspection was mutual. It looked as if he learned something satisfactory, for he relaxed slightly.

'This your beat?' he asked her.

She nodded.

'You been here all the time?'

She nodded again. 'You can check,' she added.

'Then, who's this?' he inquired, turning towards me.

'Ha-ha!' said Miss Hander, gloomily. 'Now you try your strength on it. But just before you start I'll tell you this, whoever he is, he's nuts; schizo-cuckoo like a zany in a snake-pit.' And she sat down, with the air of one taking a good ringside seat.

I looked at the loony, and the loony looked at me.

'Well, I know he calls himself Johnny Farthing, and claims he's on the staff of *Choice* – but Headquarters doesn't give any check on that,' said the loony. 'I also know he gets called Limey on account of he can't talk proper English, but – ' he turned to her ' – where do you come in on this, anyway?'

She explained about the *Snow Man*, and went on: 'So I got a guy to tag him here. Then I came along to ask him what the hell he thought he was doing going about like that – and busting in on me. And, seeing that I've not heard a word of sense since I got here, I'll hand over to you, God help you!'

'We'll clear this thing up right now,' he said, with decision. 'Your number?' he demanded of her.

'Nine-nine-four,' she told him, promptly.

'Mine's six-one-four,' he said. 'Now, yours?' he added, turning to me.

I hesitated, then:

'What's all this about? What number? You know my name, what more do you want?'

'Don't be funny. We want your number.'

I shrugged. 'I don't know what you're talking about.'

'He said two-three-seven first, but that's the room number here – and anyway it couldn't be that,' Miss Hander supplied.

'Come on. Show us your Prairie-Dog,' said the loony.

'My – my what?' I asked blankly.

'See what I mean?' inquired Miss Hander. 'Nutto-phrenic, sub-let, gone chasing butterflies some place else.'

'Huh!' said the loony. He pulled out his pistol, and gave me a good look at it. 'If we don't find out who you are in a couple of minutes, you won't be anyone much longer,' he remarked.

*   *   *

Well, approximately twenty minutes later neither of them was any nearer believing a thing I told them – and I was still failing to make sense of the questions they asked.

There came a point where they let up for a minute, and frowned at one another. Miss Hander shook her head, 'Amnesia, cerebral vacation, must be,' she said. 'The guy really is believing what he says – what there is of it.'

The furrow between the loony's brows stayed there.

'Would that mean he'd be dangerous?' he wondered.

Miss Hander shrugged. 'Could be, if he were to go around asking too many people who he is...'

'The hell with this,' I broke in. 'I've told you a dozen times who I am, and you knew it before you came in,' I told the loony. 'You don't have any right to question me, anyway. What I want to know is what goes on in back of you two? What I want *particularly* to know is what has happened to the girl you saw me with in the park?'

'What was her number?' asked Miss Hander.

'Anyone who says "number" to me once more won't have one,' I said, turning on her and for the moment she looked a little uneasy.

The two of them exchanged glances again. The loony put away his gun. He began to speak in an altogether different style.

'Now, see here, feller. You're not quite well, you know. Maybe you got a knock on your head sometime – that can play funny tricks with your memory. Doesn't do to let it go on like that, either. You ought to see a doc and get it fixed. Now, what say you come along with us? It happens I know just the feller – right here in town. A real swell worker on just this kind of thing. A taxi'll have us around to his place in five minutes. What you say now?'

I'd had enough of it. And I only go with guys who tote guns when they're pointing them. All in one sweep of my arm I swung up a small chair beside me, and smashed the light with it. At the same time I jumped sideways.

He'd not shoot. Except in the movies, where each room happens to have its own fire-escape, hotels are pretty awkward to get away from once you've roused the place. What I was anxious he shouldn't do was club me. Somewhere in all this somebody had already pulled one gag with an ambulance...

I felt my way to the wall, and got my back against it. I'd not know quite what was going on elsewhere, but presently there was a crunch and a creak, at which the loony's voice said clearly and irritably:

'For God's sake! Now you get across to the door, and stay there. And take this. If he tries that way, shoot!'

I judged that to be entirely for my benefit – meaning that he was very sensibly keeping hold of the gun himself.

I started to edge along, with my right hand outstretched against the wall. After three or four cautious steps, my fingers met a knob. I paused. Then, on an impulse, I turned it fully round, and wrenched it off its shaft.

The entire Crosby family in harmony hit the place like weather arriving at Key West. The windows rattled, the walls shivered, the floor palpitated in sympathy with that vast, superhuman boom...

In less than three seconds my door was open and my two visitors were hurrying down a corridor where other doors were opening and outraged voices were doubtless hurling abuse into the quivering gales of song...

* * *

After the light had been restored, and I had reduced the management to apologizing to me for having a faulty knob on its radio-control, I locked the door. As a further precaution, I balanced one or two clattersome objects against it. Then I prepared for bed – so, of course, my phone had to ring.

I guessed it would be Miss Hander or the loony, and thought up a few numbers to give them. But it wasn't: it was Jake, on long-distance. I got a lump of lead in my stomach the moment I heard his voice. He'd not ring me at that time in the morning for nothing...

'Yes. Johnny here,' I said.

He hesitated, then:

'I'm afraid it's bad news, Johnny. The police rang the office for you. Nobody knew where you were, so they put it through to me, here.'

I tightened my hold on the phone, and tried to do the same on my voice.

'She's not – ? You don't mean she's – ?'

'I'm afraid that's what they say, Johnny. Better come back right away.'

You can half-expect things. Try to face them in advance, case-harden your mind, you think – but when they come, it's always different. Quite a while passed before I could say:

'I'll come. – Thanks, Jake.'

And there was a longer time before I came-to to find myself still holding the handset in mid-air. A tinny voice from it was saying:

'Hullo! Hullo, there! Are you through?'

'I – I guess so,' I said, and began to talk to the night desk about planes and trains.

* * *

When they pulled the sheet back from her face I sighed. I'd been afraid to ask them about marks. The way they'd put it to me, they might as well have told me right out that it looked like a self-shooting – and the only way I'd known that done was through the head. So I was frightened shaky at what I'd be going to see when they lifted that sheet. Not that I thought for a moment she'd have done that – but if it had been made to look that way, they ought to have told me it was through the heart…

She looked what they call 'peaceful'. But that isn't right, really. What I saw there was impersonal; something less than a sculpture – more like something she'd been wearing, but left behind because she'd not be wanting it any more now…

She was pale, even her lips. Her eyelids were closed, with the lashes lying like a gold fringe on her cheeks. The shape was the same, still beautiful to look at: it was just that it didn't seem to mean much any more…

One of the men cleared his throat, waiting for me.

'Yes,' I said, slowly. 'Yes.'

They pulled the sheet up again. A cop touched me gently on the arm. We turned away, and walked up an avenue of the nameless unclaimed lying under their sheets. Our footsteps sounded gritty in the cold silence of the place.

At the door I turned to look back once more. She was just one in the rows of unmoving white sheets now. In the end, named or not, they all looked alike… looked *alike*! *Alike*!

I stopped suddenly. *Alike*!

'Hold it a minute,' I told them, and started back long the rows of sheets.

They didn't hold it. They hurried after me. The morgue attendant laid a hand on my arm in a restraining way. I shook it off.

'Her right arm,' I said. 'In the crook of her elbow there's a small mole, brown – quarter-inch across, maybe.'

We looked.

There wasn't any mole.

They turned doubtful eyes on me, and then on one another. Nobody had mentioned a mole until now – and they must get quite a few people acting strangely in that place. We examined the arm again. Then they looked at the left one, just in case. I didn't need to.

The attendant cleared his throat with some embarrassment. His eye met the cop's again. They didn't believe me. Not that that mattered a lot. I was satisfied.

'Maybe you might be misremembering – ' the attendant began.

I shook my head, looking down at her hands.

'Finger-prints,' I said. 'You'll find plenty of hers in her apartment – but you'll find they'll not match these.'

I was quite confident of that.

The cop said, peaceably: 'Sure. We'll check on that, of course.' But his voice had a humouring tone, and his eye strayed vaguely towards the attendant.

'I'm withdrawing the identification,' I told them. 'This was *not* Freda Darl. I'll go on the record with that.'

* * *

I took the rest of the day on the loose, and didn't go into the office until next morning. When I got there, Jake was tied up in one of those high-policy conferences which send rumours round the building from cellar to roof until the old paper comes out again, still looking much the same. As he'd not be free for an hour or more I went down to 'Reference'.

'Hiya, Limey! How's wolving in Washington?' Sally inquired.

'On a kind of political basis,' I explained.

'So nobody bothered to tell you what big eyes you have? – Too bad.'

'Honey,' I told her, practically, 'the reason I've come here is because of the big ears you have.' I pulled out a rough print or two of Miss Hander and her partner dancing, and put them on her desk. 'Can you tell me who the Senatorial character is?'

Sally looked down at the photographs.

'I still say she's not your type,' she observed.

'Physically you could be wrong – though on personality you happen to be tops this time,' I admitted. 'But what I want to know about right now is this personification of the G.O.P.'

'Oh, him,' she said. 'He's Paul K. Hindler, known to the boys as Pawky – Paul K., see?'

I blinked. 'Now how would you come to know that right off like it was yesterday's lesson?' I wanted to know.

'Well, I was sort of interested, so I thought – ,' Whatever the thought had been, she let it trail off. 'Just what is it that you've been doing to that young woman?' she inquired, looking up at me.

'What have *I* been doing? Let me tell you that if anybody does things to Miss Hander, it's nobody but Miss Hander. That's the way she is. Why?'

'Well, – you took this Tuesday night?'

'Yes.'

'And my information happens to be that she didn't show up on the job yesterday. So I just kind of wondered...'

'You needn't. Nothing to do with me.'

'So? Well, there it is, anyway. Pawky's head of the section. When there was still no sign of her an hour or two after time he got worried, and had somebody ring up her apartment. No answer. He sent somebody round there. Cupboard was bare: she'd skipped right out. Seems he was quite a lot annoyed.' She looked down at the picture again. 'He'd invested, maybe...?'

I recalled the bracelet-watch.

'I'd not be amazed at that. But how do you know all this?'

'How do you think I hold down this job? I just got wondering...'

'Next time I want to know what goes on in Washington I shall stay right home and learn.'

'All part of the service, Limey. Did you speak to her? What's she like?'

'Er – a decisive kind – some might put it more crudely. Speaks English and German with notable fluency, but her listening technique is hammy.'

'Could it be your approach – ?'

'With Pawky.'

'I see. Well, I did mention she wasn't your type. What you really need, I think, is the confiding kind, smaller, so that she can nestle cosily...'

It always seemed a funny thing to me that Sally, with all her information, didn't seem to know a thing about Freda...

* * *

'The morgue people didn't believe you, then?' Jake asked.

I explained that, being pretty sure they'd not, I had rung up the man Bottleton, to confirm. He said sure he remembered that mole, and he'd get right down there, and support my word. When I got on to him again later he'd sounded shaken. 'Amazing likeness,' he said. 'If you hadn't warned me, I believe I'd have identified her. But there was one other thing, though.' I wondered what that would be. 'Her finger-nails,' he said, 'they'd get in her way typing, so she never lets them grow that long.'

'Hell of a thing isn't it,' I said to Jake, 'when your girl's boss notices more about her than you do?'

'So that makes another of 'em. This is getting very peculiar indeed,' said Jake.

I told him that was one way of minimizing it.

'And this one in Washington? How did you make out there?'

I gave him an account, ending with the climax of the grand bathroom-boom.

'H'm,' he said. 'A bit before your time there used to be not unsimilar happenings presided over by certain Brothers Marx.'

'Never heard of them,' I told him. 'But nobody else ever spent a fifty minutes quite like that. I've still not figured out how many of us were crazy, or what was supposed to be going on. And now Sally in "Reference" tells me that she's vanished.'

'H'm,' he said again, 'then, purely on precedent, I should get Sally to ring up the Washington morgue.'

In connection with the self-reliant Miss Hander that angle simply hadn't occurred to me.

'Hell!' I said. 'You don't think – ?'

'I don't know what I think – except that you seem to have got yourself mixed up in something that might be a musical comedy – if it weren't singularly unfunny.'

'I?' I said. 'What have I done? These things just happen at and around me. Where did I motivate anything? Tell me that.'

Jake took a cigarette and lit it, reflectively. Half to himself, and frowning, he muttered: 'I don't see – .' Then he added: 'How many of these women do we know of now?'

I ticked them off on my fingers. 'Fire-escape, Paris, B.A., Flagstaff, Hudson River, morgue. Six.'

'Six,' he repeated wonderingly. 'Looks like somebody might be making a purge of something – only, I wonder how you even start out to find six identicals? – well, in point of fact, eight, if we count your cousin and the one in Washington. I don't see how you could do that without advertising, and pretty widely, too. And, more, *why* would you *want* to find them? I can't think of an answer to that outside of show-business – and there, the more alive they are, the better. But there does *have to be* a reason…'

'Just to complicate things more,' I told him, 'there's somebody just like me in it some place, too. I keep on being mistaken for him.'

The janitor, the nurse, the loony on the park-bench, I pointed out, had all done that. Also, Miss Hander had been under the impression that I had been spying on her for a day or two – furthermore, she had so little doubt of knowing me that she had chosen to address me in German.

'German?' Jake repeated, raising his eyebrows. 'You're sure it wasn't Russian?'

'I am,' I said. 'For one thing, I don't know any Russian, but I do know German – even quite rude German.'

He massaged his forehead with his knuckles. Maybe that's how he rubs out one line of thought to make room for another, but this time it seemed slow in coming.

'Anyway,' I went on, 'I do have Miss Hander's picture, and what I'm wondering now is whether we can run it on that page along with the rest – or might that be letting her in for the same kind of curtains some way? – That is, of course, assuming that she hasn't fetched up in the Washington morgue already. If she hasn't, I'd not like to think I might be partly responsible for even a dame like that being – '

'That's one thing you won't need to worry about,' Jake put in. 'The answer is "No" – in fact, the answer is also "No" to the whole page.'

I stared at him.

'You mean – *Life*'s scooped us on it, or something?'

'No. It's just – out. Sorry, Johnny. Might have been quite a hit – but there it is.'

'But – ' I began. Then I stopped: I remembered that there had just been that high-level conference. 'Oh, I see,' I said, bitterly, 'we're back on the better-tone policy for a spell. Murder is rough and vulgar; let's have pictures of national dances instead. Drape the dames and up the circulation in the Bible-belt. More old masters, and fewer young mistresses. That it?'

'No, again, Johnny. Not this time.'

'But, look here, Jake. It isn't only that it's my feature. I reckon that if we show those faces it'll quite likely bring out somebody who's seen Freda, and might tell us something.'

'Couldn't it work the other way?'

'I'd risk that. Hell, Jake, you owe me a reason. I'll admit it's not a top-tone subject, but it's got wide reader-interest all right – and it could be valuable if there are any more women around who look like – '

'You're way up the wrong street, Johnny. That isn't the angle at all.'

'What is, then?'

Jake opened his mouth. He scratched his cheek, irresolutely with his finger-nail, making a bristly noise. He decided:

'Okay then, but off the record, mind.'

I nodded.

'It's this way. When a fellow came around here yesterday and sent in an Office of Security card I reckoned I'd better see him. Genteel, he was – or do I mean urbane? – Smooth, anyway. The Office, he said, understood that we had it in mind to publish an article drawing attention to the deaths of certain women who bore a marked superficial resemblance to one another. I told him that even if that might be, I'd like to know just how the heck the Office came to understand it – the more particularly as we had not gotten much further than what you might call a preliminary to gestation even here. But the fellow ran true to form – that side of it, it seemed, wasn't his department. His purpose was simply to present the Office's compliments, and convey that the said Office would be greatly obliged to us if we could see our way to postponing indefinitely any reference to the matter in question, on the grounds of national security. The Office hoped that we would fully understand that only the gravest reasons, et cetera. The whole thing was very four hundred and diplomatic, I can tell you. I only just stopped myself from bowing at the end of it.'

I stared at him.

'Censorship! Here! And in peacetime, too!'

'Tch-tch! Johnny, what a word to use in a country with a free press. There's no such thing here, as you very well know. – On the other hand, of course, there are considerations of policy – deep waters being less still than they look, and all that. So, on thinking it over, I began to see that the page we thought of was not perhaps, after all, quite in accord with our policy here.'

I absorbed that slowly. Then I said:

'What's all this about, Jake?'

'You know as much as I do, Johnny – or, you might do if you'd stop thinking in such old-fashioned terms.'

'Such as?'

'Well, peacetime and wartime, for instance. We don't happen to live in a nicely docketed world like that any more. It doesn't mean that just because the noisy kinds of weapons aren't banging that we're at peace; not nowadays – they're only the last resort: the one everybody's scared of, so we fight without 'em as long as possible.'

'I don't see what this has to do with – '

'Nor do I – but if that Office is interested, it clearly has.'

I thought the situation over a bit.

'What is this Office of Security?' I asked.

'Well – kind of sixth angle to the Pentagon – with ramifications here and there.'

'I'd like to have a word with the part that ramifies here,' I told him.

He considered.

'Uh-huh. After all you're the guy working up the material for that page, so I had to hand you the tip, didn't I? Only don't – well, I mean that's one of those places they got special padded walls for running heads into. Take it easy,' he advised.

6

Disguise

Disguise fair nature with hard favoured rage – W.S.

He was right. That was just the way of it when I got there. I bounced gently from one official to another. They seemed to become more pillowy as I ascended the grades. Deviously, however, I did at last succeed in reaching the office of the man who had called on Jake the previous day. A nice office; very restful and orderly. A clear desk; nothing in the In tray, a few signed sheets in the Out. The man across it was a well-produced, pleasant-mannered, shock-absorbing character, with a quiet air of being on my side in general but regrettably propelled elsewhere by the tides of fate just at the moment. His name was Owen.

He heard me through my piece, and nodded sympathetically.

'Of course,' he said. 'One can clearly see that this must be very irksome for you, Mr. Farthing. Highly unfortunate, since I'm afraid it must mean a waste of quite a lot of your time and work.'

'It does,' I agreed. 'It means more than that, too. People have a right to know about things like this. I'd be a mighty surprised man if all those deaths turned out to be suicides – that makes a warning to be in the public interest. There's a mystery here – and a little publicity would likely produce some leads.'

He nodded again. 'Very disappointing for you, I'm afraid. But, unfortunately, I act only as a mouthpiece in the matter. Instructions come to me from a higher level.'

'Then if you can't do anything, I'd like to have a word on a higher level,' I told him.

'I'm afraid that is not possible, Mr. Farthing.'

We regarded one another for some moments. He did not seem disposed to add anything, but neither was I content to leave it there.

'*Choice*,' I remarked, 'has now declined to use my idea, so I am at liberty to take it elsewhere. It could be that a less influential paper might be less open to influence.'

'Our suggestion was a *postponement*, Mr. Farthing. And, in any case, I would not advise such a course as you suggest. I really would not.'

'Before I can accept that as final, I need more information than I have at present,' I told him. 'Frankly, I don't like the way this is being handled. Look at it from my angle. I'm damned sure that these deaths are not suicides – my own cousin who is also my fiancée has been kidnapped; and now I am semi-officially told to shut my trap. Why? For all I can tell at present, it may be that some private individual in this Office has an interest in hushing these murders up.'

'That is a quite disgraceful suggestion, Mr. Farthing,' he said, very coldly.

'Well, what am I to think? It would be a far more disgraceful revelation if it should turn out to be true, Mr. Owen. This Office's care not to put its request into writing is odd, to say the least…'

He leant back in his chair, regarding me with a small, perplexed frown for some seconds.

'I assure you, Mr. Farthing – '

'Certainly, Mr. Owen – but you yourself told me that you are merely a mouthpiece in the matter.'

He considered me for a few moments more, then he pushed over the cigarette-box.

'You will excuse me a minute?' he said, and he went out of the room, leaving me to the careful attention of a corner of his stenographer's eye.

About a quarter-hour passed before he returned, accompanied by a messenger into whose care he put me. Under escort I proceeded to upper and, apparently, still more sacred regions of the building. The room into which I was shown already contained two men.

One of them was dark, the other had greyed. They differed in build, but they had certain things in common – manner, stance, alert eyes, and an air of wearing invisible uniforms beneath their lounge-suits. They looked at me first with casual interest, then harder, with astonishment patently growing. They greeted me by name, but they went on looking puzzled. So here it was again: I supposed that shortly they'd be asking me for my number.

But they didn't do that: nor did the explanation of their puzzlement come out, though they kept on looking at me in a wondering way from time to time all through the interview. There was no doubt they had clams some place in their ancestry. The elder put it to me:

'You will understand, Mr. Farthing, that this branch of the Office takes its orders from Washington. It cannot act on its own account.'

He went on to repeat and confirm the request that had been made to Jake. After that, it was more a case of them finding out about me than vice versa.

'You are an American citizen, Mr. Farthing?' one of them asked.

'Certainly,' I told him. 'Don't I sound like one?'

'Not a lot,' he said, consideringly. 'Offhand, I should have put you down as a – '

'Limey's the word,' I suggested.

'Londoner is the one I was about to use. A Londoner, with some slight local colouration.'

'When in Rome…' I said.

'Exactly. Have you ever heard an Englishman trying to pass himself off as an Italian? Well, now, suppose we clear this up?'

I explained while the other man took notes. We went over much of my life history, but never got to my turn to have questions answered. When he'd taken it all down, he said, simply:

'I'm sorry we can't give you any information now, Mr. Farthing. But if you will call on us in a week's time, I think we may be able to put you a little more in the picture. In the meantime, we must advise you very strongly to pay serious attention to our previous *request*.' He got that 'request' into italics.

It was far from satisfactory to me, and I told them so. I might as well have talked to a ball of glass-wool; they both of them just absorbed without echo. They'd said their say, they stuck, and when I finally emerged on the sidewalk I found that all I'd done was talk plenty and collect nothing.

I turned to walk north, wondering what line I would take now. It might be that I had covered a block or thereabouts when a big black car came sliding past me along the kerb. It stopped a few yards ahead, and the rear door opened. I heard a quickened footstep behind me. Something was jabbed unexpectedly and painfully against my side. A voice said quietly:

'Inside there, pal. And no tricks.'

* * *

When, later on, I came round with a steady beat like a ship's engines inside my head, I wished I'd taken that last piece of advice.

I'd no desire to do anything but lie where I was for ever – except, maybe, to stop my pulse working. Some place, beyond the thumping, there was a sound of voices, but it was quite a while before I took any interest in them. Dimly, I did get around to realizing that they were speaking partly in German: I left it at that, until one emerged from the general background, saying, in English now:

'Waste of time, waste of transport, waste of everything. Why don't we bump him, and write the whole thing off? That's what he'll get in the end, anyway.'

Another, very similar voice replied:

'That's universally true – but it's what happens before the end that matters. He may be crazy, though I guess he's not. Anyway, something took him to the Office of Security – it'd be better to have him talk about that before he's bumped.'

A third voice said slowly, and doubtfully:

'I've no doubt that he can be made to talk. But is it worth the trouble? Those Headquarters boys are so efficient over confessions – a trifle disgusting, perhaps, but they get results, and that is the trouble. If I were to be the subject of their attentions, I haven't the least doubt that I should confess to any and everything they cared to suggest. As a system, it doesn't really bring one very much nearer the truth for certain, and drives the subject of the treatment into complete unreliability. In fact, that kind of information seems to me as dangerous as any from an uncheckable source.'

'In other words,' said the first voice, 'you suggest that for all the use he's likely to be, we might as well dispose of him right now.'

'Certainly I don't – and don't quote me as saying so. However, the instructions are that he must not be allowed to escape alive. It might save everyone trouble if he – er – didn't.'

They went on talking, and I went on lying with my eyes shut. Sometimes I seemed to be close beside them; at others I'd drifted quite a way off. And all the time my head kept on thumping.

The man who showed me into the car had meant what he said about 'no tricks'. I had found myself sitting in the back seat between two men fully my own size, being driven slickly through familiar streets. It seemed to me that my best chance was to throw myself on the driver's back at a moment when he was engaged in a tricky bit of cornering, or overtaking. The trouble was that I couldn't decide whether the man with the gun had a mind to use it or not, but I'd have to risk that.

I measured up the distance between me and the driver with my eye, and began to look for my chance. But between three full-sized men on one back seat there is close contact. Perhaps they felt my muscles getting ready for it. Anyway, the one on my right lifted his gun, and before I saw what was coming, quite simply socked me with it. And that had been that, until now.

Having, it would appear, nothing whatever to gain by showing life, I kept on lying doggo. After a while the door opened, and two of them went out, still talking. I reckoned the third was still present. Soon, I knew he was. I heard him come close up to the bed, and guessed he was looking at me. Then he moved across he room, and I risked opening my eyes a slit, without moving anything else.

When I got over the first stabbing effect of the light I saw that the place was a bedroom, poorly furnished. I reckoned it was at the top of some house, partly because the window was small, and showed nothing but sky, and partly because the stuffiness suggested that the sun might be shining on a roof just above. The man was looking out of the window, but as he turned his head I got a sideface view of him. His hair was dark and somewhat sleek, his eyebrows and his moustache, heavy. In a dark business-suit he looked as inconspicuous as anyone of his size was likely to be. Then he seemed about to turn my way, so I closed my eyes again.

When I risked another glimpse I had a shock. He was standing in front of the dressing-table, in his shirt-sleeves, revealing a holster under his left arm. It wasn't that that perturbed me, though; it was the fact that his hair, though cropped short, was now as fair as my own. The dark hair was in his right hand, hanging limp, like a fish-skin.

He dropped it on the dressing-table. Then he took his moustache by the right side, and peeled it carefully off his face. He rubbed his upper lip for a rueful moment, and then turned his attention to his eyebrows. After that he crossed to the basin, poured water into it from a pitcher, and sluiced himself. When he looked up again I might have been regarding my own reflection.

Quite likely I moved, or drew a breath of surprise, for he paused, towel in hand, to look at me.

'Oh, so you've come round, have you?' he said, in an unsympathetic tone, and in German.

'Give me some water,' I said.

He nodded towards the pitcher, but did not attempt to fetch it. With a great effort I pulled myself together and staggered across to it.

He moved back to the dressing-table and put on his jacket again; then he picked up the pieces of false hair, wrapped them carefully in a sheet of tissue, and stowed them in an inside pocket. Rather pointedly he refrained from turning his back on me: he need not have bothered – I didn't feel like doing any more than reaching the bed again and nursing the hydraulic ram inside my head. When it had settled down a bit I looked up at him.

It wasn't difficult to understand the janitor and the cleaning woman mistaking him for me. Met in a sufficiently absent-minded moment, I might have done so myself.

'Where did you take her?' I asked him.

He looked puzzled,

'Who?'

'Freda. Freda Darl, of course.'

'Her number, you sap?'

'Number?' I repeated, blankly. I was beginning to feel haunted by numbers.

He eyed me a bit more closely.

'If you want to put the old where-am-I?, you're on the way to H.Q. to answer a few questions. You know what that means.'

'What's all this about?' I demanded.

He smiled. Not a pleasing smile.

'Come, come. Be yourself. That one's so corny. And, anyway, the boys at H.Q. have proved that loss of memory just doesn't exist. It's surprising what they get people to remember there.' He paused, and looked with a thoughtful pointedness at the window. 'Not very comfortable – and can take them a long time on the job,' he added, still looking out. Then he turned back to give me a long stare. Presently he shrugged and left the room, locking the door behind him.

I went on sitting on the bed and trying to think.

The why of the whole thing was, if possible, even more obscure than before, but one immediacy was well lit up: once more, or still, I was suspected of being somebody else – and by the look of it that somebody else was in quite a spot. He seemed to have three possible courses open to him: he could be shot while attempting to escape (or framed on that); he could be taken to H.Q., wherever and whatever that might be, and uncomfortably 'questioned'; or, as the last remark clearly hinted, he could go jump through a high window.

It would seem a goodish idea, as a first step, to convince them that they had the wrong man... And that put up another puzzler: as the man who had just left the room looked exactly like me, and yet did not seem to know anything of Freda, then, some place in all this, there must be a third man, looking just like both of us. And who in heck would he be...? Once disguises and make-up came into it – well, there was the park-bench loony, for one. He'd been about the same height, and a paunch can be adopted even more easily than false hair.

And while we were on disguises, what about all these false-fronted doubles of Freda, too…?

I won't deny that sitting there with the trip-hammer still at work whenever I moved my head I did begin to get scared – more on account of what seemed to be happening to my mind than anything else. The thing had begun by my discovering quite a flock of identical women: now, after a knock on the head, too, I was starting to see identical men…

By the time my double returned, however, I was feeling at least physically somewhat better. I was able to tackle the food on the tray he brought, and between mouthfuls I explained to him who I was. I showed him my *Choice* card and other things, to prove it. I asked him who he thought I was. He listened, with the corners of his mouth drawn down, but said nothing. He stayed like that for perhaps ten minutes, then he walked over slowly to where I was sitting on the edge of the bed with the tray beside me. I looked up at him.

'God knows, it's simple enough to check what I'm telling you,' I said. 'Ring up Jake Parton there. Get him to send somebody over to identify me if you like. I don't know who your quarrel's with, but I do know you're making one hell of a big mistake over me. I can't tell you anything. I don't – '

At which point he let me have it with a drive to the stomach. All the breath went out of me in one whoosh. I doubled up, and fell from the bed to the floor. He kicked me as I lay there struggling for breath.

'Go on, whine,' he said. 'Whine, and snivel, and wriggle about that. I don't know what it is you've been pulling. You've played for something – and now you've lost out, and you've not the guts to take it straight. Gah! You make me sick!' And, with a final kick, he went out, leaving me trying to sob some breath back.

It wasn't a good line for him to take. It's in the character of many of us northerners to anger slowly, but we can build up with a cold hard force. It may have been that that blow in the car had knocked me a bit silly so that I hadn't so far got the position really life-size, but by the time I had my breath back and was feeling the bruises, I was no longer interested in who was making mistakes. I just saw a situation that was going to be radically altered.

*   *   *

What you do is review the situation in the light of all known factors. First you settle your objective, and get that clear. To begin with you think that's simple: that you could express it succinctly if not classically as 'getting the hell out of here'. Then you find it isn't quite that simple, for two reasons. One is that you have heard a man suggest that from his point of view it might be a good thing to have you try just that – and put a little fancy gunning in your way. The other is that these people undoubtedly have something to do with Freda's disappearance, and so far they are about the only link you've hooked. So you find that your object is not quite what you thought at first – simply to get over the skyline with the greatest possible speed.

Then you consider your opponent/s. There's a man who looks quite uncannily like you. Can you use that? A man, moreover, who has already conceived a contempt for you – that's always helpful in such circumstances. Finally, you get around to making an inventory of the materials at your disposal, and their potentialities. All this, of course, if you have time – and I was having plenty.

When I'd done all that, I pulled away the strip of carpet leading from the door, and turned the linoleum up. Unfortunately the boards near the door were well nailed down, so I had to abandon that variant on the elephant-pit, and think again.

Just beyond the foot of the bed, in the middle of the room there was a bit of loose board, some eighteen inches long – something to do with the electric wiring of the room beneath, I guessed. I took that out, and considered it. I put the linoleum back, smashed the glass on the washstand, and used a bit of the remains to cut away the part of the linoleum which covered the hole the board had left. I took the strip of carpet, damped the underside of it at one end, and soaped it thoroughly. Then I put it back to cover the hole in the floor, with the soaped end up by the door. The other end, near the window, I anchored as well as I could with the weight of the dressing-table. Then I sat down, with my legs dangling over the foot of the bed, to wait. On second thoughts I fetched the pitcher, and dribbled a little water on the carpet to mark the exact centre of the place where the board was missing.

When he came back, I was still sitting there in a gloomy slump. He didn't carry a tray this time. He wasn't being careless, either. He pushed the door right back as he opened it, and located me before he came in. And he did that with his right hand in his jacket opening, ready to draw.

He paused just inside. I turned my head, with a scared expression. His lip curled a bit as he stepped forward, both feet on the carpet now.

I heaved myself off the bed, and came down with my full weight on the damp spot in the carpet. The soaped end of the strip was whisked from under him, and his heels went up.

The idea had been to jump for him in as much the same action as I could make it. Luckily, seeing that my foot got momentarily jammed in the hole, that was not necessary. The part of him that met the ground first was the back of his head – with that nasty kind of soggy crack that skulls make. It kept him quiet.

I went over to him, and pulled out his gun, and waited, but no one came.

Then I shut the door and got busy. It's not all that easy changing rig with a guy that's gone away for a bit, but patience does it. When it was done, I poured some water on his face to bring him back. He surfaced pretty quickly considering. His eyes were screwed up at me, doubtless on account of it was he who had the trip-hammer in his head now, but there was no where-am-I? Instead, he said venomously:

'You'll not get away with this.'

'Maybe,' I admitted. 'But I have your gun, and your spare clip. That ought to ensure some company as I go.'

I watched him get groggily to his feet.

'Stop right there,' I told him.

He shook his head as if to clear it. It seemed to work, too; a more calculating look came into his eyes. I allowed him most of a minute to pull himself together, then I said:

'A while ago you made a suggestion to me about that window.' I turned my head towards it as I spoke.

On the instant, he dived for the door.

A fool thing to do. I could have plugged him twice. As it was, I sent a shot into the wall beside him to speed him up, and then jumped after him. I pulled to the door behind me with a house-shaking slam, and fired again as he ran down the corridor. I followed after to the turn, and found the start of a narrow stair. He was around the next turn by then, but I fired again, and yelled fortissimo. He went clattering on down the next flight of stairs at a breakneck speed. I listened... Presently there was the sound of a voice rising in a shout, broken off by the clatter of four or five shots: then the noise of a heavy thud.

I put the pistol back in its holster, and walked down without haste. By the look of things the man ahead of me had finished up by rolling the last flight. He was lying in the narrow hall at the bottom of it, with two men bending over him. Their faces turned towards me as I descended.

'While attempting escape,' said one of them, not without satisfaction.

But I – well, I wasn't fit for making any reply just then. That was because both of the men who stood there were living images of the man who lay dead – and of me...

* * *

If anyone were to ask me just where this affair passed from the scatty to the fantastic, from the merely improbable to the nightmare, I would, I think, select this spot for the X.

Hitherto, there had been a consoling mutter at the back of my mind which insisted that, out of plumb as the whole thing was, it could, once I had the right clue, be dragged into the straight. This, I suppose, was because there had, so far, been normal surroundings for ballast; plus one's subconscious feeling that however odd things might seem, they could not really be too far off the beam because nothing ever is.

That is a basic mistake. Things can, in their own right, be fearful, wonderful, romantic, fantastic, and unbelievable, and are so until they have entered this civilization of ours and happened a few times. Then the adjectives change; everyone gets on wonder-crushing terms with them as soon as possible, and fantasy and romance peel off. Primitive man would see every one of us as a magician, but being our kind of magician turns out to be a very matter of fact business once you're there. The poet dreamed of flying free as a bird – but airlines are worried by freight-rates. Seers foretold a godlike voice addressing the world – we suffer radio-announcers. The scientist saw the triumph of man's intellect in the achievement of nuclear fission – we ungratefully resent the probably concomitant fission of man, along with his intellect. So closely now has conception approached commonplace that a marvel has the lifespan of a mayfly.

I knew all this. But when I needed it, I forgot it. It is so much easier to be primitive, to doubt one's senses than to apply them. And so, standing in that hall, one of four identicals – save insofar as one of us happened to be dead – I promptly allowed my mind to deny my wits.

The other two seemed to sense something wrong in my manner. They looked up at me standing dazed on the stairs.

'How did he pull that?' one of them asked, in English this time.

I had enough presence of mind left to play for a stall.

'He slugged me – feeling a bit muzzy,' I said, not untruthfully.

They looked at me with similar expressions of sympathy; the only difference I could detect between them was that one wore a pepper-and-salt tweed, the other, a dark pin-stripe.

'You want a drink,' said the tweed-suited one.

Feeling dreamlike, I joined them, and we went into the front room. He poured the drinks from a bottle, and lifted his glass.

'Sieg Heil!' he said.

The other responded as a matter of course, so:

'Sieg Heil!' I said, too.

The drink was a good idea; I began to feel better.

'Well, that certainly simplifies things,' said the dispenser of drinks. 'He'd have had to go on a stretcher, and I never like the way a stretcher at an airport advertises itself.'

'What'll we do with him?' asked the other man.

The first shrugged. 'Just move him to the back, I guess, and turn in a report when we get there. Now that we don't have him to delay us we can get going right away, and make tonight's connection.'

I felt in my pockets for a cigarette. Apparently the late occupant of my clothes did not use them, but the action didn't go unnoticed.

'Backslider,' said the tweed-suited one. 'You'll have to cut it out soon, anyway, so you might as well start now. My only backsliding is alcohol. Have another?'

Clearly, neither of them had the least suspicion of me. I could, to some extent, choose my course: either watch for my chance to slip off, or tag along and see what followed. It was, I think, the remark about the stretcher that decided me. The last time anyone had seen Freda she had been on a stretcher...

The other two went out to remove my late opponent from his prominent position in the hall. They came back in a few minutes.

'If we don't finish this bottle the others will, rot their souls,' observed Tweed-suit. He poured another round, and we sat idly, apparently waiting for something.

Presently, the less talkative man took a long envelope from an inside pocket, and sauntered over to a wall mirror. He shook an auburn toupee gently out of the envelope, and carefully adjusted it over his own short hair. A box from his side-pocket produced other aids. When he turned round, I wouldn't have known him. The slight modifications of colouring and rounding out of features had surprising results.

Tweed-suit followed him. When my turn came, I did my best to fix the trimmings which my late adversary had worn, with nonchalance equal to theirs. I succeeded fairly well after I had corrected the slight list of the moustache on its first application. Tweed-suit looked at his watch, and then at the almost empty bottle.

'Car's due in ten minutes. Toss you for the last drink,' he said.

7

I Fly

Which way I fly is Hell – J.M.

The way things ran, there was no decision for me to make: the opportunity to dodge out on them didn't arise. A large black car – the same, I think, in which I had been an unwilling passenger before – stopped in front of the house. To my surprise, I found it already contained one passenger: a woman, to whom my companions wished 'good evening', and pursued conversation no further.

I had a feeling that there was something vaguely familiar about her, but my position on the seat, with Tweed-suit between us, prevented me from giving her close attention, and I was left with an impression of grey hair, rimless pince-nez, and an aura of respectability somewhat out of tone with her present company.

We travelled for something over an hour before we left the road and turned on to a minor flying-field of the kind largely used by private or taxi-craft. A few minutes later we were climbing into a ten-seater plane. There was already one passenger sitting up in front. She turned to look as we entered. Had there been anybody watching me, he'd likely have seen a dead giveaway. I stopped involuntarily. She was so like Freda that only some kind of inner warning stopped me from greeting her. Luckily all her attention was on the grey-haired woman just ahead of me, and no one noticed. I made my way to a seat and sat down, trembling. The woman who had been with us in the car took a forward seat across the aisle, and turned to speak to the other. As she did, I realized what had made her seem familiar. It was that if you were to take away that grey hair and those glasses; give her fair hair instead, and put some colour in her cheeks; then she, too, would look remarkably like Freda...

I held on to the arms of my seat with a feeling that the tide of insanity was about to float me off any minute now. Vaguely, I was aware that others were now coming aboard, and settling down in the rest of the seats, but even when the door had slammed shut and we had become airborne, I was still trying to screw the lid down on this thing – telling myself to wait, be patient, and all would be explained later... Though I'd not say I believed myself a lot...

To keep my mind off it, and to stop my eyes from continually scraping over the girl in front, in search of differences and similarities, I forced an interest in other things. The plane had climbed high, and was, as far as one could judge, making good speed. Our direction, guessed by the sun, now sinking, was roughly north-west. But that was about all I could tell. Gaps in the clouds were too infrequent for identification of landmarks, and soon it became too dark to try.

For further occupation, I was driven to examining the contents of my pockets. Most of what I found there was non-committal, except for a driving-licence which gave the name of Simon Salter at an address in Farmingdale, N.J. The only thing of interest that the wallet held, other than some forty dollars, was a pair of plated discs, about the size of a dime, and joined by a few links of chain. One of them was embossed around the edge with the words: 'Prairie Dog Vacation Camp: The Sun and the Saddle' framing a bronco in full bounce: on the reverse was the word 'Member', and the figures 891. The second disc was quite blank, and there was no mention of the location of this institution. I slipped it back into the wallet. I didn't see why a fellow would want to carry around a badge from a dude ranch, but then, one man's trash is another's souvenir. Likely there had been a girl at that camp...

Which got me round to thinking of Freda again, and thinking of her got me back to watching the girl up in front. Then I had an idea. That girl *could* be the redoubtable Miss Hander. With the red washed out of her hair and eyebrows, and a more subdued make-up than her *Snow Man* activities had called for, she could, I thought, look pretty much the way this girl did. The more I looked at her, the more sure I was of that, and the more relieved I felt that one, at least, of these doublings had been resolved. And though for a moment, too, I was alarmed lest she should recognize and denounce me, I soon persuaded myself that in my different clothes she was just as likely to mistake me for someone else again.

The mild gratification which came over me at my success in making two of the figments coincide lasted about five minutes. It was broken, and I was all but broken with it, by the reply to a female voice just behind me which asked:

'What I'd like to know is what goes on? Would you know about that?'

Then there was the reply:

'What, me? Hell, no. In my young life this is just one mistimed, labour-wasting, racket-wrecking, goddam crime. No less, and likely more.' As a style of conversation, it was unmistakable. I hung on to the arms of my seat and waited for things to steady up. I felt sure that however many doubles might be around, Miss Hander's vocalization of thought, at least, was unique.

'Oh,' said the other voice, and paused, apparently absorbing implications. 'That's a swell watch,' it remarked.

'Well, I'd not say that the part that ticks is all that good, but the rest's nice,' said Miss Hander, modestly. 'And doesn't that boil me up. Just as I'm all set to move into second gear, this recall has to happen. Am I fractured! Everything going along fine – kinda slow and heavy I'll allow – but mighty steady. And now it's just screwed up for keeps, I guess.

'First thing when I got one of those Father-seriously-ill-come-at-onces I thought maybe it was just me, but it seems like we all got 'em. And it had to be just as I'm getting my heavyweight jacked up into sight of a diamond clip. What's wrong with me is I got luck deficiency.' She brooded awhile. Presently: 'They put a watcher on to you?' she asked.

'Certainly not,' the other replied coldly.

'I just wondered,' said Miss Hander. 'They did on me – though they didn't have any cause. The crust! *Me*! I called him. Nuts, he was; insapient, maladjusted, sub-thyroid, you'd not believe. That's what made me wonder at first if it was only me that had the notice to come. Any report a guy like that could turn in would be feature flan.'

'Did you get his number?' asked the other.

'Did I – ? Say, listen here – ?' and Miss Hander went off into a dissertation on this recurrent theme of numbers. I ceased, helplessly, to listen. Instead, I returned my attention to the girl up front – the one who wasn't Freda, and now turned out not to be Miss Hander, either.

I felt past caring who anyone was. Let 'em play it up, let 'em bring on choruses, parades, regiments of identical girls if they liked. If they were real, the thing would resolve: if they weren't, then I was crazy, anyway, so why worry? I leant back and closed my eyes. Incredibly, I slept.

I don't know for how long, but I woke to hear a speaker announcing sharply: 'Landing in thirty minutes! Landing in thirty minutes!'

There was a stir all around the cabin. Tweed-suit slipped off his toupee, and removed the rest of his decorations. Other men started to do the same. Forward, across the aisle, the grey-haired woman arranged a small mirror, and began to put cream on her face; when she wiped it off about thirty years came with it. I watched fascinated until it occurred to me that

I, too, should perhaps be restoring myself to normal. After I'd removed the properties, I wrapped them up, stowed them in my pocket, and sat back to await developments. Tweed-suit leaned towards me.

'Not lost your Prairie-dog?' he asked me.

For an instant I was all Alice, then I noticed the metal disc that now dangled from his buttonhole; the number side was turned outwards, and showed the figures 284.

'Tch! Forgot the thing,' I said, and pulled out my wallet.

'Thought you might have lost it,' he said chattily, as he watched me put it in place. 'Had to jettison mine once. Hell of a business getting a new one. Hours of security questions.'

We came out of the clouds to see a lit landing ground beneath us. After circling once, we came in to a smooth set-down.

As in a dream, I walked with the rest across rough grass to a weather-beaten barn. We entered it through a small door in the side. The place was filled with the smell of the hay stacked at one end. There were several farm implements around. In the centre of the empty part a tractor, half strewn in bits, stood on a tarpaulin. I followed Tweed-suit past it to a door in the opposite wall. It took us into a narrow passage, brightly lit after the dimness of the barn. We descended a steep flight of stairs, and emerged through a swing-door into a cafeteria set with several long tables.

There were some two dozen people there already, the men slightly outnumbering the women. But by now I had reached the stage of just letting myself float with the incomprehensible. The nightmare would pile up as it liked: I'd given up being staggered – though I did just wonder, on the side, what Freud would have set about making of a dream in which every male in sight was me, and every female, Freda.

'Ah!' said Tweed-suit, hungrily leading the way to the counter.

I followed him mechanically. Nightmare, or what-have-you, I was hungry, too.

* * *

The coffee was good, and the steak. As I began to feel the better for it I got to taking in more of the room, and its occupants.

I would be, I guessed, somewhat schizzed. One of us kept on telling me: 'Nothing to it, old boy. All done with mirrors.' The other was sceptical: 'Huh!' it reflected. 'I'd like to meet the guy who could all do Miss Hander with mirrors.'

And yet, the first weirdness of looking from one similar face to another, and another, did begin to blunt a little, in time. And as it did, I began to perceive a new quality about the place; an oppressive something in the atmosphere. At the end of one table a group of four young men was chatting cheerfully enough in German, but they were almost the only ones. Most of the rest were holding subdued conversations in couples, or sitting alone with an air of being dismayed by their contemplations. It was so general that I could not even pick out Miss Hander. Tweed-suit, beside me, had caught it, too, and retired into himself.

Immediately opposite me a girl with hair tinted to a dark red was regarding her plate with a dull stare of introspection. She looked up while I was watching her. Her eyes were bright and shiny, with tears barely held back. I felt it like a stab – it was so hard to believe she was not Freda – and a very unhappy Freda. Then she caught my look, her eyes went hard and suddenly challenging. The lids lowered, and she was studying her plate again. Presently she moved off without giving me another glance.

Tweed-suit came out of his abstraction to mutter: 'Say, what couldn't I do to a highball!' and then wandered morbidly off to refill his coffee-cup.

I wanted a cigarette, but as no one was smoking, I judged that the prohibitions he had implied were already in force. So I sat there trying to recapture a memory – there was some other place I had known that held a similarly dispirited feeling; but for the time being it evaded me.

Tweed-suit came back with two cups of coffee, and we sat on – me with a hundred questions I was burning to ask; and unable to think of one which might not sell me short – until a hidden loudspeaker startlingly cleared its throat to say:

'Take-off will be at zero three zero zero hours. Repeat, zero three zero zero hours. Assembly at zero two three zero hours. That is, three hours from now. Repeat, assembly three hours from now.'

Tweed-suit finished off his coffee.

'Come on, let's get the hell out of this, and find a bunk,' he said.

* * *

It's the devil when the only things around you that aren't crazy are utter mysteries. 'Take-off at zero three zero zero hours!' Take-off, where to? – or, come to that, take-off, where from? Until I'd heard that, I was under the impression I'd arrived some place: now it seemed I was only on my way.

In what was quite clearly a routine for everyone else, the only answer to any questions would be trouble. I was having quite enough trouble as it was in keeping up an apathetic front to match the rest, and wondering how long it could be made to last.

Lying down, fully dressed save for my shoes, on one of a dozen iron bedsteads, I felt an increasing conviction that the time had now come for me to do something about getting out of the current. Already I had made one disappearance, presumably without trace; I had no desire to go a further stage into the blue without a trail that someone could follow. It is not a pleasant feeling to realise that as far as the world you used to know is concerned you will simply be written-off – and that, for all anyone is likely to be able to do about it, you'll stay that way. But it was necessary to wait awhile before I made any move.

One at a time another half-dozen or so stereos of myself came in and lay down. The last one switched off the lights, leaving only one dim bulb throwing a yellow pool beneath a deep shade.

I waited, considering. If the Office of Security was already interested in the similarity of a number of young women, this place where these reduplications of both sexes were gathered together was going to interest them a whole lot more. The whys of it might make no sense from my angle, but it could easily be a thing they were already scenting – for there could be no doubt they were on the track of something. Assuming this was it, then my proper course was clear – scram out of it, locate it, and tell them about it.

So simple – like if you should happen to be in jail any time and want to be free: all you have to do is get out of jail.

There was just one thing against trying to make a break for it – the feeling that this was the way Freda had come before me: that remark of Tweed-suit's about a stretcher at an airport...

If only I'd had some idea, even hazy, of what I was up against, it would have helped a lot. This was obviously a transit-station, and Security ought to know about it – on the other hand, I hoped they'd not crack down on it and close the avenue completely before I learnt where it led.

At one time, I guessed, a man in my present position would have started something, and shot his way out. But the world has changed: too much system everywhere. So the one-man crime-solvent only gets second-feature jobs, and the best the ordinary fellow can hope for is to help an organization a stage on its way. It's not so showy, and it turns the edge of romance, but you're more likely to last longer...

I gave the others a good half-hour by the clock on the wall to get off to sleep. Then I picked up my shoes and walked carefully to the door in my socks. Even if one of them was still awake there do remain reasons why a man might feel moved to go to a door. In the passage I paused to put my shoes on, and then made back the way we had come. The cafeteria was in darkness so that I had to feel my way past tables and chairs. Beyond the swing door at the other end there was still a dim light to show the stairs.

The barn above was quiet except for a sound that might have been a rat scuttling. I stood still to listen: nothing else moved. With the door closed behind me, the place was black. Then faint lines, a little less dark than the rest, enabled me to place the double doors. I groped towards them, trying to remember how the farm machinery stood. Once, my outstretched arm met a rod or lever which clanked loudly and echoed in the roof-space. It seemed not to interest anybody. I pawed my way cautiously around the implement, and went on. Presently I discovered the small door by which we had come in. The latch lifted easily, and I stepped outside under a dim night sky.

For a couple of minutes or more I stood fast, trying to get the layout of the place right. To the left was the outline of the main building, and the ridges of lower roofs beside it. In front, the shapes of a few young trees, swaying in the light breeze. To the right of them lay, I knew, the field where the plane had landed. There was nothing there to show against the sky. That, I decided, had better be my way; I would at least have a stretch of easy going to begin with. Then, just on that decision, the silence was broken by a sound away in the distance. A hollow, forlorn sound, but with an ominous quality: the bay of a hound, answered presently by another, slightly higher in pitch. I stood there, thinking it over.

No one has ever really trained dogs into knowing what's good for them, and what isn't. On the day they learn to recognize a pistol for what it is, they'll be starting to get some place. As it is, they don't have the sense to keep their traps shut and beat it, and so you have to shoot – which can be unnecessarily inconvenient for both parties. I had still got no further when a boot scraped on a stone, and a dark figure came around the corner of the barn. I reached for the gun.

His night-sight was better than mine.

'Okay, okay. Ease off there,' he said. A light flashed full at me for a second. 'Kind of jumpy, ain't you?' he added.

'Who's that?' I asked, feeling that I'd better say something.

For answer, he flipped the light on his own face for a moment, keeping his eyes closed. I might have known what he'd look like. He did. I relaxed a bit: for the time being, at least, I seemed to be in a state of freemasonry with all these symmetrals of myself.

'Not healthy out here with the dogs around,' he observed.

'What about you?' I asked.

'Oh, I'm okay. They know me.'

'I couldn't sleep down there,' I told him, hoping it would be explanation enough. 'Came up for air.'

'Uh-huh,' he said, without surprise. Come around the end.' We moved to a point where we were not in view of the main house. He put his hand in his pocket, and then held it out. 'Cigarette?'

I took one gratefully.

'Nasty job this trip?' he inquired, on a note of sympathy.

'Not too good,' I agreed, diplomatically.

'Thought so, the way you grabbed for your gun. Doesn't come easy to loosen up right away. I'd see the psych if I was you. Always makes a good move on account of any trouble you might have later.'

Whatever he was talking about, it was evidently meant kindly, so I said:

'Maybe I will, at that,' and wondered just what particular nastiness my job might be supposed to hold.

We smoked quietly for a while. Out in the darkness the dogs started to bay again, three or four of them this time.

'Restless tonight,' he observed. 'Couple of nights ago they caught some poor hobo out there. Tore him to bits. It's kind of excited them.'

'Oh,' I said, trying to disregard a small butterfly in my stomach. 'How did he come to be there?'

He shrugged. 'Could have just missed his road. Anyway, all we could find made it look like a regular hobo all right. Funny thing was the way he'd got past the alarms. Luck, most likely – on account of if he'd known about the alarms, he'd sure have known about the dogs, wouldn't he?'

I guessed that would be so, and added: 'Doesn't sound as if the alarm system's all that hot?'

'That's the way they saw it, too. Been tightening up on it the last couple of days.'

'H'm, I see,' I said.

We chatted on until the cigarettes were finished. Then I thanked him, and guessed I'd be getting back. It'd still be possible to put in an hour or so's sleep before we left.

'Best thing you can do,' he agreed. 'Sooner you than me. I hate those damned gimmicks.'

As I opened the door the hounds bayed again – not so far away this time. My hands went a little sweaty at the thought that I had all but set out to meet them. I wasn't at all sorry to reach the bed I had hopefully left. If the Office of Security was going to find this place, it would have to do it without my help...

* * *

'Fasten all belts! Fasten all belts!' ordered the loud-speaker, in German. I was finding myself just a bit tired of being herded and instructed by anonymous speakers. An hour ago one had awoken me by saying: 'Assembly in thirty minutes! Assembly in thirty minutes!' Maybe it would have been less irritating without the imbecile-child implication that repetition in exactly the same tone gives, but, not content with that, it did it again, for the benefit of those still unawakened.

Following Tweed-suit I had a quick wash and grabbed coffee and a roll in the cafeteria. We were barked out of there by: 'Assembly! Assembly! – Assembly *now*! Assembly *now*!'

In a dimly lit shed near the barn two trucks were waiting. The three dozen or so of us were counted into them, and the doors slammed shut behind us. There was an unpleasing suggestion of stockyard handling in the way it was done. In the darkness of the barn I had lost touch with Tweed-suit so that I now found myself sitting among strangers – insofar as die-stamped images of oneself can be regarded as strangers.

That stage of the journey was short; in ten or fifteen minutes we had stopped again. The doors opened on to darkness. We filed out and stumbled up a slope which seemed to be some kind of ramp. At the top of it, under a dim blue light, the men were peeling off to the left, the women to the right. I followed the man ahead of me along a kind of curving passage. It wasn't like any other place I had ever seen. The convex, vertical wall on the right was enamelled cream, as was the ceiling. The floor and the concave, left-hand wall were covered with some green composition. Against that wall, but standing a little out from it, was a row of seats with head rests. They looked something like exalted barber-chairs upholstered in black, and supported on a jointed framework. The man in front of me settled himself into one of them, so I took the next. Presently we were all sitting there in a curving line like a fantastical comedy chorus. But for the fact that some of us had dyed our hair, one might have been observing rows of himself through opposed mirrors. Then the voice told us to fasten our belts.

This, I supposed, was the 'damned gimmick' referred to by my acquaintance behind the barn. One had to assume from the announcements that it was some kind of vehicle, and also that, somehow, it flew; but, for all I could comprehend of it, it might have been some newly thought-up giggle-raiser in a fun-fair.

'All belts secure? All belts secure?' the voice inquired, peremptorily, then: 'Prepare for take-off! Prepare for take-off!' it went on, still speaking in German.

'Taking-off! Taking-off! Ten – nine – eight – seven...'

On zero, about half an invisible ton fell on me. Instinctively I had drawn breath and held it as the voice approached the end of its count. It was well that I had, but it was all I could do to keep it, and I didn't dare to let it go for fear that I should never be able to draw another against the force that was trying to push me through the seat. That kept on for what was probably a half minute, but felt a whole lot longer.

After that, it eased somewhat – not a great deal, but enough to let me feel that I might yet get through without having my ribs pushed in, and I might risk trying to snatch another breath. Soon, it eased a little more still. The man on my left gave out something which might have been a deep sigh or a mild moan. I heard him mutter in English, apparently for his own consolation:

'Anybody can have 'em! God, how I hate these damned saucers!'

* * *

I kept right on agreeing with that. The intensity of the start had been bad enough, but soon I became aware of a pervading note pitched right on the top step of audibility kind of cutting into my brain like a cheese-wire.

I tried stopping my ears until it should have passed, but it didn't. I'd have given pretty near all I had to have it go either higher or lower, I didn't care which, but no – that, seemingly, was its appointed cycle, and it was sticking to it. Stopping my ears helped scarcely at all; it had a trick method of getting into the system some other way.

After a half-hour of it, I'd given up caring where we were going or what would happen to anybody. The only thing in the world I wanted was for that infernal whine to let up – and I was way past wondering whether the word I had seemed to hear my neighbour mutter was 'saucers', or not. There wasn't a thing that could really matter to me until I had some peace from that nerve-nagging hum. When I did take a look along the row, it was obvious that it had got all of us the same way. You couldn't even think against it, and, by the look of them, nobody was trying.

I recall noticing in one lucid moment that my orientation had gone cockeyed someway: that the floor I had walked on was now steeply canted and the ceiling had moved around to become a sloping wall: but I couldn't bring myself to any real interest in that, let alone figure out how it could be. Mostly I just hung on to the arms of my chair and wondered how long it would be before I started screaming.

The thing that broke up the tension was altogether unexpected. There was a sound like a sudden, sharp slap, followed by a crash some place. Almost immediately a pressure like that at the start dropped on us again, without any warning. My lungs felt pressed flat, like empty paper bags – and not likely to open out again. Luckily the weight did not last more than a few seconds. When it eased, I could hear above my whooping efforts to re-inflate myself that the hum had done the impossible and risen to a still higher pitch, no less painful. Through it the voice from the speaker said:

'Achtung! Achtung! Air-leak. Stop that hole! Quick!'

A man two places from me was already struggling out of his chair. Near his feet I noticed a hole some two inches across in the green floor; the edges showed ragged metal, inturned. The man pulled off the raincoat he was wearing, folded it hastily, and slapped it over the hole. Up in what had now become the ceiling I could see a corresponding hole, looking neater on account of the edges being turned away. Nobody else seemed to think it worth doing anything about it, so I didn't. For some reason the speaker had in the emergency abandoned German, it said:

'Okay. Nice work somebody. Pressure now rising. One hit only. Okay! Okay!'

None in my row of companions looked in the least reassured that it was okay. Where the faces weren't consternated, they were worried. A brisk chatter broke out in German or in English, indifferently. Clearly, one man's speculations carried no more weight than another's, but they were still at it when the speaker broke in again, addressing us matter-of-factly in German, this time:

'We have encountered some kind of patrol. This would seem to have been accidental. Apparently only one of the shells fired at us has penetrated. Unfortunately it has passed through several sections before exploding and reached the fuel-tanks where it has caused extensive perforations. The resulting loss of fuel will make it impossible for us to reach our destination. We are now headed towards a suitable location for emergency landing, therefore, and may expect to reach it in fifteen to twenty minutes' time.'

The speaker clicked dead, and the babble broke out again. The man to my left sounded cynical as he spoke to his neighbour on the other side:

'That makes the third *accidental* meeting with a patrol, in six weeks,' he said.

'Only radar contacts. There wasn't any shooting until now,' the other observed.

'All the same, I'd like to know how a patrol comes to be operating accidentally at the height we travel. I don't like the taste of it. How did he come to be close enough for shooting, anyway? What was *our* radar doing?'

'Could be *they've* come up with a radar-absorbent, too. As I understand it, there are at least three possible ways of killing a radar echo. They'd be bound to find one of 'em, sooner or later.'

'But their picking us up must mean they have some new kind of detector going, too.'

'It *might* be accident...'

'Huh... with all this sky there is around here?'

The other sounded philosophical: 'Well, if they have, they have. So, we have to counter – and then they counter again. It's the way these things go. Ding-dong. Ding-dong.'

'If you ask me,' replied my neighbour, forcefully, 'all this dinging and donging has been going on a whole heap too long already. Why in heck don't we get busy? What are we forever waiting for? This way we're going to come just that much too late on the dong one time – we'll wake up in the morning to find everything's folded before it's started.'

The other grunted. 'Always in such a hurry, some of you guys. The thing is to play your own game – not let the other feller force you to what *he* wants. We hold a nice hand, a very nice hand – and seeing that what's not aces is jokers makes the game kind of unusual, too.'

'I still don't like it,' grumbled the man next to me. 'We did have time – but it's a wasting asset the way we're handling it.'

'Could look that way – seeing only part of it,' suggested the other.

About there I lost them entirely. I decided that if there was one thing about these characters that I objected to more than the personal affront of their mere appearance, it was their elliptical style in conversation – the way it kept on nearly telling me things I'd be mighty interested to know, and then, somehow, just missing. Give me, I felt, just one or two nice, clear basic clues, and I'd make a start at beginning. As it was, I kept on being left with an unattachable litter of us-they, our-their, we-them which made about as much sense as a scattered deck of alphabet cards.

But, presently, they lost interest in their discussion. The diabolical hum settled in again at its former level, and everybody gave up trying to talk or think. For myself, I ceased to care greatly whether we force-landed, crash-landed, or bust wide open, so long as it brought that fiendish row to an end, too.

8

Hard Rock

And here you sty me in this hard rock – W.S.

The end, when it came, was a lot less violent than the beginning. The humming sank gradually in pitch until it was a mere thrum on a tenor note. The deceleration was unexpectedly gentle, and our seats swung gradually through a right angle in their supports. There was a slight jar, a brief see-saw motion, a list, a bit of a slither, and we had stopped.

One thing I had to say for these doubles of mine, they were orderly. The way we lined up, I almost expected an inspection of passports, but, instead, there was a man in black overalls handing out tight strapped bundles, with a sling to put over your shoulder. The women got one each, the men, two. There was no ramp outside the door this time. You climbed down a narrow metal ladder, while the bundles swung in the way of each movement, until you found yourself floundering around on loose bits of stone, trying to get clear before the next man came down on top of you.

The first thing I noticed, once I'd scrambled across a bed of shale that ran away underfoot at every step, was that it was mighty cold out there. A fine, clear night, with stars so bright they could have been stuck on a blue-black drop, and a fresh breeze blowing in a temperature either side of freezing. I wished that the fellow whose suit I was wearing had gone in less for show, and more for quality.

In a little while I was able to see more. Above us sloped a rugged mountainside. The other way, across a narrow gully choked with boulders, rose another, looking much the same. The vehicle which had deposited us in this uncheering spot was a pallid, and, from my vantage point, oval-looking shape lodged at a point some hundred feet up the mountainside, and looking as if it might at any moment tip over and slide down. Before I had time to take in more than a general impression, a cascade of loose stones began to slither and bounce down around me. I shouted to the people who were crossing the face above me to stop, and scrambled up to join them. A little further on we found solid ground beyond the slide, and waited there for others to catch up with us. They straggled along in ones and twos while we stood, frigerating fast. Most of them had little comment to make, but there was an exception. I heard a familiar voice:

'Overlooked, that's what I am,' it said. 'Hexed, humiliated, bedeviled, and damned. Guys go nuts at me, my nicely warmed job shuts on me, even miscreated saucers die on me, and now I have to hike the hills of hell in three-inch heels. Boy, do I give value! If ever I – '

'Sh-sh – !' said somebody.

But Miss Hander in spate required more than sh-sh.

'Can it!' snapped the same voice. 'Listen!'

We listened. Somewhere, far up in the sky, there sounded faintly the scream of jets. For a few seconds it increased, then, gradually, diminished out of hearing.

'Uh-huh,' said a voice. 'Looks like the boys'll be having another think about that radar-absorbent gear.'

Presently the last of the party came stumbling up to us. One of them took charge. He said, in German:

'We're going round the shoulder of the hill. It'll be out of the wind there.'

It was a plain statement, with no touch of query. He started off at once, leading the way on an upward diagonal across the face of the slope, flashing a lamp occasionally to choose the trail. The idea I had half-formed, of getting myself left behind, and disappearing into the darkness, I dropped as impracticable at present, so I took my place in the line, and went clattering and stumbling uphill with the rest of them.

My attention was fully occupied with the places I was putting my feet to avoid a sprained ankle, so that I bumped into the man ahead when he suddenly stopped to look back. Two more men caught up with us as we stood.

'She's going,' one said.

I looked back, too. Seen from higher up, the contraption that had brought us appeared as a large disc, somewhat foreshortened. It was curiously distinct, as though faintly illuminated. As I watched, it grew even more distinct, with a pink tinge to it, and I realized it was glowing. The glow increased to a cherry-red, growing still lighter and brighter all the time. We seemed to be looking down obliquely on a shining, circular shield, with a boss of greater brilliance in its centre. Little bursts of fire began to break out beside it; flames skipping downwind from one tuft of scrawny grass to another, and then dying out. Presently one could feel the warmth in the breeze that blew towards us.

We watched without speaking. There were no tall flames. It simply went on glowing still more brightly, illuminating the tumbled rocks about it. Then it sagged, and slithered a few feet further down the hillside. Streams of metal began to trickle from it; bright when they started, dulling quickly as they ran. So far, it had still held its main shape, but then there came a change. The whole smooth surface crinkled, like paper writhing on a slow fire. Quite suddenly it caved in, collapsed, and became nothing but a shapeless glow, puddled with brighter spots. Throughout the whole strange scene there was scarcely a sound save the crack of stones splitting in the heat. The glow began to subside, but the cracking of the stones went on intermittently.

'Well,' said somebody, 'that sure has fixed that. I only hope to God the boys got us located right.'

'It's a darned shame,' said the man beside me, sombrely. 'Just a few hours' work would have seen those tanks okay.'

The one beyond him nodded. 'Still, there it is. Orders,' he said. 'We couldn't have got her off – not without fuel. And there's no way you could hide her in a place like this. Listen… !' He paused.

Again we caught the faraway whine of jets somewhere among the stars.

'So! They've got the idea, you see. Stooging around. Waiting for daylight. If we'd left her, they'd be sure to spot her – and, next thing, we'd likely have a regiment of airbornes floating down on us.'

'*If* they could do that,' admitted the other. 'I'd not know just where we are. Could be outside the territory, you know.'

'If they know what they're after, they'd likely risk it on most any territory – and there's other people got airbornes, too.'

'Well, maybe it's the *safe* thing to do – but it's one hell of a waste of a good ship.'

The party got on the move again, and the two of them dropped behind me, still arguing. I stumbled on. If I was not greatly enlightened, I was, I admit, considerably impressed. When the suggestion of an unnamed somebody using airborne troops in this affair could be made without arousing a touch of derision, the whole proportion of things was suddenly altered – and I began to feel a lot smaller in scale in relation to whatever it was I was involved in.

The leader had been right in his choice of direction. Once we were around the shoulder of the mountain we just felt cold – instead of being cut to bits with ice knives. He went on, moreover, until he had reached a spot where large slabs of rock lay piled against one another with numerous cave-like spaces between them. He waited until the last of us had come up, and then gave his orders, again in German:

'We shall stay here. These stones will give us plenty of cover. Keep under them as much as possible during daylight, and don't light fires. If you should happen to be caught in the open by aerial reconnaissance lie quite still where you are, and don't look up. Understood? Good. Now, the packs you are carrying. We have more than we require at the moment, but we may need the rest later. So open only one pack each. Go easy with the concentrated foods if you don't want to get blown out like bullfrogs – they're deceptive. Be particularly careful with water. Sip, don't drink. It doesn't look as if we're likely to find any more in these parts once that's finished. Questions?'

'Where are we?' asked a woman's voice.

'That is not important. Headquarters knows more accurately than I do. They took a fix on us while we were landing.'

'How long are we likely to be here?' another voice inquired.

'That isn't in our hands. We wait here until H.Q. fetches us. It might be tomorrow night – or in a week's time. It depends entirely on how they can arrange it. Is that all?'

Nobody, it seemed, thought it worth asking any more questions just then.

'All right, then. Find the best places you can among these stones, and open *one* pack each.'

I clambered on until I discovered a large slab lying across others to make a convenient small cavern beneath. I sat down there and opened one of the bundles. Wrapped in a waterproof sheet I found a blanket, a padded sleeping-bag, several cartons and cans, and a long metal bottle with a screw cap. I pulled the blanket and sleeping-bag around me, and sat waiting for the rest to quieten down.

I couldn't allow more than a half-hour; by the look already in the sky I reckoned I'd have none too much time, but I consoled myself by reckoning that once I could get only a little way off I ought to be practically unfindable in that stone-strewn wilderness. I could lie low next day and sleep among the jumble, and be on my way the moment darkness returned. The thing that worried me most was which that way should be. I had no idea where we were, and the starlight showed me no more than numbers of greater and lesser peaks at various distances.

I felt kind of uneasy about that. I really prefer my mountains either civilized by funiculars, or on picture-postcards. Raw mountains have a hostile feeling once you get among them; they're always a lot more extensive than you thought, and you very much need a map. Still, there it was; a chance of breaking out of this farrago back into a nice, normal, sane world – and there might not be another if I were to pass up on it. So I hitched up the pack and set out, footing it delicately on the rocks, like a cat in a pantry.

The going wasn't good. On the big stuff my shoes would slip and scrape, on the small I couldn't move without a crunch and a clatter. However, nobody seemed interested enough to call out, and I began to have a bit more confidence. After a few yards along the contour I turned, and began to make my way straight down. To keep the loose stuff quiet I did my best to zig-zag from one larger lump of rock to another. It was a toilsome method, but reasonably quiet, and okay so long as the supply of larger stepping-stones held out, I thought. As it happened, I was wrong about that.

I felt an apparently solid stone tilt as I stepped on it. I clutched at the air, and flung myself sideways. The slab slowly swung over, just missing me. It fell with a thump and a crunch, slid a foot or two to a sharp edge where it teetered irresolutely, then it upended itself in a lazy way, and disappeared. Out of sight, it encountered something with a loud crack and a rumble, then it abruptly reappeared lower down, leaping into the air as if suddenly endowed with life, After that, it set off like a runaway locomotive.

Only God knows how many hundred tons of mountainside it contrived to set in motion. A crescendo of crashes, thuddings and clatterings grew to a thunderous roar like half the world's waterfalls operating together. Great breakers of sound billowed back and forth, buffeting at the mountains and starting new falls until it seemed that I had initiated the destruction of the entire region. At last, however, the uproar gradually subsided. The echoes slopped back and forth less violently, and then rolled away in a diminishing mutter, until we were left with only a few minor landslides, comparable, in the circumstances, with tree-drippings after the rain.

A beam of light sprang out a little above me, disconcertingly close for the trouble I'd taken to get where I was, and began to search.

I hastily unslung my pack, and let it go. It followed the course the stone had taken, but without setting the landscape in motion. Presently the light discovered me, and steadied.

'Huh! And which of the four freedoms do you reckon you'd be exercising?' a voice inquired.

I looked back into the beam. 'I sort of slipped,' I explained.

'Oh, was that it?' said the voice. 'Then it'd have been God help us all if you'd sort of fallen.'

I climbed up carefully, apprehensively, too, lest I should start pulling down more of the mountain, but I reached him safely. He looked me over.

'What was the idea, anyway?' he asked.

I was ready for that one.

'I'd say there was just about one reason that would bring a man out from under a warm blanket at this time,' I suggested.

He considered.

'H'm,' he said. 'Did you ever read about Gargantua's horse?'

'No. I never did,' I admitted.

'Try it some time. Ought to interest you,' he advised.

I didn't get that, and I was in no mood for quizzes on the classics.

He turned the light on me again for a moment.

'What's your number?' he asked.

I was ready for that one, too, by now.

All the same, he looked a little puzzled.

'Sounds as if you were in the wrong area,' he remarked. 'Kind of English accent.'

'I've taken a whole lot of trouble with my American,' I informed him, shortly.

'Yeah, I was noticing that. Still, what's the odds so long as you get by ...?'

Together we hunted around with the light and managed to locate my hole. I crawled, inside, giving him a thanks for his assistance that I was not feeling.

'Oh, that's okay,' he said, 'you're welcome: comes under the heading of charity. Hope is useful just now, too. But don't you go using the other one around here any more, pal. 'Tain't safe.'

One of those wilfully obscure guys: I didn't catch up with that crack, either, until next morning.

* * *

They were right about the search. It was the sound of an airplane going over that woke me up. She was an old-fashioned craft, droning along comfortably like a well-fed bumble-bee. Just having a nice look around; no hurry at all. I watched her pass to the south of us and buzz lazily away to the west – at least, if the sun was where I reckoned it should be, that would be the west.

Then I looked out of my hole at the landscape. In front, the mountainside fell away steeply, a jostle of stones delivered from somewhere above and behind me in all sizes and shapes. Here and there, at the very bottom of the slope, one could catch occasional glimpses of a white thread which I took to be a stream. The further hillside was a similar bleak stretch of stony chaos, set here and there with infrequent patches of something which might be scrawny grass. It looked like the place they had chosen to dump all the stuff they couldn't use to build the mountains.

Beyond the opposite ridge, I could see peaks, some dark, some topped with white, receding in series into the distance. To the left, another mountain closed us in, but to the right was again a panorama of jagged ranges. I had never known it was possible to include quite so many peaks in one view.

Now I was able to see it all by daylight, my opinion of the previous night's frustration modified. What I had almost committed myself to was toiling alone through those endless miles of broken stone until I should drop in my tracks from exhaustion – if I had not already brought an avalanche down on myself, which would be the more merciful.

The more I regarded this as the terrain of a trek, the more I felt that there must have been some kindly disposed, if rather rough-handed, Interventionist at my elbow during the night. It would, perhaps, be presumptuous to think that I had twice in one night had the attention of a guardian angel, but after all, something had brought the man round the end of the barn to tell me about the dogs at a useful moment, and there could just as well be some reason why, just at the right time, I stepped on the wrong stone.

Though the prospect spread before me was impressive, it did nothing to cheer; moreover, I became aware that I was hungry, and turned to examine my packages. More than anything else, I would have liked a steaming hot cup of coffee. I did not get it. Not that the compilers of the packs had lacked forethought. There was a variety of substances dehydrated and compressed down to a consistency slightly less than that of concrete, there was glucose candy, there were some odd-looking biscuits which turned out to be solid fuel, but no coffee. The nearest thing I could find were some speckled cubes in a carton labelled 'Tea, sugar, milk'. Apparently the concocters had not felt any great pride in them, for a brief consolation lecture printed on the side of the carton explained that tea quenched thirst while coffee tended to promote it, and more or less underwrote that the drinker would take no actual harm. I set it going with a gloomy expectation which became justified. But, at least, it was warm.

While I was still sipping it, and nibbling uneasily at one of the concentrated foods, troubled by speculations on its possible coefficient of expansion, the plane came bumbling back from the west, passing right over us this time, but too high for me to make out its markings. It looked likely to be putting in a day of unrewarded futility up there. From that angle I guessed our district would seem most like a dirty grey blanket, badly rumpled, with a lot of knobs under it. The place where that infernal humming saucer had landed would now be just another dirty, insignificant smear.

I stuck my head out, and watched the craft trundle along until it was just a dot in the east. Even if there had been nobody to interfere, I'd never have stood a chance of catching its attention. After that, there was nothing to watch, or do, so I just lay back and longed for a cigarette.

Close around me I could hear the voices of some of the others talking together or calling from one hiding-hole to another, using German or English indifferently. For about the first time since I had left the Office of Security's building I had leisure for the kind of speculation which has no immediate purpose, so I tried sorting my various data round into little heaps, in the hope that one of them would suddenly mean something.

As a start, I assembled what I thought I had learned. It amounted to this. I was, fortuitously it seemed to me, entangled with some sort of illegal organization. One that wasn't only just illegal – but fairly went to town on illegality; to an extent where it seriously considered the likelihood of troops being used against it.

Now, somewhere, not only in a region unlocated by me, but also unhinted at by anyone else, there was something called Headquarters – which was our present destination. The farm, or ranch, that I had been taken to appeared to be the (or an) assembly and/or dispersal joint on the route for its agents. Connection between this and the H.Q. was maintained by these misconceived machines called saucers. The reason for the name was obvious enough once you had seen one, but how they flew was, at present, no less mysterious than why. But they did it very fast, very high, by night – and with an all crowning, hellish noise inside them. The existence of the saucers was known to some other party – so, too, apparently, was a part at least of their route – and that somebody was troubled enough about it all to fire on them without warning. Considering the accepted likelihood, among my companions, of an attack, and also the search now going on overhead, that 'somebody' might justifiably be assumed to be the U.S. Army – or maybe somebody else's army, anyway, an army. Which certainly put the whole thing on the grand scale…

And what sort of operations would anyone be likely to conduct on such a scale? The answer seemed to be espionage – smuggling on a big-business footing was possible, but less probable. The interest of the Office of Security, too, indicated the former. There was also the pointer that the voluble Miss Hander had been holding a job with the I.S.D.R.A.C. – I very much wished I knew what the other women's jobs had been, but the police had been ignorant (if it wasn't close) about that. The odds, then, were on espionage – but by whom, for whom, of what, for what?

And there I stuck completely. When I had to face the impossible reduplications of my own appearance, I bogged right down. Indistinguishable men, and indistinguishable women, all of us as if turned out by a machine, as far as physical appearance went...

Even granting for the sake of argument the absurd proposition that there was some machine or process capable of making people look alike, why, in heaven's name, bother to do it? It was, in the circumstances, just the very thing that was *not* required, so much so that they were nearly all of them put to considerable trouble to disguise their natural appearances.

And where did all that get me? Just no place at all. About all I had discovered was that there turned out to be a great many more similar men and women than anyone in his proper senses had the right to expect.

Even disregarding that, they were a queer lot on other counts, too. The one who had kicked me in the ribs had been a nasty piece of work, and I wasn't sorry he had got his, but Tweed-suit, who had been quite callously in agreement that a rubbing-out would be the least troublesome course, had turned out to be no tough gang-character after all, but a sociably-minded type, though vaguely depressed about something...

That reminded me of the scene in the cafeteria under the barn: practically everyone there had had an air of brooding privately with differing intensity. I knew now what it had reminded me of – the out-patients department of a hospital.

Perhaps one of the oddest things was how little the men and women mixed; an arrangement which seemed to suit both parties equally well. I couldn't think of any other group of young people I knew who would prefer it that way – but then, come to think of it, I didn't happen to know any other sizeable group where everybody looked like everybody else, anyway...

The day crawled tediously. The stoogers above were not easily satisfied. They came back at intervals, taking closer looks. One machine flew down the valley in front, at a lower elevation than our own. Another cruised along the other side of the mountain, over the shallower valley where the saucer had landed. I listened carefully, but it neither hesitated nor circled there, and presently the drone of it died away.

In the late afternoon, it appeared that the search was over, for we heard no more of them, and an hour or so before dusk a voice called us out of our holes.

By what authority the man took charge I did not know. He was one of four who, unlike the rest, were dressed in black overall suits, otherwise he looked like any of us, with only the figures 742 embroidered on his left breast pocket to distinguish him. When he spoke, and in German, I recognized the voice that had guided us around the mountain the previous night. He waited until we were all assembled, then he announced:

'Headquarters is hoping to fetch us off tonight. They expect to reach here four hours or so after dark, and will set down as close as possible to the spot where we landed last night. That is, of course, unavoidable; we can only move a very short distance in country like this, but if they can navigate to within our sight, we ought to be able to talk them down safely.

'There is, however, the possibility of interception. Although our radio-channel is believed to be undetected, it seems almost certain that some device which eludes the radar absorbent has been found. This is serious in several ways – it means our routes may already have been plotted. The danger to a machine actually in flight is less great than you might think. Our misfortune last night was due to our own ignorance. We could see him, but as we were unaware that he could also see us, there seemed to be no need for the evasive action that we could easily have taken. It is at slow speeds and while landing that our craft are inevitably vulnerable. Tonight's programme, then, depends on the craft being satisfied that she is not under radar observation. If she thinks she may be, she will not risk setting down, and we shall have to wait here for another attempt. That clear?'

Apparently it was, for no one questioned.

'All right,' he said. 'Then we might as well start moving back while there's still some light. It would be hopeless to try to bring them in this side. So pack up your stuff now, and don't waste a thing – we may have to be here some time yet. And remember, if that plane should come back, stand still – and don't look up.'

An efficient young man, I thought, wearing his authority easily – and with the sense to give enough explanation of arrangements to sustain confidence.

In a few minutes we had made bundles of our blankets and the rest, and were stumbling round the shoulder of the mountain again.

* * *

'She's going up,' the man with 742 on his chest told us.

He was sitting a little apart. A wire from a small box beside him led to his right ear. From time to time he would lean over and speak into the box. Occasionally he would relay the information it gave him.

We received it apathetically. It was a whole lot colder on that slope. We had found a partially shielded place in the lee of a large fall, and were sitting with blankets wrapped around us, huddled together for more warmth. Even so, I was shivering, and could feel my neighbour doing the same. With nothing to occupy us, and only the dark outlines of the mountains to look at, it felt as if we had been there half-a-dozen nights already. There was little talking. The cold and the prospect of another saucer flight combined to subdue us.

742 had given out at intervals that: the machine was on its way; it was flying at normal height; it had some new gimmick on board with which it hoped it had regained radar invisibility, and was anxious for a test. If the thing was ineffective, it would evade by climbing, which would mean a postponed e.t.a. So far, the radar screen had remained clear, and it did not expect to enter the likely interception zone for at least an hour, et cetera.

I listened to this kind of thing intermittently and with a slack interest; increasingly conscious of my deteriorating morale. You couldn't stump back and forth to get the circulation going, on account of there being no place to stump, and the second you stood up the wind got at you, and through you. I'd decided that by the time the thing arrived, if it ever did, I'd want no more than to be left where I was to finish the freezing to death process quietly.

When we'd been ossifying a couple of hours or so a jet had whined over to the south of us. 742 leant down to his box, and told it that if it was interception it was looking for, it might now be coming its way.

For a longish time after that nothing happened except that I kept on thinking how much more comfortable it would be to have my mortal freeze in a nice white snowdrift instead of on hard, sharp rocks. Then he had broken silence with the news that the new gimmick was apparently a flop. Something they had picked up on their screen had changed course towards them, so they were going up. I couldn't bring myself to care a lot.

'Sixty-thousand,' said 742. A little later: 'Eighty thousand.' After another pause: 'A hundred thousand.' Our group stirred slightly, and began to take some interest. 'A hundred and twenty thousand,' 742 added, with a touch of excitement in his voice for once. There was a longer pause, then he said: 'Levelled off at a hundred and fifty thousand.'

Somebody gave a low whistle of astonishment, and a few of them started to talk about it. I didn't. I made a rough calculation, and then looked at the stars overhead. I wondered what it would be like twenty-eight, or so, miles straight up there. All I could think of was that it probably would be colder still – but I found that hard to imagine. We went on waiting.

'They've put out decoys,' 742 announced.

Another frigid quarter-hour passed.

'Patrols are converging on first decoys,' he said. And, as if in confirmation we heard the shriek of jets travelling all-out, to the south of us.

Ten minutes or more went by.

'They're over us now. Coming down,' he said. He added:

'They say there was a fine mess round the first decoys when they lost sight. Something was going down in flames. It couldn't be a decoy, so the patrols must be shooting one another up – or colliding – Coming down. Coming down. They're somewhere – oh, it's okay; they've picked up the beam from this thing, now. Coming in now. Keep a look out for them.'

The starset sky looked just the same, and silence hung over us save for the faint whining of the wind in the crannies. The attack on the decoys must have been a long way away, for no sight nor sound of it reached us. It was, in fact, hard to believe that the man was not indulging in some imaginative game of his own. Minutes passed slowly until at last a woman's voice said.

'There he is – I think.'

We all stared into the darkness immediately overhead where she was pointing.

I couldn't see anything that did not seem to belong there, but other voices around me claimed it, too, and presently I thought I could distinguish a dim shape.

742 had been gabbling at his box for some time with a string of directions and warnings. He was still at it while I watched the dim shape become a disc, growing gradually larger. The party stirred, began to get to its feet, and to collect its belongings. The disc descended slowly now, and one became aware of a whining hum, much more subdued than, and quite different from, that of a jet. 742 went on talking, coaxing it out from the mountainside towards the valley bottom, slowing it more and more as it came until it hung over the rocky ground, almost level with our waiting place. Then he said:

'About twenty feet now. Broken rock surface. It's all yours.'

Edge on to us, the thing looked like a cigar with a rounded taper at each end. A bright light sprang out from the bottom of it, searched for a few seconds, and then shut off. The machine moved a little to the left, swayed slightly, and then sank slowly. It settled down on the stones with a faint scrape, a squeal or two of metal on sharp edges, and the humming began to die away.

There, of course, was my chance; I could have bobbed down behind a rock, and hidden out. In the general moving and collecting no one would have missed me. Had the chance offered itself the night before, I would have taken it without a doubt – but now, after seeing the terrain by daylight I had a strong feeling that if I stayed at all, I'd be staying for good…

There is a degree of odds against which a gambler becomes just another mug – so I packed up and tailed along with the rest towards the saucer.

They wasted no time. We were scarcely more than settled before the familiar invisible weight dropped on us. The infernal humming note set in again as the seats tilted, but I was past caring. I was so warm, and comfortable once the weight lifted, that not even Gabriel's own note could have kept me awake.

* * *

Though a voice called in German through my dreams, about fastening belts and coming in to land it took so long to penetrate that I was still fumbling with the buckle when a slight jar told that we were down. Every one of us was looking dazed, either from the humming, the sleeping, or maybe a mixture of the two, and it needed high-grade resolution to move at all. But somehow we made it, and began to shuffle out. I simply followed the man ahead. He was walking as if he were more than a little drunk, and no doubt I was, too. I didn't have any interest in anything, any more.

There was a ride in a kind of miniature trolley-car – a short ride, I think, but I couldn't be sure because I had fallen asleep again the moment I sat down. Then, somehow, we were in an office, in a building. A likeness of me in a black overall-suit was sitting at a desk. We were lined up there, and people were giving their numbers as they passed him. He checked and instructed from a list in front of him. I made a big effort to pull myself together, and managed to remember the number that I had found on the Prairie-Dog token in the wallet.

'Eight-nine-one,' I said, when my turn came.

He ran his finger down a column.

'Number ten. Block C,' he told me, in German.

It was luck that the man in front of me had been directed to Block C, too, so I dragged wearily along behind him.

The thing became like an anaesthetic-dream. Passages, seemingly miles of passages, with a downward flight of stairs now and then for variation. At last, in a much narrower passage than those we had come through, the man ahead pushed in a door numbered 3, and staggered past it. I reckoned that would make this Block C, so I trudged on until I found one numbered 10, and tried that. It led into a small room like a sizeable cupboard, but with a bed there. I didn't want any more. I pushed the door to behind me, made for that bed, and dropped on it just as I was.

9

Constant Image

The constant image of the creature – W.S.

You remember how it was sometimes when you were a kid? You got into bed, and then suddenly it was morning, with no interval in between. That's the way it was with me then, for the first time in years. Not that there was anything visible to indicate morning, but the speakers were at it again. The light was still turned on, as I'd left it, and a voice was saying, in brisk German:

' – thirty minutes. Breakfast in thirty minutes.'

I lay there a little, pulling out gradually; finding out that apart from a desire to go back to sleep, which could scarcely be considered abnormal, I didn't appear to have taken any harm from the cold wait on the mountain. Then, as the whole thing came back to me in more detail, I grew more alert, and sat up to take a look around me.

The place was pretty much like a cell. Clean, impersonal, bare. The floor was a polished dark wood; the walls and ceiling painted white. It had no window, but one wall showed the grille of a ventilator about a foot square. For furniture there was the bed, a chair, a wash-basin with a looking-glass set over it, and a black japanned box marked in white paint, 891.

When I felt that I had re-assembled the rambling parts of my mind, I got up and unlatched the box. In the top tray were toilet and shaving gear, and other small necessities; in the lower part, some neatly folded clothes. But they weren't ordinary clothes. There were two suits of black overalls numbered 891 on the left breast pocket, underclothes, shorts, shirts, two pairs of boots, and a flat-topped, peaked cap. There was also a polished black belt with a sheath-knife attached to it. I took out the shaving things, and considered the situation while I used them.

Sooner or later I could scarcely fail to be discovered, but, meanwhile, it seemed to me that I might as well continue my impersonation of 891 as long as it would wear, in the hope that some chance of a getaway might show up before the bluff finally folded. It struck me that it would be a comforting thing to retain 891's pistol in its shoulder-holster, too.

After I had put on a suit of the overalls I sat down on the side of the bed to wait. There was something to be said for this herding around by loudspeakers after all – they could save me a whole lot of worry – and presently did so by observing:

'Breakfast in five minutes!' and then repeating it.

I unlatched the door, and watched through a narrow crack. Another door opened somewhere, and a man walked past. I looked carefully at the way he was dressed, then I hurriedly tucked my trousers into my boots, grabbed up the cap and went out, still buckling my belt, and looking, I hoped, indistinguishable from half-a-dozen others now coming along – and the nightmare feeling began to close down on me once more, for indistinguishable was just what I was…

To sleep in peace, and resume a nightmare when one wakes, is a highly undesirable reversal of the natural order. It is still worse when the scale of absurdity keeps on rising.

The dining-hall was a large room. The men, all in black overalls, kept to one end; the women, in black skirts and white shirts, to the other. And there seemed to be several hundreds of each…

To see that each man might have been any of the other men, and each woman any of the other women, made my grip on my sanity desperate and despairing. Had I come into the room with no idea of what I might expect instead of working to it by degrees, I have little doubt that it would have slipped entirely.

The more the thing went on, the more outrageous it became. Not only were the faces alike, but many of the mannerisms were identical, too. After the first shock had subsided I tried to steady my reason a little by overlooking the similarities and concentrating on the differences – and once I started to look for them, I began to find some. It helped to fight down the frightening hall-of-mirrors effect a bit. Here was a scar, there perhaps a burn, a nose that had been broken, a hand that had been damaged; there were the heads that had been dyed, sometimes with the fair hair showing at the roots. I fancied, too, that I could detect a difference of age in some, but could not be sure of that.

There was not a great deal of general talk, but one young man near me was giving another an account of our mountain sojourn. I listened while I ate my cereal and rolls and drank my coffee.

'Pity about the saucer,' said the other. 'That's two. Was it really necessary?'

'Standing orders,' the first told him. 'And a good thing, too. They couldn't have missed it by daylight.' He added the piece about the paratroops. 'And if they'd not been able to take it, they'd have bombed it, anyway,' he went on. 'What I want to know is what happened to those patrols last night. They said there was one at least going down in flames. Was there any radio news?'

'Sure. Two planes unfortunately collided during night manoeuvres, was the way they put it.'

'That all?'

'What more do you expect? The saucers are just a silly rumour that's been going on for years. Anything they *do* know about 'em is top secret – that's partly on account of us, but mostly on account of they're scared what might happen if they admitted that saucers really exist. All their people'd jump right to the idea that they are Russian – so they'd likely have a full-size panic on their hands, and a lot of the tougher guys demanding action forthwith. They'd practically have to fight their own people to stop from having a war. So we *don't exist*. Saucers are optical illusions, spots before the eyes, meteorological balloons, refractive effects, cockeyed hallucinations – anything, in fact, but saucers. I sometimes wonder just what would happen if a saucer did pack up one time and come down some inconvenient place where they couldn't talk it out of existence. That certainly would knot them up.'

'I wonder – Might be a good thing, you know…'

'Hm… No. Better to choose your own time, I guess.'

And there we were again. One of those conversations which almost began to mean something, and then went sliding off just out of reach, but I might have begun to get more of a line on it if the announcing speaker had not cut them short there.

'Last night's arrivals will make their reports as called,' it said, twice. Then it added. '742 and 994 will report now.'

A man and a woman got up and made for the door. I could imagine the kind of concise, tidy report that 742 who had so efficiently taken charge of our marooned party would turn in. But when I recalled that 994 was the number of Miss Antonia Hander, I felt that somebody somewhere was going to have a long, lurid session.

* * *

Back again in my cell-like room, I sat on the edge of my bed, and considered. So far, I had been lucky – or should one say I'd had minor good luck within the major ill? – chiefly because I had succeeded in doing nothing to arouse suspicion, and no more had been required of me than one might ask of a good sheep. Now, however, I had the feeling of a big moment round the corner. I knew that I must have come pretty near to the end of the stretch where one could get past simply by keeping eyes open and mouth shut. This reporting business – a matter of being called up individually by number – didn't look at all good.

For one thing, I had no idea what I was supposed to be reporting about. If it were simply on the matter of my own supposed death, there might be a chance of getting away with it – I had a good enough notion of what Tweed-suit would be saying on that, and all I needed to do was to make my story fit with his. But I did not imagine that that was the only matter involved. It was my strong impression that the real 891 and the others had simply had the job of doing something about me tacked on to the end of whatever had been their real work – and as to what that work might be, I had still no clue.

And there was a practical stumbling block even before that. When the speaker should call 891, where was I supposed to go to make this report? If I were to ask, I would probably give myself away right off. All in all, the game, as I had been playing it, looked mighty near through.

What, then, to do next? There was one obvious answer; beat it while I was still unsuspected, and lodge such information as I could in the place where it would do most good.

The step after that would be to get myself in on whatever action would be taken, so that I could return here – for I was sure that it must have been to this place that Freda had been brought.

The situation was thus much as before: all I had to do to be free was to get away. But one thing was clear enough: simply sitting around until the loudspeaker called my number was not going to help. So I picked up my cap, and went out into the passage.

On the principle that if you walk briskly with an air of purpose ninety-nine per cent of the people you meet will assume it is a proper purpose, I did just that.

Vague memories of the previous night recalled that we had descended two, or possibly three, flights of stairs. Since we had arrived on ground level it was a reasonable assumption, reinforced by lack of windows, that I was now subterranean, and that the likely way out of the place would lie upwards. I worked on that, and managed to retrace successfully until I had to turn aside to avoid the reception room where a man in the usual uniform was seated at a desk, working.

I learned that I had deduced rightly, but from one faulty premise. On this ground-level there were miles of passages, dozens of doors, but still never a window to show me the world outside.

Quite a deal of activity went on in those parts. Young women, all so painfully like Freda that several times it was with difficulty that I stopped myself speaking to them, emerged from a room, on the way to another, with sheafs of paper in their hands. Occasionally, through open doors, I had a glimpse of fair heads bent over desks. But what it was all about, I could catch no hint. It might have been practically any government department doing anything. There were a few young men to be seen, too, here and there, but nobody paid any attention to me, as I passed on my purposeful way.

I started to get worried. Two or three times the speakers had called the numbers of others required to report, and there was no telling when mine might come up. If that were to happen before I could get clear I felt that the next person I met would notice my number, and want to know what went on.

And similarity of another kind was getting me down again. As if it weren't enough that the inhabitants should be indistinguishable, the passages were like that, too. Without anything to tell me where I was going, I began to develop a conviction that I was steadily marching round the same three or four, like a one-man operatic army. To break it up, I hopefully tried a few doors. Some were locked, several led into offices from which I backed out apologetically. One gave into some sort of light workshop full of benches where more young women were intensely absorbed in electronic complexities. I had begun to wonder if I were condemned to wander in the maze until exhaustion overtook me, when I at last encountered a quite different type of doors. They were the sole break in a long stretch of plain wall; they were also double, and much heavier in construction than any I had yet seen. I noticed that they were made to open outwards, and that there was a bar on them, not unlike the panic-bar on a theatre exit. I passed them by. When there was no one in sight, I turned, and walked just as briskly back again. Barely pausing when I reached them, I lifted the bar and slipped through, closing the door behind me.

*   *   *

I had no idea what I expected to find behind the doors. In general, I had just about given up expecting. But what I did find brought me up standing.

I was quite suddenly in a world of dim green shade, with the air about me thick and humid. When I looked up I could see the branches of huge trees were intermingled to make a high roof through which the daylight trickled weakly. Ahead, and extending to each side, was a broad belt of ground, cleared of all but the largest trees – but cleared some little time ago, for a fresh growth of young plants that I did not recognize had been able to cover it knee-high again.

I stood there for some moments, staring. Then I turned, and looked back at the doors behind me. They had no fastenings on the near side, and seemed as if they were just what they had appeared to be – an emergency exit, to be operated only by those inside. On either side of them the wall ran straight for a hundred yards or more, drab-green, unbroken, about fifteen feet high.

Well, to be out was what I had wanted, wasn't it? So now I had it – and what?

I wondered in what country, or, for that matter, what continent I was. I had the impression that the vegetation was tropical – that is, if tropical vegetation was at all the way I had imagined it to be. It told me something, perhaps, but not a lot – on account of there's an awful lot of tropics when you come to look at them. Still, that could wait. The immediate question was which way to go. With the canopy of leaves that the tall trunks were holding up there I couldn't even guess at the compass-points, and as one direction seemed to have nothing on any other, except that I couldn't go back, I set off straight ahead.

At one hundred and fifty yards or so from the building the clearance finished, and the natural state of things abruptly began. The lower parts of the trees were choked solid with a tangle of growth out of which thick-stemmed creepers crawled up the trunks, reaching for the sunlight far above. At ground-level a mass of saplings, bushes, lesser creepers, and fallen branches was woven into a natural fence. One might, perhaps, hack his way into the stuff with great labour, but it looked as if the only possible way of making progress would be to lay boards across the thickest part of it. A glance was enough to show it as hopeless, and I made my way to the right in the hope of coming across some kind of path through it. I was sure that if there were no other, there must at least be the trolley track along which we had come from the saucer.

At no great distance a small river cut across my way. I pondered it a bit, wondering if I might be able to make some kind of raft which would float me downstream – wondering, too, what sorts of creatures I might expect to find in the muddy looking water – and then there was also the question of finding suitable logs for a raft. I decided that there was a possibility there, but only to be investigated if other ways failed. So I made my way back along the boundary of the cleared land, hoping the other direction might offer something more hopeful.

After a time, it did. There was still no sign of a track, but the undergrowth, for some reason, became less closely knit, and presently grew still more open until at last I reached a place where I thought it might be worth my while to try to push my way through. I had been conscious all the time that if anyone should choose to inspect the cleared ground only the luck of an intervening tree trunk could prevent my being seen, and even if I did not make much progress in the thicker stuff, I should be out of sight there.

The difference between that part of the forest and the rest turned out to be relative. After a half-hour or so of continuous hacking with the knife from my belt I had covered perhaps twenty yards – at least, I told myself it must be twenty yards, but as the limit of visibility was around one yard I couldn't be sure of that, nor that it had taken place in a straight line. Already I was growing discouraged. For all I knew there might be endless miles of the same kind of going ahead of me. I was almost on the point of turning back and searching again along the perimeter of the cleared ground for a clearer place to break through, when the silence which hung over everything but my own struggles was split wide open by a fearsome howl to the right. For an instant I searched, panic-stricken, for the savage animal about to leap on me; then I realized it was a siren working up to a scream which scared me only a little less.

The thing was up in the trees some place where I couldn't see it or do anything about it. I went into a different kind of panic, and started floundering around. In about three seconds I had lost my sense of direction quite hopelessly. For an interminable time the siren went on wailing, and I went on flapping, sure that first this and then that was the way I had come. Then, mercifully, the thing began to die, sinking from a howl to a moan, to a mutter, and grumbling away into silence – so that I was able to hear voices calling to one another.

They seemed to sound from all directions. I pulled out my pistol, and got ready for the worst. I did not reckon it was going to help a lot to stay still. Sounds of slashing and cracking came from several sides. I floundered some more, trying to get further away from the neighbourhood of the siren. Then, pushing through a bush, I came suddenly face to face with one of my multitudinous doubles. The only real difference between us was that while I held a pistol in one hand and a knife in the other, he was swinging a machete, and had a sub-machine-gun slung round his neck.

* * *

The man looked surprised to see me.

'Hullo,' he said. 'Bit off course, aren't you?'

It was so far from what I expected that I hesitated.

Then I said:

'Who wouldn't be? This is one hell of a place,' I grumbled.

He nodded, understandingly. 'Better work over that way,' he told me, pointing. 'Not that we'll find anything. Those damned natives are like snakes; just slide right away even through this stuff. Lost your machete?' he added, curiously.

'It slipped,' I explained. 'Guess it must've gone down a hole some place.'

I started working with the knife along the line he had indicated while he slashed away on his own course. Soon there were thickets between us. I wormed a bit further, and then sat down under cover to rest.

The trouble about my guardian angel, or whatever passed for it, seemed to be that it always showed willing, but never did quite enough.

Somewhere a whistle blew. A voice shouted an order. The men began to crash back the way they had come. Evidently they were calling off the search, reckoning that the cause of it would be well clear by this time. I could hear them assemble and then move away. That did at least fix the direction of the cleared ground for me.

I gave them twenty minutes to get back, then I started off again.

I kept on going for two or three of the most strenuous hours of my life. Sometimes I pushed my way, frequently I had to cut through a kind of lattice-work of stems. Bushes scrabbled and grappled at me, roots tripped me. I pushed my way under fallen trees, or, in climbing over them, sank knee deep into rotten wood. Sometimes I battled on above the ground on a kind of mattress of low growths, at others I was ankle deep in slime and rotting muck. Never in my life had I put out so much energy for so little result. I became weary and hungry. I had no idea how far I had managed to struggle – though I did have a misgiving that it would probably look a sadly short distance if traced on the ground. I was now able to perceive quite clearly that no one but an utter lunatic would have started out as I had. Yet I still could not bring myself to the point of admitting defeat and going back – even if I should be able to find the way back. Always there was the feeling that perhaps just the next few yards would see me emerge upon a track – until, at last the decision was taken out of my hands. Right over my head a siren again spun itself into a shriek.

On that, I gave up. I sat down on a fallen tree, wet through from head to foot with sweat, and waited for them to find me.

But that guardian angel was still on the job, in its own, peculiar way, for they found me quite quickly – about five yards in from the edge of the clearing that I had left hours behind me.

* * *

Right back into the fantasy now. Passages obsessionally alike. Just look down, old Freud, and take a good laugh. Guards all like me, marching me along. Would I be projecting some self-assertion, Adler? Or maybe I'm compensating for my Nordic individuality by making a herd of myself, eh, Jung? Oh, to hell with it – a whole lot simpler to grant I'm plain nuts.

A door, like the other doors. A desk, like the other desks. Me, pushed forward to face the man sitting behind it and looking, of course, just like me – except that this one had some kind of emblem on each shoulder.

He let me have a very steady, penetrating gaze. It searched not only my face and eyes, but a little behind them.

'And what's wrong with you?' he said sharply, in German.

I hesitated then:

'I don't seem to know,' I said. 'I must be going crazy, I guess. I – well, things just don't make any kind of sense.'

Besides being only slightly committal, it was pretty well true. Moreover, it looked like I'd hit on a good line, for he didn't seem greatly surprised.

'Seen the psychiatrist lately?' he asked.

'No,' I admitted...

'Do that right away. Anybody who's got to the stage of going into that stuff out there needs cleaning up pretty quick. You mightn't be so lucky next time – and then you'd rot there like the rest of the stinking place, you know.'

'Yes,' I said. I believed him, too.

'Very well, then. I'll see you again when the psychiatrist has sent in his report on you.'

Obviously he was on the point of dismissing me. Then, with his eyes on my number, he paused. 'Eight-nine-one,' he murmured 'Aren't you – ?' He broke off, looking at me hard, and frowned slightly. He leaned forward to press a switch, and spoke into a desk microphone. 'Record on Male eight-nine-one, right away,' he demanded.

For a half-minute he turned his attention from me to a paper on his desk. Then a light in the wall began to blink. One of the men walked over, raised a shutter just beneath it, and took out a small loose-leaf book. He put it on the desk. The man sitting there picked it up, and flipped to the last page.

'So you came in last night, h'm?' he said.

'Yes,' I agreed.

He pressed another switch, and spoke to the microphone again:

'Has eight-nine-one made his report yet?' A tinny voice replied immediately.

'No. He's overdue. Please send him along if you know where he is.'

The man released the switch. He put his elbows on the desk, and leaned on them, watching me.

'This is different,' he said. 'This is quite different. So you dodged out just at the time when you were due to give your report. Scared to make it, h'm? Plenty scared, too, to try a fool thing like that. Well, what is it?'

There didn't seem to be a non-committal answer this time so I said nothing.

'Don't waste time acting dumb,' he said. 'What is it?'

An inspiration visited me.

'I was to bring in a prisoner. He got shot,' I told him.

'Meaning – you shot him?' he suggested.

'No.'

'Then who did?'

By an effort I remembered Tweed-suit's number.

'Two-eight-four – and another fellow. He was making a break for it,' I explained.

'Well, that's their worry, not yours, isn't it!' he said, still looking at me closely.

'He was my responsibility,' I said.

'H'm.' He looked down at the book lying open in front of him. 'There's nothing about any prisoner here.'

'It was an emergency. We picked him up after he had come out of the local branch of the Office of Security,' I tried.

The man looked surprised this time.

'What was he doing in there?'

'I guess it was to find out just that, that he was wanted,' I said, feeling I was doing pretty well. But it's when you begin to feel that way that the sticky patches show up.

'What was the emergency order number?' he inquired.

He had me there.

'I don't know,' I admitted.

'You don't know!'

His eyebrows rose, but it seemed worth keeping on trying.

'I got the instruction from two-eight-four,' I said.

I was starting to sink a bit. At best I'd be buying only a little time until they should check up with Tweed-suit.

'Without an order number!' he said, as if this were some kind of indecency.

'Well, it *was* an emergency,' I said.

He went on looking at me hard. Suddenly he said, brusquely: 'There's something very funny here.'

It didn't seem to me that there should be. In my experience about the least likely thing to have a number is an emergency. Just another specimen of the numeromania rampant in these parts. But I said nothing.

He came to a decision.

'Your finger-prints,' he demanded, abruptly.

I felt myself suddenly grow tense, and then relax. They'd taken away my pistol. There were two armed guards standing behind me.

I sighed. Here it came, at last.

When he got the prints it only needed a glance for him to see that they did not tally in any way with those in the book. He leaned back.

'So,' he said. 'So you aren't 891. Who are you? – And what the devil do you mean by wearing another man's number? There's going to be trouble about this, I warn you.'

I shook my head wearily. His eyes were narrowed, and I could see he was still uncertain. Probably on account of my doing such a crazy thing as trying to get away in the forest, he still had a lingering suspicion that I might indeed be crazy.

'We'll soon find out,' he said. He pressed a button, and spoke to the microphone again. 'Records. I'm sending you a set of finger-prints. Please identify immediately.'

The piece of paper with my prints on it went behind the shutter in the wall. The man turned back to the work on his desk. We waited. Five minutes. Ten minutes. A quarter hour. Then a buzzer sounded. A small female voice said:

'We cannot trace the finger-prints submitted by you. They are not in our files.'

The man at the desk looked thoroughly startled. He stared at the instrument, then at me.

'That's nonsense. They must be. Check again.'

'I beg your pardon?' said the small voice, coldly.

'I mean, we've got the man here, now. They *must* be.'

'I'm sorry,' said the small voice, still chilly, and certainly with no perceptible trace of sorrow in its tone. 'We have checked beyond possible error. We do *not* know them here.'

The man continued to stare at the microphone set. When he raised his eyes to meet mine, some of his confidence had gone. With a bewildered air he got up, and came round the desk slowly. Very carefully he examined the roots of my hair, and then my face, in unhurried detail. I guessed he must be looking for traces of plastic surgery, but when he stepped back his expression was, if anything, more incredulous.

'If you're not one of us, then who the devil are you?' he asked.

Remembering the attitude of my original captors I did not know what I might be letting myself in for if I were to tell him. So I did not answer.

'You might as well talk now,' he told me. 'For you *will* talk.'

Still I said nothing – which, had I known it, was mere foolishness.

'Very well, then,' he said.

He turned to the two who were guarding me.

'Take him along for questioning,' he told them.

* * *

Three replicas of myself stood round me. Each of them held an object like a section of hose eighteen inches long. The one who faced me was twiddling his in his fingers, with the dextrous air of a juggler. Suddenly, and apparently, casually, it flicked towards me. There was an excruciating agony in my left knee. I staggered, and tried to go for him. Two swift blows from behind came down cruelly on my shoulders, numbing my arms. That was just the way it began...

* * *

There was a voice saying, in a conversational, matter-of fact way:

'Your name?'

I dragged myself out of a swamp of pain and misery. It was like coming back a long, long way, crawling. I opened my eyes. They wouldn't focus at first, but after a while I forced them to it. Two men on chairs facing mine swam around a bit, and kind of undulated. After a little longer they settled down and solidified so that I could see that, of course, they were two of my infernal doubles. One of them was leaning back, his arms folded, his eyes fixed on me. The other had a notebook on his knee, and a pencil ready. The light hurt my eyes, but after I'd blinked them once or twice and got them to stay open the two were still there. The sight of them looking like enough to me for no one to tell us apart was funny. I began to laugh. The laugh sounded crazy even to me, but I had to go on laughing. The nearer man leant forward, and lifted his hand threateningly.

'Stop that!' he said, in German.

I tried to. Presently, I succeeded.

'Your name?' he said, again.

I hesitated still.

Saying 'no' had got to be such a habit by then. That, and saying nothing at all, were about the only two fixed points left to me. Then the man lifted his hand again. Well, what was the use? They'd found out I wasn't one of them, so I'd gain nothing now by withholding my name. It was the feeling of the crowbar in the first crack: once they knew anything about me, the more they'd want to know. Once they had my name, I'd be identified as the man they already wanted to question – the one that Tweed-suit thought he had shot.

But sooner or later they'd have it out of me. I realized that now. The trouble was, once I started talking where would I stop? I wanted to keep Freda's name out of it. I had no idea where she stood in this tangle: for all I knew, any discovered connection with me might land her right into something. So I would keep her name right out of it.

Shows you, doesn't it, the way you can rationalize? As long as they didn't know who I was, things didn't tie together for them. But my mind was trying to save my face – or my body. So I'd go that far: let them know who I was, but nothing about Freda...

My head had started to flop. The man with the pencil reached forward, and pushed me back into the chair.

'Come along now. Your name?' he said, once more.

I let my eyes close. 'Johnny Farthing,' I said.

It was like dropping an exhausting weight. I felt lighter and slightly drunk. They knew their stuff, those two. It was the psychologically sound moment for one of them to hold a glass of water to my lips as he did, and let me drink – a very little.

They went on. Age?

I told them.

Occupation?

I told them that, too.

Nationality?

'American – U.S.A.,' I said.

That didn't go down so well.

'You're sure about that?' the man asked.

'Sure? Of course I'm sure. Don't I talk like an American?'

'You may think so, but, frankly, you don't. More as if you tried to learn it. What's more, you don't speak like an Englishman either. *And* there's something not quite on phase with your German. So let's have it. Just who you are, what you are, and what you're after?'

I tried to explain. They wanted a lot of detail. Circumstances, place of birth, education, upbringing, et cetera, et cetera, et cetera. It went on for a long time. One took it all in, the other wrote it all down, but whether either of them believed it I couldn't tell. When we were through with that they went off on another tack, and an unexpected one:

'Now, who,' asked the empty-handed man, 'was the surgeon?'

I didn't get it. He amplified:

'Who arranged the operation? And who actually worked on you to make you look like us?' he demanded.

'Why – why no one,' I said. 'I didn't ever look any other way.'

He lifted his hand. I leant as far away from it as my chair would allow.

'You can *see* that's true,' I said. 'Look as hard as you like. Get a doctor to look. There'd be marks.'

'Then how was it done?' he demanded.

'But *nothing* was done,' I protested. 'Can't you see? It's just the way I am.'

He continued to look at me steadily, and still with disbelief. It made me go on:

'Something queer *has* been done, that's certain. But whatever it is, it's your end, not mine. How can there be hundreds of you, all looking like me? It's impossible – quite crazy!'

He was looking at me a little more speculatively.

'And if I tell you it's neither?' he asked.

'Well then – that just leaves it that it's me that's crazy. What I think I'm seeing can't be so. It's screwy – utterly unnatural.'

His mind, pulling itself round towards believing me after all, was a slow, but almost visible process. He gave me another drink for which I was grateful. I would have been still more grateful if he had also unfastened my wrists, my left hand was aching hellishly. But his conversion had not gone that far yet. Instead, he seemed to consider it the ripe moment for my philosophical improvement:

'"Unnatural",' he observed, 'is a word quite without meaning. It is obvious that whatever takes place must be implicit in the nature of the material producing the result: otherwise, it could not take place at all. Happenings may be coincidences, they may be improbable coincidences, they may be difficult to understand, they may astonish us – yet, however astonishing, they must still be a manifestation of the nature of whatever produces them. Therefore, to call them unnatural is nonsense, and, as such, is evidence of superficial and muddled thinking.'

I blinked. I was in no state to follow up a statement of that kind; muddled thinking was certainly right at the moment.

'All right,' I conceded, peaceably, 'then I'll be astonished.'

He nodded. 'But probably no more than we are,' he rejoined.

He reflected for some moments, and looked over the other man's notes. Then he resumed:

'Very well. We will assume for the moment that this astonishment of yours is real – and recent. Unless, bearing the possibility of your future discomfort in mind, you would like to change that?'

'No. For me it's all – just crazy.'

'All right, then.

'I don't suppose you want any more unpleasantness, so tell us fully – why did you come here? – And how did you get here?'

I told them. From their faces I couldn't decide how it was being received. At the end I said, a bit desperately:

'Look here. I don't know what you think I'm doing, but whatever it is, you're wrong. Don't you see, you've *started* wrong? I didn't motivate a thing. I'm just a guy who was quietly minding his own business and suddenly found it was loaded. All I want now is either to get sane or wake up; I'd not care a lot which.'

'H'm,' said the senior of the two men, woodenly. For resistance to stimulus he ranked high. All he followed up with was: 'We'll go back a bit. Now who was this Georg Farthing, your father?'

Things were beginning to swim again. I felt I'd not be able to keep it up much longer, but I did my best to concentrate.

'He was American born. *His* father, Georg Farthing, emigrated from Sweden as a young man. My mother told me he came from somewhere in Göttland, but I don't know what town.'

'And he was fair-haired, like you?'

'Yes. '

'And your mother – she was from Sweden, too?'

'Yes. Norrköping. But I think the family was originally from Norway.'

He glanced at the notebook on the other's knee. 'You say the name of your uncle in America is Darl. So that would be your mother's maiden name, too?'

'Yes, but spelt differently, of course. My uncle altered it, to D-A-R-L for convenience in America. The proper spelling is D-A-H-L.'

'Dahl?' he murmured, reflectively. 'Dahl? There's something – ?' Then he broke off, and be came suddenly very still, staring at me.

My effort to hold up was weakening. He began to go kind of wavy in front of me, but for the first time he started to look animated another way, too.

'My God – *DAHL*!' he exclaimed. His hand reaching for the telephone was the last thing I saw as I passed out.

*   *   *

I came round bandaged and poulticed, and in a clean bed. It was a room without windows, but it felt fresh and cool. One of the inevitable black-uniformed young men was there. He was sitting in a chair, reading a book, but he looked up when my head turned on the pillow. I asked for a drink. He got up, and handed me a glass of water without comment. When I'd finished, he took it from me, and went out of the room.

I dozed, I think, maybe I even dropped off to sleep again, for the next thing I knew was the click of the latch. The door opened sharply. A man entered, and stood back for three women to pass him. If they had been dressed with a bit more knowledge of life they'd have looked like a sister-act about to break into close harmony, but in the white shirts and black skirts there was more a suggestion of top class at the orphanage.

They looked at me, and I looked surprisedly back, a bit puzzled, as well as muzzy. Then one of them stepped forward to the bedside. I watched her come closer. Then I caught my breath – like a sudden flash, I knew the difference. It was in the eyes, the expression, in pretty well each movement. I very nearly said 'Freda' out loud, but caution pulled me up. I still had no picture of what went on – for all I knew it might be some kind of test or trap for her. So I lay there, doing my best to register indifference. It must, I think, have been a darned poor best, and Freda, looking down at me with concern, began to smile her way through it.

'Oh, Johnny!' she said 'Then it *is* you! It really is you. Oh, my dear Johnny!'

That let me smile back at her. I reached out my right hand for hers.

'Freda, my sweet!' I said, as I pressed it.

She put her other hand to the side of my face. It felt smooth and cool, there on my cheek.

Her brows came closer together, with a deep little furrow between them. She swayed her head a little from side to side.

'Oh, Johnny, my Johnny! What have they done to you? What have they done!'

'Sh-sh!' I said. 'Don't you cry for me, honey. I'll be all right. It doesn't matter now.'

Her hand trembled in mine. Presently she raised her head, and looked at the man who had brought them.

'Will he – will he be all right?' she said, still speaking in English.

He nodded. In an impersonal voice he said:

'He will be stiff and uncomfortable for a time, perhaps. But it is not serious. Nothing is broken, except three fingers on the left hand. They will mend well.'

'Only three fingers broken! Oh, Johnny, my poor Johnny,' she said softly, and bent down to kiss my cheek.

Then she wept, in a way that was unlike her, and for reasons much more complicated than my three fingers.

Everyone looked increasingly uncomfortable. At length the man broke in:

'Do you formally identify this man as John Farthing?'

Freda pulled herself together.

'Of course I do.'

'Very well. That is noted. And now I think it will be better for him to sleep.'

A moment later they had all gone, the other man was back in his chair, with his book, and I drifted off to sleep, half-wondering whether this were not just another of my hallucinations...

*   *   *

Adept as these people were in breaking a man, they did also display a considerable competence in mending him. It is, however, in the nature of things, a process taking somewhat longer. Several days passed before I was allowed to get up at all, but by the end of a week I was feeling much my usual self, save for a stiffness which had not altogether yielded to massage, and the plaster which encased my left hand.

The greatest disappointment was not to have seen Freda again. But each day there was a brief note of good wishes from her, and an assurance that she herself was well. My inquiries about her, and, indeed, about anything, were evaded when they were not flatly repulsed by those who looked after me. It was evident that they had orders to give me no information at all, and they carried them out, to the letter.

But there was one curious interlude. A man who might, to my eyes, be any one of them, came in with an air of authority. He jerked his head for my usual attendant to leave the room, and was obeyed without question. Then he pulled forward a chair, and sat down beside the bed, looking at me thoughtfully. On his uniform were the figures 451: I knew I had seen that particular combination before, but could not recall where.

'They tell me you are doing well?' he said.

The moment I heard his voice, I placed him. He was the last of my questioners – the one who could break off his inquisition of a battered victim to deliver a homily on loose thinking. It was not an encouraging discovery.

'I think so,' I told him, 'and it surprises me. Your assistants, you see, are so happy in their work.'

'They are efficient, of course,' he said, matter-of-factly. 'It is unfortunate for you that it was necessary. Your own fault, too. It need never have happened if you had told us what we wanted at once.'

As there could scarcely be a poorer consolation, I omitted to reply. He went on looking at me thoughtfully. Then he said:

'My name is Emil.'

'It is interesting to know you can decipher yourselves.'

'I tell you my name because you are used to thinking of people only by name, and therefore a name has more personality for you. It is a matter of habit. For us, 451 is as different from 452 as Smith is from Brown, so we use numbers or names indifferently – except in official matters. But you, I think, could easily confuse one figure with another, finding it lacks individuality. Is not that so?'

I had – while wondering if the man was given to delivering pocket lectures on all subjects – to admit that he was right. However, it soon appeared that instruction was not his main aim; he was primarily after more information. He inquired:

'Have you ever had any military training?'

When I admitted that I had not, he looked a trifle disappointed.

'Nor held any responsible administrative post?' he added.

I pointed out that I had had little chance as yet to show any capacities I might have for such a post.

He shook his head, seemingly as much over the manner of my answer as the content.

'Well, how else'd I get there?' I asked him.

'Chance,' it appeared, was the word that had displeased him.

'Surely,' he observed, 'the reasonable way is to train selected suitable persons in administration, and then appoint the best. To rely on chance picking a man out is inefficient. It must be very wasteful.'

'It works,' I said. 'Probably on the principle that the good man makes the chance.'

'Then, obviously it cannot be chance,' he pointed out at once. 'It is the good man showing up in spite of his lack of training. Therefore, why not take him young, train him, and save him wasting his time? Clearly it is capacity, not chance.'

'All right, maybe "chance" wasn't quite the word,' I conceded. 'Substitute "opportunity", if you like.'

He shook his head. 'I think you mean perception. You use words very loosely,' he said, with disapproval.

I continued to wonder what all this was about. At first I had assumed that he required amplification of my earlier statements, but though the schoolmasterly attitude was evidently natural to him, and liable to break out any time, he had abandoned the role of inquisitor. He now spoke to me more as if I were a candidate for examination, or, maybe, an applicant for a job. I thought I'd try a question of my own.

'Have you ever lived in my country?' I asked.

'No,' he admitted, in some surprise.

'I think you should. You'd find it a lot easier to understand if you took a look,' I told him. 'There's a certain organic quality there that I'm sure you'd disapprove of.'

He regarded me uncertainly, decided not to take up the point and got back to business.

'Your German is not always quite perfect, but it is very good,' he observed.

'And you have very good English,' I told him, but that was not what he wanted.

'I have heard,' he went on, 'that there are many good German communities in your country.'

'There are,' I said, 'quite a number of good American communities where German is spoken.'

'But why, if these people are Germans, do they live in America?' he wanted to know.

'Well, the purpose with which most of them came there was that of ceasing to be German,' I explained.

He frowned. 'I don't understand that. To be of a race is not a thing one can cease. One is born so, and must remain so – particularly this is true of the German race.'

'Speaking of using words loosely, you wouldn't be meaning "nationality"?' I inquired, wondering why the devil we had got into this, anyway. 'What do you fancy is the German race?'

He stared at me. 'Why, I am of the German race – it is a matter of the blood, not the nationality.'

I was puzzled. Thinking of the variety of types I had seen in Germany itself, I asked:

'Have you ever been in Germany?'

'No,' he said, regretfully, shaking his head.

'Well – ' I began. Then a sudden thought struck me. 'What countries do you know well?' I amended.

He shook his head again. On the same note of regret he said.

'Unfortunately none. I have always been here.'

It was my turn to stare at him. As casually as I could, I asked:

'And where is "here"?'

But he was not answering that one. He brushed it aside, and the whole of our last conversational divergence with it, and went on to ask more questions. He knew already that I was not married. I did not choose to enlighten him about Freda's place in my life, and as a result he wasted quite a bit of time assuring himself that I had no other intimate associations, attachments, or intentions back home, and the information for some reason pleased him.

It seemed to me to imply that I was just a person who could drop out neatly without being noticed, so I did my best to play up Jake's probable reaction to an earth-swallowed disappearance from the staff. But he was not a lot interested – nor could I make out what he was getting at, for all his talkativeness and proneness to disquisitions.

Maybe he did get something out of it: about all I learned was where we began – that 451 was also Emil.

And as if that weren't enough, I had to put up with much the same kind of thing again a couple of days later. It didn't go too well. The questioner this time was a woman. When she entered, I had the usual moment of involuntary belief that she was Freda; when I found she was not, it left me in a poor temper. What astonished me most about her was the difference beneath the similar exterior. Somehow, I found that more surprising in a woman than I would in a man – I don't know why. This particular character failed to appeal, maybe because she had the emotional drive of an adding-machine, and a soul like a slide-rule. The least deviation from the narrow answer had the effect of straightening her mouth and veiling her eyes with synthesized toleration while she waited for the froth of human folly to subside. An exhausting interview. I don't think she was pleased with the results – though it was difficult to know how pleasure would register there. All I got out of it was another item for the file – Number 932 was Miranda. Somehow it didn't suit – in spite of the fact that it means, I believe, 'admirable'.

This kind of thing did nothing to clear the fog. My status had evidently changed, but it was no less obscure. At times I was aware of a deep uneasiness – the sort of thing, perhaps, an infidel might feel if surrounded by rabid sons of the Prophet: the infidel himself being situated, inadvertently and inexplicably at the moment, upon holy ground.

But for most of the convalescence I did my best to shelve my speculation, and force a stolid, bovine patience. With patience I rested, with patience I consumed the foods and broths they brought me, and with patience I waited to see what would happen next.

Nor had it ever occurred to me before to consider what a strain on the patience patience can be.

*   *   *

The eighth day brought me a black overall uniform without a number, and a belt without a knife. There was no cap. As the man who carried these things in placed them neatly on a chair, I asked:

'What's all this for?'

He said, briefly:

'The Mother will see you to-day.'

'Indeed,' I remarked. 'And who, or what, is the mother?'

I have seen many people surprised – or, as Emil would doubtless have preferred me to say, astonished – but I have never observed quite the like of the flabbergasted amazement that overwhelmed the replica of my own face in front of me. Broad bands of white appeared suddenly above the iris of each eye, his mouth dropped loosely open, his tongue wobbled there, and over all came the vacancy of witlessness.

It was an interesting sight, if brief.

Presently it was succeeded by an expression of frozen outrage which he held rigidly as he left the room.

Part Two

10

Faded Pageant

... like this insubstantial pageant faded – W.S.

I shed my pyjamas, put on the clothes the man had brought, and sat down on the chair to wait, wishing, for the thousandth or so time in the last few days, that I had a cigarette. After a half-hour or so two men came in. One of them could have been the man who had brought the clothes: I did not know. The stiff formal air that both wore might be attributable to disapproval of me or, on the other hand, simply to some dignity in the occasion. There was certainly that in the tone of the one who informed me:

'The Mother has sent for you.'

This time I chose a pacific line.

'Ah!' I said, and let them take it how they would.

We set off, prisoner and escort fashion, along interminable passages, down occasional flights of stairs, and along exactly similar passages again. The two of them stepped out with a brisk decisiveness and spoke never a word. I thought it tactful to tone in with the mood.

After what seemed some miles of this monotonously hygienic scenery we stopped before a pair of doors. They were plain, larger than the rest, and differed from them in having no visible means of opening. A few seconds later, however, they swung slowly outwards, showing a thickness suited to a strong room.

Beyond, the character of the place changed. There were the same cream walls, but several pictures hung against them. The composition flooring was covered with a plain, claret carpet. At the far end, some forty feet away, was another pair of doors.

We went in, and the outer doors began to close slowly behind us. Again we waited, my companions standing rigidly, with an air of being on parade. I saw no reason for that, and to pass the time I looked at the pictures. They were, I found, exclusively items representing Nordic-looking persons in states of great activity and, frequently, of discomfort. One felt that if they did not all represent scenes from Wagnerian opera, it could merely be on account of Wagner not having the time to get around to them.

The second, and equally weighty doors opened in the same deliberate fashion. My companions marched smartly forward, with me a little slow on the take-off, and out of step. Only a certain compression around the lips revealed their opinion of the scruffy show I was putting up.

We entered a lofty hall, with a marble floor. A circular carpet covered the centre. On it stood a large dark-oak table and several chairs, looking hostile.

One of my escort startled me by clearing his throat. He spoke, somewhat in the self-conscious manner of one not to be frightened by hearing his own voice in a cathedral:

'When you greet The Mother you will raise your right hand, so, and say: "Sieg Heil!",' he told me, and waited for me to rehearse the gesture. I obliged, feeling somewhat foolish, but apparently achieving it to his satisfaction. Both men drew their knives from their sheaths and laid them on the table in a formal manner. We lapsed into silence again.

The process of build-up that was going on seemed to me some degrees too stagy and unsophisticated. The style of the atrium, ante-chamber, or whatever it was where we now stood was overdone for any but the naive. There were several more pictures there, larger than those outside, but similarly welterous with snorting horses, brandished swords, and streaming hair. Four intimidating creations in granite stood one in each corner. Trying to read significance into them, I was forced to the conclusion that they were impressive chiefly on account of their size and the way the muscles bulged.

But if the build-up was largely wasted on me, it was not on my companions. They stood stiffly as carvings themselves – rather as though they sensed a severely disposed Presence at hand. As far as I was concerned, the whole thing had grown tedious by the time a door opened to admit a man who beckoned silently. At that, my escorts stiffened still more, and we marched rather than walked into the room beyond.

It was a long, palatial room, and we had to march the length of it. Like the ante-room, it was windowless. Elegant chairs spaced far apart along the walls gave it a displayed, de-humanized air, but it was not oppressed by heroic motifs. The cream walls themselves were relieved by panels of light blue silk, striped in the weave, and set in narrow mouldings of gilt. The wood floor was beautifully laid. One's first impression was of a ballroom – or it might have been a picture gallery, but for the fact that there was only one picture...

It hung on the far end wall. Beneath it, upon a square of blue carpet, a figure sat bent over a large desk.

The picture itself was an extensive oil-painting. A portrait of a personage much better known to my father's generation than to mine, but scarcely likely to go unrecognized for several generations yet. It was with a peculiar feeling that I identified that lock of hair, the glittering eyes, the slightly ridiculous moustache ...

We advanced up the wood-block floor with a resonance which would have done credit to an entire company. Some ten feet short of the desk, we stopped. My neighbour on the right nudged me. We lifted our right hands.

'Sieg Heil!' we proclaimed, in chorus.

The figure at the desk lifted her head. She made a perfunctory action with her right hand.

'Sieg Heil!' she replied.

* * *

The woman looked steadily at me: and I, bewilderedly back at her. This time, I was not regarding one of the identicals – and yet there was familiarity...

The face was striking, imperious. The hair had almost lost its gold, but it had been reburnished in silver. Late middle-age had changed her looks, but not stolen them. Freshness had given way to assurance, vitality to presence. There was no smile to her lips, little expression to the whole face, save for the interest in the eyes. The features were composed – and yet I had the feeling that there was something that was not right about them, not congruous. For a moment I wondered whether my feeling could be the result of seeing lately so many faces that, though younger, were like it, and yet not quite like it – of its failure to be completely to the pattern which Freda and the others had set in my mind. But there was something else, something familiar...

Then, while I still looked at her, I had a strange sensation – as though, well, almost as though I were watching a 'dissolve' on a film. As if the whole face underwent a subtle remoulding, and for a brief, vivid second I saw my mother looking at me through it...

The effect was sharp, almost like a physical pricking. I shut my eyes, and then opened them again, staring at her. I could not have spoken if I had tried.

Nor did she say anything. She simply made a small motion of her hand to wave my escort away. They did a sharp turn about, and their footsteps diminished down the long room behind me. By the door they stopped with a click, but she gave another gesture of dismissal, and the door opened and shut.

She beckoned me closer to the desk.

'So you know me!' she said in German. It was a statement, not a question.

'I know who you must be – my Aunt Marta,' I told her.

'Near enough,' she agreed. 'Though it sounds strange. I ceased to be Marta Dahl so long ago – years before you were born.'

She paused, looking me over closely. Then she nodded, to herself.

'Yes. Now I see you I can well understand the mistakes. I think I would have been deceived myself.'

She withdrew a little into contemplation for a moment. Presently she said:

'Freda has told me about your mother – I am sorry.' She paused again. 'Adela … It seems strange now to think that I ever had a sister – or a brother. Adela and Nils… It was all so long ago and far away. In another life.'

She lost herself in thought once more. I stood there, remembering things I had heard of her – my notorious, yet unmet, increasingly fabulous Aunt Marta. She emerged now from a page that was almost fiction; a legendary character come impossibly to life… And yet, not to real life: such figures remain in one's mind, unageable – could one's Robin Hood ever mumble in the chimney-corner? Aunt Marta was still the golden child of the picture in my mother's locket; always, as my mother had told me, 'like a young goddess from one of the old sagas.' So strongly drawn was the picture in my mind that I would, I think, have been less surprised to encounter the same face under a winged helmet than I was to meet the woman before me, with all the changes of the years upon her. And yet, from the first moment, I had no real doubt – it was, rather, that I saw her with a double-vision which I have never yet quite reconciled: the golden girl is still there; the real Aunt Marta never supplanted her entirely.

'And Nils?' she said. 'Is what Freda has told me right? Is he a stubborn old man now?'

'He – has some unreasonable opinions,' I admitted. 'But we're both very fond of him.'

I imagined that Freda had not mentioned the old man's resistance to the idea of cousinly marriage – and the strain of instability which was exemplified for him in Aunt Marta herself. I certainly had no intention of bringing that in.

'I remember him as the correct and earnest young man, who came from America to see us,' she said. 'He was afraid of me, too, while I was still a schoolgirl. I am sure he must have led a nice, dull, worthy life, poor Nils. He still believes that I am dead, of course?'

'Yes,' I told her. 'For a long time they hoped to hear that you had escaped somehow. But they never did. And there were witnesses who swore you had been there in Berlin, right until the end. So, in spite of the doubts about identification, they did decide at last that you must have died there.'

'If they had heard anything, it would have been that I was being dragged to those ridiculous trials at Nürnberg. They must have known that I was on the list.'

'I put it badly,' I admitted. 'But naturally they hoped that you had escaped. I know my mother used to wonder sometimes if you hadn't got away after all, like Borman.'

She frowned.

'I regard "like Borman" as a somewhat offensive expression,' she remarked.

'I'm sorry,' I said. 'I never knew him. All this was somewhat before my time.'

'But, in the end, they came to think that perhaps I had died there after all – and that it was better that way?'

'Well – yes,' I admitted.

'They need not have worried, you know. I should never have played my part in that farce. I should have cheated them, as Hermann did – but earlier.'

'And yet,' I put in, curiously, 'the witnesses cannot all have been false. You *were* in Berlin. You *were* in that bunker, weren't you? So it was reasonable to assume that you had died there with the others, but unidentifiably.'

She looked at me sombrely, but out of eyes that were remembering, rather than seeing.

'There was a great deal that died there,' she said. 'A new world, as well as those who had fought to bring it about. There was a number that let their vision die, and then followed it with their bodies – but I was not one of them: not I...'

Again she paused for some seconds, then she went on:

'It has been convenient for me to have it thought that I died there. But *I* am not a hysteric. I see death as the worm's opportunity. It is defeat. You can dress it as you like, with drama, or glory, or pomposity, and perhaps deceive yourself for the critical moment – but, nevertheless, the same worm comes – it is defeat...

'*I* was not defeated. We had lost a battle; the greatest battle there ever was – and *some* of us were defeated. *I* was not! I did not then, and I do not now, admit defeat...'

I watched her as she spoke. Her eyes still looked towards me, but beyond me. It was not to me she was speaking, nor to anyone. She was reciting a conviction. After she had paused again she seemed to slip still further away from the present into reminiscence, as if she had discovered in a corner a once familiar thing she had not seen for a long time.

'Yes, I was there with them,' she said. 'I went there a few days before the end. You could hear the guns day and night. Every hour they seemed to grow a little louder and closer. The aircraft came, too, as they liked; with none of ours to stop them.

'The city all round was falling to pieces. The sky was full of smoke and clouds of dust all day long. And the buildings burnt like funeral fires all night. Houses would suddenly spout with dust and dirt, and when it cleared away there were frozen cascades of bricks there instead. Everywhere, the Reich we had built was blowing away in those clouds of dust.

'There were still a lot of people down in the bunker. Some of them had already lost hope, some of them had hope but no plans; most of them had plans, though – plans that sounded like whistling in the dark. The largest party was desperately urging that we should go south and make the mountains a redoubt, from which we could still fight on as guerrillas. They kept on pressing the Führer, but he still knew better than that, and scarcely listened to them.

'He was not easy to see. Everybody was wanting to put suggestions to him. But at last somebody contrived an interview for me.

'I was shocked when I saw him close to. He was haggard. His face was so thin that his eyes looked huge and bright. He was close to exhaustion. He could not keep still. He looked around him continually like a man pursued. I don't believe he had a great personal fear – or, if he had, it was submerged in something much greater. He was split in two. Even then he could not believe what he had always denied as possible. He could not fail to know that the Greater Reich was broken into pieces; and that the enemy was already in the eastern part of the city. The conviction of defeat was already deep in his soul, but his mind was still tight-cased against admitting it. He was so torn and distraught that for some seconds he did not seem to know me. Then he pulled himself out of his private anguish to say, bitterly:

'"You, too, Gerda? And with *another* plan to save Germany?"

'I reminded him of this place: a retreat from which he could, perhaps, continue the fight later. When I told him that there was already a nucleus of followers waiting here for him, he became angry. He would not see them otherwise than as rats who had deserted. When I protested that they intended to carry on the fight by other means, he sneered. But for a moment he dropped his front, and let his real feelings speak:

'"Then, if they are not knaves, they are fools," he said. "We *won* our war – but again the gods were jealous of our genius: they turned on us. Destiny is a cheat. She promised, and when she had fooled us into staking all we had, she went whoring with the Mongols. Very well, since that's the way of it, let them bring down the world in flame and ruin and finish it. We have been cheated – cheated once again. There is no justice for Germany – nor ever will be."

'I talked, but I could do nothing. The light of his leadership had dwindled to such a little spark in all the darkness of defeat that it was past saving.

'I had tried what I had to try. Then I went away, leaving him, and the rest, there in the bunker.'

She stopped, and sat silently, lost in thought.

Old wars can be very stale – and, stalest of all, the one that happened just before one was born. As a child, I had found my elders' talk of it exceedingly tedious and hard to bear. For me, it was a done-with thing, and dull, at that. Yet, as I listened to my Aunt Marta, it took on colour. I glimpsed the mood of that last, stricken gathering in the bunker. I could see the drawn-faced man with hag-ridden eyes, still only half-comprehending while the last of his empire was crashing about him and blowing away on the wind.

'You believe that he did die there?' I asked her. 'Some people say – '

'There are always some who like to make a mystery – but they are wrong,' she said. She turned her head so that she was able to see the portrait on the wall. 'That's how they think of him. But he did not look like that when I left him. He was broken: there was death in his face already. No – you can depend on it, he died there.

'Someday,' she went on, 'some one – some German – will write a great tragic opera laid in that bunker. The last scene will be set in the courtyard, with the flames curling up round his body, and Eva's. That will be true. Everything else in it will be heroically and magnificently false, for it will deal with the death of a great man. But real tragedy, you see, lies not in the death of the man, but in the death of the leader within the man. If that had not already happened, he would have come here to plan the next battle.'

'And where,' I asked, trying not to sound too eager, 'where is "here"?'

The question broke her mood. She turned back to face me, and shook her head slightly.

'Only a very few of ourselves know that – and you are not one of us. It is a question that one does not ask. You can just call it Headquarters.'

That was the flat answer. I had to accept it.

'Very well,' I agreed. 'But would it be against the rules to help me get my reason on the rails again? Ever since I fell into this it has had me wondering whether I'm entirely crazy, or just crazy in parts. These men and women, so like me and Freda that I can't tell any of us apart…? If that isn't some kind of hallucination, well, it just doesn't fit in with anything I ever heard of. It's something outside all my thinking patterns – if you understand me – and that's a pretty alarming thing to run up against.

'Then there's this enormous place, like a self-contained city, apparently hidden away in a forest. It's quite improbable, but not quite so bad as the other because it is at least possible – it doesn't quite outrage my reason – only totters it on the edge. And yet, it does have more sense than a nightmare. I do get a feeling that maybe there is a kind of core of sense about it that I've not got near yet.'

She regarded me, and then nodded slowly.

'There is,' she said, ' – though I doubt whether you will appreciate it seriously. You seem to me to have been educated along very conventional channels.'

'Try me,' I suggested. 'It could be that what has been going on around me lately has kind of softened up my mental resistance.'

'Very well,' she agreed, and appeared to fall into meditation for some moments, still looking at me. Then she said:

'We, in this Headquarters, represent a new Germany – and the core of purpose you have been looking for is our intention to build a *great* Germany.'

Her eyes kept on watching my face steadily.

I shifted my gaze up to the picture behind her for a second, and then back again. I hesitated. I realized that she was a formidable person here, and I would do well to be tactful. I said:

'*New*?' and let my gaze wander back to the picture again.

She took the point. 'That is only a symbol. I mean a *new* Germany – the Germany that would, in time, have existed, but for the Mongols…

'I expect that because our territory is so small, and unknown, it seems absurd to you that we should call ourselves the new Germany. I hope it does. A great deal of our strength lies in the obtuseness of people who would not take us seriously enough even to dream that we exist.

'Nevertheless, it is *not* absurd. In quite a short time the world has changed a great deal more than most people find it convenient or comfortable to admit. They are very stubborn about this – and they find it less alarming to brush away the few who do try to explain it as alarmists and defeatists: and, luckily from our point of view, there is always a percentage of hare-brained fools who can be shown as such. So people are reassured, and obsolete formulas and lines of thought continue, for a number of reasons.

'Everyone, you see, fears to disturb seriously *any* part of the foundations lest the whole system should suffer from the chaos that might ensue. The attitude continues to be acceptable because dislike of change is inherent in most people, and the usual forms of education deliberately tend to foster that dislike in order that the community shall be stable. The one in a million who does not accept, and tries to warn of dangers is regarded defensively as an unreliable crank – or, if he has the means of making himself better heard, as subversive.

'Now, in effect, you will see that that means that any body of people which faces the facts and accepts the logical developments implicit in the present has the advantage of immensely greater freedom of mental movement. Not being concerned to preserve the obsolescent they become a mobile force able to attack how and where they wish while their opponents are hampered by the necessity of holding on to preconceived ideas.'

She was facing me as she talked; ostensibly she was speaking just to me, but her style was scarcely that of conversation. I was receiving an address, and I felt that if she did not quite harangue me as if I were a numerous audience, it could only be because she felt more at home in the style of a broadcaster. I did not mind that. I had a feeling that, at last, I was going to learn something – and something, I suspected, pretty cockeyed. I started her out of another long pause by prompting:

'The new Germany – I don't understand that. This place can't be in Germany: I've seen the forest outside.'

She made an impatient, sweeping movement with one hand.

'Are you really so literal? Germany is not just a geographical expression. It is a faith, an ideal. Of course this place is not in Europe. The old body of Germany there is still very sick and very helpless at present, – crushed between the jealousy of the West, and the barbarism of the Mongols. It must be liberated and healed before it can throw them off.

'It is from our new Germany that the liberation will come. Then Germany will be born again, as the world leader.'

I had read things like that from time to time. For me they had always had the musty smell of a generation gone – but not enough generations gone to have become romantic. Dry and stale in fact – and therefore sounding the more oddly old-fashioned since they seemed to contradict fairly precisely the things that she had been saying just before. Indeed,

I perceived that we had in some way switched from a eulogy of logic to a declaration of faith. Very interesting. Yet, she was not speaking like a visionary or an hysteric. Her manner was convinced and calmly confident. Then I reminded myself that I had once interviewed a man who had been just as calmly confident that time would show the Earth to be flat.

'I'm sorry if I seem dense,' I said, 'but this whole idea is new to me, and rather surprising. I grasp the general sense of a party of liberation, but who are your group? He – ' I nodded towards the picture ' – is not here, you say. So who constitutes this New Germany?'

She looked at me steadily.

'I do,' she said. 'I, Gerda Daele, am the New Germany.'

I held my pan steady. Inside, I told myself: 'Uh-huh! Here it is! I might have known.' It's kind of regular for people to get around to thinking they are Germany from time to time. The funny thing is it doesn't seem to make much difference if they aren't even Germans, either. Aunt Marta was Swedish. The last one in a big way had been an Austrian house painter. But though I could keep a hold on my face, I didn't seem to come by any suitable comment to make out loud. She amplified for me:

'I created it. I control it,' she said.

'That must have been – must be – er – quite a job,' I ventured.

'You don't believe that?' she said, challengingly, and very coldly.

Her expression, too, made the warning note inside me tick louder. I tried to temporize:

'No, it's not that. It's just – '

'That you don't think I mean what I say?'

'No – I guess it's that what you say hasn't quite registered yet. It's a new idea to me – and it sounds like a big thing: the kind of thing that takes a while getting itself absorbed.'

'It's a great deal bigger thing than you imagine,' she assured me.

Her attitude didn't exactly alter, but I had a feeling we were relaxing slightly as she looked at me reflectively for some seconds.

'I will tell you something about it,' she added, with abrupt decision. I saw that I was in for another spell of her microphone technique. I could have done with a chair, for I was not yet feeling completely recovered, but it did not occur to her to offer me one. Nor did I like to ask for it: the air of the place suggested that one did not sit when in audience with The Mother. And on that thought a possible explanation of the title occurred to me – had she proclaimed herself, perhaps, The Mother of the New Germany...?

'I expect you will have heard quite a lot about me up to the time I came here from outside,' she began. 'Much of it, from what Freda has told me, quite untrue. But one thing you cannot have known is how I felt when I first left Sweden and went to school in Germany – how, almost at once, I felt a call that seemed to run through me in my blood.

'I knew, almost from the first day, that I had come to my rightful home among my own people. It was undeniable. With complete certainty I *knew* that Germany was my country, and her ideals were my ideals. There was something so fundamental about it that I knew I must, by blood, be German. Later, I found out by investigation that my instinct had been right. My Swedish nationality was simply a geographical accident. Our stock is from Marienwerder – the pure Nordic strain, from East Prussia.'

I forebore to correct her. She quite obviously believed what she was telling me. She went on:

'Within a few months, I could see my duty quite plainly. I left the school, and went to live with friends who belonged to the Party. Soon I was accepted as a Member myself. Then, as the Party rose, I rose within it. I saw Germany growing once more into a Great Power: and I was proud, for I believed then, as I have never ceased to believe, in the destiny of Germany.

'Do not mistake me there. I am not a mystic. There were altogether too many mystics in the Party. When successes come so rapidly one after another it seems, to some kinds of mind, too much to be merely the reward of courage and skill; they become dizzied and likely to believe all kinds of strange things. I do not. What I believe is that organized genius must in the end be irresistible. And *that* is a belief based on reason.'

I nodded. Given competent organization and an adequate supply of genius, it appeared more than likely.

'Then the war began,' she went on. Still successes came to us in an unbroken chain. We won the war within a year. Those parts of Europe we had not conquered, we controlled. We could, and should, have consolidated then. But the successes had altogether turned the heads of our mystics; they became like gamblers on a winning streak.'

She paused, and sighed.

'Three years spent then in consolidation and planning, and who can say where we might stand now? But, instead, a year was spent in hurried preparations to launch our next war while the luck still held. And, indeed, just at first it seemed that it might go on holding – but, in forty-two, some of us already began to see the end coming.

'No one dared to say that to the mystics, of course. And so no plans could officially be made to meet it. But I happened to be one of those who knew of this place.

'It was much smaller then. The Führer had said that it was to be a headquarters for a later campaign. But in my recollection it was started as a possible retreat at a time when there had not been so many successes as to make defeat seem impossible. In forty-two, nothing more was being done about it. With the big men following their stars, even to think of anything but final and absolute victory had become treachery. Nevertheless, a few of us began to take notes of likely personnel.

'For several reasons we did not choose the important men with the well-known names. Those we went after were the young men of promise who worked with them. Chemists, physicists, biologists, bacteriologists, metallurgists, engineers – the kinds of people who are the real builders of the modern world… We found out what they would need, we started to ship it here, and, in secret, we began to enlarge this place.

'It was not easy to get all the things we wanted, but we did acquire a great deal. The departments concerned knew of it only as a top-secret project of some kind, for which we took our orders directly from the Führer – and at a later stage that was, in a way, true when the Führer consented for a while to entertain the idea of a great Southern Redoubt in the Austrian mountains. We did our best to encourage and spread that idea – farcical though it was – and the supplies and materials allocated to it were nearly all of them shipped here instead.

'By the winter of forty-four only the most devoted of the mystics could believe in victory any more. The Reich was beginning to break up. I started to send out our selected technicians, along with as much material as we were still able to lay hands on.

'Things became more disorganized. There were still people who went about talking darkly of wonderful weapons that would save us yet, and some departments were still supposedly working on them. There were by now some almost official schemes for survival in defeat, and the confusion of the demands on various ministries helped us almost as much as the shortages hindered us.

'My approach to the Führer had to be left until the last possible moment. I was so unsure of him. I thought that if he were to learn of this place while he still had enough power to order its destruction, he might do so as a gesture of immolation. So I waited as long as I dared – until even he must have lost faith in miracles.

'Then, when he refused to come, I was free to go my own way. None of the others in that bunker would have been of any use to us.

'I was flown out of Berlin in a small plane. Then I transferred to the big aircraft that was waiting for him, if he had wished to come. When I arrived here, we cut ourselves off from the world for a time, except by radio. We burnt our aircraft, let the jungle grow back over our flying-field, and started to work for the New Germany.'

I had listened to her without, I hoped, anything but interested attention in my expression.

There are so many views of any situation. It was clearly her intention to tell me of a picked community dedicated to a single purpose – I wondered how true that was now. I recalled my Uncle Nils' accounts of the groups of refugees who had fled years ago from Austria and Czechoslovakia, and how they had clung together, trying to keep up their habits and customs until history should go backwards for them, and allow them to return home. Indeed, the world is still over-full of people unconvinced of the irreversibility of history. It looked as if I had happened upon a tight pocket of this particular futility. To recall that it was she herself who had earlier stressed the weakness of trying to maintain obsolete forms in a world that had fundamentally changed, only made it the more odd. I did not see how the two could be made to fit. But then, I suppose we all have a number of carefully furnished, non-communicating rooms in our minds. I came out of that reflection to find her regarding me closely.

'You are thinking – ?' she prompted.

I hesitated. My gleanings from history suggested that directness with potentates was generally inadvisable – and a potentate here my Aunt Marta undoubtedly was. I avoided direct comment.

'You spoke of preparing for the next battle. Did you mean that literally?' I asked her.

'Certainly – quite literally,' she replied.

'Then there is one thing that strikes me right away,' I said. 'I know nothing of your resources or how you propose to use them, of course. But, if you do, I very much doubt whether you will be regarded as conducting a war. A certain scale of operations seems to be required before trouble graduates to war status. I'd say you would be viewed not as the New Germany, but as bandits. As such, you cannot expect either allies or any other support. You'll be a small terrorist group, with every man's hand against you. And, frankly, I see a very brief, if lively, future in it.'

She did not resent that answer, but she shook her head slightly.

'We have a semantic difference there. When I speak of war, I mean an all-out attack by the best available means, with serious intention. But when you say the word, you not only require a certain scale; you also, have a geographical concept of bases from which armies, navies, and air-forces are set in motion. Isn't that so?'

'Well, roughly – yes,' I admitted.

'Good, I only hope that is the way most of your country thinks. But consider why that concept arose. It is that shape only because the original fighting power was man-power. The leader must control a geographical area large enough to supply enough man-power – or have enough money to hire it. In general, then, the richer his geographical area, the stronger his fighting forces. And that principle has gone right along – only modified, slightly, by the ability of an industrially wealthy nation to produce a better armed soldier.'

'Fair enough,' I agreed.

'It *was* – but today it has ceased to hold true. There is, as our great German philosopher Hegel showed, a point where sheer quantity produces a change of quality. When this happens, you have a new substance which you must then consider on its own merits. It has now happened to war. Man-power as the decisive factor, has given way to brain-power. Those who perceive that, also perceive that the effect of it is radical.

'A number of brains working together produce a fission-bomb. When that bomb drops, a million men under arms can offer no more resistance to it than one man can. Furthermore, the more men that are put in its way, the more it kills – with no more output of energy or cost.'

'You might say that the same is true of a shell, on a smaller scale,' I suggested.

'It is there that the qualitative factor operates more strongly. Few men, comparatively with the damage it can do, are required actually to make that immensely destructive bomb. And they are not subject to wastage. The only way you can stop them making more is to find them and prevent them – but the greater the forces you collect to do it, the better targets you provide. Think of a simpler example of the same kind of change. Which has the better chance of disabling a heavy tank, ten thousand savages with spears, or one man with a bazooka?'

'Uh-huh,' I said, 'And so – ?'

'And so it follows that fighting forces organized as we have known them are obsolete.'

'Which,' I remarked, 'is something that I have heard before.'

She nodded: 'It is so obvious that you must have done. But what are the results? You see, so few people are going to admit that the jobs they have been trained in for years are really a waste of time. So, alongside the new weapons, there will go on being big, expensive armies and navies – the more expensive, the more important – until something actually happens. Then the bluff will break down – quite shockingly and horribly.'

'I'd protest that. You must have ships to counter submarines, for instance.'

'Must you? When submarines can be found more easily, and dealt with more simply, from the air? – And how long will a radio-active submarine be useful?'

'Well, the generals maintain that you must have ground forces for occupation purposes, at least.'

'But why occupy? If your aim is conquest, bomb the enemy into surrender. Then issue your orders, and if they are not obeyed to your satisfaction, bomb again. Occupation forces are wasteful.'

'But they maintain that bombing can't win wars.'

'That is sheer job-holding nonsense now. Even when it was true it only meant that no one could deliver powerful enough bombs fast enough. But when you have reached the point where all the cities and most of the factories can be annihilated by bombing, and when you have done that to enough of them, you've won your war. In any case, that is academic; it would be unnecessarily expensive.'

'You're willing to contemplate annihilation, then?' I said curiously.

'Our aim is complete victory. The amount of destruction necessary depends on the enemy's will to resist.'

It was not, in this secluded hideout, easy to take what she was saying very seriously. We were, I saw, getting back once more to the old megalomania of world-domination – and not, this time, even by a nation, but, from what I understood, by a group of a few hundreds, or maybe thousands, hidden away in a forest some place. It could, and should, have been laughable, and yet I found, facing this calm and perfectly serious woman, that it was not. I began, indeed, to have a creepy, uneasy feeling that there was not only a hard centre of theory, but an equally hard intention. It was at any rate, wise on all counts to give credit for that, so I asked:

'But questions of production, logistics – ?'

'We can produce what we need. The breeding of bacteria, for instance, does not require either great plants or great outlay. We already have some very interesting bacteria.'

'Spreading plague is not my idea of war,' I said.

She nodded.

'That is exactly what I have been trying to point out to you – that your idea of war has become as obsolete as the crossbow. But even your own military are not altogether neglectful of that. If you were to look into the records of the work done at Camp Detrick, Maryland, among other places, I think you would be astonished. Still, if it is any consolation to you, we shall not start with that, nor with the viruses, nor the fungi. We shall start with the satellites, and the rest may be unnecessary.'

'The satellites!' I exclaimed. 'But all they do is to re-broadcast television programmes.'

'So? No, they don't tell you much about the others, do they? Your own faults, of course. You all made so much sentimental fuss about the atom bomb, and later about the hydrogen bomb that they not surprisingly found it caused less trouble not to tell you about the things they were doing. But I assure you there are quite a number of them – and quite a lot more being added each year. Whether they would ever dare use them or not I don't know – some of them are really very nasty – but each one has to have them because the other does – and they have to put into them whatever they think the others may be using – not just atomic heads. So you see why we think it may not be necessary for us to use our own dusts, viruses and fungi?

'It is only the people and the traditional forces that have completely fossilized in their strategy. The others have set quite a celestial arsenal revolving around us, just idling along up there until the time comes. A flock of Damoclean moons.

'The course of each projectile has been corrected and carefully charted by the dispatchers. All that is needed to bring it down at any place along that course is the transmission of the right impulse at the right moment. What could be simpler? Nothing to do but wait for that moment, press the button – and death and destruction rain down on your enemy from vasty space.

'It is a beautiful impasse. Nobody dares to give, for fear of what he will receive – just as nobody dares to be without satellite weapons, just in case he should receive.'

She paused for a moment, apparently to contemplate the pretty perfection of the stalemate. Then she went on:

'Naturally, we were interested. We made technical investigations of the situation. As a result, we find ourselves very conveniently placed. None of the present satellite tracks passes within a hundred miles of us here, for one thing. Another is that we have acquired enough information to enable us to drop any one of five hundred satellites at least, out of fifteen hundred whose orbits we have charted, with a fair degree of accuracy. You will see what that means?'

I did.

'That you could start a war tomorrow, if you wished to?' I suggested.

'Exactly. Each side would think the other side was dropping satellites upon it – and each would hurry to finish off the other before the damage at home became too serious. In fact, the ingenious satellite idea was not quite clever enough to be safe. As it stands, we can choose our own time, and afford to wait until we are quite ready. The satellites will still be there when we feel that it is the right moment to use them, because there is no way of getting most of them back other than dropping them.

'I am still waiting for recent devices of our own to be perfected. Then, during some convenient crisis, we can start it off, and let them hammer one another. With present weapons, that should soon lead to a complete breakdown; if it does not, we shall begin to use some of our own weapons to make sure that both sides collapse. It needs relatively few men and craft to blast or poison a whole country now. Large forces have become just a liability, and a logistic nuisance.

'And then, when the disorganization is complete, we shall come into the open, and begin to take over.'

She went on talking and explaining. Faced by her calm assurance, which she might have been applying to some big business deal, I began to lose a lot of my earlier scepticism – and my confidence. It was perturbing to recall how an originally small but ruthless party had succeeded in mastering first Germany, and then nearly all Europe – and to reflect how a small group in the Kremlin had shown itself capable of controlling one-sixth of the world. I knew, of course, that the potential power of destruction had increased immensely, but now, for the first time, I began seriously to envision what might be done if all the means available were to be employed without scruple – if there were a group determined and unprincipled enough not to care what was wrecked and how many millions died as it made its coup. The prospect horrified me – but not, apparently, her.

'Scarcely anything is impossible now,' she said, 'It is not the ifs that delay us; simply the techniques. Had Germany recognized that fact years ago instead of engaging in a foolish competition between better conventional weapons and better conventional defences, she would have produced fissile material when it was needed, she would have won her war, and all history would have been different. We concentrate on the unexpected, or at least the improbable, for our own weapons. We don't intend to waste ourselves by attacking defences, even inadequate defences – it is elementary for anyone but a professional soldier to attack where no defence has been prepared, and we differ from him in another way: we are not interested in fighting a war – our concern is all in *winning* it.'

'At *any* cost?' I asked.

She nodded, deliberately.

'But if you were to win it by the means you have been talking about, you'd inherit a world that was ruined, decimated,' I pointed out.

She shrugged.

'All the old orders are breaking up, in any case. Science has seen to that. Even without us there would inevitably be havoc and chaos sooner or later. Surely it is better that it should come while we are organized and prepared to handle it?'

'That means accepting your premise that it *is* breaking up.'

'Well, isn't it? Where can you see light and a way out?'

'I have always been an optimist,' I told her.

She shrugged again.

'There are several types of optimist – I, myself, am the reasoning kind. The world itself will soon recover. Repopulation has never been a problem – and if it should be, our scientists could look after it. We shall be able at last to build a modern world – one that is not shackled by all manner of traditions and outworn systems. And German genius can administer it...'

She spoke coldly, unemotionally. It gave me a creepy horror to realize that she was meaning every word of what she was saying. There was no compassion there. No trace of regret for anything she believed must go. She saw herself as capable of bringing forward the time of an inevitable cataclysm, and making herself its fulcrum. Her conviction that she and her group could reshape the world after it, however monstrous, was sincere; and in that conviction she was perfectly prepared to administer the first push towards destruction.

And not the least horrible aspect to me were the questions it raised. How far was she right in her assumptions? To what extent would the nations dare to make use of their powers of destruction? That seemed to me to be the crux of it. She thought that both sides would go all out to win. But she was ready to sting them on if they did not; and to prevent them coming to their senses before it was too late. And I could see – or thought I could see – that, with the tempers of countries as uncertain as their fears, a fair chance that her assistance might not be needed at all... I felt that I had suddenly been brought face to face with something I had been dodging – and it was a face I didn't like at all.

I became aware that she was watching me, and waiting. Just because I felt that she was expecting an outburst of moral indignation, I restrained it.

'Why,' I asked her, 'should you be telling me, a stranger, all this?'

If that reaction disappointed her, she gave no sign of it.

'Partly because I wanted to see what impression it makes on an outsider to whom it comes as a novelty,' she told me. 'And partly because you are no stranger. Being one of my own blood, the true German race, and now here with us, I think it better that you should have some understanding of what we are doing.'

'Even risking that I might not be sympathetic? If I were to tell someone –?'

She looked at me surprisedly.

'Who would you tell? You don't suppose you will be allowed to leave this headquarters, do you? – And even if you were, who is going to take you seriously? Are the Americans likely to listen to you when the Mongolian satellites begin to fall on them? Or the Mongols when the American satellites destroy their cities? You will stay here while we do. But it will not arise. You will marry Freda, as she tells me you intended. And we shall find useful work for both of you to do.'

'And suppose that we should not care for the kind of work you choose?' I suggested.

'It will not greatly matter – I do not suppose that either of you has the training to make any important contribution, in any case.'

That had not been quite my slant when I put the question – but, anyway, it had been a foolish question. It was not at all difficult to imagine after my recent experiences the kind of thing which might be expected to happen to an active non-cooperator, or a saboteur. She went on bluntly:

'It is not yourselves who interest me so much as the children you will have. We are badly in need of new stock in the true Nordic strain. Anyone more mystical than I might say that it is the hand of destiny that has brought you both here.'

I told her, with some soreness: 'A hand with some quite modern strong-arm methods behind it. Furthermore, you seem remarkably assured that we shall be content to have children to your orders.'

'Content or not, you will,' she said calmly.

With some difficulty I reminded myself of my resolution to step carefully.

'I don't understand your remark about "new stock",' I told her. 'This place simply teems with healthy, sturdy young men and women. In fact, ever since I came here I've seen nothing else but, until now. They look, since we are using such practical terms, fine "stock" to me.'

Her expression softened, for almost the first time in our interview.

'Yes. They are fine children, aren't they? They are all I hoped of them – the true Nordic strain.'

'Then,' I said, puzzled, 'I don't see your problem. Why shouldn't they have pure Nordic children? – Or is there something queer about them?'

At that, and also for the first time, she looked really angry for a moment. I didn't care for the glimpse – there was a flash of the authentic off-with-his-head. Then it passed. It even gave way to a half-smile.

'Do you mean to tell me that you haven't yet seen that they are all brothers and sisters? Why do you think they call me The Mother if it is not because they are my children?'

She must have summoned my escort while I was still staggering under the impact, for they came thumping up the room to halt at each side of me.

'And now I must get on with my work,' she told me calmly, in dismissal.

I suppose I sieg-heiled with the others. I don't remember: I ended the interview much as I had begun it – with my eyes popping and my mouth wide open.

11

Not Nature

Accuse not nature, she hath done her part – J.M.

Once one had left behind the sprightly scenes of carnage among thunderclouds, the passage outside wore an even more bleakly hygienic aspect than before. But the contrast helped to steady me. Indeed, it promptly gave to everything that had taken place beyond the heavy doors a comforting quality of unreality. I felt that noticeable lift which I usually ascribe to the third or fourth glass. What I had heard would no doubt return to disturb me later, but for the moment I pushed it aside. I was aware of feeling fatigued and hungry, and ceased for the moment to care whether my doubles had occurred naturally, parthenogenetically, or out of a stamping mill.

On leaving The Mother's suite we turned not by the way we had come, but to the left. In that maze of a place I was unsurprised: I simply hoped we were on our way to the lunch-room.

In the first passage there was no one to be seen. At the end of the next, however, stood two young men in the usual black. They had an air of waiting, and as we came round the corner they started towards us. We met halfway, where they stopped, barring our progress One of them said, curtly:

'We are taking over this man. Orders from Ulrich.'

In a voice no less short the man on my right replied:

'We are in charge of him. On orders from 451.'

The two pairs stood quite still, facing one another. 451, I recalled, was Emil. Who Ulrich might be I had no idea.

'You had better let us pass,' added the man beside me. The other looked back at him steadily.

'Ulrich requires this man,' he said.

My neighbour put out his arm to press me back. He did not take his eyes off the other. As far as I was aware, it wasn't my quarrel – or maybe it was, but as I didn't know which side I was on, I stepped back out of the way.

The hand of the Ulrich partisan was already at the hilt of his dagger. My escorts reached for theirs, crouching a little. But nobody drew.

'Ulrich is the senior. It is his order,' repeated the man who bad spoken first.

'His authority does not run. Come with us to Emil, and tell *him* what Ulrich's orders are.'

It was queer to watch them, almost as if the two with their back to me were acting into a mirror. The watchful, tense expressions on the faces of the further pair were identical, and, I had no doubt, reduplicated in front of them. By the look of it they should have started simultaneously, done all the same things, and ended up even.

But in fact, it was the man who had spoken first who acted first. His knife flicked out of its sheath and flew at the man opposite almost in a single movement. And as a part of the same action he jumped. But the man with his back to me was quick too: he must have known the move. He warded the flying knife with a jerk of his left arm, and drew his own. Before he could use it, the other was on him, gripping his wrist. They swayed, one struggling to bring the knife into use, the other to get it from him.

I had not seen how the other two began their scrap, but by now they were rolling on the floor together, breathing hard as they tussled. The flung knife had fallen close to my feet. I picked it up, noticing a little blood on the blade where it had grazed the man's arm. With the help of it I could easily have settled the matter. But which way? How was I to know whether to prefer Tweedledum to Tweedledee? I was still watching the contestants contorting themselves and wondering about it, when a hand fell on my shoulder. I swung round, still holding the knife, and on the instant it was knocked out of my hand. I found myself gazing into a pair of steely eyes. I looked down to the number on her blouse; it was Miranda, all right, and behind her stood two more young women looking almost as efficient. All three of them were holding pistols. Miranda made a movement with hers.

'Come along,' she said to me.

I glanced towards the combatants. They were still at grips, all four on the ground by now, and each too much occupied to notice anything but his adversary. We had got well started on our way back up the passage before anyone of them did. Then there was a sudden cessation of turmoil, and they came running after us. Miranda swung round on them.

With the pistol facing them, they stopped.

'Mista has sent for this man,' she told them.

'To hell with Mista. Ulrich wants him,' said one of the four.

'Emil put him in our charge,' objected the one with the slit sleeve and the blood trickling on to his hand.

They came a step closer.

'Back!' ordered Miranda. 'And drop those knives!'

Her eyes flickered from one to another. They did not get back: on the other hand they did not advance. Nor did the three who were holding knives drop them.

'You have no right. Mista's authority doesn't run,' said the man who had no knife.

'Tell that to Emil,' said Miranda. 'I've Mista's orders. Now get out – all of you.'

The four faces were similarly obstinate. Miranda moved the pistol suggestively. They looked as if they were trying to make up their minds to rush us. There was a sudden sharp movement. Quick as a flash Miranda jerked her head aside. The knife sailed by, hit the wall, and fell with a clatter which mingled with the crack of Miranda's pistol as she shot the thrower in the leg. The other two dropped their knives, and, at the motion of her pistol, stood back. She picked up the knives and threw them along the corridor ahead of us. Then she turned contemptuously, and we went on again.

My new escorts tucked their pistols away into pockets in their skirts as we went. It was unreasonable, considering the calm accuracy with which Miranda had fired, and that her companions were probably as good, yet I could not help feeling that my doubles had put up a pretty poor show.

We went back past the door which led to The Mother's apartments, and turned off from the route by which I had come. Presently we were in a wider corridor where there were more people about, mostly women.

'And who,' I inquired of the girl on my right, 'is Mista?'

She pressed her lips together, shot a quick glance at Miranda, and did not reply.

'Miranda,' I said, 'Who, please, is Mista?'

'She will tell you herself,' she said, without turning her head.

'There are times,' I remarked, 'when I get a bit weary of this mysteriosissimo approach.' But nobody took any notice of that. We went on.

The only Mista I could call to mind was one of the more notable of the Valkyrie. An adept, if I recalled aright, at scavenging battlefields in search of dead heroes for onward shipment to Valhalla.

I did not altogether – oh, well, doubtless we should see...

* * *

'What you very obviously need, Johnny, is a drink,' said Freda.

'More than one,' I agreed. 'But in this place – ?'

Freda smiled. She crossed to a closet, and came back with a bottle and glasses. The stuff she poured out didn't taste like anything I knew or was anxious to switch to, but it had the needed characteristics. After a couple of glasses I began to improve.

While she went out to tell someone that I was also hungry, I looked the room over. It was adequately furnished, although with the air of a hotel. Even that, however, was luxury compared with the bareness which seemed to prevail everywhere but in The Mother's suite. Freda came back. She was wearing the black skirt and white shirt of the place, but with no number on the pocket.

'I suppose you wouldn't be Mista, darling?' I inquired, hopefully.

She shook her head, and laughed: 'Why?'

'Well, I gathered I was being taken to see someone called Mista, and expecting to find her twice as frozen as Miranda on account of she seems to be higher up the ladder, and what I find is you. I don't get it. In fact, there's darned little I do get, around here.'

'Oh, you'll see her later on. This is just a bit of a wangle. I thought you might be glad to see me.'

I went over and kissed her again.

'Just in case you didn't notice the first time,' I told her. 'And, my sweet, even in the most nightmarish of nightmares I'd be glad to see you – though I can't help admitting I'd sooner it was a nice summer's evening back home.'

'Me, too, Johnny. How's your poor hand?'

'I'd not know. But I could pack a lovely punch with this plaster – if only I could find a guy it seemed some good punching.'

She shook her head.

'Primitive. Much too primitive for this place,' she said.

'You mean they're culturally advanced – Got to the knife-fighting stage?'

'That was just a bit of brawling,' she said, and changed the subject. 'You really are better?' she asked.

'Physically I'm pretty near okay again – or will be when the plaster comes off,' I assured her. 'But I'll admit that mentally I do feel pretty unreliable. Whenever I do find out anything around here, it turns out to be more screwy than it was unfound-out. I've come to the conclusion I'm probably just some kind of male Alice – so I'm trying to take no notice.'

I perched myself on the arm of her chair, took her hand in mine, looked speculatively at her a while, and then around the place again. 'I suppose this *is* all true? This is part of the same fantastic place, and there *is* a jungle all around outside?'

'Quite true,' Freda said. She added: 'I think this particular section must be a kind of distinguished guests' apartment – or you might call it a very superior sort of cell.'

We looked at one another for some moments. Her hand tightened on mine.

'Honey,' she said, 'I'm – rather frightened.'

She leant her head against me. I stroked her hair. There was no reassurance I could make that wouldn't sound fatuous. I went on stroking. Presently she reached up both arms, and put them round my neck.

'It'll come all right somehow, won't it?' she said.

So I had to be fatuous.

'Of course it will, sweet – sure, of course it will,' I told her. I probably said it with as little conviction as I had ever said anything in my life. But she didn't seem to notice that.

We had to break up on account of somebody who came knocking at the door. Freda did a quick-change act into brisk self-reliance as she went across to it. She took in a tray from the someone outside, and brought it back to a small table for me.

'Funny kind of food they give you in this place,' I remarked, as I got down to it. 'One of the advantages is that you can tackle it single-handed, anyway,' I added, forking into a pale green, pâté-like substance.

'It's all right – but I prefer real food, somehow,' Freda said.

'How do you mean?' I asked, through a mouthful.

'Our German genius can solve all problems,' she replied, with a nice imitation of The Mother's manner.

'It's – kind of fake?' I asked.

'Photosynthetic,' she said.

I finished the mouthful. Somehow the flavour had deteriorated. I turned over a bit of the stuff on my plate, with curiosity.

'H'm,' I said, dubiously.

'Go on now. Eat it up,' she said, as she would to a child.

I did because I was hungry, but my appetite was kind of lowered in voltage. All the same, when I laid down the fork I felt the better for it, synthetic or not. I leaned back, longed for a cigarette, and resigned myself to doing without it.

'Now tell me some things,' I said. 'It needs a lot of dewrinkling. First, where *is* this incredible set-up?'

Freda shook her head.

'I don't know. Nobody I've asked seems to know – they're kind of conditioned not to be interested. Of course some of them must know, but it's a sort of state secret. My guess is somewhere in South America – but it may be Indo-China for all I've been able to find out. All I do know is that it isn't the kind of place you can run away from.'

'I've found that out,' I agreed. 'It's about all I had found out until an hour or two ago. But since then I have been received in nightmare audience by an unbelievable character called The Mother – who, no more believably, turns out to be our legendary Aunt Marta. I doubt whether my tottering mind will stand much more.'

'I know. They wouldn't let me see you again until she had talked to you.'

'Talked! My God, the woman emits! Cracko, too – crazy like a goat.'

Freda said, judicially:

'Fantastic lots of ways, yes – but not really crazy.'

'Well, maybe we differ kind of technically about the level that craziness sets in. But I say she not only suffers from delusions of grandeur – megalomania quite on the grand scale – but she has hallucinations from the repression of her natural instincts – also on the grand scale. Do you know what her final announcement to me was? – It was that all these people here, and there must be hundreds of them, were her children – and the way she said it, she wasn't meaning it figuratively, either!'

Freda looked back at me a moment, and then smiled. 'Well, how else would you account for them?' she asked.

I stared at her.

' "Else?" "Else" doesn't come into it. I can't account for them at all yet. Though, God knows, I've tried hard enough. '

'Then don't you think,' suggested Freda, 'that you had better try believing just what you've been told? Because they *are*, you know.'

There was a pause – the kind that keeps on awhile. I did have the sense not to say any of the things I was thinking. Presently Freda added:

'She *was* being quite literal – besides, you've only got to look at them to see it.'

'You can't sell me that one. We look just like them – but we certainly aren't her children.'

'Well, anybody has only his parents' word for it – and, we were both born late in our parents' married lives, weren't we?'

Some sort of indefinite panic swept over me. To make it worse, Uncle Nils' inflexible opposition to our marrying jumped into my mind. I couldn't say a thing. I sat there, like a lump, staring back at her. The meaning of my expression suddenly came to her.

'No, no. It's all right, Johnny. It is really,' she said. 'I'm sorry, I shouldn't have put it that way. Sooner or later the idea was bound to occur to you, as it did to me. But I checked on it, Johnny, with The Mother. We aren't brother and sister. Looking just like all of them is just an accident – well, not quite: a sort of very strong family strain.'

I wiped my brow.

'It's all a sort of strain,' I said. 'My God. Did you turn me over? For heaven's sake, isn't everything around here crazy enough without you letting off things like that? I don't see an idea like that getting set to begin to occur to me. Well, for the Lord's sake!'

'It could – might: After you've heard the explanation of *them*. It did to me.'

'Then let's get down to this explanation. Right now I've reached the point of understanding that they are her children because they look like her – but that we aren't her children although we look like them. Would you mind telling me just who is trying to demonstrate just what?'

'Now, now, Johnny, Take it easy.'

'I asked a simple question.'

'And I shan't answer it if you shout at me,' she said, steadily.

'All right. – Sorry,' I said.

'That's better.' She considered. 'Well, it's – er – well, you know what fission is?'

Of all the unlikely beginnings! But I tried to take it.

'Certainly,' I agreed. 'All you have to do is take two suitable pieces of plutonium and –'

'Oh, dear. Not *that* kind of fission. The natural sort – the way a cell divides. I mean, you know how identical twins happen?'

'Why, sure,' I said, 'the thingummy, the whatsit – what do you call the fertilized ovum? – anyway, it splits up.'

'Zygote, is the word,' she said. 'And it divides into exactly similar halves – so what might have been one foetus becomes two. And if those cells divide again, it becomes four. Now that's quite simple, and been known for a long time. What nobody was quite clear about was why one zygote divides, and another doesn't. But there wasn't any reason why some method shouldn't be found which would induce a zygote to divide…'

'You're not going to tell me – '

'Shut up! I *am* telling you. The trouble was almost the same as with nuclear research – it was quite obviously possible in theory: what had to be found out was the technique – the know-how. There were two main things to be worked out: one – a method of persuading the zygote to divide: the other was to provide some system of incubation for after it had. They tell me that the groundwork for the incubation was done years ago in Germany, and was mostly a matter of adaptation. But the other part of the work was done here. And these cousins of ours are the result. – You needn't look at me like that.'

'You – you'd not be fooling me?' I said. 'How can that be possible?'

'Well, naturally I don't know a lot about just *how* it's done. I think carefully controlled hard rays – or was it gamma rays? – come into it somehow. Anyway, what they do is persuade the original zygote to divide; divide the resulting pair again, divide the resulting four, and so on, dividing and dividing, and then each one can grow into an individual.'

I considered.

'That should amount to quite a lot of zygotes before you get far,' I suggested.

'It does. At the ninth division it ought to give five hundred and twelve – only the final figure never works out quite right, apparently. For one thing, it seems that you always get a few zygotes that can't be induced to divide, for some reason or other; then there are some losses, mostly during early incubation. So altogether they reckon on about a ten per cent error.'

I avoided her eye for some seconds.

'I suppose you've seen all this happening?' I asked.

She said, irritably: 'Oh, loosen up your mind a bit, Johnny. You have to take in a new idea sometimes. Show me what's wrong with it – given the know-how. Or maybe you've thought up another way of accounting far them?'

'No,' I said. 'But I do reckon I've seen a lot more than five hundred and twelve less ten per cent of them.'

Freda regarded me, compassionately.

'At the very least there would have to be two sexes, one of men, and one of women, you goof,' she pointed out. 'As a matter of fact there are several sets, and only the last few are nine-division sets on account of the quantity of incubating equipment needed. They all look just alike to me, but each of them can tell another of his or her own set on sight – though they can't always be sure which set anybody else belongs to.'

I recalled Miss Hander's prompt 'It can't be that' when I had given her my room-number.

'All the makings of a highly confusing family life,' I suggested. 'And all of them with the same parents?'

'So I'm told. But who the father is, is The Mother's secret.'

I poured myself some more of the local fire-water, drank a little of it, and contemplated the opposite wall for a while. Then I contemplated the drink, swirling it round in the glass. At last I looked back to Freda.

'It's no good,' I told her. 'I can't take this. If it were true, it would be as dangerous as the other kind of fission – maybe more so.'

'That's a pity,' she said, 'because I'm afraid you've got to take it. Snap out of it, Johnny, boy. You don't have hardening of the mental arteries yet – or do you? Or – ' she looked at me a little harder '– or are you just wanting not to believe it?'

'I'm not sure,' I said.

'Oh, come along, Johnny. When we were kids we learnt about a whole heap of things that nobody would have taken a century before – there was anti-sepsis, brain-surgery, nuclear fission, artificial insemination; flocks of things. None of those things were "invented" in the ordinary sense. They were found out. All the possibilities were always there: all people did was to develop the means of carrying them out. It's just the same with this.'

'No,' I told her. 'It isn't, you know. If it is true, it's something *different*. It's a kind of tampering... Something too – too *basic*.'

'Johnny, dear, it's no good shying at the thing, like that. Be yourself; you're talking like an old, old grandfather. Tampering, indeed! Good gracious me, what is any civilization but a tampering with natural conditions? Why, every time anyone is cured of sickness the course of nature has been tampered with.'

It was natural, I suppose, for Freda to take my reaction for the regular obstruction to any novelty – the same kind of stupid prejudice which automatically opposed the use of anaesthetics in childbirth, for instance; and pretty nearly every innovation, good or bad.

But that was not the whole of it. I *wanted* not to believe it. I can't pretend that I grasped many of the implications in that first few minutes, but I did have the feeling that they were there. After all, if it were true, the first results of its application had led a fantastic woman to face me and say in all seriousness: '*I* am Germany'.

It was a perturbing enough symptom. I fancy it was the darkling hint it gave me that made me say then:

'It's a revolting idea – monstrous!'

That did sound just the conventional, emotional response. As such, it made Freda give me a smile in which there was something maternal. She said, gently:

'If men weren't always so shocked by all the processes of creation that they must sentimentalize over them: and if they could manage to be a little *more* shocked over the processes of destruction, the world might be a more sensible and comfortable place to live in.'

'Not if every birth were to be multiplied by five hundred and twelve,'

I suggested. And I let the emotional recoil have its say, too: 'That sort of interference with natural processes *must* be repulsive to civilized taste – it's a version of the conveyor-belt.'

'Now that *is* nonsense,' she said, as if to an obtuse small boy. 'You complain of having your *primitive* instincts upset on the grounds of your *civilized* taste.'

'I – well, I strongly disapprove of it, anyway,' I told her.

'Oh dear! And they talk about the illogicality of women! Nobody's going to ask whether you approve or disapprove of it. What you wanted was an explanation of how all these doubles of ours came to exist – so I've given you it.'

I considered for some minutes. I still had only the vaguest hint of further implications, mostly I was feeling as if something fundamental had been snatched from under me, leaving me, as yet, suspended.

After a while, Freda said in a different tone:

'What are you doing, Johnny? Dangling a carrot in front of your prejudices? I know it is a bit of a facer at first, but you do get used to the idea, if you try.'

'As a matter of fact,' I told her. 'I'd just got around to being thankful that neither the Germans nor anybody else developed this thing before – back in the cannon-fodder days.'

'Not a bit profitable,' she said. 'You could waste time just as well in being thankful that the Romans didn't have aircraft.'

'Devastatingly logical. All right then, what should I be thinking about?'

'The consequences to us.'

Still the implications were coming to me only in penny-numbers.

'Well, I can see that it would have delighted old Malthus in his gloomier moments. After just a bit of it there'll be a world-wide famine, and everybody'll starve, and – '

'You're forgetting the photosynthesis.'

'Okay. Then suppose we go right ahead until there's standing room only...?'

'When I said "us", I meant us, personally.'

'Well...?'

'Didn't she tell you that she expects us to marry and have children?'

'She – ' I began. Then I paused. 'Good. God! You don't mean – ?'

'Five hundred and twelve little boys!' she said, reflectively. 'It makes me feel quite queer to think of it.'

There was a pause. I broke it:

'I'm not at all surprised,' I told her. 'And less ten per cent would bring it to four hundred and sixty and four-fifths of a little boy – which ought to make you feel even queerer.'

She looked at me. I answered what she didn't say:

'But, damn it all – it's too utterly fantastic!'

'It isn't any good being an ostrich over it, or trying to laugh it off. Sooner or later we'll have to face it.'

'All right, then,' I said. 'The motion is that we shall have an unspecified number of children, batched up in batches of five hundred and twelve, and subsequently reared on the Führer principle. Do we agree to that? – And, if not, what are we going to do about it?'

She shook her head.

'I don't think our views are likely to carry much weight, Johnny. It's what Aunt Marta thinks that goes, around here.'

'Uh-huh.' I leant back, and looked the room over.

'Maybe it would be wiser not to continue. The setup here seems to run pretty true to type, so there should be microphones some place.'

'Quite right, Johnny – but microphones and recorders need monitoring. The human element...'

'Oh,' I said. 'Do I begin to see something...?'

'Dimly, perhaps. You see, even if you do mass-produce human beings, you mass-produce the human element, and human error, too.'

I frowned. 'If I were using mikes, I might use two sets as checks,' I observed.

'Only if you were very suspicious of danger. And what possible danger could there be inside a fortress, dedicated like a monastery, and buried in a jungle?'

I looked at her again. There was something in her tone.

'I'd not know. Suppose you tell me?' I suggested.

* * *

Freda explained: 'There was some kind of muddle about me. I was mistaken for one of them. You see, in spite of the training, not all the agents they send out from here are a hundred per cent reliable. Sometimes the contrast between this place and the world outside goes to their heads – and sometimes they fall in love. I don't know whether any of them have actually tried to turn their coats: I fancy not. But there are others who keep a watch on them, and if they are thought to be weakening they are recalled, and given a going over. Sometimes they are too scared to come back; they refuse, or try to make a break for it. It's not at all a healthy thing to do, but there seems to have been quite a bit of it going on lately.

As a result, there was a sort of purge. That's why those girls were found dead. The chance of the likenesses being noticed was one that had to be taken. It was either that, or let the girls break right away – and they couldn't risk that on any count.

'Well, that's it, you see. They somehow mistook me for one of the girls who had been backsliding. They had two tries at finishing me off, and very nearly did it the second time. Then somebody must have checked up and found out the mistake. After that, they decided to bring me here. For one thing they didn't want people asking me questions; and, for another, they wanted to make quite sure that I wasn't one of them at all. They didn't really have anything against me except the confusion I'd caused by looking like one of them, and once I was in the airplane they treated me all right.

'When they really did find out who I was, everything changed a lot. You know what a thing The Mother has about the purity of the strain, so once she had been satisfied about my mother's family she was all over me. I was half the answer to her pure Nordic blood problem – but only half of it. You see, if I were to be married to one of her brood, then all my brood would be nephews and nieces to the rest; so that wouldn't really be a lot of good. However, being half the answer made me into something between an honoured prisoner and a sort of potential queen-bee.

'But now you're here, the whole thing's as good as fixed, from her point of view. A trifle close, perhaps, but permissible – and with the essential Nordic purity preserved.'

'It must be most satisfactory for her,' I observed.

Freda disregarded that. She went on:

'When they came across you poking round and asking questions they were badly puzzled. They couldn't see why, if you were a renegade, you were going undisguised – unless you were crazy. Then they wondered if you were trying to lead them into some kind of trap, so they watched you very cautiously. They didn't like what you were doing – particularly they didn't like you photographing that girl in Washington: it made them pretty sure you were collecting evidence. So you were, of course, only they didn't know it was simply for your paper. But then when you went along to the Office of Security they decided to do something about you, fast. They must have been pretty much puzzled about you to have brought you here – it'd have been more like their way to have got rid of you for keeps right then.'

'Well, in theory, that's just what they did do,' I told her, and explained the circumstances in which the real 891 had been shot while 'attempting to escape.' 'I've had the rest figured out much as you say,' I added. Then

I hesitated. I didn't much care for the idea of those listening microphones that might or might not be there. I leaned forward to speak quietly. 'It's obvious that the Office of Security are on to something,' I said, and told her about the cancelled feature-page on the dead women. 'But the devil of it is I don't know what they're on to. They may have the right line, or they may be way off it, puzzling over a lot of bits that don't fit together.'

'They didn't tell you anything?'

'Too much damned security. I'd no idea at all what they were getting at then, and they'd no intention of giving me a clue. They kind of walked round me, like dogs sniffing. The most I had was a hint that they might tell me more in a week's time – when they'd done some more checking up on me, I suppose. But there's one thing, it does suggest that this organization isn't quite so well under the hat as The Mother seems to think. And then there are the patrols that are trying to keep tabs on those infernal saucers, too. So it looks as if they have at least two lines of approach. Was that the danger you meant?'

Freda stayed thoughtful for some seconds, then:

'There may be some trouble that way,' she admitted, 'but it wasn't the kind I was thinking of. What I meant was something more subtle, right here in this place – in the centre of it: The Mother, herself. You see, she likes to be called The Mother; it flatters her. But when you get right down to it, what is she Mother to?'

'Well, from what you've told me, I'd say plenty.'

'In the most technical sense, yes. But that's all. Chiefly, she is a female ruler. They'd have had a more suitable title if they had called her Führerin. She doesn't act towards them as a mother – how could she? She doesn't feel about them like a mother, or think about them like one – come to that, she doesn't even think like a woman. She has an excellent mind, she can plan and apply principles, she has an astute perception of possibilities; in fact, considering what she has done, she must have genius. *But* she's mighty short in one thing – human understanding. It has never in her life been necessary for her to understand. She has always simply issued her orders.'

Freda was speaking with a calm assurance that surprised me, for I was still fresh from the impact of our Aunt Marta's personality. Whatever I might feel about her plans, morals, and views, I could not help being impressed by the woman herself. The build-up she had acquired in my childish mind as one of the inner circle of that band of buccaneers that had driven Germany into the old madness may have predisposed me to some extent. And though the setting she had made for herself now was stagy, there was an impressiveness about the woman herself. If one could not laugh off the width of her ambition and her confidence – and I was not able to do that – then one had to be awed by it.

Nor did it seem to me, recollecting the last part of the interview, that Freda was on quite firm ground when she accused The Mother of not feeling like a mother.

'And,' Freda added, 'she is a mystic.'

'She took some trouble to point out to me that she is not, and that the mystics were the weakness of the Party,' I told her.

'Nevertheless, she is. There is this racial strain business – the blood – as one obvious indication. When she denies it, it simply means that she is aware of it as a danger that does exist. She's an idealist too.'

At the sight of my expression she added:

'We may detest her ideals – but that doesn't alter the fact that they are ideals. She has worked quite ruthlessly to find a means of carrying them out, and she'll be just as ruthless when the time comes. Everybody here is selected and trained for their jobs; most of them to run this headquarters, some to guard it, others to go out and spy for it. It's all closely in mesh. As a piece of organization, it's wonderful.'

'All right, you must know more about it than I do, but if it's all so wonderful, where is this danger you talk about?'

'It's because idealists are, paradoxically, so mechanistic. Somewhere along the line they always lose sight of the fact that human beings are human. I admit that most of us are pretty sheeplike if the basic needs are satisfied, but only *if* they are.'

'Meaning, when you bring it down from these fine generalizations, just what?' I inquired.

'Meaning chiefly the women here.'

'Oh,' I said.

Freda moved impatiently.

'I'm not altogether a fool,' she said, shortly.

I hastened to agree.

'Then why "oh", in that tone?' she asked.

'Well – I guess the way you seemed to be leading made me expect something bigger – more definite, I mean.'

'There's not anything much bigger,' she said. 'Why do you think it was women and not men who fell off fire-escapes and were found in rivers? The oldest batch of women here is nearly twenty-eight now. I suppose even you can see that that begins to mean something? They've all been well trained in their jobs, I've no doubt – but there's one thing you're never going to train out of a woman, and that's the consciousness of time streaming away under her feet...

'Our Aunt Marta's a freak. She's outside all the normal rules, so she doesn't understand what she's doing. These women here may have abnormal origins, but they are women, nevertheless. She's got most of them believing completely in her cause – but that hasn't stopped them at the same time wanting babies, husbands, homes of some kind. What our Aunt Marta has done is construct a wonderful machine – and leave out the safety-valve.'

I was feeling a bit let down. I'd been expecting something much more concrete.

'But if she's been training them from childhood – ' I began; then I noticed her expression. 'Okay, okay. I'm in no position to know. I'll take your word for it. You think there might be an explosion?'

'Might be! Why, with the amount of suppressed hysteria there is in this place, I wonder it hangs together at all.'

'I can see that it might be troublesome at times. But the way the place looks to be organized – '

'"Troublesome"!' she repeated. 'What she's up against is fundamental. It's what makes the dandelion split the paving stone.'

'Uh-huh. You don't think you're – overestimating this thing?' I suggested. 'Suppose the – er – dandelion had become a bit domesticated; or the paving-stones were, maybe, ferro-concrete?'

She regarded me with contempt.

'What's the good of trying to explain to a man?' she inquired of some unseen presence.

'I'd not deny it,' I told her. 'The force may be as strong as you claim. But if it is, it just seems kind of funny to me that millions of women in ordinary life manage to sublimate it by reading or seeing love-stories of drivelling innocuousness – wouldn't you think they'd at least demand them tough, to match?'

Freda moved impatiently.

'All right, be smart about it, if you like – .'

'I'm not, I'm only pointing out – ,' I began to protest, but she swept right on:

'What I'm telling you is that this place is ready to rip on account of it – and before very long, too.'

The memory of the cafeteria beneath the barn, where we had eaten after our plane trip, recurred to me. The reluctance, the dreariness, the abstracted air which had hung over almost all of them there. The tears in the eyes of the girl who had sat across the table from me... But I still thought Freda exaggerated...

Then I suddenly found myself impatient with all of it. Whether it blew up or didn't blow up lay outside my immediate interests. What I wanted to find right now was some way of getting us both out of it; and I told Freda so.

'The forest is hopeless. We'd be worn out in less than a mile of it. If there are tracks, I'll bet they've fitted them out with alarms and booby-traps. I'll try to find out about the river, but somehow I don't see them leaving that open. So far as I *can* see, that leaves just one thing – to try to get hold of one of those damned saucers someway.'

Freda looked doubtful.

'I don't see how you'd expect to get away without it being known.'

'Would that matter a lot once we were away?'

'I think it would, Johnny. You'd lay information about this place, wouldn't you?'

'I certainly would – and tell 'em to come and bomb it to hell.'

'Exactly. And that's what these people would expect you to do. So what? Wouldn't you be forcing them to put their plan into operation right away whether they're ready or not? And once things do start dropping, I very much doubt whether anyone's going to listen to you, Johnny. With great nations hammering away, a story about a small group here stage-managing the thing is going to sound a bit thin, isn't it?'

'They'd think me just a crackpot, you mean?'

'Well, it would take some putting across even when people were calm, you know. What was your own reaction when you first heard about it?'

She certainly had something there.

'All the same,' I said, 'we've got to try something. I do believe that woman means to have a shot at it – and we can't just sit here doing nothing.'

'My feeling is that the way to do it is from inside, Johnny.'

She might be right about that. I didn't know enough of the setup to say. All the same, I wanted to know more about the saucers. Even if it weren't practicable to make off with one, there might be a chance of smuggling aboard.

Freda conceded it as a legitimate interest.

'Well,' she observed, after some reflection, 'the only person we can trust to help us there is Hilda.'

'H'm,' I said. 'I like the tone of this place increasingly less. Wasn't Hilda another of the Valkyrie?'

12

Hideous Dream

Like a phantasma, or a hideous dream – W.S.

The next few days found me with little occupation, and plenty to think about. Immediate authority clearly did not know what to do with me, and higher authority appeared to be stalling; so I roamed on a loose tether.

From Freda's quarters I had been conducted back to Emil, this time without incident. He regarded me in perplexity. When he wanted to know what The Mother had said to me, I hesitated. He perceived the reason.

'You can talk to me,' he said. 'I am in charge of security and order here. That puts me in The Mother's confidence – as far as anybody is,' he added, with a trace of bitterness. 'I know who you are, and quite a lot about you. I imagine that it is intended that you shall marry your cousin?'

'Then you know most of it,' I told him.

He leant forward a little.

'Did The Mother give you any hint regarding the day?' he asked, intently.

'Why, no,' I told him. 'And it could be that my cousin won't agree, anyway.'

He moved impatiently.

'I don't mean *that* day – I mean the Day of Action.'

'No,' I assured him.

He frowned. 'You're certain? Not a hint?'

'From the way she spoke it might be next week, or in five years' time,' I told him.

He toyed with a pen on his desk.

'It gets more difficult,' be said, rather to himself than to me. 'A date ought to be fixed – it *must* be fixed soon.'

'Who is Ulrich?' I asked.

He looked at me, slightly startled, as if I might have been linking with his thoughts.

'What do you know about Ulrich?' he asked, sharply.

'Nothing. That's why I'm asking. He's just a name to me – but, after all, some of his people fought some of yours, apparently to get hold of me. So I'd just like to know.'

He nodded reasonably.

'Ulrich holds the fighting command. His time will come when action starts – or so he thinks,' he said, and brooded on it.

'I don't see – . What was that little fracas over me, then?' I inquired,

'I don't know. I'd like to,' he admitted. 'He says now that his men misunderstood his order and exceeded instructions. They were simply to request you to see him, in case you could give him some useful information.'

'It didn't strike me quite like that.'

'It didn't strike Mista like that, either. She's been raising hell,' he said, gloomily.

The familiar feeling of frustration was coming over me again.

'I wish,' I said, 'that there was a beginning to this that somebody would begin at. Where does this Mista come into it, anyway?'

He looked shocked. 'Where does Mista – ? Why, Mista's the works. She's The Mother's right hand. Technically she's head of Intelligence. Under her, I am responsible for the internal security and discipline of the men. Sigrid does the same job for the women, and Griselda organizes the external work for both.'

It just got more complicated. I asked how it was, in the circumstances, that his own men had seemed no less willing than Ulrich's to attack Miranda and the two women with her who had quoted Mista as their authority. Emil shrugged.

'It was unfortunate,' he said. 'They had my orders to bring you here. Naturally, with a perfectly legitimate excuse like that you could scarcely expect them to resist the chance of beating up those women.'

I blinked.

'Er – that's usual here?' I inquired.

'By no means. Very seldom happens,' he assured me. I didn't really suppose there was a tinge of regret in his tone, but there was something. 'For Ulrich's men it was a bit different. He is responsible directly to The Mother,' he explained.

I was, by now, so well bogged down in the hierarchical arrangements of the place that I could think of no comment. He looked at me reflectively, and went on:

'I'm responsible for your safety now, and, frankly, I can see you being a nuisance. I think the best way will be for you to disappear as soon as possible. It's a choice between that and having you constantly guarded. I shall put it round that you are imprisoned in Mista's section, but in actual fact we'll give you the number 891 again. If anyone asks what you're doing, tell them that you've been recalled for a special secret course, and if necessary refer them to me. Got that?'

In a bewildered way, I had: anyway it seemed a better prospect than being under constant guard.

* * *

The room they gave me now was not large, but it was an improvement on the cell-like cubicle in which I had spent the first night. As well as the bed and washing facilities there was a reasonably comfortable chair, a writing table, and even a shelf with a few books. The books turned out to be the safer German classics, with one or two pieces of National Socialist philosophy, and some slabs of Geopolitics. *Mein Kampf* was not present: I wondered whether it was the author's mystical strain that had told against him.

I was left pretty much to my own devices. The loudspeaker kept me informed of mealtimes, and I would emerge to become an inconspicuous member of the crowd in the nearest dining-hall. Occasionally a young man would put his head into the room, apparently to check up that I was still around. Otherwise, I had no sense of surveillance. It seemed strange at first that there should be no restrictions on my wandering about the place, but when I came to think it over, there were at least two good reasons: for one thing, I could have done little damage if I had tried, and, for another, everybody I had encountered so far had simply taken it for granted that I was not hostile to the main plan – with them, if not of them.

Prospecting about on my own, I began to form clearer ideas about the Headquarters.

The first discovery was that I had been deluded in thinking it continuous. In fact, it was constructed in blocks. Some had an upper storey above ground, in the manner of the one where we had arrived, and whence I had made my excursion into the jungle, but most were entirely subterranean, with only ventilation ducts appearing above surface. Many of the long corridors which I had assumed to be passages within a single building were actually connecting ways between the separate blocks. Once one had grasped that, it was not difficult to identify them by the heavy doors, recessed into the walls, which could be closed to isolate any block completely. The overall pattern of the layout still eluded me – largely because there were parts into which either one did not go, or was not admitted.

Apart from the exclusively female blocks, a whole further region was barred off by closed steel doors. Admission was only on one level, and then only on production of a pass shown to the guards. Later it was explained to me that the scientists and technicians who had been brought from Germany, and their families, lived and worked in parts strictly segregated from the administrative headquarters. Those of my multitudinous cousins who had been selected to help them, also lived in these further parts, and only a few accredited workers passed between the two sections. It must have been a community only a little less curious than Headquarters itself. Some of the early-comers had succeeded in bringing their wives, and formed a kind of colony, while others had married some of those drafted to help run the place. In the eyes of the H.Q. staff they formed a corps of gifted inferiors whose presence was a regretted necessity – a class which, however ingenious, was still untouchable. Draftees there became contaminated by non-Nordic association, and did not return. Indeed, it appeared painful for the elite of H.Q. to have to admit that it was from this region that the synthesized food and all the other major products of research emanated.

When, more than once, I tried unsuccessfully to get a pass that would take me into those parts the refusal conveyed that my request had been a social gaffe. The severance was kept as complete as possible. The draftees were sacrifices to circumstances. The blood over there was not pure enough for Aunt Marta to risk a trace of it in her super-race.

Behind the work that went on there, there must have been some source of materials, but neither then nor later did I find out how the supplies were shipped. According to Freda, organizations of companies held lucrative patents in various countries and presumably passed shipments under cover of legitimate business.

One of the points which had puzzled me when I had talked with Freda now cleared itself up. She had spoken of the unrest among the women, but she had said nothing of the same trouble among the men. It had seemed to me that this would present an even tougher problem, but here, I had underestimated The Mother. I discovered one whole block devoted to relaxation and entertainment for the men. Possibly it owed its existence to Aunt Marta's not inconsiderable experience of male organizations, and I had the impression that it was provided with some contempt.

I grew to realize, too, that there was a greater antagonism than I had suspected between the men and the women – the reason became clearer as I discovered the large number of higher administrative posts that were in the hands of the women.

Rightly or wrongly, I found myself tracing that back to The Mother herself, and her experiences. The Party, in its last stages, had dissolved in weakness. It had fallen apart in mysticism, fatalism, and intrigue. But long before that, there were many who stood high in it and yet lacked single-ness of purpose. At the end, she, almost alone, had retained determination to continue. That, I felt, could, not surprisingly, cause her to see whole-hearted loyalty and practical purpose as predominantly female virtues.

I'd be the last to dispute that many a woman can put into a single channel an intensity and devotion which few men achieve. It was, perhaps, reasonable for her to decide, after her experiences, that the generally more diffused interests of men led to unreliability. But it was less reasonable for her to assume that every daughter of hers would develop her own undeviating dedication to the cause. So, though she provided diversion for her male troops after the immemorial way of armies, she seemed to have deduced out of her own singlemindedness that diversion was unnecessary for women – and maybe she was half-right there, too: they'd most likely be wanting diversions with more stability.

And then, of course, there was the Race. The Mother and her daugh-ters would keep the strain pure. The men, after all, were secondary, and largely dispensable.

This reversion to the matriarchal system, with descent traced through the female line, should, I thought, interest an anthropologist. It was in keeping, too, with The Mother's professed logic – leaving so much less room for argument than there could be under our own, rather curiously trustful, system...

The application, further confused by the biologists' triumphant contri-bution to the population question, would interest a psychiatrist no less – and probably reduce the poor fellow in a short time to a state of all wires crossed. For myself, I came round to Freda's contention that the cardinal error had been the assumption that the women would be content to dedicate themselves exclusively to the cause for as long as should be necessary.

For the moment I hung on to that, and left out the lesser factors. It did seem to have the makings of enough trouble to be going on with...

* * *

After several of my schemes for finding out more about the saucers had fallen down for lack of suitable means of bribery and corruption, I put the problem to Freda at one of the short meetings we managed to have each day. She passed it on to the as yet unseen Hilda. The answer was practical, if not to my taste. The negative, rather than the positive approach. I suppose, if one were not squeamish about words, it might have been called blackmail. I received one or two numbers, and certain information about the holders of them.

Number 562 turned out to be less easy to locate than I had expected. It was astonishing, once one began to notice numbers, how many people turned out to be the same fellow over again. But once I had found him, I tagged along closely, waiting for the moment when he would be as near alone as anyone could be in that place. It seemed likely to me that the dining-hall might be as free of microphones as anywhere, and I took my chance at the end of supper. The rest had left. He was on the point of going himself when I slid along the bench to his side. In a voice that reached to him, but not much further, I said:

'Hullo, Mike. How's Susie?'

It rocked him so much I was half sorry I'd let the clutch in that fast. I watched his fingers clench on the table, and then gradually relax. His jaw took the shock the other way round: it relaxed, and then tightened. Once he'd got all that over, he started pretending he'd not heard me.

'And how's little Willy?' I added.

That jolted him about as much. He rescinded his deafness, too. Without looking at me, he muttered:

'What do you know about that?' He gave a swift glance up and then down again.

'Not a lot,' I said. 'But the man who put me on to you knows more.'

It struck me it might be better put that way, on account of the nasty, nervous flash in his eye. 'He just turned me on to asking you a few things.'

'What about?' he asked, apprehensively.

I thought maybe I'd better soften him up a bit more. 'There's enough known to start them questioning you. They'd not like it if they knew you were married to Susie, would they?'

'It gives me good cover when I'm out there,' he said, defensively.

'Well, then, let's say they'd not like it if they knew you were in love with Susie. How much have you told her about this place?'

'God!' he said, looking scared. 'Nothing at all. You don't think I'd risk that? When I have to report, all she knows is that I go away on business.' He was desperately earnest.

I nodded. '*I'll* believe you. But I wonder if *they* would? Most likely they'd get hold of her and bring her here for questioning, if they knew. A cover is one thing – a settled family life is another.'

It was not difficult to see the official view about that: if his family was in a large city, the temptation to get it out when he knew trouble to be imminent would be irresistible.

He turned his head towards me, taking notice of my number.

'What is it you want?' he said, wretchedly.

'First, I want to know something about the saucers,' I told him.

He looked a little relieved. 'I can't tell you.'

'Come, come. You must be something of a technician, or you'd not be working on satellite information.'

He faced me more steadily.

'What's all this about?' he demanded.

'The less you know, the better for you if anything were to go wrong. What I want to know is how to operate a saucer.'

'I don't know.'

'Now, look here –'

'That's true,' he said, decisively. 'There are only a few full pilots. And before this interception started they had about as much scope as they would with an automatic elevator. The whole thing was sealed in, with radio controls. The pilot pressed the starter. She lifted vertically. At a pre-set height she flew automatically on a tight beam. Near the destination, side beams picked her up and brought her in. The pilot was only there for emergency, until interception and jamming made them go back to manual control, and I don't know anything about that.'

'And the power units?' I asked.

'Some kind of jets – but I don't know what kind.'

I looked at him, and he looked right back at me. I reckoned he was telling the truth. I'd not really expected a lot. I'd begun to grasp the principle that the less anybody knows, the less any squealer can give away. Indeed, a motto for the H.Q. Staff might well be, *Noli investigere*, meaning, 'Not my department'. And it was easy to see that in a place where questioning was liable to assume the aspect of a blood-sport, the less one did know about other people's business, the better.

'What you can do, is draw me a rough interior plan of a saucer, giving some idea of the layout of power units and control sections,' I said.

He did that. Very rough it was, too, and not much of a contribution.

* * *

The nights troubled me more than the days. The air conditioning was good, but I find that unless I have been working hard, I need rest-conditioning, too. And there wasn't that.

The whole sense was that of waiting – I did not know what for. The work that The Mother had spoken of did not materialize. Maybe somebody somewhere was trying to figure out how such a type as a news-picture man could be fitted into the organization – and I'd allow that'd be quite a job. As it was, I'd a lot too much time to brood.

All the time, too, there was a guilty feeling that I ought to be doing my damnedest to disorganize the outfit. And never did I seem to get any nearer to seeing how one lone man could give it anything but the smallest pinprick.

I did have romantic moments when I felt that a sub-machine-gun would be a nice, comforting thing to possess. With a toy like that, you can cause so much bother with so little thought and trouble that it ought to be quite a relief, but in my more sober moments I recognized that it would be a stupidly futile gesture.

Once more, I considered my former idea of floating down the river – and, once more, thought little of it. It might be a thousand-mile journey for all I knew. And these people weren't fools. In their place I would have rigged photo-electric cells to guard that river – maybe in intimate connection with machine-guns...

In fact, every idea that looked bright for a moment got a quick tarnish on it.

And at night, when I was trying to get to sleep, my mind kept right on squirrelling.

At first, it was the prospect of what Emil had called Action Day that obsessed it. Aunt Marta could have had no purpose in telling me anything but the literal truth about the satellites, and her conclusions struck me as uncomfortably sound. Push-button warfare is the blitzkrieg carried to its logical conclusion. Once it starts there can be no time for consideration. Up among the high-brass plans A, B, or C have been approved for immediate application in given circumstances. If the enemy is going to hit fast, then the counter plans have to hang on a hair-trigger if they are to operate before he delivers a knockout.

A projectile falls. It might be a mistake, or an accident but the hand must go forward to give the alert. A couple more projectiles fall out of the sky. There may be a dozen more on the way down at the very moment. There is nothing that the man with the hand can do but guess, and guess fast, who sent them – he *dare not* delay any further. There's no time to consult. Even the loss of a minute may mean disaster. He must make his decision *at once*. He does. And Plan A, or B, or C goes into action, in the ultimate analysis, on one man's guess. The show is on – who started it no longer matters.

Aunt Marta and her gang having provoked the whole thing then watch comfortably through a telescope while the giants batter themselves into bloody, tottering wrecks; just shying in a cracker now and then when the party looks like getting stale.

Plan for chaos – and, as far as I could judge, just about perfect.

And how, once the push-button principle had been applied, such a thing could be countered, I simply did not see.

The more I thought of satellites, the more I began to understand the feelings of the people who had wanted the atomic bomb 'outlawed'. That certainly was a nice idea – the only snag about it was that if sensible international arrangements had ever been enforceable, the atomic weapons would never have gotten themselves invented, anyway.

The satellites, however, were up there, ready, and being added to.

For a couple of nights I was preoccupied with this theme, and when I did sleep there were nightmares wherein characteristics from Wagner, Nietzsche, Spengler, Hitler, H.G.Wells, Clausewitz, and, very likely, Freud, were dynamically, if improbably, combined. Then it became modified by an even more disturbing speculation.

One had to assume that The Mother held a detailed plan for taking charge of the chaos she proposed to create, but so far I had acquired no more than an airy impression that the chosen would sally forth, establish themselves as Authority, take to themselves such warranted Nordic mates as had chanced to survive, and forthwith organize and rear the New Germany, while preventing what was left of the rest from reorganizing themselves. There was a large generality about it, and it was while contemplating the possible details that I began to perceive the likelihood of a force more potent than the satellites. That the implications came to me so late, I can only attribute to my preoccupational worry over the more conventional forms of doom. But, when the implications did come, they smote with all the vigour of a good, old-fashioned revelation.

One moment I was pondering upon the acid tests of Nordicity, and wondering whether there would be enough certified and approved Nordics to provide all my cousins with suitable partners – the next, I perceived that it was entirely unnecessary that there should be. I sat up in bed abruptly, and stared into the darkness with a feeling that all I had known had been suddenly kicked away.

I had a shocking glimpse of an immemorial pattern dissolving.

The reproduction of any species is a very hit and miss affair – very predominantly miss. If all the millions of spawn in the sea were to grow to maturity, it would take remarkably little time for the oceans to become solid fish. There always is, and has to be, some check on the realization of the full potentialities; if not natural enemies; then food supply, or climate – or it may be the physical constitution of the species itself … A mammal, it seems to me, might be regarded as having, by its evolution, obstructed the immense fruitfulness which it still potentially retains. Heaven knows why things proceed in this muddled fashion. Maybe they seem less muddled to a biologist, or to a philosopher – but for a mere observer, a guy who just uses a lens for recording, there's plenty to grade as crazy.

Yet, even to an uninstructed fellow like me, the obvious becomes visible, in time, once I get around to mulling over it.

And now I suddenly saw, quite brightly lit up, that the human creature had built his institutions the way he had on account of his limitations. Because the female could have only a few offspring, and those weak, he had built on the family unit to protect them. Gradually, in the course of time, he had thought out local and national organization, and right now some of him was fumbling around with the idea of world organization – and leaving it pretty close to twelve o'clock, too – but back and base of it all was the foundation unit, the family.

Until now…?

But now what would happen to human relations? The biologists had let out something to attack them right at the roots. No institution we had could deal with such a factor. The whole pattern of every race had been built up to deal with the normal cycle of birth, life, and death. Tampering with death had brought problems enough – because the old no longer died fast enough there were famines in which many of the young died too early; because the figures of infant mortality improved, the problems of food supply grew worse every year.

Jokingly, Freda had referred to herself as a 'potential queen-bee': it hadn't seemed funny to me then; now it was even less so. Behind it, I could half-glimpse a world where that might become possible – where mothers could be a chosen few, and the human pattern might turn to the beehive, or the termitary. Why not? Once the symbol of the mother holding her child ceased to have universal significance for the race, anything might happen. There was not a standard, not a value that could not be changed.

My views on the sanctity of human life are, I think, about average – that is to say, in honesty, not very high, for, if people felt the reverence for it they profess, I guess we would be having no wars, and a lot fewer accidents, but, even so, I found myself shocked by a new prospect of cheapness. If human beings could be turned out by – well, mass-production, it wouldn't be long before the individual had scarcely any value at all… the ant-heap trend again…

What difference that might make to the planet, no one could foretell, but I saw now that I had been righter than I knew when I said that for the race the new fission was more dangerous than the old.

Visions of a regimented world, of corps fitted, as among ants, to work or guard, and with no other interest or purpose in life, came into my mind. I saw how easily, with an unlimited supply of material from which to draw, it could be built up. God knows, we have learned that a fanatic corps can be created even in the present world – and that, with the dropping of a few moral scruples, unwanted persons can be disposed of in large quantities. And the moral scruples certainly were not going to remain intact when the whole pattern changed...

I know well enough that the small hours distort – but I know, too, that the world has become pretty well distorted. Out of the recent past, out of the discoveries, something more than clumsy compromises has to come. It is quite close now, waiting round the next corner to overthrow our system – but we still cannot see what it is. Once, it looked as if it might be communism – before that faith produced a strange hotchpotch of industrialized state-feudalism out of the process of keeping its chosen wandering and uncontaminated more than forty years in the desert – but it had not been that. The veil on the face of the future is as ominous as ever – and as opaque. And now I had a vision of what it might be – and what, at all costs, it must not be...

Just one invention too many...? People had thought that about nuclear fission, of course – and they might yet be proved right – but even if they were not, here was something worse...

So simple, too. You stimulate the zygote – that's all you have to do. You just irritate a single cell so that it divides into two – and you split the foundations of human life...

I lay awake a long time, and I couldn't see anything but retrogression and loss: the path leading steeply down from all dignity to the termitary...

And then, sometime when the small hours had got around to enlarging, it came to me that there are more kinds of fission still... Freda had said that the women were restless. But there was more than that: the men, too, were restive – under the authority of the women. Clearly there was resentment of Mista whom I had not yet seen, and, it might be, of The Mother herself. More than that, there was enmity between the followers of Emil, and those of Ulrich; which would derive, it was fair to guess, from a rivalry of their leaders...

The more I considered it, the more I seemed to perceive quite a quantity of inflammable material lying around and waiting to be blown upon. And very likely there'd be more if one started looking deeper... It might be that, working carefully, I could do something about that...

13

I Go About

Sometimes I go about and poison wells – C.M.

I sat depressedly through my breakfast with the rest. Their company had a withering effect on the bloom of my nocturnal plots. The utilitarian, purposeful, sterile quality of my surroundings oppressed me with a sense of being too late: so much that properly belonged to a termitary seemed already to have taken form around me.

I found myself wondering again whether I could not somehow manage a pass into the technical regions and grab myself a weapon. It could be simple – one really good bomb now might still fix it – idea and all. But once the idea should get outside the place, no one would be able to scotch it…

I was still pondering over my third cup of coffee, alone at the table, when a man came up. As usual, he might have been any man.

'The boss wants to see you,' he told me.

'When?' I asked.

'Soon as you like.'

'Okay. Might as well make it now,' I said, and got up, leaving the coffee.

My guide was no talker. After leading me through a number of passages, he opened a door. I went in.

The man seated behind the desk looked up.

'Morning, Emil,' I said, politely.

He went on looking at me. Then he said:

'I am not Emil. I am Ulrich.'

I ought to have noticed the 523 on his chest where Emil wore 451. As it was, there did not seem much to say but:

'Well?'

He continued to look hard at me. He must have known that no difference from one of themselves would be apparent, yet he seemed surprised to find that so.

'You say your name is Johnny Farthing?' he asked.

'Yes.'

'You were received by The Mother a few days ago?'

'Yes,' I said, again.

'I would like to know some of the things she told you.'

I let my eyebrows lift slightly.

'I understood that my audience was private.'

He frowned, keeping his eyes steadily upon my face. 'There are certain things that it is important for me to know.'

We went on stalling that way a while. Then I said:

'Look here, if Emil doesn't know about this spiriting away already, he soon will, and he'll have a pretty good idea where to look for me. Tell me what it is you want to know, and I'll consider it.'

Evidently one did not speak in this way to Ulrich. His eyes bulged a little.

'I could put you where he won't find you,' he said.

'And I could give you some funny answers to your questions,' I replied.

He was less certain how to deal with me than I had supposed. I reached a chair forward, and sat down.

'You sent a couple of toughs to get hold of me right after I had seen The Mother – only Mista's women turned out to be tougher.'

I was pleased to see that that didn't go down well. He still seemed doubtful how to lead on, so I did it for him:

'You're going to ask me when the Day is?' I suggested.

He became more alert.

'She told you?'

I shook my head.

'No – but from what she implied, and from what I've overheard from Emil, it's going to be soon.'

'"Soon" might be a week, or a year.'

'More than the first, and less than the second.'

'Late February, or early March?' he guessed.

'My impression from Emil was –'

'Why in hell should Emil know anything? I shall be in charge of operations when the time comes.'

'There has to be security – that's his department. Besides, he does have certain personal interests, you know…'

'Meaning...?' he asked, coldly.

I let myself disclose motives for Emil which clashed very nicely with what I imagined his own to be. I also invented a later consolidation in which Mista's authority would exceed his own. It went down quite gratifyingly well.

All in all, I had a busy day. On leaving Ulrich, I visited Emil and let him have a disturbing account of ambitions revealed by Ulrich, and his determination not to stand Mista's authority longer than necessary. I followed that up with a call upon Miranda to whom I dropped uneasy hints of the male restiveness under female domination. And I reckoned I had put that across well enough to cause her concern, for presently I was being shown into the presence of Mista herself.

One thing I never could get used to – the multiplicity of minute variations which could be found in what, at a distance, was always Freda's face. And Mista was an extreme example. There was the same gold hair, the same colouring, the same features, even familiar movements of the head. Yet the composite effect, and the manner, was so different. A touch of The Mother's imperious assurance made the features tauter, and more controlled. The mouth was, in an indescribable way, hardened. In a face less mobile the same eyes were sharper – at least, they were the same-coloured, same-shaped eyes... But what is it can make some eyes the windows of the soul, and others the weapon of the basilisk? I'll never know – but I did have a sudden feeling that any opposition to Mista, including myself, was up against something far tougher than I had expected.

She looked at me from a long way off – and yet as if I were under a microscope. It was not the pose that the underling adopts to reassure his little ego. There was the habit of authority. She examined and evaluated in detachment.

The start was sticky, but I got my piece said, in the end. It was a complaint regarding certain factions which, assuming me to have influence with The Mother, were pestering me to join with them. I had no wish to be mixed up in the internal politics of the H.Q. in any way, and still less to have it thought that I was in sympathy with movements which seemed to me subversive.

I could not tell how that was received. Mista's expression told me nothing. When I went, I had to leave with the unsatisfactory feeling that it had all sounded rather better inside my head than it did in words. Her dismissal was simply:

'Very well. Should you come by any definite information, you will please report it to Miranda.'

It seemed to me that I had now reached the stage where I should consult with Freda, but at her rooms I was told that she had been sent for by The Mother, and no one knew how long the interview would take.

To kill time, I put in some exercise in a gymnasium. Stimulated by that and a shower, I withdrew to my own room to concoct schemes for my next moves. I felt none too happy about the Mista attitude, and reckoned the best line might be to concentrate on fertilizing trouble between Emil and Ulrich. I was still thinking up ingenious disguises for mischief when the speaker announced the evening meal.

After a few minutes in the dining-hall one could not help noticing a difference. I looked around curiously. There was an inescapable impression that everyone in sight had been given a few extra volts. They moved more briskly as they walked to the cafeteria counters. There was a whole lot more talking than usual, too. After I'd watched them a bit to make sure I wasn't mistaken, I asked my neighbour:

'What goes on? Public holiday, or something?'

He looked surprised.

'Why, haven't you heard? General address by The Mother tomorrow.'

I stopped chewing, with a sudden, apprehensive feeling.

'What about?' I asked.

'There's nothing official yet, but – well, what do *you* think?'

'Not – not the Day?' I said, uncertainly.

It was clear that I had not used the right tone.

'Why not?' he demanded, looking hard at me.

I tried to deaden the pan.

'Kind of hard to realize,' I said. 'You get so used to just expecting it someday... This is only a rumour though?'

'You can see what everyone's thinking,' he said.

He pushed away his plate.

'Well, I'm for the Amusement Block while there's still time. There's that nifty bunch of new girls arrived just right, bless their brown hides. Coming?'

'Later,' I told him.

'Better not leave it too late,' he advised, as he got up. 'You'll find the doors shut. By the look of things it's going to be a big night.'

My appetite left me. I sat on, feeling more and more as if I were the only one out of step.

After a bit, I pulled out, and made my way slowly to the block where Freda's rooms were. She was back now, and one of the girls showed me right in.

She didn't look pleased to see me – in fact, I had a wavy moment thinking she might be one of the others. But it was her voice, even though it did have a kind of edge on it just then.

'I've been waiting for you,' she remarked, irritably, and without welcome.

'Oh,' I said, 'well, it was you who wasn't here when I came. But have you heard the news? They're all saying – '

'I know,' she said. 'Happens about once every six months, they tell me.'

I deflated a bit, but:

'Maybe it is right this time,' I suggested.

She brushed that off with an impatient shrug.

'What I want to know right now,' she demanded, 'is why you've been going round playing the goat all day?'

I blinked. 'What – me?'

'Yes, you, Johnny. What's all this fidge-fudge you've been dishing up to Mista?'

'Fidge-fudge! You mean she – ?'

'I certainly do. Really, Johnny, of all the childish, irresponsible ways of going on! What on earth made you – ?'

I came back a little.

'Now you listen here,' I told her, and I explained my idea of spreading uncertainty and suspicion, with particular reference to Emil-Ulrich, and male-female, enmity. 'It just needs working up gradually,' I said.' There's plenty of jealousy around, and I reckon that if some of them were handled right, they might fetch up one day at the idea of deposing The Mother. But, of course, if this rumour is right – '

I let it tail off, partly because that was what would happen to the idea now, anyway, and partly because her expression was kind of sorrowful.

'My poor Johnny,' she said, with just that note that sets up a nasty resonance.

'I don't see why, at all,' I replied, shortly. 'Properly planted, it could help disorganize things quite a bit. *She's* what holds them together.'

'Of course she is, Johnny – That's why not one of them would want her deposed. For one thing, she *is* The Mother of all of them. But, more than that, she is Authority here. What is there to choose between them? But she appoints some of them to act as her instruments – and that's why any of them have any authority. Without her commission, they'd all be equal. But there'd be no reason at all for anyone of them to obey any other – and so, pure chaos, utter democracy – '

'Here, hold that,' I protested. 'Utter – what?' But she swept on.

'No, you listen to me. Don't you see, whatever they may feel at times, they *know* that only she gives them any stability. And even if anybody did want to make a coup, he'd have to have supporters – and why, as he isn't any different from themselves, should any of them support him? For them The Mother is the symbol of all the law and order there is here. Why, Miranda tells me that Mista actually laughed for the first time in months when she heard the recordings of your talks with Emil and Ulrich – and I don't wonder.'

I stared at her. I could almost feel myself dwindle. I had forgotten about microphones, and even if I had not, I'd scarcely have thought eavesdropping on the higher ranks in order. I said so, too.

Freda looked scornful. 'Surely it is only there it would be worth bothering with it – particularly when there is this antagonism,' she remarked.

I broke the pause that followed by requesting a drink. I knocked it back, and poured another.

'All right,' I said. 'Maybe I have made a fool of myself. But I couldn't go on just hanging around: I had to try something. Anyway, it's too late to matter now. How long do we have before the atoms get popping?'

She shook her head. 'I don't know anything about that. All I do know is that she's going to announce about us – you and me – tomorrow.'

I looked into the drink a bit, and then swallowed it.

'So?' I said. 'Just like that, huh?' I examined my fingers a mite. 'Darling,' I told her, 'I'm sorry about this.'

'Are you, Johnny?'

'You know the way I mean. All this is rather – well, not exactly romantic. How much were you set on the bells and rice and Niagara Falls?'

'You know me, Johnny.'

'That's the trouble – I don't come near it. All the same, I do, in my humble way, keep on loving you.'

'That's all you've got to do, Johnny – only maybe, not *too* humbly. Perhaps if you let up worrying about mights, and fixed it that the chief point for us is us…?'

'I'll try that,' I agreed.

'And, Johnny,' she added, seriously, 'will you promise me to stop playing the fool?'

'Meaning?'

'Meaning, Johnny, that you throw out all snap ideas the minute you get them. You see, even if this isn't going to happen for us just the way we had in mind, I'd – well, I'd still a lot rather have you whole than partly broken up. This time Mista and the others thought it funny – next time they might not.'

'But look,' I said, 'we can't simply let this thing go ahead and not even try to do anything to stop it.'

She looked at me seriously. 'I know the way you feel about it, Johnny. But you have to be a realist. You're just one man – if you were a woman you might understand a bit more about living as fully as you can within the limits allowed. But you are only one man, and this isn't the age of St. George, either. Nowadays all the things that get done are done by teams, not individuals.'

'Except, of course, Aunt Marta,' I said. 'But, in general, I agree – only, show me where to team up. I've an idea that you know.'

'I'm afraid they'd not be very pleased to have you now, Johnny – not after your turning this spotlight on yourself. You'll have to lay up for a while, and live that down.'

'But there's no time for that – no time at all. It may be too late now. It depends on what she announces tomorrow. Ulrich thought February at the earliest. Do you think – ?'

'What I'm asking you is to leave it alone, Johnny. For a bit, anyway. You've had the luck that Mista thought it funny to-day. Now, please –'

'All right, then,' I allowed. 'For the present I'll do my best to re-establish confidence. Does that suit you?'

'You'll keep to that?'

'Yes.'

'Good. Now then, let's talk about us, instead.'

So we did that.

14

Expectation

Now sits Expectation in the air – W.S.

The day began, just like any other, with instructions from the speakers – but that was about the only similarity. The sense of suppressed excitement seemed to penetrate in some ineffable fashion even to my room where I lay alone. Once I stepped into the passage outside, there was no disregarding it. The men on the way to the dining-hall were walking more briskly, and holding themselves more alertly. When one entered the place the wave of chatter smote surprisingly by comparison with the desultory talk that was normally even more characteristic of breakfast than of other meals. The women were no less animated than the men, and now that a number was gathered together one could feel the tension gradually rising.

Just as I had collected my coffee and rolls, the speakers clicked, and announced: 'Allo! Allo!'

Silence fell on the room as though a switch had been turned. Everyone froze, listening. In German, the voice went on:

'There will be a General Assembly this morning. All personnel not designated for special duties will attend at the Great Hall at eleven hundred hours.' It repeated that, and then clicked off. There was a moment of silence. Then the chatter broke out again, twice as loud as before.

I was back in my room again, waiting, when the summons came.

'General Assembly in thirty minutes! General Assembly in thirty minutes!'

I went out, and joined a stream of black-suited figures all moving in the same direction. There was some little distance to go from our block. On the way we descended two or three levels lower. Along the route, doors opened, and more men and women came out to join us.

The speakers had just got around to announcing 'General Assembly in fifteen minutes' when we came in sight of a large pair of double doors, open, and folded back.

There was already a crowd ahead, so that we checked, and then began to filter forward more slowly past a point where sharp-eyed guards pounced every now and then to remove a knife from the belt of one of the absent-minded.

A few minutes later, we were entering an auditorium, capable of seating, by my rough guess, some three thousand people. It was something like half full already: men on the right, women on the left. I followed the man ahead of me, and sat down next to him.

In style the hall was plain and Germanically massive; its floor was somewhat raked to give a good view from every seat. The platform in front of us was backed by long, grey curtains, and there were doors set in the forward-sloping walls to either side of them. The roof arched over us in a single span pierced with ventilation grilles. The sole attempt at decoration was mounted on the wall above the curtains – an eagle, wings outspread, perched upon a wreath; but a wreath, I noticed, that contained no swastika.

While we waited, I turned to look over my shoulder at more of us still filing in. In the last few days I had almost succeeded in overcoming the feeling of nightmare, but now, watching row after row fill up with replicas of Freda and myself, I began to have a touch of lightheadedness again. I wanted to shout at them so that they would vanish, and I should wake up.

A few minutes later, with the place almost filled, the doors were closed. We waited for something to happen: for quite a time, nothing did. I recalled that though punctuality may have been the politeness of kings, it had been the custom of the upstart dictators to enhance the moments of their appearance by delay. The audience was fidgety, though somewhat subdued, and the buzz of talk small, considering the number there. One could feel that the first excitement had given way to more serious tension.

The sight of the repetitious faces was becoming obsessive, and I turned to my front. That wasn't a lot better, really: all rows of fair heads matched for height. The rare breaks in the monotony were where old dye was being allowed to grow out.

We went on waiting patiently: evidently there was a technique for a formal occasion. Suddenly, as if at some signal that I failed to notice, the whole place fell quiet. There was a pause. Then, a single voice rose, loud with the professional violence of a drill-sergeant:

'*S-i-e-g HEIL!*'

A long drawn first syllable: a bark on the second. Twice more it was repeated, as a kind of introduction. Then a drum began to beat, giving the time. The audience took up the call, staccato now:

'*Sieg-Heil!-Sieg-Heil!-Sieg-Heil!...*'

It was, in its peculiar way, a most frightening sound. Neither a chant nor a paean, but something with the insistency of the drip-drip-drip which wears stone.

A battle-cry is the yell of hot blood, defiance, and fury. But this was something quite different. It was not a sound to send the spirit vaunting: it was the hydraulic pump, working up pressure. It was the left-right-left of marching boots; the thud-thud of the power-hammer; the champ-champ of Moloch's jaws. No flame, no fire, no spark... Just the implacable, pounding steadily to crush and obliterate...

A trick, of course. The deliberately inexorable quality of it: the sense of the machine pulsing with irresistible power... Effective, too – but where are we going when men and women increase their self-confidence by imitating machines?

The thing settled in to run like an engine at its most efficient speed – thump-thump, thump-thump!

Presently, lights flooded the platform. The beat of the vocal engine became sharper, and more decisive.

Then, from the door on the right of the platform, The Mother made her entrance.

She was bare-headed, and dressed entirely in black. A silver Maltese cross, hanging on a silver chain, glittered against her chest. She stopped, and stood gazing at the audience with perfect confidence and composure. When she stepped forward again, she moved with almost the carriage of a young woman. An escort of three women and two men followed her closely. She reached the centre of the platform, and raised her right hand in salute. For four or five repetitions the 'Sieg-Heil!' increased in volume. Then it stopped so absolutely dead that the silence came like a slap.

The Mother – it was impossible in that setting to think of her any longer as our Aunt Marta – lowered her arm, and remained standing quite still, with her escort ranged behind her. In her own time, without haste, she began to speak. The audience sat bound in an utter silence of expectancy.

The style of her oratory had not been modelled on that of her late Führer. Possibly she regarded his hysterical passion as a part of his deplorable mysticism. Her own method was clear, simple, and, at carefully chosen moments, high-lit by an incisive phrase. Above all, it conveyed supreme self-confidence.

The first sentences were general; somewhat in the nature of a benediction upon us all. The audience sat patiently waiting for the great moment. The hand of the man beside me was tense upon the arm of his seat. Hundreds of similar faces wore expressions just like his own. I looked round on them. I must have been the only one who was not concentrated on the figure on the platform, with eager eyes and slightly parted lips. In looking, I lost the thread of The Mother's words. I was still watching, and waiting for the outburst of cheers that must surely come, when I suddenly knew that the atmosphere had changed. I hurriedly turned my attention back to the platform.

' – and this can be no greater disappointment to you than it is to me,' she was saying. 'Yet, it is unavoidable. When we strike, we must be absolutely sure. We must be able utterly to overwhelm our enemies. Twice before, Germany has failed in her intentions. Each time she has failed because, although she was strong, she was not strong enough. The strokes were swift and skilful – but they lacked the *extra* care, the *extra* preparation that could have made them completely decisive.

'The first stage we could win tomorrow. Of that I have no doubt whatever. But that is not enough. Triumphantly, magnificently, Germany has *always* won the first stage. *But* twice, after such triumphs, she has gone down in ruin and degradation. This time, we have to be *certain*. Whatever our feelings, we must hold our hands until we are coldly, scientifically *sure*. This means that I must tell you there has to be a postponement of our plans.'

A strange sound rose from the audience: the release of held breath was almost like a great, composite sigh. It had, moreover, an indeterminable quality. The faces were curiously blank and relaxed, as if the morale which had been so high had all gone up in that sigh.

It was a bad, a thoroughly bad, bit of staff-work. A dangerous misuse of secrecy. For more than twelve hours the place had been allowed to buzz with rumour and rising excitement. A gross mismanaging: the let-down was too sudden, too big, and altogether too unexpected. With many other groups I had known it would have been dangerous, but with these, it was hard to tell. I still could not judge how strongly the regimentation held the rank and file, but somewhere there must be a breaking point, and I felt that they had been brought close to it.

The Mother's confidence, however, was not in the least abated. I could see no change at all in her expression or her manner. She had made her decision, and announced it. That was that. Now, after a short pause, she gave some of her reasons: the loss of several saucers; the loss of radar invisibility, most particularly; other technical advances elsewhere.

'If we were to move before we regain our lead, we should be wiped out
– and, with that, our trust and our hopes for a re-born Germany would be
gone, too – this time, for ever.

'Therefore, we must wait upon our technicians. When they can give us
counter-measures, they will find us ready.'

To me, it sounded a reasonable enough statement of the position, but
I half-expected the frustration I could feel about me to break out into
demonstrations. And yet, when I looked round, I could see that most
were taking it with a dull, unvocal fatalism. Then I thought I perceived
also part of the reason for it: dotted here and there among the audience
were heads turning this way and that, as if they might be alert for any
source of trouble. Possibly members of Emil's corps of thugs, I guessed.

The Mother allowed another longish pause for her words to sink well
in. She still appeared perfectly unmoved and untroubled. It was difficult
to decide whether she was indifferent or insensitive to the atmosphere
she had created. A little of both, I thought. There was something barely
human about her detachment from all the feeling in the place.

The moment for an outburst passed. The surge of disappointment ebbed.
When she began to speak again, she was no less assured, but she had adopted
a slightly different style. The public meeting, the official pronouncement
was, one felt, over: now the Matriarch spoke to the clan.

Her theme this time was the Nordic stock, and its destiny. Expressions
of resignation or frank boredom settled in. A glazed look came over many
eyes while the minds behind them thought of other things. It remained
there while she disserted on the heritage of blood, and while she spoke,
addressing herself to her multitudinous daughters, of the sacred duty of
non-contamination – for the sake of the race of supermen and super-
women that was to come – by any type outside the elite of the proven
Nordic.

It might be old stuff to her listeners, but for her it had lost no vitality
– or reality. She would, I am sure, have been utterly uncomprehending
had anyone suggested a strain of mysticism in her thesis. Meanwhile, her
listeners went on fidgeting, the men slightly more than the women.

The Mother propounded the problem that had confronted her in
launching this super-race – and then announced that she had found the
solution.

There was a stir. The whole audience sat up as if pins had been stuck
in it. Its members looked slightly shocked, as if by a breakdown in a well-
known pattern. All attention was once more concentrated acutely on the
platform.

The Mother turned. With a movement of her hand, she called forward one of the girls who had been standing behind her. Until then, I had paid them little attention, they were the same face repeated. But now, with a slight shock, I noticed that the girl who stepped forward was wearing no number, and realized that it must be Freda.

The Mother took her hand and drew her beside her. The audience was sharply interested; clearly, something right outside their experience was taking place. Deliberately, The Mother introduced Freda to them. For once, there was a trace of emotion in her voice. One could feel that she presented one whom, in part at least, she regarded as her successor. Every eye in the place was fixed on Freda's face while The Mother went on to explain how Freda was of the true strain, and would mate with her cousin, who was no less impeccably Nordic.

(Here I dismissed the thought that I, too, might be summoned to the platform for inspection by the assembly. After all, it's the bride that gets the columns any place. And here the gynocratic control was evidently strong enough for the male concerned to be taken entirely for granted. I wasn't sorry.)

We were then treated to an interesting account of my hypothetical children's future. She had the whole thing pretty tidily arranged for us. Whatever Freda's and my views might be was, apparently, of no interest to anyone. We would acquiesce as a matter of course, and then, with the ardent midwifery of science, would have an extremely numerous progeny. These would be able to mate with The Mother's progeny, to whom they would stand as first cousins, once removed. That was all fixed and fine. Some people, The Mother conceded, might think it a trifle inbred. But they were wrong. In other races it could very likely prove so, but among true Nordics, such as ourselves, the dominant characteristics were the finest, et cetera, et cetera.

If it is possible to be progressively stunned, the audience was. Maybe The Mother attributed their glassy fascination as a tribute to her organizational genius.

The progress of science, she went on smoothly, had obviated the necessity for such a scheme as far as mere increase of population was concerned, but she had several times been informed by the psychiatrists and medical advisers that the institution of marriage exerted a socially stabilizing effect upon some types, and was, therefore, to be recommended. And though she herself had never felt it necessary to dilute her devotion to the cause by merely personal affections, she could scarcely doubt the value of advice from trained observers. Therefore it made her happy to announce this solution of what had evidently been, to some, a problem.

She paused.

While a clap or a cheer might have seemed a shade off-key with the circumstances, one did, nevertheless, feel that some audible token of approval had been expected at this point. But the audience remained indecisive. It flashed across me that perhaps it knew no other form of mass-expression than 'Sieg-Heil', and vaguely felt that to be inappropriate. At any rate, for some seconds the silence hung unstirred. Then, abruptly, it was shattered.

There came a very odd sound indeed. It began on a non-human note, like the scream of a radio-tube. From there it took on a curdling quality which shocked everyone motionless. In the silence it went on rising higher until it broke suddenly into a sob, and then became shrill, hysterical laughter. It ended quite abruptly; as it might with a hand over the mouth.

But it had been something wild, broken loose. Unnerving in its abandoned shredding of restraints. In several different parts of the left section a number of other women began to laugh and cry. A group of men in the middle of our side had the presence of mind to get the 'Sieg-Heil' going again. Those around them took it up, and champed away with it as if by sheer persistence it would wear down the merely human sound of a dozen and more women releasing hysterics.

Rarely indeed, I imagine, had The Mother been caught off balance, but this was one such time. Not that she descended to anything so unleaderly as confusion, or even discomposure, but there was a flat, glazed look about her eyes, and there could be no doubt that for once she was disconcerted. She had made her announcement with the air of one conveying a boon. Without doubt that was what she had seen herself as doing – and the reception of it baffled her completely. I honestly believe that it simply had not occurred to that incredible woman that her older listeners would be not a lot short of fifty before the first batch of husbands she was generously offering them could come to maturity. And now she stood there, patiently wondering beneath the calm schooled by habit, what on earth could have come over her audience.

Meanwhile, the sieg-heiling, while a good enough idea in one way, was proving to have the disadvantage of giving cover under which more of the women could let their feelings go. The original anti-climax, when the expected announcement of the Day had not been forthcoming, probably had a lot to do with it. But for that, the heiling might have prevailed enough to steady many of them; as things were, it seemed to lose power after the first minute or so, and become a mere percussive background to the scattered outbursts of emotion.

The Mother's eyes looked, perhaps, a little blanker, as though her bewilderment might be growing. But there was no alarm in her expression –

and that meant no perception of the shrill note of desperation that was beginning to dominate the uproar.

Possibly she had never learned to be alarmed at the sound of a crowd getting out of hand, and so was slow to understand. But down in the body of the hall one could feel the coming of that unpredictability which is greater than the sum of the individuals. There is a sense of reason's finger-nails scrabbling to keep their hold, as one slides towards something which is not accountable; not, by ordinary standards, quite sane...

But there were attempts to restore order. Some of the crying women were getting what looked to me like unnecessarily brutal handling as they were passed along the rows to the gangways: nor did the groups of Emil's young men who hurried across to receive them there treat them kindly. Indeed, the very crudeness of the treatment defeated its object. It helped to break through the thin restraints that had been holding yet more women from hysteria.

A dozen or so of the unfortunates arrived in the gangway, and were dragged towards the back of the hall, some still screaming or crying, one or two unconscious. It was not pleasant to watch. A number of the young men were only too clearly seizing their chance to work off some of their wider resentments.

There was an infection in the slipping of self-control; a feeling that the discipline of the women's side of the hall was cracking up as the luxury of freed feelings tempted them all. The unsteadying effect was mildly apparent on our side too but, as yet, the men's sense of order was only slightly impaired.

It was when those engaged in dragging the women away reached the exits at the back of the hall that a new source of commotion occurred. The first comers tried to push open the doors, and failed. They dropped the girl they were holding and tried again, more vigorously. The next pair also discarded their burden, and joined them. Presently, all four of them were barging their shoulders at the jammed doors, in unison.

After the third combined onslaught, it came home to them with visible astonishment that the doors were not simply stuck, but fastened against them. They stood back, conferred, and then, still disbelieving, tried once more.

Most of the audience other than those in the rear rows remained unaware of the trouble at the back. Several sturdy contingents of reliables went on trying to pound order in by sieg-heiling, but the uproar continued to grow, as much, seemingly, from the anti-hysterical as from the hysterical themselves. The Mother remained standing like a statue, as if waiting for her presence to recover its domination and quell them all. But there was no sign whatever that it would succeed.

After another puzzled exchange two of the men left the main doors, and hurried to another, single, small door in one corner of the back wall. It, too, refused to budge for them. They looked at one another, identical expressions of ludicrous bewilderment reflected on their faces. By common consent they hurried right across to a similar door on the other side. They did no better there.

By this time, more of the audience had become aware of what was going on. A queue of frustrated bouncers and potential bouncees extended halfway down the central gangway. People all over the hall began to stand up to see what was going on. A buzz of speculation grew. Fresh peals of overwrought laughter broke out on the women's side. Then, quite unexpectedly, one of the few things that could have quenched the developing mood in a moment, happened.

I had just time to disbelieve the fact that I had felt the floor lift under my feet, when there was a deep boom. The building shook all around us. On the instant, every voice in the place ceased, and there was silence...

I looked quickly at The Mother. For once, there was a truly human expression on her face; a look of bleak alarm. She covered it quickly, but anxiety stayed in her eyes. I saw that Freda was looking at her watchfully.

The first astonished silence was beginning to break into mutterings when two more explosions occurred in rapid succession. Either they were less violent, or they were further away than the first. The tremble in the building was only slight...

The audience looked speechlessly at one another, eyes slightly widened, as if expecting more. And more came: a hard, sharp slap this time, without the rumble of the others.

The Mother's face now was simply a mask. Her eyes, hard and bright, were seeing nothing. She stood as if frozen, listening and waiting...

A group of men in the section where the heiling had been most steadfast was the first to recover its wits. They piled out into the gangway, and began running towards the rear exits still, apparently, unaware of the state of things at the back. They became entangled with the queue of strong-arms already silted up there, and tried impatiently to plough through them. Several more sharp explosions sounded somewhere outside.

The Mother moved for the first time since she had stopped speaking. And it was not a purposeful move. One could see her trying to make the decision – whether to stay where she was as the symbol of imperturbable authority; or to appease her curiosity by discovering what was happening outside. Another sharp explosion made up her mind for her – wrongly. The gesture with which she ordered her escort to accompany her was all right. Her mien as she moved was unhurried and dignified. The unfortunate anti-climax occurred when it was discovered that the exit doors from the platform, also, were locked, and she was forced to return, now in no better plight than anyone else. The only course for her was to take up her pose again. We all waited.

By this time somebody should have taken charge. In any ordinary gathering there would have been stewards, and someone in authority over them. But this was by no means an ordinary gathering: it was a family affair, if somewhat irregular in scale. Not only had no one visualized a need for stewards – if one except the officiously self-constituted bouncers – but the leaders, Mista, Emil, Ulrich, and the rest were not in evidence. Possibly, as members of the inner circle, they had been informed first, and the general meeting was simply for the rank and file. It was left, therefore, to The Mother herself to take charge. With her voice still under good control, she gave the order:

'Break down the doors!'

Half-a-dozen men cleared a space, and lined up. They charged forward, crashing their shoulders against the panels like a single thrust. The doors shook, but did not give. The men stepped back to re-form. Outside, there was a muffled clattering. A line of holes suddenly appeared, low in the doors. Two of the lined-up men subsided. On account of the rake of the auditorium floor several bullets whistled harmlessly above the heads of the audience and smacked on the opposite wall, above the platform.

After an indecisive moment, two more men replaced those who had fallen with bullets in their legs. The doors shuddered again under a second charge, but held. There was another chattering burst outside. A second line of holes appeared. The wounded were dragged aside, and direct assault on the doors suspended.

Cautious approaches to the side doors were no more successful. Not only were they constructed to open inwards, but single, warning bullet-holes abruptly appeared in them, too.

The Mother's face was grey. A few minutes had added twenty years to her looks. Once she swayed, but she mastered herself as though fainting were a weakness beneath her. Somehow she drew fresh strength to take a hold on her nerves and remain standing. There was still, intermittently, the sound of small explosions outside.

What was in the minds of most of us, I have no idea. Many, without doubt – and possibly The Mother was among them – must have thought that the H.Q. had been discovered, and was under foreign attack. For all I knew, it had, but the most important thought in my mind was that the closer I should be to Freda, the more we would be able to do together.

Accordingly, and little noticed now that most of the place was on its feet, I began to worm my way down the gangway towards the platform.

When I got there, it was hard to attract Freda's attention; she was watching The Mother carefully as she stood, tensely still.

Our Aunt Marta was stricken. Capacity for decisive action had deserted her. I do not think for a moment that it was the prospect of personal danger that paralysed her so much as the far more devastating fear that her plan had been imperilled – worse still, she could not tell how, nor how much, it was jeopardized. She did not know whether the danger came from within or from without. At first, it might have been that one accidental explosion had set off others – but now there had been bullets to settle any doubt.

I rapped on the edge of the platform, and managed to catch Freda's attention. She spoke to the woman who had the figures 462 on her blouse, beside her. The woman nodded, and Freda beckoned me up.

Seen from there, the audience was a mass of bewildered faces. Some were making their way towards the already crowded central aisle, but the majority stood indecisively waiting for a lead. It would have been easy for anyone to take over. I asked Freda:

'Shall we quiet them?'

She shook her head.

'No,' she said. 'Better let it work out.'

She seemed to know more of what was afoot than I did, so I let it go at that.

The woman wearing the 462 was watching The Mother intently. I searched my memory, and recalled that her name was Hilda – it was she who had given me the tip on which I had tried my little piece of blackmail regarding saucers. I wondered if I was right in fancying an off-colour smell around…

On the other hand, I was close enough now to have discovered that the third woman was 932, which meant Miranda. She, too, was regarding The Mother closely, but with a far more personal concern than the other two. I could have imagined that, outside her character though it seemed, she would have liked to put a comforting arm around her – except that to take such a liberty with The Mother was just beyond the range of credibility.

So we stood, in a tableau, with everywhere a marked disinclination to take command over The Mother's head. In the end, it was Miranda who became decisive. She walked to the front of the platform, and raised both arms.

'Stop!' she shouted, in a voice of astonishing power.

That was all that was needed. Every head turned towards her, and the babble diminished into silence. From outside sounded a distant stutter of shots.

'Back to your seats. At once!' she commanded in a cold voice, for all the world as if they were a set of displeasing children.

It was as if a sudden shamed awareness had come over them at the voice of authority. Automatically they began to obey her.

Miranda watched them for a steady moment, and then turned back to speak to The Mother.

Aunt Marta seemed to shiver slightly. She had altered. It was not simply that she looked grey of face. She had changed from an ageless to an old woman. She still stood straight, but now she was held stiffly. The carriage which I had thought so young for her years had lost its pliancy. The confidence which had radiated from her like an almost visible vitality had gone. And, as Miranda spoke to her, her face relaxed: the token of command fell from it. The austerity of a Brunnhilde gave place to an expression softened, and humanized, much as I had seen it for a moment at the end of my interview. With a gesture quite unlike her, she rested her hand on Miranda's arm. Then she stepped slowly, as though only half-conscious, towards the front of the platform.

In the silence that had fallen over the hall, those who had not found seats again stood motionless, watching. Even the clatter of firing outside had died away now.

The Mother stopped, and stood quite still. Then she turned her head slowly, surveying her whole audience from side to side. The line of her mouth was softened, but not quite smiling. Her eyes were shining, but no longer hard. She moved her hands, to clasp them in front of her. We were close enough to see that she was trembling. Again she swept her eyes across the whole width of the hall. She drew a breath. Her mouth opened. But no words came.

She put one hand up to her eyes, and turned. Tears were running down her face. Miranda stepped forward again, but with the other hand The Mother waved her back. Presently, she lifted her head. In a strange, quiet voice she began to speak:

'My children,' she said. 'Oh, my beloved children – '

The sound of a door closing behind us cut her short. We turned. With his back to the door through which The Mother herself had entered earlier, stood a man, looking at us. In the crook of his right arm he carried a sub-machine-gun.

15

Treachery

Hollowness, treachery, and all ruinous disorders – W.B.

A face, right outside the pattern that had been endlessly and exclusively repeated before me for many days, took me aback. It seemed unnatural.

Moreover, it was a striking face, with an ascetic, somewhat severe, quality. The hair, above a broad brow, was plentiful, though greyed. Equally grey eyebrows jutted out in bushy ridges over dark, intelligent, sunken eyes. The cheekbones were high, the nose prominent. Grave lines curved down to the corners of a well-shaped mouth with lips that were neither too thin, nor too thick. It was the mouth, and the radiations of wrinkles at the outer corners of the eyes, that relieved an effect which might otherwise have been harsh, and so balanced intellect with feeling.

The man was not tall, and he was dressed in a suit of faded blue overalls, yet he had presence. It was the man, not the machine-gun, that held our attention as he stood looking at us for some seconds. His expression did not change as he gravely inclined his head to The Mother in a courtesy which consorted oddly with the gun upon his arm. Then he looked out over the auditorium, and for a brief moment his brows contracted slightly as though the sight of all those rows of similar faces disturbed him.

When he stepped forward to the middle of the platform he moved confidently, and without haste. Not a sound broke the silence of the hall as he stopped there, and stood looking back into the hundreds of expectant, puzzled eyes.

I took a swift glance at The Mother. She was staring at him, horrified, and she swayed as she stood. Miranda's awe of her had softened. This time, she did put an arm round her to steady her. We all waited.

At last the man spoke, in German. He used no oratory and no violence, but his voice carried clearly.

'Sons and Daughters of The Mother,' he said. 'The time has come for me to speak seriously to you. Few of you know me, though I have been here longer than any of you. I have, indeed, been here longer than The Mother herself. One more reason why you should listen to me is because it is I, Eidermann, who am, in the greatest degree, responsible for your very existence.' He raised his voice slightly to quell a murmur that began to rise. 'Do not misunderstand me. I do not mean that I am your father: that is a privilege which belongs elsewhere. But I do tell you that without my work you would not, any of you, exist at all.

'I did not wantonly make your existence possible: I was working with a purpose. Thus far I am responsible for you. But for what has happened to you since you achieved independent existence I am *not* responsible – nor would I have had it that way.

'Had you been educated, rather than merely taught and trained, it is possible that some of you might have read some of the works of the English writer, Swift. Since it is thoroughly improbable that you have, I will quote you a passage of his which has remained in my memory for many years, and may help to show that my work was no idle, ingenious meddling. It is this:

' *"And he gave it for his opinion, that whoever could make two ears of corn or two blades of grass to grow upon a spot of ground where only one grew before, would deserve better of mankind, and do more essential service to his country than the whole race of politicians put together."*

'*Two* ears of corn, *two* blades of grass. Too modestly put, perhaps – every couple that has produced four children has done as much as that. But the principle remains.

'Now, my colleagues and I have achieved a great deal more than mere doubling – and our purpose in it was to do just such an essential service to our country: but "our country", as we see it, is the *whole world*.

'It was our belief that we had done such a service. *Was*, I repeat... For we now see that it is by no means unlikely that all our work will be ruined and wasted by the "race of politicians."

'I am a scientist: I believe that, ultimately, reason is more powerful than physical force. Now, you are the most powerful family that has ever existed – *but* someday someone is going to contrive a family that is just as numerous, but composed entirely of geniuses: and for that reason, that family will be a thousand times more powerful than yours. Nevertheless, there are stages when the application of mere physical force is essential, whether it be fire to soften, a cyclotron to divide, or – weapons to conquer...

'I was a young man when I came here. I had witnessed the failure of a great attempt to unite the world by conquest. For a time I was a little weakened in the belief that unity could be achieved by force. But since then, watching history unfold, I have become convinced that so great is the stupidity, the self-seeking, the credulity, and the immorality of peoples, that union, which must be achieved if we are to survive at all, cannot now be attained by any means that does not entail the application of crude force.

'Furthermore, it must be attained *soon* – before the means available to resist it have the power utterly to wreck the world.

'*Soon*, I tell you. *Soon*! *Soon*! – If, indeed, it is not already too late.

'Many of the best brains in Germany came to this place. We worked hard. We developed new weapons. We produced *you* to operate them.

'You can call yourselves the New Germany, or the New Atlantis, for all we care. We don't mind what silly playacting and racial mysticism runs in your minds, so long as it does not clog them. Our purpose is quite clear. It is Domination for the sake of Unity, for the purpose of Salvation.

'This has been obscured and muddied for you by considerations of race, nationality, and other nonsense. But I tell you now that delay – any delay at all – is *dangerous*. Any further advance in the potential powers of destruction, and not only your Nordic super-race fandangle will come to an end, but, very likely, the whole planet with it...'

I looked round while he paused, to see how they were taking it. It seemed to me that they weren't taking it at all. They were looking at him, all right, but as if fascinated by a strange apparition. I doubted whether his words had meant anything to them. It jolted me to realize that there must be many of them who had never seen anyone not of their own kind. Perhaps he himself became aware that his reasoning was going to make little headway against their conditioning, for he went on:

'Three times now we have been on the point of action – and, each time, for one reason or another, there have been postponements. This time, there must be *no* postponement. Delay is not only dangerous in general, it is dangerous in particular, to *us*. Our lead in weapons has narrowed, and seems likely to narrow more. You have been told that new radar-absorbent devices must be found. They *may* be found, but by the time they have been, something else will have become obsolete. Already we have had far too many obsolescences due to these postponements. Time is on the others' side, not on ours. If we go on any longer like this we shall find ourselves faced before long with the supreme calamity – the discovery of this H.Q. Then one or two hydrogen bombs – and that will be the finish...'

He looked from side to side across the rows of faces.

'*That* is not going to happen. We must strike – *now*, within a few days. If we do not, it is probable that we never shall.'

Again, he paused, his eyes darting here and there, trying to sum them up.

Then he said:

'That is my reason for announcing to you that we have taken command of this Headquarters. Control has now passed from The Mother's hands into ours.

'The Mother – ' He turned, and inclined his head towards her ' – will be treated with all respect and honour. But she will no longer exercise political authority. She will not be C-in-C operational forces. She will *not* be a member of the planning staff. We have been reluctant to take this step, but practical considerations have forced us to it. We have to work upon facts; we cannot risk depending upon intuitions and mystical doctrines.

'I therefore declare The Mother deposed, and all authority vested henceforth in the Council of Scientists.'

His statement died away into a dead silence. The idea he proposed was so utterly outside the mental range of The Mother's children, that I doubted whether five per cent of them ever began to grasp the position. The Mother, for them, was Authority incarnate – always had been, always would be. Their response could only be blank, uncomprehending.

The Mother herself was looking pitifully white and drawn. She braced herself, and moved forward, away from Miranda's protecting arm.

'My children,' she cried. 'Oh, my children. This is treason. This man is a traitor to us all. I implore you not to listen to what he says. He endangers everything you were born for. Before we strike we must be entirely, absolutely *sure*. He is making the old mistakes over again. Everything he says is treachery – treachery!' She buried her face in her hands.

Eidermann nodded Miranda forward to her. He turned back to an audience which seemed, if possible, more bemused than ever.

'This is not a matter for debate,' he said. 'It is an accomplished fact. I have explained to you why – .'

The crack of a single shot cut his sentence short. I did not see where it had come from, but he, without hesitation, lifted his gun, and stuttered a string of bullets into one of the roof ventilators. He watched it, his finger still on the trigger.

A queer sound came from the audience, making me look down. Their bemusement had broken at last; every face was turned towards The Mother. I turned, too. She was clinging to Miranda, who was supporting her. And, as I looked, one of her arms slipped down, to swing loosely.

Somewhere outside the hall the firing began again, in muffled bursts. Inside, all was petrified. Then there came a little moaning noise, like a voice calling far, far off. It grew, a mingling of pity and anguish.

Some of the women jumped from their seats, and began to run towards us. One of the men beside me stepped forward, hands extended, to ward them off. They came to the edge of the platform and stopped, a row of anxious faces, distressed, in pain.

Miranda lowered The Mother gently to the floor. Eidermann crossed over, and knelt beside her to examine her.

I looked again at the rows of familiar faces, some with tears running down their cheeks, craned forward in concern. The look upon them suddenly stabbed me. For the first time I understood that for all these my Aunt Marta, the tyrant, the dictator, was, above all else, The Mother...

I could not understand what it was she could mean to all these children of hers, but I could see now that it was something intensely personal to each of them. There was the anguish on the faces, and the sound of sobbing on the women's side. I was an alien. I did not understand. That austere woman... these unnatural children... I shall never understand...

Eidermann stood up.

'It is not fatal. It may not even be very serious,' he told us.

A sigh went up from the whole hall. He turned to Miranda:

'Get her to bed as soon as you can,' he directed.

Hilda and one of the men stepped forward to help. Then they paused. A louder burst of firing reminded us that the situation was not yet clear.

Eidermann hesitated, then, with his gun tucked beneath his arm, moved towards the door by which he had entered.

It opened while he was still several yards from it. A black-uniformed young man appeared, pistol in hand. With a sound like a single shot, he and Eidermann fired together. The young man sagged against the doorpost, and began to slide down. Before he reached the ground came the sound of another shot. Eidermann staggered, and then crumpled, falling where he stood. We turned, and saw another black-uniformed figure standing in the corresponding doorway on the other side of the platform, a trace of smoke coming from the pistol in his hand.

He watched Eidermann's body for a second or two. It did not move. Then he saw The Mother where she lay.

The shock showed in his narrowing eyes.

'What's happened here?' he demanded.

It was Miranda who explained to him that The Mother must be taken to her room, and attended. He nodded.

'Wait!' he said.

He went to the other door, and pulled the body of his fallen brother aside. He stepped out, with his pistol held ready. We could still hear a scatter of shots, but they were further away now. The man came back, and beckoned with his left arm.

Miranda, Hilda, and the two men raised The Mother gently between them. I looked at Freda. She gave the faintest nod. I picked up the dead young man's pistol as we followed.

*　*　*

A smell of burnt powder was still hanging about the passage There were several scars and furrows in the plastered walls. Three figures lay on the floor: two in soiled brown denim, one in the familiar black. .

The young man with the pistol scouted each corner ahead of us. Sporadic firing was still going on somewhere, but it was difficult in the echoing corridors to tell how far away.

There was no great distance to be covered before we reached the outer doors of The Mother's suite. We passed through the entrance gallery – with its scenes of romanticized slaughter seeming particularly nonsensical at the moment – and into the high ante-chamber where I had waited before. There, the party broke up. The man with the pistol said something to one of the men who had been on the platform, and they went off together by the way we had come. The other man and the two women carried The Mother through a door on the right. Freda and I stayed where we were. Presently the man who had helped with the carrying re-emerged, and hurried off, taking no notice of us. We looked at one another.

'Just what's supposed to have been going on?' I inquired. 'I think you know something about it.'

But she shook her head.

'Not now. Something's gone terribly wrong. I don't know what's happened.'

'Who started it all?'

'Why, Hilda, of course.'

'Hilda!' I stared at her. 'But she –.'

'Didn't you see her face while Eidermann was speaking? She was – .'

She broke off suddenly as the door through which they had taken The Mother opened, and Hilda herself came out. She walked slowly towards us. She stared at Freda for some seconds, but as though she were looking through her.

'They cheated us!' she said, bitterly. 'They double-crossed us! I'm *glad* Eidermann was killed. I hope a lot of them get killed.' She looked round.

'Where's Mista?' she said.

'She should be here.'

'I expect they went to fetch her,' Freda suggested.

'The Mother's asking for her,' Hilda explained.

'How is she?' I asked.

'The wound's below her right shoulder. I don't think it's dangerous. Shock is the trouble – a lot of shocks.' She clenched her hands together. 'Tell Mista and the Doctor to come in at once,' she told us, as she went back to the room.

'That just makes it more difficult,' I said to Freda. 'Who's double-crossing whom?'

'She means her lot has been double-crossed by the scientists and technicians,' Freda explained. 'Hers is a sort of peace-at-any-price faction – they simply want to get out of here, and live their own lives. As Hilda sees it, the only way they have a chance to do that is to stop operations starting – somehow. Once they do start, you see, it's either win or lose for The Mother. If it's lose, they'll all be wiped out: if it's win, they'll still be under The Mother's control. *But* as long as the crisis can be staved off, there's always a slim chance that they may be able to get out, in some way.

'So, when she thought, like the rest of us, that The Mother was going to announce the Day, she made contact with the technicians. They had been telling her that they weren't ready for the Day – and now it looks as if they were just fooling her, and using her. She agreed to have some of her girls open the doors and let them into this section while nearly everyone was gathered in the hall. Hilda thought Eidermann was going to appear on the platform and announce a postponement on technical grounds, over The Mother's head. When it all happened the other way round, Hilda must have had a bigger shock than anyone. But what all the noise was, I don't know: perhaps they had to blast their way in, and then fight.'

I thought that over.

'Where did you stand in all this? You seem to know quite a lot about it.'

'I was on Hilda's side, of course – anything which would delay the Day looked good to me.'

With that, at any rate, I could agree.

'Then who's been doing all the shooting on this side?' I inquired.

'How should I know? Ulrich may have kept some of his men out of the meeting – or it might have been Emil. Of course, Ulrich may have thought it a chance to take over military command and force a cancelling of the postponement – or Emil may have thought he was going to try that, and decided to stop him. Or they may have been working together for once, to get control over The Mother – and Mista.'

My head was beginning to whirl.

'The way you talk, the whole place could be shot through with plots and counterplots from cellar to attic,' I remarked.

Freda nodded. 'The way I see it, it just about is. That's how dictatorships seem to go.'

'Well, now, which of all these would be likely to shoot The Mother?' I asked.

'None,' said Freda, promptly. 'It wouldn't suit any of them. They'd have to fight it out after that. What each of them wants is to control The Mother – and then, through her, control the rest.'

'Then how do you account for this shooting business? Would there be still another faction that *does* want her out of the way?'

'There couldn't be. It'd mean simply chaos here.'

'Well, that would suit a number of people in the world outside if they knew about the place. But if they *do* know about it, they're likely to take much more drastic action.'

'It might have been a mistake,' she suggested. 'It *might* have been meant for Eidermann.'

It might. In such a setup pretty nearly anything might have been meant for anyone – except, apparently, the one hit.

Mista came sweeping into the ante-room. It did not need her number to identify her. She had thunder on the brow, and lightning in the eyes. She was accompanied by another woman, and two men hurried along slightly behind her. The second man was not of the mother's brood. He looked about sixty or sixty-five, and was dressed in a baggy suit, with a white handkerchief worn as an armlet. They disappeared into The Mother's room without a glance at us. I guessed the man would be a doctor, from the technical side. The door closed behind them.

'You know,' I said to Freda. 'I can't help feeling that we ought to be making some good use of all this – if only we knew where the hell it's got to.'

I went over, and looked into the entrance gallery. The outer doors were closed now, cutting off all sounds from beyond. Three men and three women, all with sub-machine-guns, were loitering there.

'What goes on?' I inquired, in German.

One of the men shook his head.

'I couldn't tell you. Last thing I heard we'd pressed them back quite a bit towards the technical blocks. Maybe we can hold – .'

The ringing of a bell interrupted him. He went to a scanning device, and spoke. Then he said:

'451 outside, wanting to see Mista. Better open up.'

They opened the door narrowly. Emil and another man slipped in. It was promptly shut again. Emil looked over the guards, and frowned.

'You three come with me,' he directed. 'The women can hold the door, if necessary.'

The three hesitated. They looked at him, at the pistol in his hand, at one another.

'Our orders from Ulrich – .' one began.

'This is an emergency,' Emil snapped. All five of them went towards the ante-room together, leaving the three women looking somewhat bewildered. In a moment Emil's companion came hurrying back. He said:

'Ulrich's not to be allowed in – nor any of his men,' and disappeared again.

Nothing seemed to be going to happen where I was, so I strolled back to the ante-room again. The men had gone. Only Freda was there, sitting in an ornate, uncomfortable-looking chair, and regarding three machine-guns which now graced the centre table.

'This gets worse. Curiouser and curiouser,' I observed. 'Whose are those things?'

'Emil and another man took them off the guards – and then locked the guards in there,' she said, pointing to one of the several doors.

I regarded the weapons. Nice handy thing to have one, but right now I did not quite see what I would do with it.

'I reckon I'm a move or two behind,' I said.

'It's Ulrich. I think he must be parleying with the scientists. It might suit him; he's all for action as soon as possible.'

'Splitting The Mother's brood wide open?'

'Well, splintering off his combatant section.'

'That seems to put us on The Mother's side – for the moment,' I suggested.

'Um,' said Freda. 'I think we'd better keep to our own side. Nobody seems to be interested in us, and it'll be less confusing.'

One of the women came from the entrance gallery, and hurried across to knock at the door of The Mother's room. Emil came out.

'What is it?' he demanded, irritably.

'A party of Ulrich's men outside. About twenty of them,' she told him.

'Keep them talking,' he directed.

He made for a telephone in the corner, and we heard him giving orders to someone for the party outside to be taken from both flanks: no shooting unless absolutely necessary.

'We seem to have a nice ringside seat here,' I remarked to Freda. 'Do you suppose – ?'

I was interrupted by the approach of Emil. He looked at us, without saying anything. Then he thoughtfully collected the guns that were lying on the table, and took them with him.

'If – ,' I began again. But as I opened my mouth, Mista emerged from The Mother's room, hurrying towards the entrance. We watched her shoot past, and then looked inquiringly at one another. It couldn't do any harm to know as much as possible of what went on, so I left Freda there, and followed Mista back into the entrance gallery.

One large rendering of the Nordic Gods' pastimes had been taken down, revealing an instrument panel. Mista had already seated herself on a stool in front of it, and was peering at a series of small, illuminated screens. They gave, in sections, a vertical view of the passage outside the doors, and all were criss-crossed with red lines which meant nothing to me. Along a sloped panel beneath the screens was a row of numbered press buttons, looking like organ-stops. Only the central panel of the screens showed movement. In that, one was looking down on a semi-circle of heads: men clustered round the door, pointing weapons at it. They appeared singularly futile when one remembered the thickness of the doors. Mista, said, presumably into a microphone:

'Get back from there! If Ulrich wishes to see The Mother, he may come in – alone. Send and tell him that. The rest of you get back now, or we shall shoot.'

The group hesitated. Then it divided, standing back against the walls on either side of the doors to be out of a possible line of fire from there. A voice said:

'We have Ulrich's orders to find out whether The Mother is alive, and, if so, to protect her.'

'You can tell Ulrich that she *is* alive, and that Mista is protecting her. And hurry up – we don't want to hurt you.'

There was a pause. They must have been uncertain to what degree they were observed, and from what direction. Then one man edged past the others, along the wall towards the door. He carried a small black box in his hand.

'Stop that!' Mista said.

He hesitated. The others began to run back along the passage, in both directions. The man took another step towards the doors. He was close to one of the red lines drawn on the screen. Mista's hand reached towards the knobs.

'Stop!' she repeated. 'Get out, and take that thing with you.'

The man's only response was to crouch lower. Another step brought his image across the red line on the screen.

'Very well,' said Mista, harshly.

She pressed a knob. There was a brief, distant hammering. The man twisted. As he fell forward the box slithered in front of him, and came to rest just outside the doors.

Mista jumped from her stool. 'Back! Back, all of you!' she cried.

We pelted without hesitation for the inner doors. Beyond them, we turned, and pulled the heavy weight of them shut behind us. There were only three or four seconds to wait. The floor heaved beneath us. The walls shook. The sound of the explosion came, thunderous, but muffled. Large pieces of the ante-room ceiling smacked down to the floor sending up clouds of powdery dust.

We looked around. No one was hurt. Mista and the rest of us had been against the wall, out of the way of falling plaster. Freda and another woman had taken cover under the central table. Through the fog of dust I could see that they had their hands over their eyes, and were coughing. Then the wave of dust reached us, too, and we began coughing.

'Open the doors,' directed Mista, when she had her breath back.

All pushing together, we succeeded in forcing one of them open a little, and a fresh billow of dust rolled out of the gallery at us. We had to wait for it to settle before we could see the damage. When we did, the power of that small explosive box amazed me. The massive outer doors had been driven in, but the space they had left was entirely blocked by masses of fallen concrete.

'We'll not have to worry about that for a bit,' said the man who had come in with Emil.

Mista had already reached the telephone, and found it still working. Emil, emerging from The Mother's room, made towards her, but she waved him away impatiently. Freda had crawled from beneath the table, and was wiping the dust out of her eyes. We were all still coughing intermittently.

'Yes! 523 – Ulrich,' said Mista. 'Yes, at once. I don't care if he's talking to Wotan himself. This is Mista. Cut him off, and put me through to him.'

Several more women emerged from other parts of The Mother's suite. Most of them seemed to have been where more plaster had fallen. I recognized one complaining voice:

' – thirsty like a bag of cement. If I don't get a drink right soon, I'll just parch and desiccate and – .'

'Silence!' snapped Mista, with enough force to dismay even Miss Hander.

Mista's connection came through.

'Ulrich?' she asked.

Nobody could hear the reply, not even Mista.

'Will you stop that coughing, or get out,' she told us furiously, and coughed herself.

Some of them went, the rest of us did our best to suppress ourselves.

'Ulrich?' she said, again.

This time, the room was quite quiet enough for us to hear his irritable answer.

'Who's that? You're cutting in on a – .'

'I know. This is Mista. Listen. I've had to kill one of your men already – and very likely some more were killed when his bomb went off. I don't want to have to kill any more.'

'In that case, you'd better surrender,' came Ulrich's voice.

'Don't be a fool. This is suicidal.'

'I agree – if it is allowed to go on. All that is needed is that The Mother shall definitely announce the date of the Day. Any date within the limit of one month. If she does not do it now, we shall see that she does before very long.'

'You propose to use force on her – if you've the chance?'

'She *must* be persuaded. Everything was ready months ago. But she went on waiting – until this radar business cropped up. Next time there will be some other excuse. The scientists are right: all the time we are losing our lead. You *must* see that, Mista.'

'I can see that you are a traitor, Ulrich.'

'Words like that aren't going to help. I'm holding to the plan. It's The Mother who keeps on postponing it on one pretext or another – she's getting too old.'

Mista said, impatiently:

'You renounce her leadership, then?'

'No,' said Ulrich, after a pause. 'I say that she must take the advice of her experts. And we shall see that she does. She can't be allowed to wreck her own lifework – and us with it.'

'Listen, Ulrich. You know The Mother's section is self-supporting. You can destroy it, but you won't do that, because you would destroy her, too. You may have, perhaps, one-third of the Sons. But the rest are loyal to The Mother; so are all the Daughters.'

'We have the scientists.'

'Their only influence among the Children is over you.'

'Without them, this place couldn't go on. They have the whip hand, and you might as well accept that, Mista.'

'If they are going to operate the Plan, we're just as necessary to them. And we're not afraid to fight you, Ulrich.'

'Not now. But wait until the women's blocks begin to get hungry. It'll make a lot of difference.'

'It will pay you to see that they don't get hungry. If they do, my departments will begin systematically to destroy information that is vital for the Plan. If they are attacked, destruction will take place at once. Without that information, you can't move. It would take years of work to replot the satellite orbits alone… So you'd better see to it that they get what they ask for…

'And, by the way, in case your friends the scientists should think of putting something unpleasant in the ventilating system, you can tell them that I thought of that, too, some time ago – and made my preparations.'

She put down the instrument, and stood for a moment in thought.

'Fetch Miranda,' she instructed, and turned to Emil. 'You know the plan of this block,' she said to him. 'I'm putting the defence of it in your hands.'

Emil blinked. Clearly, he would have preferred the commission expressed differently, but he made no protest.

Miranda came up, and she and Mista went off together through the doors leading to the audience-room where I had first seen The Mother.

Emil pulled out of his reflections, and walked over to have a look at the fall which had blocked the main entrance.

'Very useful,' he said, as he came back. 'Nobody's going to move that lot without noise.' And he began to take a roll of those present.

After posts and duties had been allocated to the rest, he found himself left with the two of us. He regarded us thoughtfully, his eyes lingering longer on me.

'I don't trust you a lot, after yesterday's antics,' he observed.

I said that it was pretty obvious on which side my bread was buttered in this affair.

'I have never understood the phrase,' he said. 'Not only can bread be buttered with equal facility on either side, but it can be eaten upside down without the least inconvenience.'

'Suppose we cut the pocket philosophy this time,' I suggested to him, 'and just say that I'm naturally for anything that delays the big bust-up.'

'H'm,' he said, dubiously. 'I think we'd better see Mista about you. And you, too,' he added, to Freda.

He led the way to the door through which Mista and Miranda had passed a few minutes before. The audience-room was undamaged, and unchanged. The long, shining floor stretched bare before us. On the end wall the portrait of the original Führer looked back at us, commanding, and pop-eyed, but there was no figure seated at the desk below it this time. There was, in fact, no one in the place at all.

16

Grief

This is the poison of deep grief – W.S.

Emil was disconcerted. His gaze roved up and down the long room. There was, perhaps purposely, no possible place of concealment.

'Funny how the patterns repeat,' I said. 'No self-respecting tyrant ever overlooked the line of retreat. I've often wondered why he – ' I nodded at the portrait ' – didn't have a private way out of that bunker. Maybe he did, but with Russians at the other end just when he needed it most.'

Emil took no notice. He was frowning, thinking.

Freda observed:

'The way out should be somewhere at that end, to be handy.'

We waited for Emil. He had a problem. There was nothing to show whether Mista and Miranda had made a voluntary or involuntary disappearance. Private passages can be tricky things if the wrong person happens to know about them.

I beckoned Freda aside.

'If Mista has been snatched, would the women take orders from *him*?' I said, quietly.

'I imagine that's what he's wondering – and I'm pretty sure the answer is "no",' she whispered. 'Maybe if he co-operated with Hilda... *if* she would...'

'Just one big happy family,' I said.

The possibilities of the situation seemed to have put Emil into a trance. Presently, though still without any air of decision, he made his way up the length of the room. Standing in front of The Mother's desk, he reached towards the telephone. Then he changed his mind. He withdrew his hand, and stood looking over the walls, thoughtfully. We followed him up to that end. I started to rap here and there with my knuckles. Everything sounded very solid and unrewarding. Freda's curiosity took her to the desk itself. She examined the fittings, and looked thoughtfully at a row of push-buttons there.

'Don't you think one of these might open something?' she suggested.

She reached out a finger, and pressed one, experimentally.

There was a sudden shattering roar. Something whistled past my ear. In the instant the place seemed to be filled with explosions and the whizz and smack of bullets. Emil and I flung ourselves flat. The whole thing ceased abruptly, just as we hit the floor.

'Oh, dear!' said Freda, rather inadequately. Her finger moved towards another button, just as we started to get up.

'Stop! Get right away from there!' roared Emil.

Freda pulled back her hand. Emil produced a handkerchief, and patted his brow with it.

The fire of several machine-guns seemed to have been concentrated down the full length of the room on the entrance. Metallic splashes showed on the doors where a thin veneer of wood had been ripped from solid steel. Gobs of shiny metal lay on the floor in front of them. Emil went round the desk and shooed Freda further away from it.

'Wotan knows what the rest may set off,' he said, looking at the row of buttons nervously.

Then he sat down in The Mother's chair, and picked up the telephone. He dialled a number.

'I want to speak to Miranda,' he said. 'Yes – 932, Miranda.' There was a pause. 'Oh, I see. I was informed that she was with you.' – 'No. No destruction so long as the doors are holding them off. Mista's in charge, for The Mother. She'll let you know details.' – 'The Mother? Oh, yes. It isn't serious. She'll have to rest for some days.'

He pressed down the bar, and then dialled another number. Much the same conversation followed. He was on the fifth or sixth inquiry when a voice behind us said:

'You're wanting me?'

We jerked round to see both Mista and Miranda standing there.

Emil all but dropped the telephone.

'How did you do that?' he demanded, looking bewilderedly around.

'Never mind. What are you doing in here?' Mista countered.

One could see Emil repress a sharp reply. Neither her tone, nor her assumption of an exclusive right to the place suited him, but he chose, with an effort, to be tactful. He explained that Freda and I, as the original problems, had been supplanted by his anxiety over her disappearance. She heard him with faint amusement.

'A touching concern, Emil.'

'If you had been kidnapped, who would be in charge? Would the Daughters recognize my authority?'

'My dear Emil, what a question! Certainly not. Would I incite the arrangement of my kidnapping?'

'That's an outrageous suggestion,' protested Emil.

'I'm glad to hear you say so. Now what about these two?'

'Yes. What about them?' Emil echoed, sulkily.

All three of them regarded us reflectively. We might well, I could see, be an awkward problem. We were, so to speak, of the local blood royal, and, though it might be argued that all the Sons and Daughters were, too, Freda had already been presented as virtually The Mother's successor, socially, if not politically. And me? Well, I was at least the prospective dear Albert of the setup. Quite apart, too, from the fact that The Mother's aegis was over us, there was no pressing reason for getting rid of us – indeed, we might even turn out to be useful in some circumstances. Perplexity showed on Mista's brow.

'If he were trustworthy – ' Emil began.

'Look here,' I broke in, 'I've had that out with you already. Now that The Mother has postponed the Day, obviously I'm on her side. And as for trust – is there anyone in this asylum who trusts anyone else? But I *am* against anyone who wants to declare the Day. Does that help?'

Mista looked at Miranda, who nodded. She turned back to me. 'Very well,' she said. 'But any more of this childish mischief making...'

'Certainly not,' I agreed, readily. 'I know when I'm outclassed. Never did I – ' I broke off as one of the big doors opened. A man came in, and closed it behind him. He was the man with the baggy suit, and the white handkerchief tied round his sleeve. He stood for a moment, looking the audience-room over, and then shook his head slightly as if reproving a foolishness.

'Megalo. The same hoary technique. They all go that way,' he observed, seemingly to himself. He came ambling up the room towards us and stopped a few feet away from our group, surveying us.

'Would one of you be Mista?' he inquired, in English.

Mista enlightened him, in a cold, authoritative voice. He studied her, without haste.

'Good. Then, I'd like a word with you,' he said, quite unimpressed by her tone.

He pulled out a case, took a cigarette from it, and lit it.

'This is The Mother's room,' Mista told him, coldly.

'Whose else could it be?' he inquired, looking from side to side.

'The Mother does not permit smoking.'

He regarded her through the smoke.

'The Mother,' he remarked slowly, 'is in no state to prohibit or permit anything, at the moment.'

'I represent her, and I prefer you to respect her wishes.'

The man smiled slightly. He shook his head with the same reproving gesture as before.

'Drop it,' he suggested. 'It does not impress me, young woman. Stiffen the sinews, summon up the blood, lend the eye a terrible aspect... Uh-huh, we all do it when we're young – but some of us manage to grow out of it.' He drew on his cigarette, and regarded the glowing end. 'Nor,' he added 'do I place great value on your neo-Spartanism. So perhaps we could – er – abolish the usual scenery?'

Mista was looking at him in genuine puzzlement, as though she had encountered a new species. He sighed.

'Oh, you monstrous regiment of women – and men, too. How shall a mere human being reach you?' he asked, bleakly. 'Listen to me. I have come to talk to you about The Mother. I want you to try to understand what I say, not to have half your mind wondering about my motives, your opportunities, and everybody's factions. You can go back to all that afterwards. First, simply try to understand what I am telling you – it may be shocking for you, but it isn't very difficult. The Mother – ' he hesitated, looking from one of us to another, 'The Mother is – finished.'

We stared at him. Emil said:

'You don't mean – '

'No. She's not dead. That might have been better... No, if she is kept quiet she should get over the wound. But – there's been too much shock...' he shook his head, slowly...

For some seconds nobody spoke. Then Miranda said, in a harsh, unnatural voice:

'It's not true. He's lying, Mista. Can't you see he's lying?' She went closer to the man, glaring at him from narrowed eyes. 'You're lying. You're trying to tell us she's mad, aren't you? I know. I've heard it before. The little people like to think that. She's too big for them to understand. How can *they* judge *her*?' Her hand went to the pistol on her belt. 'Say it, you liar. Say The Mother is mad, if you dare!'

The man did not move. He said nothing. Without a change of expression, he looked steadily back into her eyes. The lines of Miranda's face altered slowly. A shudder shook her. Her hand dropped limply from the pistol butt. She drooped. She put her hands to her face, and swayed.

'No, no, it's not true,' she said, in a muffled voice. 'Tell me it's not true.'

But the man said nothing. He put out a hand to steady her, beckoning Mista with the other. Mista made no move. It was Freda who stepped forward and put her arms round the wilted Miranda. The man was looking at Miranda now with a puzzled wonder. He shook his head slowly as Freda led her aside, amazement, almost disbelief, in his expression. Mista's voice, speaking coldly, recalled him:

'*Is* that what you mean? That The Mother is mad?' she demanded.

'That's a loose, almost useless word, relative at best – still, in the sense you mean it, let us say; yes, The Mother is mad.'

Mista almost echoed Miranda:

'There have always been people who said The Mother was mad – people who thought themselves wiser than she.'

The man shook his head.

'I am a medical man. I have attended The Mother for a number of years. It is *now* and for the first time that I say she is no longer rational.'

'But she was shot in the chest – how can that have harmed her brain?' Emil put in.

The man opened empty hands, in a hopeless gesture.

'With all that that remark implies, where do I even begin to explain?'

He looked over us slowly. 'How can I explain? Oh, you – you unhappy monsters; with your minds out of Hegel, your morals out of Plato, and your bodies out of – bottles. How – ?' Then he paused. He looked at Miranda, weeping on Freda's shoulder. His look of puzzlement returned. 'I don't know,' he said. 'I – I'm out of my depth with you,' he admitted, still watching Miranda.

'I think we might understand: Johnny and I,' Freda said.

He looked at us, and noticed for the first time that we wore no numbers.

'Oh!' He looked more closely. 'Oh. So you must be Freda, heaven help you. Eve to The Mother's Lilith in this new creation – and mother-to-be to a host of Cains?'

Freda ignored that. She asked, curiously:

'And what are you doing here?'

'Oh, me. I'm just a prisoner. I am something futile, something which is dying slowly, smothered by these – ' he swept a hand towards Mista and Emil,' – something ineffective, a mere unmechanized human being.'

'Democritus?' suggested Freda, surprisingly.

He looked at her with more interest.

'H'm. Never a popular philosopher. No flags, no drums, no solvent slogans. Rather short on sales-technique, don't you think?'

'Closer to the human heart than materialistic nonsense,' said Freda.

'So. But who cares about the human heart any longer? Do they feel passionately now about anything but the collective mind? No, we may become sick at heart, but hearts don't matter. What you must do now is to believe, with blind faith, that one or other of the advertised patent cure-alls is going to rejuvenate the world with a magic touch. Not such a very new idea, either, but more insisted upon, now that what used to be Lethe, or baptism, have become membership of a party. In all countries you must believe in magic spell-words like freedom, democracy, justice, destiny – but in all countries you must for safety attach different meanings to them. And your motives must always look high and resound nobly – on the collective, not the human, scale. Even these – ' he glanced again at Mista and Emil' – intend to bring down their horrors upon the world in the name of inspired destiny, liberation, and the – very eventual – good of mankind, as they see it – God save their souls.'

Mista had been watching him as he spoke, uncomprehending, but curious. She watched him much in the way the audience in the hall had watched Eidermann: as a phenomenon for which her experience provided no measuring-rod. Now that he had paused, she reached out, and wrenched the subject back into place.

'What is it that has made The Mother mad – if she is mad?' she demanded, sharply.

The doctor came out of his reflections. He pondered her.

'Very well, then,' he said. 'In a word – conflict. The old, old irresistible versus the immovable.'

'You mean Eidermann and his scientists?' Mista said.

'I don't – and I don't mean the bickering of your factions, either. I mean conflict within herself.'

Mista frowned back at him.

'I don't understand that,' she said.

He shrugged. 'I didn't expect you would. But I'll try to explain simply.' He closed his eyes for a moment, and then opened them again. Not looking at any of us directly, he said: 'Very many years ago – when, in fact, she was little more than a child – The Mother adopted as her supreme conviction that it was the destiny of Germany to rule the world. This curious obsession, which has attacked a number of people during the last century, appears to be contagious, and sometimes attains the degree of mania.' He turned to regard the portrait on the wall reflectively. 'In The Mother,' he went on, 'though it was obsessive, it did not reach mania. The easiest way to think of it, perhaps, is to realize that her mind was hag-ridden by the sense that it was both her duty and her destiny to be one of those who should bring it about. Personal will to power, megalo-ambition, and that kind of thing came into it, of course, but they were subsidiary to the main driving force.

'That drive did not desert her even when everything seemed lost for ever. She withdrew perforce, but her determination was unweakened.

'At first, this place must have seemed to her little more than a refuge and a waiting place. But Eidermann's work altered everything. It gave her a sudden sight of herself with a new destiny – which was the old one, magnified by a few thousands. She determined that it should become fact.

'Nobody but The Mother can know how it seems to become a mother on such a scale. She, who must already have been made aware of the smug self-satisfaction with which the most brainless breeder feels herself entitled to patronize the childless, in part-pity, part-contempt, and – could it be, in part self-consolation? – she, now suddenly surpasses them all, biologically as in other ways.

'That increased her imperiousness, but it must have created a still more profound change in her orientation towards the world. And, perhaps most important of all, there was no one to claim a share in her children. The father was, and remains, unknown. They were hers, and hers alone. So, to the imperiousness and the knowledge of biotic supremacy, add possession and domination.

'Do you begin to see the shape?'

It was clear enough that Mista and Emil did not. He went on, speaking more to us than to them.

'So, what do we have? On the conscious level, still the old determination that she, and they as part of her, shall conquer the world. In the subconscious, the desire to possess and dominate them.

'While they are in here, she can still do that. But if she sends them out to fight some of them are bound to be killed. And it is worse than that for her. If they lose, then everything is lost: if they win, she will no longer be able to dominate them as she has, and some of them, at least, will slip out of her control.

'On the other hand, if she does not send them out to fight, she is frustrating the very dynamic of her life.

'So, what does she do? What *can* she do...?

'I'll tell you. She does what we all do. She rationalizes. When her conscious mind tells her that *now* is the time for them to strike, her subconscious thrusts up reasons and excuses for delay. And so, each time the fatal order is almost given, there is a postponement. Something is not quite propitious; the occasion, for one reason or another, is found to be *not quite* ripe.

'And so on, and so on – with, each time, the conflict more bitter and acute... Until, today, there came Eidermann.

'No conciliation was possible, you see. Sooner or later something had to break. Her mind couldn't resolve the conflict, and the strain grew until it gave way. It's as simple as that.'

He glanced questioningly at Mista, to see whether she had understood. Her eyes were a little narrowed.

'Your people have often hinted before that she was mad – sometimes they have even said so,' she observed.

He shook his head reprovingly at her.

'Can't you think in anything but plots and factions? I am not responsible for what other people say. I am giving you my professional opinion And, if it is any consolation to you, I wish to God that I could give you another. So long as The Mother held control, there was little chance of this damned folly ever taking place. But now – ' he shrugged ' – I don't know how long it can be held off.'

Mista considered him, detachedly.

'It sounds as if you were loyal to no one.'

He gave a wry smile at her.

'I have my standards of integrity – but you wouldn't understand them. For you, loyalty is something owed to a dogma – never to yourself: personal responsibility is shifted on to the leader.

'I am a man of reason. And in the fullness of reason I detest and despise this age of squabbling Faiths. Your pseudo-political religions interest me only as evidence of the crass gullibility of the majority of my fellow men. I look at what I am offered as clearly as I can. I find no satisfaction in granting demi-divinity to a dogmatist, whether his name is Aristotle, or Marx – or Hegel. And so I am the despised outcast of my century – the man of no faction.'

Mista clearly made nothing of that. It was Freda who said:

'But, since we find you in this place, a pragmatist, perhaps?'

'To hell with your labels. As a young man, I was invited to come here. As I told you, I am a man of reason, and as the alternative, apparently, was to be shot, I came.'

Emil spoke up, with the air of one who has kept a firm grasp of the needle while the haystack was built.

'You are claiming that The Mother is not fit to hold authority?'

'I am.'

'We had better see her,' Mista decided.

'It would be kinder to let her rest for a while,' the doctor advised.

'You don't want us to see her?' Emil said, sharply.

'Oh God! You and your eternal piddling intrigues. Go on then! Go and see her if you like, and be damned to you. It can't make much difference now. Better take this girl with you.'

'No,' said Miranda, 'not if she's – '

'It might be better if you went along with these Spartans. She may need someone who's fond of her.'

As we watched the three of them make their way to the door, he shook his head again.

'And she *is* fond of the old tyrant,' he mused. 'How does that come about? It doesn't make any real sense, you know, not in this setup.'

'You weren't there when The Mother was shot,' Freda told him. 'It – it sort of clutched at my heart to hear them. I don't suppose we can hope to understand how they feel, but she does mean something tremendously important. She *is* The Mother, but she's more than that – something like Isis, or Freyja, perhaps...'

The doctor nodded, thoughtfully.

'Or maybe simply – Stability?' he suggested.

'But not to Mista,' I put in.

'Yes, Mista, too,' Freda corrected me. 'She was *acting* the Spartan – she thought that that was what The Mother would have done in such circumstances, so she did it.'

'These twisted Children,' said the doctor. 'They plot, and they intrigue endlessly, they lie, and they bully – and yet I believe you are right: not one of them would really do The Mother harm, knowingly.' He looked uneasily at the door that had closed behind the other three. '*Knowingly*,' he repeated. 'But, maybe I'd better go along. You never know, with these young fools.'

I didn't want to let him go like that. He was the first normal human being, other than Freda, that I had spoken to since I had been in the place. There ought to be a lot of important things I could learn from him.

'Just a minute, Doctor,' I said, as he began to walk away. 'There are some questions I want to ask you.'

'Just hold 'em over till I get back. Those two are very likely exciting my patient,' he said, scarcely pausing.

'But at least you can tell me where this place is,' I said.

He was a few feet from the door, and turned to look back at me, in surprise.

'Why, haven't you found that out yet? It's –'

The click of the doorlatch cut him short. The door opened, and on the threshold stood The Mother. She was wearing a plain white nightdress. Her hair was caught back by a white silk ribbon. It was she – but, in some way, with the illusion of youth spun about her. The light glistered the faded hair back into gold. The lines of her face were relaxed, and softened.

I caught the beauty revived there, and remembered my mother's locket, but it was a fragile, fugitive beauty. The eyes had softened, too, – too much... The lips were a little apart. I was afraid that they might speak:

'They say the owl was a baker's daughter.'

Oh, pretty Ophelia...

Behind her, half-a-dozen identical faces peered in through the doorway, marked with identical consternation. The doctor was taken aback for a moment, then made up his mind and he walked calmly to her.

'You should not be here. You must rest,' he told her, quietly.

She seemed neither to see nor hear him. He went closer. He laid his hand gently on her left arm:

'Come back to your room now,' he said.

The touch changed her in an instant. All the old imperiousness was back, more than life-size. She became aware, too, of her surroundings. Arrogantly, she ordered the doctor out of her way. He stood back, at a loss. On account of her wound he dare not use, nor provoke her to use, any physical pressure. He said again:

'This is wrong for you. You must rest quietly.'

But, for her, he had ceased to exist. Her gaze swept hither and thither about the big room as if she were remembering, recognizing the place by degrees. It came to rest at last on her chair and desk, at the far end. She started to walk slowly up the middle of the floor, her bare feet silent on the polished boards.

Through the open door behind her Mista, Miranda, Hilda, Emil, and others came crowding in, subdued and alarmed. The doctor was watching her intently. He made a motion with his hand to keep the rest back, and shot a quick frown at them, in silent warning.

The lonely white figure walked on, down the long room. We had no existence for her, Freda and I, but she did seem to be seeing things or people that we could not. She passed by us, walking slowly, with immense dignity. Her head was held confidently high. Occasionally she turned her face to one side or the other. What figments were lining the walls for her progress we could only guess. Not, I think, the ranks of her fantastic Children, for her expression was haughty, almost contemptuous – and I remembered how it had softened when she said to me: 'They are fine Children, aren't they?'

And so, I fancied that she had gone further back; back before the Children who now watched her with such anguish and distress had come into her life. For her, I think, the walls were lined with figures from her past; an assemblage in uniforms that glittered with orders and medals; the pirate-adventurers with whom she had once set out to conquer the world, recalled now in a great ghostly rally to do her homage…

She walked on, a solitary white form reflected in the shining floor. We knew she was not asleep, yet all of us feared that she might wake.

A few yards in front of the desk she stopped. She stood quite still, looking up at the portrait, studying it. We looked at it, too; that undistinguished figure with the bulging eyes and the ludicrous moustache; the very aggrandizements of the artist emphasized it for what it was – the little man's dream of power; the apotheosis of the mediocre…

There was a sound of shots, so distant that it might have been raindrops pattering on leaves. No one stirred. The Mother stood as if frozen, in contemplation of the portrait. The seconds lengthened. A tiny moan came from one of the girls in the doorway. She wrung her hands, helplessly. The doctor signed again to the rest to keep back, and began to walk quietly up the room.

Suddenly, The Mother laughed. It was a shocking laugh, hard and harsh, a queer mixing of mockery with despair. The doctor stopped, uncertainly.

The Mother moved swiftly to the desk, and sat down there, upright against the high, straight back of the chair. She remained for a moment staring down the long room, and beyond it, her own arms resting along the carved arms of the chair. She tried to stretch forward her right arm. It seemed to puzzle more than pain her that she could not do so. She gave up the attempt, and brought her left hand across towards the row of buttons. There was the faintest trace of indecision in her choice, but, when she had chosen, her finger pressed firmly, and held the white button down. She waited, lips apart, eyes focused far beyond the walls.

The floor surged a little under us, the building trembled slightly. Seconds later, there came a slow, swelling rumble…

The Mother withdrew her hand, and regarded the row of buttons selectively. The doctor began to cover the rest of his distance from her at a run. Her hand reached across again.

'Stop!' he shouted. 'Stop!'

It was as if the violence in his voice had hit her physically. She stopped in bewilderment, her hand poised in mid-air.

The doctor reached her, and manoeuvred himself between her and the row of buttons. She looked up at him, all arrogance suddenly lost, from a child's eyes.

'Gerda,' he said, gently, 'Gerda Daele, you are sick. You must go back to bed, and rest.'

She looked puzzled, but she nodded obediently. He helped her from her chair, and, with his arm supporting her, they moved away from the desk. After a few steps she paused uncertainly. She spoke, plaintively, like a little girl – and in Swedish.

'Jag är mycket trött – förtrött,' she said. 'I am so very tired.'

She managed two more, hesitant steps, and stopped again. Her eyes opened wide, blue, and intense. Her lips parted, but no sound came. She shivered violently, and then went limp.

The doctor reached down his other arm, and lifted her. He walked swiftly down the room, carrying her. With a shake of his head he motioned the group at the doors out of his way, and strode past them. Mista and Emil turned to follow him. The rest stayed huddled in a forlorn little knot.

None of us spoke. From somewhere outside came the crisp explosion of a small bomb, followed by a rattle of shots.

But that kind of thing didn't sound very important just then.

17

Not To Die

Give her the wages of going on, and not to die – A.T.

Fully half an hour passed before Emil reappeared. He looked at the subdued group near the door, and gave them a reassuring nod, but did not speak to them. Then he observed Freda and me where we were making the best of chairs designed entirely to impress the eye. He came across to us.

'The Mother wishes to see both of you,' he told us, speaking with great distinctness, and in the manner of one conveying a command.

We followed him out. We crossed the familiar ante-room, looking less impressive now in its coating of plaster-dust. At the door of The Mother's own private room he stood back for us to precede him. He closed the door carefully behind him as he came in after us.

I don't know quite what I expected to find there, except that it would be grandiose. More pictures of those not very couth Nordic gods diverting themselves, maybe; statuary muscle-bound with heroic implication; banners and emblems fixed like college pennants? There was none of it. The place was all white. Walls, ceiling, carpet, and hangings. The chairs were upholstered in white leather, with gilt piping. The toilet table, with its triptych mirrors in narrow gilt beadings, was flounced in white spotted muslin, patterned a few inches above the hem with gold thread. The bed against the opposite wall was similarly flounced, and the cobwebby white drapes that rose to a peak above its head were trickled sparsely with the same gold thread.

My first impression was of asceticism broken out into frills. But then I saw that that was wrong. Asceticism is aware of what it resists. This room was not – it was virginal, very private, a young girl's room.

I looked to see how Freda was taking it. I caught there an astonishment even greater than my own, and then a look of pity coming into her eyes.

The doctor was sitting in one of the white leather arm chairs. Mista stood a little distance from him. Her hands were clasped together, her gaze fixed tragically on the bed. I glanced at The Mother's head lying on the pillow, and then at the doctor for confirmation. He gave a slow nod, without speaking. Emil came and stood beside Mista. The doctor got up, and beckoned us over to a corner.

'I'm sorry we had to mislead you,' he said.

'I more than half expected it,' I told him. 'The Children are not to know?'

'Exactly. She died, of course, back there in the audience-room. I knew that when I carried her out.'

'Then why – ?' Freda began, lamely.

The doctor pulled at the lobe of his ear, thoughtfully. 'The question is whether we can afford to let her die. Is it *politic* that a demi-god should be allowed to die? For that is what she is here, you know – a demi-god, and a most powerful symbol... That is one point. The other is that this is quite the most difficult moment in the whole of the place's existence for it to lose its symbol.'

'I can see that it's awkward,' I admitted. 'But – well, even leaders have to die sometime. Whoever follows has to do his best to keep the tradition alive.'

'You can't carry on being the first and the source, as a tradition,' he pointed out. 'And to become a demi-god takes time – you have also to be exceptional; and that's exactly what none of these reduplicated Children is.'

'I understood that Mista was more or less appointed by The Mother as her – well, her *administrative* successor,' Freda said.

The doctor pulled at his ear again. 'You are overlooking the expression I used quite advisedly – demi-god,' he said. 'We can't see her as these creations of hers do – particularly, I think, the Women. She is, as I said, something symbolic – and fundamental to them, she has the kind of extended motherhood with which one speaks of Mother Nature, or Mother Earth. How can I put it?' He reflected a moment, then he said to Freda: 'Let me alter my greeting to you. Try to think of The Mother not as Lilith, but as Eve. Now, before Darwin began correcting our family tree for us, Adam and Eve were pretty important symbols. Eve, the personi-fied mother of all mankind, meant a lot. Well, here you have the symbol and the fact combined. For, however we may feel about it, The Mother *is*, or was, the Eve of a new order. Other women after Eve continued to bear children, but that did not alter her position as the unique, symbolic first –

and just so stands The Mother. I assure you that to call her a demi-god is no exaggeration of their feelings about her. And that goes for Ulrich and his lot, too – opposition to a god is certainly not a denial of his existence.'

He paused, looking at Freda, and leaving an inconclusive feeling hanging over us.

'And so – something?' I suggested. 'What if she does mean all that to them?'

'Dying,' observed the doctor, 'is such a very ordinary thing to do – and the discovery of clay feet in a demi-god, so profoundly disturbing. The mother-symbol is significant to all of us, but here it is raised to the n-th. There – ' he glanced towards the still figure on the bed, ' – there lies the emotional centre of all these frustrated women.

'Miranda has shown, surprisingly, I must admit, that some of them love her. Possibly, some of them hate her – though I've noticed none – but that doesn't matter. She still forms the emotional focus for them – and for many of the men, too.

'Well, what happens when that focus is suddenly lost – and in such a normally mortal way? What do *you* think happens?'

Freda frowned. 'From what you've been saying, I should think – well, I should think the bottom will drop out of their lives – for a time, anyway.'

The doctor nodded. 'Just that, I should say – until they learn a way to do without her.'

Freda looked round at the hangings, the bed, the flounce-skirted stool before the mirror. She said, inconsequentially:

'There's something here that makes me want to cry. She must have been – over sixty. Were they right before? I mean, *was* she a bit mad?'

'Mad? Oh, no – unless you would call a failure to grow up a kind of madness – in which case there would be very few sane people. No, one overwhelming passion left no room for the rest to develop – so she never matured.'

'But that conflict you spoke of?'

'Oh, she was possessive, all right. Intensely possessive. That doesn't require maturity. Her Children did not have independent existence for her. They were her dolls. They had to play her games. They were *hers*. She was fond of them, oh yes. Little girls can be greatly attached to their dolls and do dreadful things to them.

'The other rooms are all part of the game she was playing with them – this is what she was really like.'

He looked round at the setting again. Then he went on:

'I don't suppose she could admit to herself that she could die with her task unfinished – and in that she did them her last great disservice. She has made no provision; nothing more than that Mista should act for her in an emergency – no building up, no formal declaration of succession, no laying-on of hands. And so, as well as depriving them of their emotional focus, she leaves them leaderless – only, they don't know it yet.

'Now, our feeling – that is, Mista's, Emil's, and mine – is that an announcement of the death at this moment would leave them so confused and emotionally shaken that they would be unpredictable. The only way we can see of preserving unity and order among them is to ensure that, for the present, at least, they do not learn of The Mother's death.'

I began to perceive that there was a purpose of some sort emerging.

'If you three – and, maybe, Miranda – are the only ones who know, why bring us into it?' I asked him.

'I can tell you that quite briefly. We want Freda to impersonate The Mother.'

Freda looked startled.

'Me? But I – I – Why on earth me?'

'Well, for one thing, you're like them, but you aren't one of them; you're detached. If we got one of them to do it, those who knew her best would soon be asking what had happened to her. Also, there would be the emotional strain and significance. I'm not sure that we could depend on her. She might make a slip – or she might easily be suddenly overwhelmed by her own presumptuousness, and flunk it at a critical moment.'

'But why do it at all?'

'Don't you see? None of them is happy about The Mother's decision to delay the Day, but she ordered it, and, in duty and faith, all, except Ulrich's lot, support her. But take her, the uniting factor, away, and they'll all fall apart. Some of them will change sides, and without a united opposition the technical faction will easily have its way. It might have to delay a little after this rumpus – God knows, for instance, what The Mother may have blown up when she pressed that button – but the time could be profitably used to improve solidarity.'

He broke off to glance across at Mista and Emil who were now talking quietly together.

'Those two undoubtedly have more ideas further up the sleeve – everyone has, in this nest of intrigue. But the thing we are all agreed on is that this is no time for The Mother to die.'

He looked questioningly at us.

'Clear enough to me,' I said.

Freda demurred.

'I couldn't keep that up for long – if at all.'

'You'd not have to. What we want to do first is to get over the immediate crisis. We want it thoroughly established by witnesses that The Mother is alive – although, of course, in a weak condition. After that, we can consider the next step.'

'But there are so many things – is my German good enough, for instance?' Freda said, uncertainly.

'It'll pass. A few essential words are all you'll need. Very weak and sick, you see.'

Freda still hesitated. She looked at me. I did not see how it was likely to involve her in any danger. In fact, she ought to be the best protected person in the place. Also:

'Anything that helps to delay hell popping is a gain,' I remarked.

Freda considered for some moments, then:

'Very well,' she said. 'I'll do my best.'

The doctor looked relieved. He beckoned the other two across.

'She'll do it,' he told them as they came up. Mista nodded, looking at Freda without smiling. Emil brightened slightly. His gaze rested on my bandaged fingers.

'So much better when there is mutual consent,' he said. 'I should have disliked having to beat up Mr. Farthing again as a means of persuasion.'

* * *

The next time I went into that room, The Mother's body had vanished, and it was Freda who lay back in the bed. But, unprepared, I would never have known it. Somehow her face seemed to have thinned. It had been given that imperious mien of The Mother's, and then had it modified by tiredness and sickness. Some of the hair had faded, the rest gleamed silver. I stared at her, finding it hard to believe. The smile that came to the mouth was Freda's, though.

'But what did you expect?' she said.

I had, of course, expected just that; but it was disturbingly like the real thing. Luckily I was wise enough not to say so. After all, however distinguished she may otherwise be, a girl's elderly aunt is still that.

'I'm trying to decide where art ends and craft begins,' I told her.

The girl who had produced the transformation was just finishing her work. She studied each visible part with an intensely critical eye. Not all of it satisfied her.

'Hands,' she said, 'are very difficult. You had better keep them under the sheet as much as possible.'

Her standards were high. For me, the hands had just the texture and

quality to be expected in the late fifties or early sixties. The rest, she passed.
She looked at Mista, standing on the other side of the bed, for approval.

'Excellent. Very, very remarkable,' Mista told her, in a troubled voice.

'May I see?' Freda asked.

The girl handed her a glass. Freda studied it carefully.

'Queer,' she said. 'Now I know that I look like that, I know how I have
to feel.' She settled back against the pillows, and closed her eyes.

'I'll get by,' she said.

18

Mischiefs

And some ... have in their hearts ... millions of mischiefs – W.S.

I was left supernumerary, with nothing to do but hang around. At first I thought we were all holed up in The Mother's suite: I should have known that she ran truer to type. Before long, I came across one unobtrusive exit recently opened; probably there were half-a-dozen more, suited to various contingencies. I made my way through the narrow passage it served, thinking I might be able to sneak back to my own quarters. It landed me in one of the women's blocks, and when I tried to leave there I found a steel shutter across the passage, with two young women brandishing sub-machine-guns, to turn me back. In the opposite direction it was possible to travel through several blocks on several levels before my idea of working round was frustrated by another steel shutter. I began to realize that The Mother's supporters were in charge of a larger section than I had supposed – probably several sections, interconnected by emergency passages.

I turned back again, and tried another side corridor. It was some hours now since there had been any sound of firing or explosions, and I began to wonder whether I had missed the declaration of a truce. But I had not. On turning a corner, I encountered a pair of steady blue eyes looking along a pistol barrel. The owner of them seemed undecided about me for a moment, then she noticed my lack of a number, and regarded me more closely.

'Oh, it's you,' she said, with an intonation which I could not consider flattering. 'You'll get yourself shot, snooping around like that. Better get right away out of it.'

'Listen,' I said. 'I've nothing to do, and no place to go. My quarters seem to be in either enemy territory or no-man's-land. What happens?'

'Sigrid is allocating billets. You'll find her in Room 15, Level 3, Block 16,' she told me briefly, and dismissed me.

Eventually I found the room, and there, behind the desk I found just such another of them, impersonal, detached, on the job. She told me where I could sleep, where I could eat. And while I listened, I found I was hating her – hating all my stock-faced, stock-sized, stock-numbered cousins with such a silly, futile anger that I hurried away before I should make a fool of myself.

The next day I sought Emil. He was a subdued man. Not at all the old confident deliverer of pocket-lectures.

'Look,' I said. 'For God's sake give me something to do. I'll go nuts, just hanging around like this.'

'What sort of thing?' he asked.

'Hell, how would I know? But you have a kind of civil war on your hands, haven't you? You must want some help some place.'

'It's a stalemate. They daren't attack for fear we'll destroy the intelligence reports and plans.'

'It might stay like that for weeks,' I said.

'Quite likely,' he agreed. 'After all, that's what The Mother wanted, isn't it? – A postponement.'

'Well, if you can't think of any way for me to make myself useful, I'll go and see Mista.'

'I don't think that would be any good,' he said.

'Why not?'

He looked down at his finger-nails.

'Mista's – Well, she's out of a job now,' he explained.

I stared at him.

'But she's the works. She's The Mother's chief executive.

'Was,' he said.

'For Pete's sake, is everyone crazy around here? Did Freda – ?' His look of sudden alarm stopped me, and I remembered the prevalence of microphones in those parts.

'You mean Hilda,' he said, hurriedly. 'Yes, Hilda's taken over from Mista now.'

I shook my head. 'I give up. I just don't get any of it in this crazy dump.'

He looked as if he might have said quite a bit – but there were still the mikes. I took myself off.

The mess-room, in the way of mess-rooms any place, was enjoying rumours. Several limelight-loving types were holding forth with an air of knowledgeability which might or might not be spurious. Everyone apparently accepted the fact that The Mother had fired Mista; it was the reasons for the firing that were in dispute. A suggestion that Mista had plotted the shooting of The Mother in order to usurp power found practically no takers. That she had schemed to gain ascendancy over her was scouted, too – for it was difficult to see how one of the Children could hope to maintain an ascendancy without outside help to enforce it. Possibly it was this angle that generated the theory that Mista was simply a tool – the scientists had attempted to assassinate The Mother because they had thought they would be able to control Mista when she succeeded her. There was a lot of argument as to whether Mista was likely to have known about this or not. The balance was generally in her favour, but there was a feeling that if the opposition party held that her succession might be useful to them, then she was not suitable for the role of heir-apparent.

The whole thing was in the air, right from the assumption that the shot had been intended for The Mother and not for Eidermann, but a few lacunae like that matter little in mess-room logic.

There was far more astonishment over Mista's successor. Miranda was the obvious choice. Her genuine devotion to The Mother had never been questioned until now. But, too, of course, she was Mista's official second, and pretty well in cahoots with her...

And now Hilda had the job. Why Hilda? She hadn't been in favour for quite a while – or would that be a cover? Maybe she had been on provocateur work...? It was a suggestion that made one or two of the listeners thoughtfully uneasy. But they were distracted when the question of repercussions on Emil came up. He had been working with Mista, and if he were to lose his job, too, would his staff sympathize with him, or remain loyal? Or, if he held on to his job, would he switch allegiance to Hilda, or might he not work underground for Mista still?

There were so many cats among the pigeons that an hour of this kind of thing added nothing but confusion. I decided to go to see Freda, and find out what really was happening.

But at the entrance to the suite they were firm. 'The Mother', they told me, was resting. Only the most inconsiderate of persons, they indicated, would think of trying to disturb her after all she had been through. Maybe in a week or two she would be enough recovered to give short audiences. Meanwhile, if it were anything important, Hilda might consent to see me sometime, by appointment.

The pistol I had picked up on the platform was still in my pocket, but the three young women who inflexibly barred my way in a determined sister-act all wore pistols holstered to their belts.

So I went away.

* * *

Many times, in works of fiction, I have been struck by the uncannily acute perception of the central character. He may be a G-man, or a cop, a gangster, an eye, or a spy, but, having the author on his side, he has a pretty good idea of the setup, animate and inanimate, which includes him. He has a wide comprehension of the purposes of his captors – and of their weaknesses; also, a rapid discernment of error in his opponents, a comprehensive understanding of their organization, and the perception of a hawk for the obscure potentialities of a situation. Thus equipped, he is able to select the exact moment and place which will make it possible for him to triumph over what, to a lesser man, might appear dismayingly unreasonable odds.

It must be very comforting for a character to know he has the author on his side. The trouble about my situation seemed to be that, if there was an author, he was on somebody else's side, and/or crazy.

Here was I, dragged into this thing more or less by accident, a potentially disruptive force set down in the middle of this deplorable organization.

All the time there had been a voice inside me saying: 'Go ahead now, get on with it, disrupt,' and so far, I had done about as much disruption as an egg-whisk in a foam-bath.

And now the place was split wide open between two main factions, spiky with splinters, too. The disruptor's harvest home, you'd say? Just play off one against another, and everything'll be fine. Uh-huh... uh-huh...

You have to start some place, you know. It kind of helps if somebody'll take you seriously, too. But if all you can raise is a sort of oh-run-away-and-play, if it is made abundantly clear to you that you are only around at all on sufferance as a procrastinated biological convenience, if you have become uncomfortably aware that when your myriad matriarchal cousins identify you they tend to snigger to one another, and if, on top of all this, every current that you perceive has half-a-dozen cross-currents beneath it, then, where *do* you start?

I didn't know.

When I went to bed, I lay there wondering whether I wasn't maybe getting a preview glimpse of The Mother's intended order. I envisioned its extension. For quite a long time I contemplated the prospect of a gynocracy where the few males that it was necessary to preserve led their largely ornamental existences to the accompaniment of unpleasing giggles and derisive, feminine wolf-calls, until, somewhere in this swirl of horrid imaginings, sleep mercifully took over.

* * *

They were infuriatingly tolerant of my inquiries the next morning. The Mother, they told me, was doing nicely: it was quite likely that she would be able to receive me in about a week's time. I went off to Emil. Bearing the microphones in mind, I said:

'Look here, I want an order that'll get me past those b – , those female watch-dogs, and an interview fixed up with The Mother. And if I don't get it in a few minutes, I'll start raising a particularly ruptious kind of hell for you.' I looked meaningly at him so that he would get the idea.

He did: and I got my order.

Faced with that, the guards reluctantly passed me into the ante-room. But nobody was being precipitate. I had to cool my heels and shorten my temper there for close on two hours before I was beckoned across and admitted, with warning frowns and do-not-excite gestures, to The Mother's room.

Freda's appearance, sitting up in bed against a tier of pillows, was so uncannily that of The Mother, and the presence of two other young women in the room so unexpected, that I was left with nothing to say. I stood there feeling, and, doubtless, looking, a fool.

She was toying left-handedly with an invalidish-looking mess on a tray. As she lifted a spoonful, her eyes met mine, with just the faintest trace of amusement in them. She put the spoon down on the plate languidly, and looked at the stuff with distaste.

'Ach! 'S ist genug,' she said.

One of the girls put the tray beside the bed, and took the plate away.

Freda closed her eyes while the other fussed over smoothing the sheet and pillows. The first came back, and set a glass and saucer on the tray. Freda motioned both of them to go. They hesitated, looking at me doubtfully.

'Zehn Minuten,' she said, with an irritable frown.

She waited a moment after they had gone. Then she lifted the glass, regarding me over the edge of it.

'How'm I doing?' she asked.

'That kind of depends on what the devil you think you *are* doing,' I told her.

'You sound peevish, Johnny. The capricious despot – with the added advantage of a weak condition; that's me. It's an almost unassailable position. Has it ever struck you what an enormous number of mediocre women must owe their strength entirely to their weakness?'

'What's troubling me – ' I began.

'It's really quite a delightful sensation,' she went on. 'People anxiously hurry to do the most ridiculous things for you for fear you should relapse on them. I never knew.' She sipped at the contents of the glass, and then frowned at it. 'Not so good. Still, there has to be give and take, I suppose. Il faut souffrir pour être impératrice. Now, there'd be something on your mind, Johnny?'

'Listen,' I told her. 'I've never claimed to understand more than about one per cent of what goes on in this nuthouse, and now the decimal's shifted further west. What's all this about Mista, for instance?'

'Oh, I had to fire Mista,' she said.

'Indeed! You just – had to fire her?'

'Well, you see, she thought that The Mother might have a change of heart. It occurred to her that if The Mother could make some face-saving discovery which would enable her to patch things up with whoever is leading Eidermann's lot now, we might make much better terms than if we went on being obstinate. Then we could all happily get on with the plan to start the rest of the world throwing bombs at one another. And I didn't think that was a very good idea, so I fired her.'

'And she just took it?'

'What else could she do? She can't afford to let out that The Mother's dead, because her authority would then be undermined. And if it were known that she was trying to force The Mother to surrender, she'd be all washed up, right away... Oh, dear, you'd think they could make some *nice* tasting medicines nowadays, wouldn't you?'

'But putting up Hilda! They're all absolutely staggered by that.'

Freda chuckled. 'So's Hilda. She probably thinks the shock has knocked The Mother a little silly. But Hilda is the works of the let's-get-out-of-this-and-live group. I'm hoping that once she gets over the surprise it will occur to her that she is now in a position to plan a break out on quite a big scale. The awkward thing is going to be if Emil's agents get on to it while she's preparing.' She pondered. 'Of course, I could sack Emil, too. But there doesn't seem to be anyone I could usefully put in his place. It's a pity about your hand.'

'I'm no candidate for impersonating Emil in this infernal tangle, if that's what you're thinking,' I told her. 'Let's get back to Mista. She's not the sort to take this lying down.'

'What can she do? The civil war is suspended – it's just an armed truce now.'

'But if she could somehow guarantee the preservation of those intelligence reports, she might make terms,' I urged.

Freda drank again. 'This is the most disgusting stuff,' she complained, 'but there's nowhere else to pour it. Would you like to finish it for me?'

'No,' I said. I took the glass from her, and put it back on the tray. 'Now, if they could be sure of getting hold of those intelligence reports – '

She looked at me, vaguely.

'You don't need to worry about that. When The Mother pressed that button quite an important laboratory went up. They daren't make a move. All they're interested in right now is dashing madly around figuring out what else she may have mined. Still whole row of buttons... she might... They're scared... Don't think they'll touch... Johnny...'

'They – what?' I demanded, baffled.

Then I saw she was resting with her eyes closed. She opened them.

'What?' she said.

'You said they were scared.'

'Did I? Who?'

'The scientists. Eidermann's lot.'

'Eider – oh, yes,' she said, vaguely.

Suddenly she sat up.

'The papers, Johnny. You must have them.' She fumbled at the front of her nightdress.

'What's wrong with you? What are you talking about?' I demanded. 'What papers?'

She went on fumbling clumsily, tugging at something caught in the folds there.

'The papers, Johnny. You must take them. Keep them for me.'

'What – ' I began again, just as she succeeded in juggling up a packet of papers held together by a band.

'Pocket, Johnny,' she said, holding them towards me. I came closer, and took them from her.

'Pocket,' she insisted.

'All right,' I said, impatiently.

She watched me while I stowed them in the inside pocket of my jacket.

'Now, about Eidermann's lot – ' I started once more. But she wasn't listening. She was leaning back on the pillows, with her eyes closed again.

I was alarmed. I took hold of her shoulder and shook it.

'Freda, Freda, darling, what's the matter?'

Her eyes reopened, but they didn't focus properly.

'Sleepy,' she said. 'That medicine. Silly of me, Johnny.' And her lids dropped again.

There was a hard knot in my chest. I kind of froze up where I was. Maybe it was only for a second or two, but it seemed a whole lot more than that before I could move. Then I grabbed her shoulder again, and shook her. This time her eyes didn't open. She slithered down sideways against the pile of pillows, and lay that way. I bent over to look at her, hating the make-up that hid her real face from me.

'Wake up, Freda. You must wake up,' I pleaded. But she didn't move.

There was a noise on the far side of the room. I turned round quickly to see the doctor closing the door behind him. He started towards us. I remembered the pistol in my pocket. I had it out in a flash, and pointing at him.

'You've poisoned her,' I said. 'By God, I'll – '

He gave me a weary look.

'Don't be a fool, man. What would I want to poison her for? Put that thing away.' He advanced with calm disregard of the pistol, and passed me by. He reached for Freda's wrist, took her pulse, and said 'Huh', as if not unsatisfied. Then he turned back to me.

'Do put that thing away,' he said, again. 'You're not a schoolboy now,' he added testily.

Well, after all, I could pull it out again if necessary. I demanded:

'What have you done to her?'

'It won't hurt her, but it will keep her out of mischief for a time – and I do mean mischief.' He turned to regard her again. 'It would seem as if the unusual talent for intrigue shown by this family extends to the collateral branches – though, maybe, with an exception in your own case.

'This young woman has regrettably turned out to be a veritable menace – and without in any way disturbing the required impression that she was an elderly lady playing a close game with eternity. In two days she has succeeded in concocting a variety of snarls, snarls within snarls, and sheer goddam bedevilments that are going to need months of tact and work to smooth out. It has become quite clear to certain persons that if the social system here is not to be reduced to ruins in a couple of days more, she must have a relapse. To their great relief, she is now having it.'

'It did seem to me she had been – er – going it a bit,' I acknowledged.

'A conservative expression,' the doctor assured me. 'I doubt if you know the half of it.'

'Well,' I said. 'I'll take your word that whatever you've given her is harmless. And I can see that it could be safer for her if she is kept quiet.'

'It certainly could. There's a lot of latent energy around here looking for a place to expend itself.'

'But what follows? She can't simply go on having a relapse.'

'Ah, that's just what she must do – though she can't do it here, of course. In fact, the sooner she is out of this place, the more easily a number of people are going to breathe. Therefore, I, her physician, being worried by her relapse and the state of her general health, have decided that she must have a change of climate and surroundings. Some place that is drier and more bracing. Accordingly, she will leave here this afternoon – indeed, in a few minutes' time.'

I was taken aback. 'Now, look here, wait a bit – ' I began.

He raised his hand. 'Easy, now. You're going, too, don't you worry. The way you held up Emil to get that permit has made him feel you might work around to more troublesome ideas on the same lines. So you're both being sent off to one of the small assembly stations for a while. You'll be able to cool-off safely there while they get to sorting this place over, and putting some stability back into it.

'And you can thank your family connection and irreproachable Nordic blood for that; otherwise, there would have been a much more messy kind of solution. As it stands at present, you will both, in due course, be brought back here. Nobody will, this time, make the mistake of giving Freda authority of any kind, and the programme envisioned for you by The Mother can then begin peaceably.

'The Mother motif will be sustained, so long as it is preservable, in the form of the cruelly exiled invalid whose greatest hope is to return one day, when her health is good enough to permit it, to her devoted Children. If they work it carefully, they ought to be able to keep that one up for quite a spell, don't you think?'

'Somebody,' I said, 'has been quite busy, inventing this lot. Was it you?'

His look reproved me.

'I? My dear fellow! For this kind of thing one requires either experience in the immediate entourage of a dictator, or a certain something which is characteristic of your illustrious family – omitting, again, your own branch. Emil and Mista qualify on both grounds, but I would guess that her contribution was the greater.'

I turned to look at Freda, and wondered whether she would have any ideas for dealing with this situation. I didn't.

I sat down on the side of the bed, and took one of her hands between mine.

'You are quite sure – ?'

'Don't worry. I know what I'm doing. And she only drank about half of it. Two and a half to three hours, and she'll be quite upsides again – except, possibly, for her temper.'

'Where's the place we're being sent to?' I asked.

He shook his head. 'That isn't the kind of information they give,' he said.

'You still haven't told me where *this* place is,' I reminded him.

'I thought you'd have worked that out by now. You've seen the forest outside? Well, now, there's only one part of the world where you can find the *paramecium reticulata* growing wild, isn't there?'

'Oh, is there?' I said. 'And where would that be?'

'Do you mean to say you don't – ?' he began. Then he broke off as the door opened to reveal an ensemble of my female cousins.

'Ah, the stretcher party,' he said, with satisfaction. 'Now we can get on with it.'

* * *

Word had evidently been put around. There were over a hundred of the Children, three-quarters of them women, waiting in the ante-room when our little procession emerged from The Mother's bedroom. An intake of breath broke the silence as they caught sight of the stretcher and its load. They came crowding closer. The doctor waved them back with a gentle motion of his hands.

'Don't disturb her,' he told them. 'She has taken something to help her sleep, so that the journey will not tire her too much.'

He allowed the stretcher to pause for almost a minute while they looked down on her in a mute farewell. It was subtly done. They were all witnesses to the slow rise and fall of her chest as she breathed. Not one of them, I am certain, had the least suspicion that it was not actually The Mother who lay there. Numbers of the women were crying, the tears rolling silently down their cheeks. A few wrung their hands, with little moaning sounds; some clenched them, white-knuckled. The men were solemn faced, with troubled eyes; some with mouths that quivered slightly. There was none of them who wasn't deeply distressed, many were more than that – they were dismayed. I remembered Freda saying: 'She means something tremendously important to them – something like Isis – ' and I hoped that none of them would ever know this last sight of her for a hoax.

Then the doctor told the four girls who held the stretcher to move on, and the crowd parted to let us through. The doors of the audience-room were opened, and as we followed the stretcher through them a multiple, ghostly whisper sounded behind us in farewell, sibilant and aspirate reciprocating, like a slow turning steam-engine – *Sieg Heil!* – *Sieg Heil!* – *Sieg Heil!* ...

The doors closed behind us, cutting off the sound, and we walked up the long room in silence. It was a small party. Two young women with pistols in their belts led the way. Four more carried the stretcher. Emil walked directly behind it, flanked by two of his henchmen. The doctor and I followed, and the procession ended with two more of Emil's men. The group seemed to me as notable for its absentees as for its components. It would presumably be Mista's political eclipse that prevented her attendance, but one had expected Hilda in place of her. I wondered, too, what had become of Miranda. By popular report she was closest of any to The Mother – too close to be safe, perhaps, for, now I came to think of it, I had seen nothing of her since Freda took up the impersonation.

We proceeded down the middle of the room with much the air of a cortège until we neared The Mother's desk. There we paused while one of the leading young women went ahead, and began to search for something on the end wall.

It occurred to me suddenly that here was my big chance. If I were to move fast, I ought to be able to press half-a-dozen or more of the white buttons on the desk before anyone could stop me. It might be that I would only set off a few machine-guns, as Freda had done, but, with luck, there could be serious damage somewhere – though with less luck, of course, we might all be blown up where we stood. If one could be sure that the place would be effectively wrecked any risk was worth taking. And then, while I hesitated, eyeing the desk and judging the distance I noticed that somebody else had, in a negative way, thought of the same idea before me – and had screwed a wooden cover over the whole row of buttons to protect them. I'll never know whether he prevented me from becoming a fool, or a hero just then.

Our pause drew out while the girl in front fumbled at the wall with increasing exasperation. To her left, the painted leader glared out above our heads. Amazing that such a figure should have commanded such fanaticism, destroyed whole nations, made a sharp elbow in the world's history. Maybe *that*, after all, was the real symbol of the Century of the Common Man... For the common man wants his God. And if his celestial God is taken away from him then he compensates by setting up his own local god to admire, fear, and obey.

But the god of the crooked cross was an amateur, a too jealous god, running a one-man show; writing his own scriptures, doing his own evangelism – and neglecting his own fundamentals. The Russians, I felt, were making a better job of it on more orthodox lines; the only serious omission from their pattern is the female principle; a mistake which they will doubtless rectify in time – if they have time...

Emil, in front of me, started to fidget. The second girl went forward to join the first, they conferred, and they poked about at portions of the wall together. We waited.

The female principle, I reflected, was going to be established with a vengeance if the Children of The Mother ever brought off their coup – and possibly, once the means was known, even if they did not. What was going to happen to any other principles under the impact might be difficult to see, but that did not make it comfortable to contemplate.

'Vitality in women,' Shaw once said, 'is a blind fury of creation.' And I guess he had something there, for they do go right on doing it in the damnedest circumstances. So, keep the blind fury, but remove the current disabilities, and what do you have? When you come to think of it, the female toad doesn't need a *reason* for laying seven thousand eggs at a time, nor the salamander for producing fifty young at a birth; it's simply that, being *able* to do that kind of thing, they just naturally do it. So, if –

'Ah!' said Emil, with a tinge of relief in his voice.

I looked beyond him, and saw that the piece of wall below the portrait was opening towards us, showing a passage beyond. The party re-formed, and got moving again.

Very few doors broke the plain walls of the passage. It stretched before us dead straight, diminishing in the distance like a surrealist perspective. When we came at last to the end of it, there was a flight of concrete steps. We walked on up them, to come out right in the forest, where a dozen more young men and women were waiting for us. There was a faint thud behind, and the hole from which we had emerged had vanished with only a rotting log to mark the spot. A few yards further, and we reached the narrow-gauge line where a few trucks stood waiting.

At the end of the line there was only one man to receive us. By the number 742 on his chest I recognized him as the resourceful character who had taken charge of the stranded party on our incoming journey. He singled Emil out of the group, and tackled him.

'Look here,' he said. 'Somebody rang me to stand by for a trip to Assembly Six. Your authority, she said.'

'That is right,' Emil agreed.

'It's *not* right,' countered the young man. 'It means crossing an interception belt. What's more, Assembly Six is right in one of the areas suspended from use by The Mother's own order. And I'm not disobeying that for you or anyone else.'

'Not for The Mother herself?' Emil asked, pointing to the stretcher.

The man stared.

'Nobody told me about this,' he said, uneasily. 'I knew she had been hurt, of course, but – '

Emil explained about a warm, dry climate.

'It may be a good climate – but it's a bad area,' said the young man, still uneasily.

'Very well. If you refuse to fly The Mother there, we'll get someone else,' Emil told him.

The young man thought for a moment.

'No. I'll do it. I'm as good as anyone else. If we are intercepted, well, I've some experience to go on.'

He led off on a path through the trees. Presently I had my first sight by daylight of a saucer – and not very informative, even then. Just a curved, overhanging wall of blue metal, nestled into a clearing barely large enough to hold it. The place was roofed with netting for camouflage, but it looked as if, when that were removed, the thing would only be able to get free by rising vertically, pushing aside overhanging branches as it went.

We followed the pilot round the curve to the entrance. The stretcher was manoeuvred inside, and slung to hooks. The doctor fussed over measurements to make sure that it had room to swing centrifugally. The rest of us chose our seats. This time there was no attempt to segregate us as on the previous journey. The doctor examined Freda again, took her pulse, and nodded to himself. Then he sat down in one of the padded pivot-seats nearby. Emil finished off a briefing colloquy with the pilot, and looked round. Then he abruptly stood to attention. The rest of us caught the implication, rose to our feet, and did likewise. Gazing down upon the stretcher, he lifted his right hand.

'Sieg Heil!' he said, in salute.

'Sieg Heil!' the rest of us echoed.

Emil, with his two henchmen, turned to go. Everybody else sat down again, and began to reach for the safety-belts. Emil looked back. He hesitated.

'Come along, doctor,' he said.

The doctor looked up, in innocent surprise.

'Me?' he said.

'Yes. You're not going.'

'But of course I am,' the doctor told him. 'I can't desert my patient in her present condition. It's out of the question.'

Emil frowned.

'You can't have forgotten the edict which forbids any staff technician to leave the H.Q. for any reason whatsoever.'

'Of course not. But, unfortunately, when the edict was made, an emergency in which The Mother's life would depend on the constant attention of a "technician" was not envisaged.'

Emil regarded the doctor grimly. The doctor looked blandly back at him. Emil said, shortly;

'The edict stands.'

'I take the spirit rather than the letter. The edict was made for the good of the community: I regard care of The Mother as of paramount importance to the community.'

'You are not to go. That is an order, and the edict is my authority.'

'That is your considered decision?'

'It is.'

'Very well. I see I have no choice. But, for my own protection, professionally and otherwise, I shall need that in writing.' He pulled a notebook out of his pocket, and held it against the wall, speaking as he wrote:

'I, 451 (Emil) hereby agree that I have this day deprived The Mother of the services of her medical adviser, against his will. He has advised me that in his view the condition of her health is such that it may well prove fatal for her to undertake the present journey without expert medical attention at hand. In rejecting his professional opinion I accept sole responsibility for her welfare. For any deterioration of her health, or for her death, on account of this deprivation of medical assistance, I shall be entirely to blame. Signature there. Date. Witnesses. Now, if you would be so good as to sign that…?'

Emil did not move.

'It is ridiculously tendentious,' he said.

'But is it untrue? I have my reputation to think of.'

Emil glared impotently at the doctor. For a moment he seemed about to make an angry reply. Then, abruptly, he became aware of the attitude of the rest. It needed no more than a glance at any of the faces to warn him against doctrinaire persistence at the moment.

'I will not sign that,' he said.

'Then you agree that I should go?' asked the doctor.

'I don't agree to that, either. I tell you that the penalty for trying to disobey the edict is shooting.'

The doctor looked him in the eye.

'But duty to The Mother surely stands higher than mere duty to the law?'

Emil quivered. For a moment, I expected him to spit. He was cornered. Whether or not any harm should come to 'The Mother', it would stick to him that he had been prepared to endanger her life for a technicality, and her intended long 'relapse' would, without doubt, be ascribed to his interference.

Without trusting himself to say one word more, he turned on his heel, and left.

The doctor dropped into the seat next to mine.

'Poor fellow,' he said, 'he'll have to face Mista when he gets back.'

'That was quite a swift one,' I told him. 'Why do you want to join this picnic, anyway?'

'I don't know that I do,' he admitted, 'though there might be an outside chance of making a break. No, it simply occurred to me that I was likely to have a nasty accident on the way back from here. You see, with you and Freda shipped out, and the girl who did the make-up presumably well taken care of, it should be that the only people who know about this little charade of ours are Mista, Emil – and me. I might be an embarrass-ment one day, so why take a chance on me. So I thought I'd not risk that accident.'

'Fasten all belts! Fasten all belts!' a speaker directed. Somewhere a faint humming began.

'He might have signed, and taken the paper back after the – er – accident,' I suggested.

He shook his head. 'No. He knew when to get out. He knew my next move would be a direct appeal over his head, and he was pretty sure they wouldn't back anything that might harm The Mother. So he saved half his face, and kept his authority.'

'All belts secured? All belts secured?' asked the voice.

'It's a funny thing,' I observed, 'the way everybody around here, except me, seems to be a graduate in diplomacy. There must be – .'

'About to take off! About to take off!' said the speaker, interrupting.

19

Away

They never see us but they wish us away – D.G.

I watched the doctor give Freda something to drink from a small glass. She looked gratefully at him, and they exchanged a few words. I couldn't hear what either of them said, above the noise of the craft. When he came back and slumped down beside me, I asked how she was.

'Fine,' he said, gruffly. 'Better than I am. She didn't have to try to hold out against that damned acceleration at the start.'

'How long is this supposed to go on?' I asked.

'How would I know? The infernal thing can drop any minute now for all I care, as long as it stops that whine.'

'I didn't mean that. I meant Freda's Mother-act. It'll have to stop soon. And what's going to happen when they first find out? I don't think this lot's good for a big laugh.'

He agreed, abstractedly. I said:

'The more I think of it, the more I don't like it.'

'Huh,' he grunted. I glanced at him.

'I know it's hell to try to think against this row,' I said. 'But this affects you, you know. Seems to me they're quite as likely to think you finished off The Mother, as anything else.'

That did prod his attention somewhat. 'Why the devil should I?'

'That's not the point. The thing is that Mista and Emil do have a purpose in keeping Freda and me alive,' I went on, rubbing it in, 'but they'd rather dispose of you – you'd make a very handy scapegoat. How much would you be prepared to bet that Mista isn't radioing some kind of warm reception for you right now? And there's Emil sore enough, too. It wouldn't be hard to turn these cousins of mine lynch-minded where The Mother's concerned.'

'I hadn't thought of that,' he said, and his lethargy dropped from him as he began to think of it, with some intensity.

'H'm,' he said, a minute or so later. 'Yes. The time would be just as soon as we land. Make a bolt for it then; before they're expecting anything?'

'That's what I thought,' I agreed. 'We're bound to arrive in the dark. It ought to give us a start, anyway.'

'Us?' he repeated.

'You, me and Freda,' I said. I went on to explain.

The moment the door was opened, he was to run for it, and I would be close behind him. Immediately he was out, he was to turn to the right, and make off. I would stop in the doorway, fire several shots to the left, and do my best to add confusion as the rest followed up. In that confusion, Freda and I would also slip round by the curve of the machine, and then beat it as fast as we could. It was, I had to admit, not much of a plan, as plans go, but it was the one chance we were likely to have before they got us into whatever arrangements for safe-keeping they had ready. It might be no good if, say, the place was fenced, or the going too bad, but it was worth trying.

'Where I don't see my way, is over Freda,' I admitted. 'She can't leap right off a stretcher and tear across country in a white nightgown and bare feet. She has to be got mobile some way.'

'H'm,' said the doctor. He considered further, then: 'I think that might be fixed,' he decided.

A few minutes later he went over to inspect his patient. He frowned, displeased.

There was a short consultation. Presently, the stretcher was unslung, and carried up the curving floor out of our sight between two young women, with the doctor following. Before long, one of the young women came back. The other did not.

* * *

Either the patrolling was not as good as had been feared, or we were flying too high to be reached; at any rate, we had no warnings or alarms. nothing was heard from the speakers from the time we started until they announced: 'Landing in fifteen minutes! Landing in fifteen minutes!' This seemed likely to be our most vulnerable time, but the minutes went sliding past without interruption.

By instruction, we fastened our belts. The note of the whine altered. The seats began to tilt in their brackets as the centrifugal force decreased. Again, one had the uncanny experience of watching the floor become wall, and the wall, floor. The whine sank still lower, presently there was a faint jar, a settling, and we were at rest.

Thankfully but dazedly we unhooked our belts. A young woman several seats away clasped her hands to the sides of her head. 'And some guys say these things are spots before the eyes, or met balloons,' she said bitterly. 'They ought to try riding one, sometime. Of all the infernal, brain-swirling, gut-wrecking, bone-screwing, muscle-squashing, goddam contraptions that a misdirected, ill-conditioned, infra-quota intelligence-surrogate ever evolved, this wins.'

I had not previously noticed that Miss Hander was one of us. It was almost like meeting an old friend. She appeared to have some further observations to make on the shortcomings of saucers, but her attention was caught, as was everyone else's, by the sight of the doctor hurrying round the corner, wearing an expression of alarm.

'Open the door, quickly,' he ordered with an air of authority which brought the nearest man jumping to the job without question.

He passed me. I thought the girl who followed him was Freda, but I could not be sure. The moment the door was opened the doctor disappeared into the darkness outside, leaving a bewildered look on the faces behind him. I let the bafflement grow for a moment, and then jumped forward to do my stuff.

The thing was pretty gratifying. A few yells and shots brought several of them after me, peering bemusedly into the blackness while others behind them jostled to see what went on. A babble of questions added to the confusion. I eased off to the side as one or two more pushed forward. Then there came a tug at my sleeve. I grasped a hand in mine, and dodged from the lighted entrance into the shadow. We ran a few yards close to the curving wall of the saucer, and then lit out for the open.

It was then that the programme began to go wrong.

I must, I guess, have been in a pretty high-octane state, because I'd already been able to get around to wondering what some sharp flicks of light might be before I heard the sound of the shots. Several bullets went p-hew! p-hew! p-hew! close to us. I dropped flat, pulling Freda with me.

Over on the left, a machine-gun opened up, firing tracer, and, by the look of the angle, aiming at the open door of the saucer. Bullets smacked at the metal walls, and whirred off on ricochets. Screams and shouts arose from some place. Then there was a thud, as if the door had been slammed.

Almost simultaneously, a light blazed out on the left, its beam was right on the saucer, flooding it brilliantly. The firing went on; bullets pinged and clanged on the metal surface without apparent effect. Then something with a bright tail to it whizzed over our heads, and went off with a whoompf a few yards short of the target. It threw up a geyser of dirt which came pattering down on and around us. The saucer swayed, and started to lift. Another of the bright-tailed things came over, and burst just beneath it. The whole craft rocked with the concussion as if it would sideslip back to earth again. Then it righted, and shot away up, like an express elevator.

The light lost it in half a second, and began to fan around wildly, trying to pick it up again. There were one or two hopeful discharges into the air, then silence fell all around us. The whole thing had been so short, sharp, and unexpected as to leave one somewhat numbed, and not quite credulous.

It left me, also, disinclined to move lest things should start up again. The light laid-off whipping uselessly about the sky, and brought its beam down to the spot where the saucer had rested. Three or four bodies lay there, and it steadied, floodlighting them.

Freda stirred, as though making to get up. I caught her arm to stop her. We should be silhouetted against the lit background the moment we moved.

'They seem to shoot first in these parts,' I said. 'Better wait.'

Whistles began to blow in different directions. Voices gave orders, but the words did not reach us. They might have been military voices any place. Presently there were sounds of movement, voices calling to one another, occasional lights flashing. Dim figures began to emerge from the darkness, closing-in in ones and twos, each with a weapon ready. One pair was coming straight towards us. I let them get within a dozen yards or so of us, then:

'Hullo, there,' I said, and sat up.

They stopped, startled, and turned their guns at us. One of them flashed a torch. We stood up.

'Stick 'em up,' said a voice.

We stuck 'em up.

'Better frisk 'em Bill. Could have ray-guns, or somethin',' said a voice, with an unfamiliar intonation. To us it added: 'One move out of you, chums, and you'll have bought it.'

The torch was held steady, dazzling us. I heard a man walk round behind. He patted my pockets, found the pistol, and pulled it out with a grunt. Presently, he said:

'One squirt between 'em.'

'No ray-guns?' inquired the voice behind the torch. It sounded disappointed.

'How in hell'd I know what a ray-gun'd look like, if there was?' replied the man behind us, in a lazy drawl.

''F you got any ray-guns, better drop 'em right now,' the voice in front advised us.

'Oh, my word! What's the good of expecting them to understand English?'

'Well, he said "Hullo", didn't he, and – '

'What,' asked Freda, coldly, 'is all this rubbish about ray-guns?'

There was a brief silence.

'Cor!' said the torch holder. 'Sort of like a Yank.'

'Good-oh! Five quid from you, Dig,' said the lazy voice.

'Hell, now! Ain't that a fair cow?' asked the other. Then, on a note of regained hope, he added: 'Could have learned it by radio, though.' He looked at us. 'Short waves'd reach Mars. That's the way you learned it, isn't it?' he persisted.

'Mars?' I repeated, blankly. 'What goes on here? What the devil are you talking about?'

'Huh,' said the slow voice. 'The bint's a Yank, but this one sounds like a Pommy to me.' He poked me in the back. 'Are you a Pommy?'

'What's a Pommy?' I asked.

'See, he don't know. A Martian wouldn't know, either,' said the man in front, darkly.

'Will someone talk a word of sense?' I demanded.

'Sure – seein' I win five quid on this,' said the voice behind me. 'It's this way. My cobber here fell for the furphy that them there bloody saucers come from Mars. Me, I said, hell betcha, no. It's either Yanks, or Ruskys. And five blisterin' weeks we've been bivvied down here waiting for one of the bloody things to come so as we could find out. Well, it's bloody come, and it's got a-bloody-way again – but I win my bloody bet. And now we'll get movin'. There's some folk over there mighty anxious for the oil on this lot.'

We started to walk towards the searchlight site. We'd covered about half the distance before the torch-holder spoke again, evidently out of a process of close-reasoning.

'It still don't follow that the bloody saucer itself has to be a Yank or a Rusky. Either of them might have captured it from some bloody Martians,' he pointed out. He prodded me in the back again. 'Just where did you get aboard it, chum?'

'I don't know a question I'd sooner answer,' I told him.

Freda sighed.

'I've a feeling too that's a question we're going to get mighty tired of mighty soon,' she said, gloomily.

20

Finality?

Finality is not the language of politics – B.D.

'In general,' said the High Pentagonal, facing me across his desk, 'we have to thank you both. You have at least enabled us to assign places in a pattern to a number of puzzling and isolated phenomena. And that, of course, is to the good. Unfortunately, however, it has to be admitted that though you have narrowed the location of this Headquarters to the Tropics or sub-Tropics, that still leaves us with a very large area of choice.'

'But surely – I mean, I told you what the doctor told me.'

'Er – I'm afraid that hasn't quite supported our hopes.'

'No?'

'No. In fact, I am advised that *paramecium reticulata*, if it existed at all, would be something at the other end of a microscope.'

'Well, I know it was *para* – something, and I'm dead sure it was *reticulata*,' I told him.

'Possibly,' he agreed.

'If only those fools hadn't shot the doctor – ' I said.

'If you hadn't started the shooting, they'd quite likely have netted the whole lot – *and* the saucer.'

'How was I to know they were there waiting for us?'

'Exactly.'

We considered one another.

It was, I understood, my final interview with him and his kind – and I was heartily glad of that. It had taken the Australians several weeks to be sure that they had pressed out every droplet of information that we could give. After that, we had been handed on to a cluster of Pentagon ornaments and F.B.I. illuminants, and the whole thing had started again, from the beginning.

I had seen little of Freda because they preferred not to have any 'confirmatory influences' around as they put it, and our only time together in several weeks had been a short spell out when Freda's father, my Uncle Nils died suddenly. They let us go up for the funeral – but, even then, they saw to it that there was always someone near enough to listen.

You couldn't blame them for that. All the evidence remaining was us, the bodies of five of the Children, and that of the doctor. The radar-controlled rockets sent up after the saucer had been deflected by some kind of metallic dust-cloud it put out, and it had got clean away.

The officer now in front of me had chaired the inquiry from the start, and was a somewhat disappointed, though patient, man. He said, not very hopefully:

'Before you go, I want to ask you once more: are you absolutely sure that there is no single detail connected with this business that you have not given us? Some little thing that may have come back to you, perhaps?'

I shook my head.

'Not a thing. There's nothing whatever that I haven't told you a dozen times.'

'It's a pity,' he said. 'I'd like to get around to clearing things up there as soon as possible.'

I said that he put it in a way that seemed to me to undervalue the urgency of the position.

He opened his mouth, and scratched his cheek, reflectively.

'Well, by your own account, there has been considerable damage there, the whole place is badly disorganized, and lacks any strong unifying influence. Also, by your account, they are aware that they are falling behind in scientific devices. All that gives us a margin of time to find them before they can be really ready to start anything.' He paused. 'And, strictly between ourselves, I'm not quite sure how much it matters, anyway.'

I stared at him. He grinned wryly.

'I help to delay the evil hour – but sometimes I wonder whether I'm not helping to make the hour more evil when it comes.'

'*If* it comes,' I suggested.

'Oh, it'll come, all right. Once the satellite weapons were put up there, it was certain they would have to come down one day.' He frowned. Then he went on:

'Besides, Gerda Daele – your Aunt Marta – wasn't very original in her plan, you know. There are half-a-dozen ingenious small nations who would be only too happy to start us smashing one another to bits – if only they could be sure that they would be left intact, and sitting pretty on the sidelines when the dust cleared. So we've had to make it quite clear to them that if anything does start, something is going to happen to them, too. The only real difference between them and these others of yours is that we have them taped; whereas we are not, for the moment, in a position to turn the necessary heat on your lot.'

'I wish you wouldn't call them "my lot",' I protested. 'They're nothing to do with me. I simply – '

'I know – I didn't mean it that way. Now, what I want to know from you is what you are proposing to do? It might be safer for you to have one of our men around, for a time at any rate.'

'Well, first we are going to get married. Then, as my uncle Nils has left his farm to Freda, we are going to live there and work it. – It strikes us as a good place to raise children – if your department will see to it that there is a world left to raise them in.'

'Er – an ordinary family? Just three or four, I mean?' he asked.

'Yes,' I said. 'And before I go, I'd like to tell you one more thing – on the record, too.'

'Sure. Go right ahead,' he invited.

'It's this. All the time this inquiry has been going on, nobody has paid more attention to the chief danger than to grin at it, and then skip over it. God knows, I have tried to put it across enough times.'

'I agree, Mr. Farthing. You certainly have.'

'And yet not one of you seems able to take it in. Why can't you see that though bombs may wreck the world for a bit, it'll get over that, but that if this Eidermann business were once allowed to start it would wreck the whole race.

'I know I've stumbled through it all like a mug, but that doesn't matter if I can help to stop this thing getting out. Once that H.Q. is found, it should be utterly destroyed, at once, and all knowledge of the Eidermann process with it. I can't help it if that would entail the deaths of hundreds of my cousins – the thing's too dangerous for that to count. Even as it stands, it's much too dangerous – and it won't stop there, either. The next step is as plain as a billboard: in no time at all somebody ups – with a scientific method of activating the ovum. And then where are you? No need for men at all, so no men – a monosexual race – an entirely female – '

'Mr. Farthing, don't you think you're slightly – ?'

'No I'm not. This thing is the first stage in a potential destruction of the species. It is our duty to scotch it completely at the outset. Surely you can see that!'

He shook his head.

'Frankly, Mr. Farthing, I can't. To put it on the most practical basis, that kind of stonewalling never works for long: somebody else would be bound to rediscover it quite soon. But, in any case, I think you exaggerate the danger very greatly. It could be very usefully applied to stockbreeding, for instance. Think of the quantity of veal we could – '

'I'm not thinking of stockbreeding: I'm thinking of us,' I told him.

'All right then, surely all that is necessary there is to get it interdicted for human use on religious grounds. Set up a taboo. That'd be a pushover. Good heavens, man, if perfectly healthy women can be persuaded to immure themselves in convents, there'll not be much difficulty in handling this. You needn't worry. It'll be taken care of, all right.'

'You're an optimist,' I said. 'Suppressing it could just as well be denounced as a form of birth-control. And there's instinct. There's this "fury of creation"'.

'I don't think Miss Darl agrees with you on this danger?' he suggested. 'She's outside, waiting for you. Suppose we have her in, and hear her views.'

I recalled Freda's expression, the reflectively odd look in her eyes when she had said: 'Five hundred and twelve little boys! It makes me feel quite queer to think of it.'

'Women's imaginations work kind of differently,' I said. 'Besides, I've wondered once or twice whether there mightn't be something – nothing much, you understand, but sometimes just the slightest, the faintest trace of course, of – er – Aunt Marta's influence…'

'Nevertheless, I think in fairness she is entitled to give us her own opinion,' he said, and picked up his desk-phone.

Half a minute later, Freda was shown in. He rose to greet her, and pushed forward a chair.

'Mr. Farthing has told you his views on the Eidermann process?' he inquired of her.

'Oh, yes. A number of times,' said Freda.

'He has just told me that he thinks that the Headquarters should be bombed to destroy the details of the Eidermann process, if for no other reason, as soon as we locate the place.'

'Isn't that rather academic, in the circumstances?' Freda asked, with a touch of surprise.

'Possibly. But I'd like to hear your own opinion of the process – I mean, do you think that to make use of it would be disastrous?'

'That, disastrous?' she exclaimed. 'I'll tell you what is going to be disastrous: bigger bombs, long-distance rockets, satellite weapons, biological warfare, radio-active dusts – *they're* disastrous. But the Eidermann thing! For heaven's sake, if anything *ever* was *con*structive, surely this is. Johnny doesn't approve of it. Men are like that – they suddenly decide that something or other is "meddling with nature", so they pompously can't approve. But they meddle enough with it when they want to. They call in all kinds of sciences to help them kill people in more than ones and twos; and then, when something comes along that will help women to have children in more than ones and twos, oh, no, – oh dear, no! *They* don't approve! Here for once, is a scientific discovery to *bring* life – and, automatically, people like Johnny oppose it. Can you wonder that – '

'I'd point out,' I said, 'that like all inventions the very first thing that has happened to it is that it has been adapted to – ' But she was still on her way, not listening.

'Whatever else the Headquarters has done, and whatever it may do,' she went on, 'this one thing is enough to offset all the rest. The Mother, of course, was not the right person – she wasn't even a normal person, but if this is handled properly we might be able to create a super-race, physically and mentally – '

'You've got it all wrong,' I protested. 'There are too many people already.'

'Too many fourth-rate, fifth-rate, yes.'

'But how do you know they won't all be – ?'

'Haven't you any imagination?'

'Haven't *I* any imagination. I like that – '

'Well, if you can't see it, I can. I decided that if everything else in the Headquarters was wrecked, the Eidermann process at least must be saved.'

'You decided! Freda, you don't mean – ?'

'But I do. I had two days and nights in The Mother's own room. I was pretty sure she'd have her own private copies of all the really important records. And when I found them, I took them.'

'All of them?'

'Good heavens, no. There was a closet-full. I only took the Eidermann packet – the rest was mostly weapons, circuits, chemical formulae, and things like that – but I'd have taken the photo-synthesis ones, too, if I could have found them.'

An unpleasant suspicion was coming to me.

'What – what did you do with them?'

'When I realized I'd been doped, I thought they might find them, so I gave them to you.'

A silence set in. It lengthened.

'The Australians took them when they searched you?' the officer suggested.

I nodded, dumbly. I'd forgotten about them. And there'd never been a quiet moment alone for me to look at them, anyway.

I guess I was looking in need of consolation, for he said:

'You know, I think you're taking a pretty morbid view, old man. I don't say it's a very moral world, but there are plenty of things we might have done and didn't, and could do and don't, on account of ethics. You can depend on it, this'll be another of those.'

* * *

H'm... Well, I suppose it had to come; science being what it is... And I suppose he *could* be right – though it seems to me scientists mostly have one ethic, which is science... Women have two, of course; one is respectability, but the other is babies...

I shouldn't think there would be many women who would... but then, I'd not have thought there'd be any...

It's likely Freda will get around to seeing things differently when her baby comes – particularly if it's only one. I mean, it can't help but be pretty offensive to a woman's sense of personal achievement to think that some other women... Well, I mean, five hundred and twelve...! Even less ten per cent...

Anyway, I've taken out subscriptions to a few Australian papers. After all, it's an under-populated country... I wonder what they'll call them?

Multiplets...?

Note on the Text

Plan for Chaos was written mainly during an eighteen-month break in the composition of *The Day of the Triffids* beginning in 1948. John Wyndham completed a final revision by 1 September 1951, just after the UK publication of *Triffids* in August that year. *Plan for Chaos* survives as a ribbon and one corresponding carbon typescript, now part of the John Wyndham Archive, which was purchased by the University of Liverpool in May 1998 from an anonymous previous buyer, with assistance from the Heritage Lottery Fund. The carbon copy is entitled *Fury of Creation*, the initial working title; the ribbon title, *Plan for Chaos*, is that under which Wyndham's then American agent, Frederik Pohl, attempted to market it as the follow-up to *The Day of the Triffids*.

Both typescripts include corrections (not always the same corrections) in pencil and various different inks, clearly used on different occasions. Most of them are very minor: the cutting of a word, rewordings, corrections of punctuation, spelling or grammar. This text is the result of collating these two typescripts. In addition, a few very obvious typos such as 'on' for 'of', and spelling/punctuation mistakes have been silently corrected. Like *Triffids*, *Fury*/*Plan* was originally written with a US publisher in mind and the American spelling in the typescripts has here been changed to British (e.g. 'color' to 'colour'). The numbering of the final chapter has been altered from the probable typo '22' to '20', as given in the *Fury* typescript insert list of chapters. The five substantive deletions made in the *Fury* typescript are retained as they appear in the text of *Plan*. In addition, some typographical errors and misreadings have been corrected from the Liverpool University Press first edition (2009).

We decided on the title *Plan for Chaos* because it is the one Wyndham settled on in his correspondence with Pohl, and because we think it is suggestive of the catastrophe novels on which Wyndham's reputation is based, as well as hinting at the relationship between this novel set in 1973 and *The Day of the Triffids* set in 1976.

In his daily life, Wyndham used the first and last two of his six names: John [Wyndham Parkes Lucas] Beynon Harris. He published under various combinations of all six. *Plan for Chaos* is here published as a 'John Wyndham' novel, like all of his novels from 1951 onwards, as was his original intention.

The chapter epigraphs are all from Shakespeare, with the exception of those for chapters 2 (Sir Thomas More), 7 and 11 (Milton), 13 (Marlowe), 17 (Tennyson), 19 (Garrick) and 20 (Disraeli).

For a full account of the composition of *Fury of Creation*/*Plan for Chaos*, an analysis of its relationship to *The Day of the Triffids* and much else, the reader is referred to http://sfhubbub.blogspot.com/ (search for *Plan for Chaos*), which includes the corrected and expanded text of David Ketterer's introduction to the LUP edition.

David Ketterer and Andy Sawyer

JOHN WYNDHAM

THE DAY OF THE TRIFFIDS

When a freak cosmic event renders most of the Earth's population blind, Bill Masen is one of the lucky few to retain his sight. The London he walks is crammed with groups of men and women needing help, some ready to prey on those who can still see. But another menace stalks blind and sighted alike. With nobody to stop their spread the Triffids, mobile plants with lethal stingers and carnivorous appetites, seem set to take control.

The Day of the Triffids is perhaps the most famous catastrophe novel of the twentieth century and its startling imagery of desolate streets and lurching, lethal plant life retains its power to haunt today.

'One of those books that haunts you for the rest of your life' *Sunday Times*

'Has captivated readers for over half a century' *Guardian*

JOHN WYNDHAM

THE CHRYSALIDS

David Strorm's father doesn't approve of Angus Morton's unusually large horses, calling them blasphemies against nature. Little does he realize that his own son, his niece Rosalind and their friends, have their own secret aberration which would label them as mutants. But as David and Rosalind grow older it becomes more difficult to conceal their differences from the village elders. Soon they face a choice: wait for eventual discovery or flee to the terrifying and mutable Badlands …

The Chrysalids is a post-nuclear story of genetic mutation in a devastated world, which tells of the lengths the intolerant will go to to keep themselves pure.

'Remains fresh and disturbing in an entirely unexpected way' *Guardian*

'Perfect timing, astringent humour . . . One of the few authors whose compulsive readability is a compliment to the intelligence' *Spectator*

JOHN WYNDHAM

THE MIDWICH CUCKOOS

In the sleepy English village of Midwich a mysterious silver object appears and all the inhabitants fall unconscious. A day later the object is gone and everyone awakens unharmed – except that all the women in the village are discovered to be pregnant. The resultant children of Midwich do not belong to their parents: all are blonde, all are golden eyed; they grow up too fast and their minds exhibit frightening abilities that give them control over others. This brings them into conflict with the villagers, just as a chilling realisation dawns on the world outside …

The Midwich Cuckoos is the classic tale of aliens in our midst, exploring how we respond when confronted by those who are innately superior to us in every conceivable way.

'Exciting, unsettling and technically brilliant' *Spectator*

He just wanted a decent book to read ...

Not too much to ask, is it? It was in 1935 when Allen Lane, Managing Director of Bodley Head Publishers, stood on a platform at Exeter railway station looking for something good to read on his journey back to London. His choice was limited to popular magazines and poor-quality paperbacks – the same choice faced every day by the vast majority of readers, few of whom could afford hardbacks. Lane's disappointment and subsequent anger at the range of books generally available led him to found a company – and change the world.

'We believed in the existence in this country of a vast reading public for intelligent books at a low price, and staked everything on it'
Sir Allen Lane, 1902–1970, founder of Penguin Books

The quality paperback had arrived – and not just in bookshops. Lane was adamant that his Penguins should appear in chain stores and tobacconists, and should cost no more than a packet of cigarettes.

Reading habits (and cigarette prices) have changed since 1935, but Penguin still believes in publishing the best books for everybody to enjoy. We still believe that good design costs no more than bad design, and we still believe that quality books published passionately and responsibly make the world a better place.

So wherever you see the little bird – whether it's on a piece of prize-winning literary fiction or a celebrity autobiography, political tour de force or historical masterpiece, a serial-killer thriller, reference book, world classic or a piece of pure escapism – you can bet that it represents the very best that the genre has to offer.

Whatever you like to read – trust Penguin.